Legends LOST

Legends
LOST

Mark –
Are The Best –
(and I do look good
in a dress)
Charlie Mac

Charlie Mac

FILTER PRESS, LLC
Palmer Lake, Colorado

Library of Congress Cataloging-in-Publication Data
Mac, Charlie.
Legends lost / Charlie Mac.
p. cm.
ISBN 978-0-86541-126-5 (hardcover: alk. paper)
ISBN 978-0-86541-140-1 (paperback: alk. paper)
1. Cassidy, Butch, b. 1866—Fiction.
2. Sundance Kid–Fiction.
3. Outlaws—Fiction. I. Title.
PS3613.A216L44 2012
813'.6–dc23
2011047775

Published by Filter Press, LLC, Palmer Lake, Colorado
info@FilterPressBooks.com / 888.570.2663

Publisher's Note: *Legends Lost* is a work of fiction. Names, characters, incidents, and places either are the product of the author's imagination or are used fictitiously.

BOOK & COVER DESIGN by Robert Schram, Bookends Publication Design

Printed in the United States of America

To my wife, for all her support.

And to the memory of Paul Newman.

Acknowledgments

MY THANKS TO Blake and Melyssa Ankrum, Corey and Shannon Arnold, and Scott and Shelley Zyber. My children not only support my writing, they offer great insights.

Thanks to Tom and Doris Baker of Filter Press, who had faith in the project and transformed my manuscript into a book. Tom's sense of history gave a greater verisimilitude to the setting and times. Doris took on the tough job of editing, an invaluable contribution.

Thanks to Bill and Lesley Bickers, Mark and Helena Trudell, and Chuck and Glenda McLaughlin. They've always been there.

Thanks also to Bill Scott, author extraordinaire and generous friend to whom I go to for writing advice. He never lets me down.

And to Dr. Dave Wolf, who not only worked on the editing of *Legends Lost*, but is a great friend and tennis partner.

And special thanks to my wife, Sharon. In spite of innumerable readings, edits, and rewrites, she never lost her patience and was always there to boost my confidence.

Bolivia, South America—1908

From behind a water barrel, El Capitan *screamed*, "FUEGO!" *And again*, "FUEGO!"

His voice scattered and ricocheted like the rain of bullets around him. When he found the courage to lift his head, he saw his soldiers' aim had not found their targets. The outdated and abused weapons—to say nothing of lack of training—was too much to overcome. His men had followed his lead and fired from behind their barricades without exposing themselves to the Bandidos Yanquis.

The onslaught had the bandidos *pinned down, pushed back through the doorway of the* cocina *in the first moment of gunfire. Doors and windows long gone, bullets pounded the adobe walls, each bullet tearing away another piece of the flimsy protection. Inside, two men lay behind an overturned table that for the moment shielded them from a stray bullet. Once the shooting stopped, one of the men rolled over to catch his breath. "You alive?" he asked.*

A voice answered, "I'm working on an idea."

"Well, make it quick," said the first man. He poked his head around the edge of the table for another glance through the door. "Australia won't work."

The partner shook his head. Drops of sweat mingled with the pooled blood. "One idea and it's like there's never been another." He used his sleeve to wipe the salt from his eyes.

"The army's not gonna put up with this much longer. They're gonna storm us. So whatever you come up with will be all right with me."

The partner sat up and examined the front of his leg. The wound in his butt would have to wait. The hole in his thigh wouldn't keep his leg from supporting him when they made their next run. With an effort, he pulled himself into a squatting position and forced himself to stand.

"Easy," cautioned the first man. "They aren't much as shooters, but one of them could get lucky."

The partner ignored the advice. He walked in a circle to loosen his knotted buttocks and test the bleeding from the bullet hole in his thigh. Surprisingly, there was more pain in his right hand where a fragment had hit a knuckle. In frustration he kicked a stool through the shattered doorway. A new volley of shots rang out—some actually came close to the door. The partner ignored the bullets as he looked around the room. After a time he said, "This town is built on the side of a mountain."

"Skip the town description," the other man retorted. "Give me a plan. I'll watch for a rush."

"Great. Out of the hundred or so out there, you oughta be able to pick off a couple," said the partner. He went down on his stomach and left a trail of blood as he slid toward the corner where an old sheepskin covered a wooden section of the floor. He shoved the sheepskin aside and found a trapdoor, which he yanked open. Peering into the hole, he said, "I got a plan...if this hole is a tunnel, one of us has got to go down there." The first man glanced back, nodded, and then resumed staring out the door.

"Right," said the partner. He paused for a second, then grabbed a few of the twisted-root torches from next to the hearth and reached into his pocket for a wooden match to light the torch. As he lowered his body, he took care to put his weight on the uninjured leg. He found himself in a small cellar. The sound of scurrying feet let him know that he was not alone. Just before the torch burned out, he waved it one last time startling the rats piled on top of each other in every corner of the cellar. Now surrounded by darkness, he was reminded that where there were rats, there were snakes. He stuck his head out the trapdoor. "Why don't you go check this out?"

"I got your back."

"That's comforting," the partner mumbled to himself before using his last match to light a second torch and ducking through the trapdoor. Following the slanted floor, he slid down to the middle of the cellar, waving his torch at the squirming shapes in the corners. The high-pitched squealing set his nerves on edge more than the bullets had.

He lit a large hanging torch from his smaller torch. The shadows receded as the dry wood caught and the flame lit up the room. On the opposite wall he saw another torch and limped over to light it revealing a blanket hanging on the wall next to the far corner. With more light, the rat population thinned. He waved his torch again, sending the rest of the vermin scurrying under the blanket.

The partner found a bundle of torches on the floor in the corner and stuck one in his belt and ripped the blanket off the wall in one quick motion. As if by magic or an answer to unspoken prayer, there before him was a passageway, three feet wide and five feet high—large enough for anyone who didn't mind walking hunched over. The partner figured it must be used to deliver supplies from the road below.

His speculations were interrupted by a hissing voice from above. "They're getting ready to rush us."

"I think I found a way out," the partner said. "Fire a few shots to keep them busy, then jump down here. And get this place ready to burn." He hoped the tunnel led to a way out beyond the militiamen covering the back of the cocina. Bent over, he followed the tunnel until he saw a glimmer of light. He set his torch in the dirt, pulled his gun, and made his way to the cellar door.

He pushed the creaking door aside and peeked out, hoping he wasn't sacrificing the top third of his head. No shots. He dashed for the protection of the wall that surrounded the neighboring building. It was then the partner heard the voices. He edged around the wall and behind the two soldiers who had ambushed them. More from instinct than thought, he slammed the butt of his gun into the head of the man closest to him. The other private grunted in surprise as the unconscious soldier fell across his legs; he turned his head to find the barrel of a gun crammed against his cheek.

"Silencio, amigo," said the partner. To emphasize the point, he thumbed back the hammer. "I don't have much of your language, so I'll just say you're within one move of having your brains splattered." The soldier understood the meaning of the gun in his cheek, if not the words, and threw up his hands. The partner grinned and pulled the bandanna from the soldier's neck as he casually asked, "Como se llama?"

"Miguel, por favor—," answered the soldier. It was all he got out before the partner stuffed the bandanna in his mouth and tied it behind his neck. The partner pointed at the cellar door—Miguel understood that he was to carry the unconscious soldier.

On the town square, the militia repositioned anticipating the order to storm the building. The man inside the cocina thrust torches in the embers watching the dry wood ignite. He threw the rest of the touches on the fire, then stepped to the door and emptied his guns in the direction of the soldiers. As he reloaded, he sneered at their reluctance to risk exposure— those unfortunate enough to show themselves had already paid dearly for their courage.

"Hey?" the partner called from the beneath the floor.

The man glanced back to see a sweating soldier dressed in army tan and blue come through the hole in the floor. "Damn," he mumbled to himself. "I believe we got a plan." He stuck his gun to Miguel's head and peered down into the hole. The partner was dragging a barely conscious soldier up the incline. The man nudged Miguel with his gun. "Help him."

The private dropped to his knees and grabbed his friend's collar and lifted him into the room. Once the body was flat on the floor, the partner pulled himself through the trapdoor.

Wiping his face on his sleeve, he said, "I thought we'd borrow their uniforms and get the hell out of here." The soldier on the floor moaned and held his head as he slowly sat up.

"That's your idea?" asked the first man.

"So far," he replied.

In rudimentary Spanish the partner ordered the soldiers to remove their clothing, and in no time the soldiers were naked. The partner pulled the army blouse over his head and then stopped. The soldiers had not availed themselves of a bath in quite some time. "Forget it," said the partner, throwing the *foul-smelling shirt on the floor. "We either get out of here in our own clothes, or we don't get out at all. I'm not gonna die smelling like this."*

"Fine by me. What's your plan for them?" he asked.

"Tie 'em up," said the partner. He grabbed some rope hanging next to the hearth and was tying Miguel's hands, when once again El Capitan *screamed, "FUEGO!"*

The Americans dove behind the overturned table. Slower to react, Miguel and the other soldier fell to the floor, cut down by their compadres *gunfire.*

Once the fusillade ended, the Americans stood and emptied their guns out the door—the screams of the soldiers let them know some of the bullets had hit their mark. Then it was quiet again. Stepping around the dead soldiers, the partner said, "We're going out the back. Throw the rest of the ammunition on the fire. A burning building will keep them busy."

When the partner was halfway through the trapdoor, the other man suddenly asked, "You didn't see rats, did you? I thought I heard rats."

"I can't believe this," said the partner. "You're worried about rats?"

"I can't stand them."

"I thought you couldn't swim." The partner thought and then said, "I can honestly say I didn't see a single rat." He disappeared into the tunnel.

The other man pulled the burning torches out of the fire and threw them around the room. Instantly, the tables and chairs burst into flames. As he bent down, pain shot though him. He had taken a hit, but like the partner, believed he had a flesh wound. The partner would eventually cauterize the wound with gunpowder, but for now he ignored the pain. He tossed the rest of the bullets and ammunition belts into the fire before lowering himself through the trapdoor.

The other man slid to the floor. As he did he heard noises that sounded like rats—he might have stopped to investigate, but the bullets in the fire began to explode with a fury that sounded as if the army was already attacking. The pain in his back heated up as he crossed the cellar and yanked the burning torch out of the wall. He ran toward the opening at the end of the tunnel. As he raised his head, he heard a whisper. "Over here."

The man was not able to stand. He stumbled through the yard to where the partner was waiting with the soldiers' horses. He managed to lift himself into the saddle. It was impossible to sit straight, and he leaned over his hands to grip the saddle horn. It was then the partner saw the blood dripping from the front of his shirt. "You gonna be all right?"

"You sure there weren't rats in that tunnel?" he asked. As a new spasm of pain hit, he sucked in air, "You lead." The partner mounted; he leaned over to take the reins and guided the horses down the narrow alleyway. They would have to take it slow.

In the cocina, the fire had nearly destroyed the small cafe. The exploding bullets in the hearth added to the noise of the shots the militiamen fired into the burning building. It sounded like a war. "Hang on," the partner said. "We'll keep to ourselves until we're healed up. Then we're going to the ranch, and then back to the States."

The other man groaned, then asked, "Aren't we...asking for...trouble going back?"

"Don't see how," said the partner. "We just got killed."

I

New York City—1909

He was a man people went out of their way to avoid. One look at his face and most turned away—but not because he was ugly or disfigured.

It was his eyes. Dark, piercing, devoid of life except for a cold fury. His eyes were the eyes of a hunter, and the world was his prey.

Elias Kotkin wore an unbuttoned overcoat with the collar turned up. His bowler hat covered dark hair that hung below the brim, and thin bloodless lips formed a slit of a mouth. The color of his skin resembled the pallor of death. A childhood bout of smallpox had left scars on his cheeks. He could have been twenty-five or forty-five.

His clothing was impeccable, and he walked with a confident air. He had the look of one who dealt with death, perhaps a mortician or a coroner. In truth, he added to the job security of coroners and to the wealth of morticians. He was an assassin, plying his trade on behalf of a number of pillars of the business world. Morgan, Rockefeller, Harriman, Mellon, Carnegie—all part of a select group whose endeavors were directed toward complete control of their respective interests.

Each month throughout Kotkin's life, one of these pillars of business had sent his mother an envelope containing five-hundred dollars. Sometimes the courier also delivered a detailed letter. Adele Kotkin burned the letters in the fireplace and used the money to maintain her comfortable home near Central Park. Elias always assumed that the money came from the person who was his father, but Adele never explained or identified the sender.

Elias graduated from The Cholise School for Young Gentlemen at the age of fifteen in 1892. Shortly after, he received a letter from Princeton University informing him that he had been accepted for the fall class. Elias hadn't applied to Princeton and was in the process of destroying the letter when Adele informed him that he was expected to attend—in addition, he would be on an accelerated course of study that would cause him to graduate in three years. But he had already decided that he was entering Harvard University to study the law—whether his mother liked it or not.

Adele recognized that the days of arbitrarily controlling her son's life were coming to an end. She penned a note and had the building doorman deliver it to a Madison Avenue address, ordering him to wait for the reply. Within two hours, the doorman delivered a three-page response and a separate envelope for the boy.

Still, Adele remained unwilling to reveal who Elias' father was. It was enough that Elias knew his father was a businessman who had plans for his son. Passing herself off as a widow, Adele had continued as the businessman's mistress, never wanting nor expecting to be part of his public life. It was a credit to her devotion to Elias that he'd remained unaware of her secret life as she was careful to shield the boy from scandal.

Elias read and burned his letter and never discussed the contents. The only change his mother noted was that he now agreed to attend Princeton. For the first time, the young man had the feeling he was part of something.

At Princeton, he had no more of a social life than at Cholise. His course of study was laid out for him, and he was afforded the finest in tutors and mentors to ensure his quick matriculation. International law, economics, and philosophy were his principle courses of study, along with highly advanced courses in hand-to-hand combat, and extensive work with firearms. With one hundred and ninety pounds spread out over his six-foot, four-inch frame, Kotkin combined natural quickness with a ruthless personality nurtured by years of loneliness.

Kotkin's life was puppet-like. Upon graduation, he was

offered a position with a detective agency which his mother advised he accept. He did, after receiving another letter from his unknown father. Three years later, just shy of his twenty-second birthday, he received a substantial sum of money to start his own investigative agency. With the money came a long-term contract to provide security, should the need arise, for a corporation he had never heard of. He would not be in need of employees as there would be little paperwork— all paperwork would be for his unknown employer's eyes only. His work would be sporadic, but necessary to the continued success of certain enterprises. His first jobs were following and submitting detailed reports on individuals who meant nothing to him, but were of upmost importance to his clients.

A year later, Kotkin was ordered to attend an elegant event, the opening of an exclusive museum. There he met Charles Bates—the first time Kotkin had met a direct representative of his employers. Shortly after, Bates contacted Kotkin and gave him a letter detailing how the young man would permanently relieve one Robert Albright of his earthly obligations. There was two thousand dollars enclosed in the envelope.

It didn't take Kotkin long to figure out the significance of this request. He had been following this man for two months. Albright was a powerful aide to the governor of New York and entertained thoughts of his own political career at the expense of the burgeoning international trade industry centered in New York City. Kotkin was aware of the man's propensity for late-night visits to the opium dens of Chinatown where he sought both the drug and one of the working girls. For his first job at killing, Kotkin found it quite easy to strangle his victim in the private room the man always reserved, leaving the police to come up with an explanation for the aide's death. The revelation of the man's personal habits insured the investigation would be cursory.

Over the next six years, Kotkin's skills were used and refined. He made a habit of reading about the new science of criminology to keep ahead of any threat to his livelihood. He eventually concluded it was far more efficient for a target's death to be attributed to an accident, a robbery gone bad, or even suicide, anything to keep even the scent of scandal away from his employers. By now he had several employers, but his only contact with them remained Charles Bates. He rightly guessed Bates was the intermediary for several powerful men because many of the scenes occurred in cities other than New York.

In some respects it was a simple life. Should some unfortunate soul interfere in the growth or plans of one of Kotkin's barons, Kotkin removed him and made sure the trouble went away permanently. Afterward, the family of the individual who hadn't been amenable to a buyout or merger was approached by one of the companies that had been negotiating with their late relative. It had never taken a second "accident" to help the loved ones recognize the need to acquiesce.

By 1909 Kotkin was a wealthy man. He had invested wisely and enjoyed some financial success. With no help from Bates, he had identified his employers, always wondering which one was his father. As insurance against his own eradication, he made it a policy to investigate each of his employers and develop a less-than-flattering dossier that could be used as barter. This information was in the hands of two well-paid attorneys. If he didn't contact each at least monthly, the lawyers were to open the information and deliver it to a federal attorney Kotkin had once met at a charity event. However, unknown to Kotkin, events were occurring which would soon eliminate the necessity of this security measure.

Receiving instructions to meet Bates was not unusual for Kotkin, but the meeting place was strange. A public place such as the Waldorf-Astoria was a break in protocol. Ignoring the scores of pedestrians, he arrived ahead of schedule—Kotkin was always early—at the main entrance of the hotel, where the doorman opened the door and tipped his cap in one motion.

Kotkin stepped into the ornate lobby, removed his hat and, as instructed, sat on the settee that faced away from the registration desk. He pulled his watch from his vest pocket, noting that it would be a few minutes before Bates arrived. As he collected his thoughts it occurred to him that he should be more concerned about this meeting. Always before, Bates would insure privacy by arranging to meet in an out-of-the-way restaurant. Kotkin's slight unease made him unconsciously reach for the holster under his right arm. Reassured, he touched the inside of his left ankle with his right foot, making sure that the hidden derringer was accessible.

Bates entered the lobby from the lift in the corner. He paused to run his eyes around the room, coming to a halt when he spied the young man. To Kotkin's surprise, Bates suddenly smiled and walked directly to him. "So good of you to meet me," he called.

Kotkin rose with his hand extended. He was rewarded with a firm handshake, surprised when Bates patted him on the shoulder. "I think it's time you call me Charles," he said. "Would you join me?" As the lift groaned its way to the top floor, he said, "Forgive my methodology. I assure you it is necessary, and I believe you'll be pleased at the outcome."

"I am curious," Kotkin admitted and was then silent.

"As well you should be." Stepping off the lift, Bates waved off the guard in the hallway with a glance. They reached the end of the hall where a double set of doors opened outward—Bates ignored the second guard and gave a knock with the lions-head doorknocker. A coatless man, pistol holstered under the left arm of his shirt opened the door and stepped aside. "He's waiting for you, sir," said the man.

"Thank you, Andrew," said Bates. Turning to Kotkin, he said, "Please take a seat." He looked toward the guard, "Make sure our guest is comfortable."

Kotkin knew better than to ask questions. He shook his head at Andrew's offer of refreshment and sat on a couch, crossing his legs and keeping his hand near his left ankle. Taking his cue from Kotkin, the guard returned to his chair next to the door and sat with arms crossed.

The immense room was overly decorated with exquisite wall coverings and gilt-edged crown molding. The hand-carved trim could only have come from the finest of craftsmen. A clock quietly ticked off seconds in the corner, waiting to announce the time with its deep-toned chime. Fresh flowers were arranged in crystal vases throughout the room giving off a slightly sickening smell.

Aside from the clock, the only other sound came from Andrew shifting in his chair as he searched for comfort by continually changing positions—an indication he had been on the job too long. Without appearing to do so, Kotkin watched the guard. While not being overly large, Andrew was solidly built and appeared quite strong. As Kotkin studied the man, he was struck with the notion he had seen him before. Concentrating, he had almost decided he was incorrect when the sound of footsteps caused him to unconsciously straighten. The door swung open and Bates said, "He's ready to see you."

Kotkin followed Bates down the hallway to another set of double doors before asking, "Who am I meeting?"

Bates was opening the door as he quietly said, "Your father."

II

Kotkin entered a bedroom as ornately decorated as the rest of the suite. A bed had been moved to the corner near the window where a man was lying against a half-dozen pillows. His long-sleeved night shirt was buttoned to his neck, and the silk sheets extended from his chest to the end of the bed. The flower-filled vases couldn't hide the malodorous stench that hung over the room. Kotkin recognized the impending smell of death and wondered why the guards were necessary. The old man confirmed this when he turned his pallid face toward the door as Bates and Kotkin made their way to the side of the bed. What remained of the old man's thin hair was long, scraggly and gray. His face was deeply lined; his mouth pinched from constant pain.

The old man fixed an intense stare into the eyes of his son. Kotkin now knew his father was E. H. Harriman, founder of the Union Pacific Railroad and one of the wealthiest men in the world. The knowledge caused him to come to a stop as the old man haltingly raised a liver-spotted hand in greeting before rasping in a barely audible voice, "That will be all, Charles."

"I'll be outside when you need me," said Bates. Gesturing to another man who sat in the opposite corner of the room, he said, "Come, Doctor Peterson, let's give Mr. Harriman his privacy."

The doctor frowned. He picked up a book sitting on the table next to his chair and was following Bates to the door when he turned and said, "You must stay calm, Mr. Harriman."

Defiantly waving his hand, Harriman said, "Get out." The old man watched Kotkin as the others were leaving, his eyes bored into the young man as if he was trying to see what was there. After a time, Harriman pointed to a chair and said, "We have much to talk about."

Kotkin did as directed. Effortlessly lifting the heavy chair with one hand, he swung it around next to the bed before lowering himself into it.

"Strong," said Harriman, before a coughing fit overtook him. Pointing at the bedstand, he indicated for Kotkin to hand him a crystal goblet filled with water. Even taking small sips, it was minutes before the red in the withered face subsided and he was able to talk. He took a deep breath and laboriously exhaled before saying, "I'm dying."

"Yes," agreed Kotkin, slowly nodding.

"You must have questions," said the old man in his gravelly voice. Since the coughing fit, he seemed to grow in strength. He forced himself up against the pillows.

"Are you truly my father?"

"I am," he replied. "Your mother and I have been together for thirty years." Peering at his son, he asked, "Did you know Adele was once an actress?"

Kotkin shook his head.

"It's true," said Harriman. "I saw her at the opera house in some damned play and fell in love with her." He answered the question before it was asked: "Because I was already married and had a family, that's why. My business would have been ruined with the scandal. There wasn't a thing we could do about it." He stared up at the ceiling. "No...couldn't be done...impossible."

"So you supported her."

"I did...and you also," he said. Watching his son, Harriman's lips twitched in the beginning of a smile, before he asked, "Are you going to kill me?"

"There's not much point, you're almost there."

A gasping laugh nearly caused another coughing spasm. "That's right," Harriman agreed. "I don't have much time. That's why I had Bates arrange this meeting."

Kotkin smiled for the first time. "So now you need something from me," he suggested. "And I suppose you're prepared to pay dearly." He pursed his lips in thought before going on. "Although I cannot think of a single reason why I should help you."

The ghastly laugh reappeared. "You will if you want your birthright," Harriman said. "That, and your inheritance."

Kotkin was stunned. Never in his wildest dreams did he ever consider the possibility of being given a name—particularly one that would elevate his status to the highest levels of New York society. His father watched as he wrestled with the idea. The younger man swallowed and said, "Perhaps you should explain."

"I've prepared a document, now in the hands of Charles Bates, which will reveal to the world that you are my son. As a result of this, you will receive your share of my fortune," said Harriman. Beginning to breathe heavily with the effort of talking, he sipped his water, and then went on, "However, regardless of your decision, arrangements have been made to deposit one million dollars into the bank of your choice."

Kotkin was unable to remain seated. He rose, stepped to the window and stared at the busy street below, his large hands in constant motion as he clasped and re-clasped them behind his back. His mood changed from confusion to anger and back to confusion at the thought of such a sum of money. Turning from the window, Kotkin leaned over the end of the bed and asked, "What's to stop me from taking the money and doing nothing?"

Expecting the question, the old man nodded. "That's up to you," Harriman said. "But I'm betting that a name is more important than the money. Besides, I'll expect you to take care of your mother when I'm gone."

"That would happen anyway, and I don't need anything from you to do it," said Kotkin. Still in shock, he slowly moved back around the bed and reclaimed his seat. Harriman nodded in agreement, so Kotkin demanded, "Then why? What do you want?"

The old man shrewdly asked, "Then you agree?"

"I agree to listen to your proposal."

"Very well," said Harriman. He smoothed out the sheets before he began to speak. "From the society page, you probably know you have a younger brother. What you don't know is that I've slated William for a life of public service, perhaps as high as the presidency. However, I will not live to make that dream a reality, and that's where you come in."

"Doing what?"

Voice rasping, Harriman said, "Removing obstacles."

Kotkin leaned back in surprise. "Obstacles? Your son has not reached his majority."

The old man tried to sit up, but was overcome with another coughing fit. Kotkin handed him the water goblet and waited; when Harriman was able to speak, he set the glass down before daubing his lips with a linen handkerchief. "Yes," he agreed. "William is only eighteen, but I already explained that he's being groomed. Understand that he'll have unlimited funds and, barring a disaster, complete backing from my business associates and their families. But even so, there are always obstacles. Over the years, he'll be subjected to forces that will both help and hinder in his development. That's where you come in."

"Surely you have professionals who can help William."

"I do," agreed Harriman. "However, there will always be problems. One in particular."

His son began to understand. "Is there someone who has a gun to your head?" he asked. "In a manner of speaking."

"In a manner of speaking," repeated Harriman. "You see, when I was younger, I kept detailed journals of my life. Unfortunately, it was very detailed." He noted Kotkin shaking his head and angrily went on, "I wasn't always so smart. Everyone makes mistakes, especially as a youth. Anyway, during a robbery, my first journal was stolen. Quite frankly, not only was I stupid enough to record my dealings, but I carried the journals with me when I traveled."

"What sort of robbery?"

"I'm getting to that," said Harriman. Reaching for his water, he took another drink, but this time swallowed with great difficulty. "Damn," he swore. "Get me brandy. I'm damned if I'll go to meet the Lord with nothing stronger than water on my lips."

Kotkin went to the sideboard and brought back a decanter and two glasses. After pouring, he handed one to his father, obligingly returning the salute the old man gave him as Harriman swallowed half the contents of the glass. "Ah," gasped Harriman. Taking his time, the old man drained the glass before setting it on the table. "Much better," he said, color rapidly returning to his face. "Now, you were asking what kind of robbery when I lost my journal." He shook his head before continuing. "It was a train robbery near Denver in 1898. A gang of thieves had been hounding my railroad for years, but in this case they were lucky and not only made off with a large amount of cash, but also a box of papers. The box, unfortunately, included this particular journal."

Kotkin was becoming intrigued with the story. "What kind of papers?" he asked.

"Some were important, others not so. There were land grants, rights-of-way, trust deeds...those were important papers. The rest don't matter because there's no one alive to contest them. But it's the journal that's the diamond in this case. That journal could bring down the entire family."

Kotkin was dubious. "After ten years, logic says facts would have come out by now. So what makes you believe someone even has it?"

"It's not a belief, it's a fact. A young man from Colorado recently appeared with one of the land grants, along with a number of the rights-of-way. He and his brother are suggesting that in some cases we never paid for the use of the land." With an ironic wave of his hand, he added, "They're correct, of course."

"Why don't you simply pay them what they want?"

"I considered the possibility, but concluded it could open a door," Harriman said. "The fact is, if enough of these claims come to light, it would seriously injure the company financially. But that's not the problem." He paused, before adding, "They also brought proof of my journal's existence."

"The government isn't going to let anything happen to the railroad. You're too valuable to them."

"Alive, yes...dead, no," he said. "Once I'm gone, with this information those vultures—along with others—will pick the company clean."

"That's always a possibility," Kotkin conceded. "I suppose everyone could turn on you."

"Or me on them," growled Harriman, feistiness showing despite his infirmity. "I can take some of them with me. However, not enough to stop the ruination of my business and my family." He peered at his son again and said, "That's where you come in."

"In what way," Kotkin demanded. Without being asked, he picked up the decanter and refilled both glasses.

Grasping the brandy goblet again, Harriman drank. As before, he had to wait before he could say, "Tasted better the first time." The old man fixed him with a glare. "What is your part?" he asked. "I've already told you...remove any and all obstacles. You have ten years to do it."

"Why ten years?"

"Because William will be ready for public office by then. Worst case, I estimate he'll be elected to the House of Representatives by 1920," he said. "During that time, you will determine what help to give him."

Shaking his head, Kotkin returned to the window to stare out onto the street. "I surmise you want me to eliminate these brothers," he said. "Along with anyone else who might make a claim based on the journal, and to a lesser extent, the missing papers."

"In the long run, the papers mean nothing. But as to the journal—," Harriman stopped. After a minute he asked, "Can you suggest an alternative?" Kotkin was silent so long the old man asked again, "Well, will you do it?"

"I'll consider it."

With a faint smile, the old man reached under a pillow and with great effort pulled out a thick file. Unable to lift the file, he slid it across the silk comforter toward Kotkin, who grabbed it. "In here is an accounting...of the missing documents," he said, now wheezing. "They're important, of course, but as I said, the journal is the key."

Kotkin sat on the end of the bed. Lifting the file, he held six inches of papers tied with a ribbon. He briefly examined the document on the top of the stack—a yellowing newspaper clipping—before flipping through to hand-written documents. "I see what you mean," he said, without looking up.

"You see why the lost documents must be found," agreed Harriman. "But I would be remiss if I didn't warn you that by taking this assignment, you're putting your own life in jeopardy." Kotkin looked up in surprise as the old man went on, "The associates I referred to as vultures would be extremely agitated if this information becomes public knowledge. Each of them would be implicated in schemes that not only would bring down my business, but virtually every major corporation in the country." Smiling at Kotkin's obvious skepticism, he said, "It puts you in a tenuous position."

"Are you suggesting there are others like me?"

Harriman hesitated. "Yes and no," he said after thinking a moment. "There are others who have had results such as yours, but none as advanced." Once again, he had trouble breathing. "Keep...keep in mind...that...that you were trained from birth to do this job. Comparatively speaking, the rest were simply hired thugs. You're the only one with... the...ah...the intellectual brilliance to go along...with your physical...training." In spite of himself, Harriman offered a weak smile before gathering himself by taking deep breaths.

Kotkin actually laughed. "So," he said, "I'm at the top of my profession."

"Even you...could fail. And failure would...result in you...become a target for revenge," said Harriman. He gathered himself once again, before saying, "But it's my...opinion that only you have a chance to...ah...solve this problem. Although I...I...must admit I didn't plan on bringing you to...this point quite so soon. After all...I didn't...plan on dying."

Kotkin warily watched his father. "And you think you can buy me with a million dollars?"

Harriman shook his head. "It's true that every man has his price," he replied. "This may not surprise you, but I know your financial assets...all my...ah...associates know...so I doubt the money means...much to you. I think...you...*need*...to be my son."

Showing for the first time where his thoughts were, Kotkin said, "You won't be able to control a thing from the grave, so what makes you think your family will accept me?"

"I won't...have to." Losing his breath, Harriman audibly wheezed and then haltingly said, "In addition...to your mother ...my wife knows everything...and is prepared...to...follow through...on my wishes." Kotkin could only stare while the emaciated old man controlled his breathing. After a time, Harriman asked, "Satisfied?" Once again, he seemed stronger.

"I'll have to speak with Mother."

"Of course," agreed Harriman. "Adele will verify everything. And once I'm gone, she'll arrange a meeting with my wife."

Kotkin picked up the decanter, but this time absentmindedly poured only for himself. Harriman pointed at his own glass, which Kotkin immediately refilled, murmuring an apology. He slowly sipped the brandy, before asking, "Do you always think of everything?"

"Not always," admitted the old man. "But in this case...I've tried to cover as much as possible. You realize, of course, I'm asking for your life...something I have no right to do."

"True," agreed Kotkin. "On the other hand, you're offering me the one thing I truly covet. I'll admit to that." Coming to a decision, he asked, "Hypothetically—if I were to do this—where would you suggest I start?"

"South America," said Harriman. He pointed at the file. "This is where the story supposedly ended. But we can't afford to leave anything to chance—a few minutes ago you saw the reason why in the clippings."

Kotkin removed the newspaper clipping. "I don't understand," he said. "What does the death of these outlaws have to do with you?"

Harriman groaned and forced himself to breathe deeply before saying, "Those two were part of the gang...of thieves...who...kept robbing my trains. I decided that even if we could capture...ah...them, no court would be of real help, so I took matters into my own hands." Kotkin gave him an inquiring look. Harriman's voice was raspy as he went on, "I assembled the...the... finest officers to...destroy those bastards. My men...did their job...wiped out the entire gang— except for these two...and maybe a couple others."

"Robert Leroy Parker and Harry Longabaugh...known as Butch Cassidy and the Sundance Kid," said Kotkin. "Interesting nicknames. It says they were killed in a gunfight in Bolivia?" In disbelief, he repeated, "Bolivia?"

"I don't believe they're dead," murmured the old man. "That notice is from a Denver newspaper."

"What's the significance?"

"Why wasn't this reported here in New York? Or perhaps in San Francisco? I find it significant that their...deaths were reported in a nondescript newspaper in...ah...the part of the country...they used to operate in. It makes me...think something is amiss."

Kotkin smiled. "It would have been more logical if the reports emanated from New York," he admitted, "since that is where the news from South America would arrive first."

Harriman fought through another coughing fit before he was able to gasp, "Exactly." He struggled for control before saying, "There's another...factor."

"Which is?"

"Longabaugh's woman, Etta Place," wheezed the old man. After another sip of brandy, he was able to say, "She returned to New York...ah...Longabaugh brought her himself...and it's believed she was ill...ah...there's even the possibility that she's dead."

"Go on," urged Kotkin, now impatient with his father's struggle for breath.

Harriman explained. "She...she dropped out of sight. Even the Pinkertons couldn't find her...and they searched every hospital...and graveyard. But I don't think she died. In fact, I believe she came back...with enough money to...to help Parker and Longabaugh return."

"If she returned ill, it's more than likely she did die," countered Kotkin. "Particularly if she came back from Bolivia with some unknown disease."

"Yes, but—," said Harriman. He stopped to breathe and reached for his brandy. "But there should...have been a way to verify the...death. The detectives...followed the trail of the woman...to a New Jersey hospital, although they admit it was...impossible to positively identify Miss Place. Unfortunately, whoever this woman was...had already disappeared. She...she left in the middle of the night. Ah...the...report is...in the file." The brandy brought color to his face.

Kotkin leafed through the papers until he found the notes. Taking his time, he read the section pertaining to the woman who could have been Etta Place leaving of the hospital, then looked up and said, "According to the report, the doctor didn't think Miss Place would survive the night. May I point out he says it was unlikely she could have even walked without assistance." Harriman nodded and took another sip. Swallowing was difficult, but his son was too engrossed to notice. Kotkin said, "Here it is: the report further says a back door was found unlocked, and there is the possibility she was taken out that way."

"Yes," agreed the old man, voice reduced to a whisper. "You must...admit it's strange."

Kotkin again shook his head. "On the other hand, there are two factors that must be considered. In the first place, no one knows for sure if this was Miss Place. Second, according to the doctor's statement, the lady in question had little chance of surviving the night."

Harriman's voice became stronger. "I've read the report...and I know all of that." Pointing a bony finger, he said, "But if you wished to disappear, and guarantee no one would look for you, wouldn't the announcement of your death be the surest way to eliminate curiosity?"

"I suppose. Particularly if one intends to establish a new life."

Harriman sank further into the pillows. "I suspect that Miss Place might have knowledge of...or even possess...ah... my journal." The old man's face had lost all color and was now as pale as the silk sheets. Kotkin hadn't noticed, such was his concentration on the papers in the file. He was a little perturbed when the vein-lined hand grasped his sleeve. Harriman whispered, "...the doctor."

As Kotkin crossed the room to the door, he wondered if the doctor would be of any help. He opened the door and found himself face to face with Peterson. "He wants you," said Kotkin.

Dr. Peterson hurried into the room. He leaned over Harriman and felt for the pulse in the old man's neck; almost immediately, he reached into the bag for a small bottle. Using his teeth, he pulled the cork and poured a sweet-smelling liquid in the old man's mouth, Harriman immediately began to choke and tried to regurgitate the potion. Peterson clamped his hand over his mouth, trusting the body's natural gag response to force the liquid back down his throat.

The doctor's ministrations were effective and Harriman began to breathe easier. Peterson reached for the pitcher and poured water into the goblet, gently coaxing Harriman to swallow, and within minutes the old man relaxed. He was soon asleep. "Mr. Harriman will be unavailable for the rest of the day," Peterson said to Kotkin.

"Will we be able to speak later? I consider it crucial if he won't live through the night."

The doctor shook his head. "I estimate Mr. Harriman will be with us for at least a week—possibly longer—so you'll be able to speak with him tomorrow. But quite frankly, within a few days he'll have to be sedated." Kotkin's eyes bore into Dr. Peterson, causing the doctor to needlessly add, "It will be for the pain."

"That's your concern. But understand that I must speak with him at least once more," Kotkin harshly said. Without waiting for a response, Kotkin wheeled and stalked into the living room, where he confronted Andrew. "Where's Bates?" he demanded.

The guard handed him a slip of paper. "I was told to give you this message. Mr. Bates asked you to meet him at this location." Kotkin unfolded the note and looked up at the guard. "I didn't read it," the guard said in answer to his look.

"I should think not," he said. He folded the paper and put it in his vest pocket.

Once again, Kotkin stared at the guard. "How long have you worked for Mr. Harriman?"

"I work for a private agency and am on assignment," said Andrew. "I've been with the firm for two years."

"Pinkerton?"

"Yes. As are the gentlemen in the hall."

Kotkin changed the subject. "Make sure the doctor informs Mr. Harriman that I'll return in the morning." As if suddenly remembering the message from Bates, he walked past Andrew and closed the door behind him.

Staring at the door, Andrew found he was standing at attention. When Peterson eased back into the room, the guard delivered Kotkin's instructions. "Who is he?"

"I wouldn't know," said the doctor. "But if I was to hazard a guess, I'd say it is someone of great importance to Mr. Harriman. He was quite agitated until Mr. Kotkin made an appearance."

"Kotkin," repeated Andrew. "I don't know the name."

"Nor I," agreed Peterson. "But it isn't something I intend to pursue."

III

New York Harbor—1910

It had been seven months since they'd met, but Kotkin had little trouble picking out the familiar face in the crowd of people gathered on the dock. He waited impatiently for the walkway to be lowered, savoring the thought of never spending another minute on the ship he'd placed two rungs above the depths of hell. Before the return cruise, he'd thought nothing could be worse than the months spent in the jungles of Bolivia.

"There cannot be a more disgusting place," said the wife of a man Kotkin had made a point of avoiding the last fourteen days. "Thank the heavens this is over."

Her husband nodded. "My dear, we're never going out of this country again."

Before the walkway was completely secured, Kotkin pushed his way to the front of the crowd and in two bounds was on the dock. Bates patiently waited at the back of the crowd as Kotkin shouldered his way through.

"Welcome back," said Bates. "How was your trip?"

Kotkin fixed him with a glare. "You cannot begin to imagine how despicable that country is," he said. "The innumerable bugs, filth, and heat compete with the snakes, lizards, and spiders to see who can make the kill."

Bates smiled. "You didn't enjoy the hospitality of our southern neighbors?"

"The fact is, Charles, if I didn't know better, I would think my father ordered me to Bolivia because he wished to kill me," Kotkin replied.

"Perhaps," agreed Bates. Leading the way to a carriage, he said, "I've arranged to have your baggage delivered to the Waldorf. Your father's suite is part of your legacy."

Contrary to Dr. Peterson's prediction, Harriman had

lived another ten days, refusing all pain medication until
the last days when he was in such agony it became impossible for him to communicate. During this time Kotkin had
thoroughly reviewed the contents of the file and come to
agree with his father's assessment that the Harriman
empire was in peril.

Kotkin preceded Bates into the carriage, arranging his
long legs as comfortably as he could in the confined space
while Bates instructed the driver to deliver them to the
Waldorf-Astoria. The driver turned the carriage around on
the dock, cracked his whip, and put the horses into a trot.
Bates looked Kotkin over before he commented, "Besides
your lack of a beard, you seem different."

"After I started shaving daily, my scars disappeared,"
said Kotkin. "The beard was unbearable in the heat, and I
didn't like giving a home to several species of insects."

"Yes, that would be it," agreed Bates. "How did you manage
to get rid of the scars? If I'm not being intrusive?"

Rubbing his now smooth face, Kotkin said, "Not at all.
Perhaps it was a combination of shaving, a native potion,
and the intense heat." He didn't add that once the suntan
had replaced his pallor, he had become particularly fond of
studying his reflection in the mirror.

Bates asked, "What sort of potion?"

"I'm damned if I know," he admitted. "A whore I visited
a few times brought the salve to me. It could have come from
tree bark, or for all I know the excrement of a poisonous
snake." With a laugh, he said, "Her uncle made it—probably
some sort of untrained healer that passes for a doctor."

"Is Bolivia as primitive as that?"

"Very primitive," said Kotkin. "It's beyond me as to how
a county so rich in resources can be so far behind modern
times. Do you know how much gold and silver is being
mined there?"

"I understand it's considerable."

"They have security problems," he said. "If I could stand
the bugs, I could make a fortune importing detectives to
safeguard the mining and banking industry. Perhaps we

should expand our business down there."

"A thought," agreed Bates. He swiveled and faced Kotkin. "Let's move on. Do you wish to discuss what, if anything, you discovered? Your last letter arrived two months ago and at that point, you had little to share."

Kotkin lost his smile. "We'll wait until tomorrow. For now, I intend to settle into the hotel and have a bath to scrub away months of filth. Will this be a problem for you?" The way he asked the question left little doubt that he could have cared less about the other man's scheduling problems.

"No. I anticipated you would want to relax. Tomorrow is soon enough," he said. "Do you want William to join us?"

"Absolutely not," Kotkin quickly replied. "I don't want him near me at all. Surely you understand that he'll never be a part of this."

"I do," said Bates. "I just wanted to see if you did."

Now it was Kotkin's turn to study his companion. After a pause, he nodded and said, "Let's make sure we understand each other. For now, although you run the business on behalf of the family, I have control over matters of security. This is my job, and the perpetuation of the family is my primary consideration. I don't wish to alienate you, but the fact is, you can be replaced. I cannot."

With a smile, Bates said, "I couldn't agree more."

"Then you will also agree there will come a time when I assume complete control of the company. But you know that, don't you?"

"I promised your father," he said. "Rest assured, it's my job to turn everything over to you—when you're ready."

"Excellent," he said. "I have plans once we have young William launched on his political career. My brother will be the lightning rod for the family. He will be the public Harriman."

"Deflecting trouble from you, quite the opposite of now," said Bates. His thoughts turned inward before he murmured, "In choosing you, your father chose wisely."

The driver brought the carriage to a halt in front of the hotel. Bates remained seated as Kotkin stepped down to the

sidewalk, turned, and said, "I won't be in the office until ten.
It will give me time to prepare." Closing the door, he kept his
hand on the polished wood. "I hope I wasn't overly offen-
sive," he said. "I appreciate all you have done...and what
we'll do in the future." Kotkin turned toward the hotel.

Acknowledging the salute of the doorman, he walked
into the lobby, and stopped to take in the smells and look of
civilization. Pampered women with Gibson Girl hairstyles
glided on the arms of gents in waistcoats. He was finally
home with only the potted palms to remind him of seven
months spent without stepping on a carpet-covered floor.
Suddenly, he was hungry. At the manager's desk he placed
an order for dinner in his suite. He'd start with Malpeque
oysters, cold partridge with German asparagus, chocolate
Russe, and end with Turkish coffee. It pleased Kotkin that
the lift operator was waiting for him, eager to deliver the
young man to his magnificent suite of rooms.

⚬

Kotkin languished in the bathtub until he was satisfied
that the stink and stains of Bolivia had lost their battle with
the bath water, then he donned a brocade robe to enjoy his
dinner.

Dinner done, he opened the desk humidor and selected
one of Harriman's expensive cigars. Lighting it carefully to
achieve a perfect draw, he began reading the extensive notes
spread in front of him. The file his father had shown him
months ago had grown satisfyingly large, four times its
original size. The Pinkerton Detective Agency had not sat
still during his absence. The information collected everything that could be found about the two outlaws and the
woman Etta Place in addition to other gangs associated with
Parker and Longabaugh.

Kotkin believed that two men had died in the village
shootout in the mountains outside La Paz. However, even
though both bodies had been burned beyond recognition, he
didn't believe either was Parker or Longabaugh. Having discovered both outlaws were thought to have been wounded,

he used a significant amount of cash to persuade the village leaders to have the bodies exhumed. Although his examination revealed multiple gunshots in each, the size of the bodies caused Kotkin to deduce there was little chance the bodies were those of the Americans. Further, while descriptions of Parker and Longabaugh were sketchy, Longabaugh was known to have blond hair, Parker's was light brown. The hair remaining on the two corpses was dark.

This information led Kotkin to focus on the few known facts about Etta Place.

It had been documented through the New York Port of Entry that Miss Etta Place returned to New York in December 1907 accompanied by a man named Carver. Miss Place had been taken first to a hospital in Manhattan then moved to the facility from which she disappeared. Assuming she was still alive, it was conceivable Miss Place assisted Parker and Longabaugh in their return and assumption of new identities.

Kotkin also considered whether Etta Place and Harry Longabaugh were still together, maybe married. Longabaugh was born in Pennsylvania but grew up in New Jersey. It was entirely possible he had stayed on the East Coast because of his notoriety out west. According to the Pinkerton report, Longabaugh had once been arrested for horse stealing in the small town of Sundance, Wyoming, and served eighteen months in the county jail. He took the name with him when he left. It was unknown what education or skills he possessed, besides robbing banks and trains. However, it was noted that Longabaugh was deadly fast on the draw, possessed a sure shot, and had survived numerous gunfights—one of which was with a man who had sworn to kill Parker.

Less was known about Robert Leroy Parker. He was thought to have been married and have children, but the whereabouts of his family was unknown. If there was a family, they may no longer be alive. Parker was also reputed to be good with a gun but not in the same class as his partner. Smart and tough, he was a good-natured man who was generally well liked. Reports compiled by Pinkerton agents through local peace officers indicated Cassidy was the leader of the Hole in the Wall Gang. The hideout was thought to be located in Wyoming but could have been in Utah or Colorado.

Parker and Longabaugh were partners for a number of years before disappearing in 1899—or 1900, or even 1901—depending on which story one believed. Accompanied by Etta Place, the outlaws left for South America after Harriman's hired posse came too close to killing them. Most people assumed Harriman wanted to find Parker and Longabaugh because they robbed his trains. That was true enough, but Kotkin knew the real reason for his father's obsession was that the outlaws most likely had his journal.

Returning to a stack of papers that dealt with past members of the gang, Kotkin had a thought. After a few moments, he found what he was looking for. One member of the gang, William 'News' Carver, had been killed by the posse after a train robbery in 1899. "Not very smart of Longabaugh," Kotkin said aloud. Carver was the name used by Etta Place's escort upon her return to New York. Making a note, he decided to use the Pinkerton Agency to search the records for anyone named Carver in New York or New Jersey. He now had a starting point for his investigation.

Kotkin stared at the ceiling as he thought. *Parker could be more difficult to find. Assuming he rejoined his wife and children, he could be located in a number of the western states.* He felt secure that Parker, as Longabaugh, would return to a familiar location if they planned on starting over with new identities. *Yes,* Kotkin continued thinking, *Parker would remain in the West.*

In South America, the two outlaws tried their hand at cattle ranching before returning to bank robbery. Kotkin searched through his notes again. The Yankee bandits weren't mentioned again until 1906. If they gave ranching a chance, five to six years would have passed before they started robbing again. During the next three years, banks throughout Bolivia and neighboring countries had been robbed, most more than once. For a price, the captain of the militia provided Kotkin with old wanted posters that had sketches of two men who could have been Parker and Longabaugh. The men in the sketches were not named, but the one with the drooping mustache resembled Longabaugh.

Kotkin based this on the only known photograph of the outlaws made with three members of their gang, one of whom was identified as William Carver. Of great interest to Elias were the allegations of a sixth man, who was not pictured in the serigraph. Because the other members of the gang were identified, he wondered if it were possible this man was connected to the brother who had approached Harriman with the missing papers. Kotkin decided he had to start somewhere in his search for Parker and it might as well be by finding the missing sixth man. In the notes from the managing director of the Union Pacific Railroad he found the name of the brothers. The name was Brannigan, and they lived in Colorado.

Even though Parker and Longabaugh had been back in America for only a few years, Kotkin was under no illusions about the chances of finding them. If Etta Place were involved, it was likely that she had established identities for the outlaws. *What if Miss Place had brought back their money? What if she was sent back to set up a new life?* Other questions came to Kotkin. *What if he could find the shipping line Miss Place and Longabaugh used for their return? After all, she was rumored to be a beautiful woman with a flowing mane of dark hair, and Longabaugh, based on the serigraph, was a handsome man. Is it possible that someone would remember the couple?*

The clock chimed midnight. Kotkin sat back and rubbed his eyes that ached from the reading in the dim light. He put the papers back in precise order in case he needed them to explain his conclusions to Bates. Finished for the night, he rose and stepped to the sideboard to pour a brandy. As he drank, he caught his reflection in the mirror, causing him to set down his glass.

Kotkin no longer looked like death. With his tanned skin he had become a handsome man. The color in his face had softened his sharp features. As with his beard, he had discovered long hair was not conducive to insect-infested countries, and he had shaved his head after the onset of a scalp rash. When the hair grew back, it was much lighter. He crossed to the doors of the bedroom where his father had died. He settled himself in the soft mattress and thought again that Bolivia was behind him. His thoughts then turned to the importance of tomorrow's meeting.

Charles Bates would go along with his plan. But only to a point.

IV

Gunnison, Colorado—1911

Josh Brannigan threw down his pitchfork as soon as he heard the buckboard and hurried to the front of the barn, his breath visible for an instant before the howling wind blew it away. "Where's Pa?" Josh took the reins as his older brother climbed down from the buckboard.

"Still up to Crested Butte," Will Brannigan replied, taking back the reins and leading the team into the barn. "And he's madder than hell."

"Uh...is it about the money?" Josh asked, concern in his voice. He quickly added, "Pa ought to be proud of us getting that money."

Two years older, but half a foot shorter, Will paused to look up at his brother. Searching for an answer, he said, "Yeah, it's the money. I've been arguing with him the whole trip, and all he keeps saying is we should have kept this to ourselves." Neither spoke as they removed the bits and harnesses of the matching grays and led the horses into stalls. Will was forking a load of hay into the manger when he said, "Now that I think about it, Pa almost seemed more scared than mad."

The younger brother looked up in surprise. "Horseshit," he said. "Pa's never been scared of nothing."

"That's what I've always thought, but I'm telling you something is up." After Josh pushed the wagon to the back of the barn, the brothers closed the double doors, and before they turned for the house, Will paused to look at the cloudless sky. "Pa said for us to do nothing 'cept keep our mouths shut about the money." Josh waited for his brother to continue. "Pa said he'd be back to the ranch tomorrow. He's gonna talk to Silas, and then he said he might have to go on a trip."

"Where to?"

"Wouldn't say. He was acting spooky, so I decided to shut up and do what he said." Will looked at his brother and said, "And that's what you're gonna do too."

They reached the back porch and went into the kitchen pausing to shed coats, gloves, and hats on hooks. The heat from the wood-burning stove warmed the room. A large kettle of stew simmered next to a coffeepot. Josh's bride of three months greeted them. "About time," said Molly, setting a plate of sourdough bread on the table. "When I heard you drive by, Will, I thought you'd be right up."

"Sorry," said Will. "We got to talking while we put up the horses." He smiled at his sister-in-law as Josh gave her a peck on the cheek and sat down. Will grinned and said, "You two better keep your hands to yourself if we plan on having supper."

Molly blushed and dished a mountain of beef and gravy stew onto her husband's plate before giving Will an equal share. She and Josh had been married after the New Year— neither could wait until June. They had been childhood sweethearts, spending many an agonizing hour in the woods and haylofts before finally tying the knot. Tall and pretty, brown-haired Molly had grown up on her father's neighboring ranch with five older brothers from whom she learned to respect and like men. She was good natured and didn't care who knew she adored her handsome six-foot, four inch husband with muscles her brothers envied.

Will Brannigan was Gunnison's most eligible bachelor and Molly intended to have a say in picking her future sister-in-law. While Josh was an outgoing young man and knew his mind, his older brother tended to be ponderous and hesitant. Will had inherited his father's dark hair and short muscular body, along with the older man's disposition.

The fact that he was Tom Brannigan's son helped Will's marital prospects. At forty-seven, Tom owned the largest cattle and horse ranch in Gunnison, and was not only respected, he was assumed to be the richest man in the

valley. His other business, however, gave him a certain notoriety. He was owner of Brannigan's Saloon and Gaming Hall
in Crested Butte, a mining town twenty-five miles north of
Gunnison, located at the base of Mt. Baldy in the Redstone
Mountain Range. Brannigan had grubstaked well and now
had interests in mining claims. Even more revenue flowed
his way from his percentage of the many whorehouses that
dotted the back streets of the small town. People didn't talk
about this side of Tom's business, at least not in Tom's presence.

In any case, now that Josh was safely married to Molly
Hutchinson, Will's future was a topic for speculation. The
fact that the older brother had just turned twenty-six and
was still unmarried—to say nothing of the fact that all three
lived at the ranch—caused mothers of eligible young ladies
of Gunnison to consider it only a matter of time before Will
would take a wife and move into his own house. Because the
elder Brannigan spent significant time in Crested Butte,
coming to the ranch every few weeks, he left the daily running of the ranch to his sons, with Will as manager.

Molly set the kettle back on the stove and returned to the
table. "What were you talking about that you couldn't get up
to supper?"

"Pa's upset about my trip back east. He doesn't want us
doing any more about it." Will answered without looking up
from his stew.

Molly looked at her husband. "You never told me exactly
what you were doing. How come Daddy Tom's upset?"

"Damned if I know," admitted Josh. "I can't see the problem. You remember that box Will and I found when we were
tearing down the old storeroom a couple years ago?" Molly
nodded. "Some papers looked important, and we thought
they might be valuable. So Will took it upon himself to find
out if there was anything to them."

Will, in fact, had become obsessed with the official-look-
ing papers. In the fall of 1909, Will took them to the Union
Pacific office in Gunnison. The local agent, Al Bellison, told
him there wasn't anything he could do about the papers. In

January, when he took cattle to Denver for the stock show,
Will visited the Denver station with the documents. Horace
Akers, the district manager for the Union Pacific, who was
formerly of the Gunnison station and a long-time friend of
the Brannigan family, telegraphed the New York office.
When Will came back that afternoon, Akers said there were
no missing documents of value. When Will persisted, Akers
said the only way to get any information about the grants
was to contact someone at the Union Pacific headquarters in
New York. Akers figured this would be the end of it for Will
and was surprised when Will asked, "Where 'bouts in New
York?" Will finished the cattle sale, then wired Josh that he
was heading for New York.

Four days later, Will was standing in the Madison
Avenue offices of the Harriman financial empire. After pre-
senting himself as the spokesman for the Brannigan Cattle
Company, and after a long wait, Will was ushered into the
richly appointed office of Charles Bates.

Bates was polite, but clear. There was no value to the documents, and the company had no intention of offering a
reward. Since he hadn't asked for money at this point, Will
became suspicious and pushed forward with his questions.

Bates continued to rebuff Will and called for his office
assistant to escort young Brannigan out when Will blurted
out, "There's more. There's a bound journal with initials
stamped in the leather." With that, Bates excused his assistant and ordered the young man back to his chair. The questions that followed were pointedly about the journal. Bates
decided he needed time to corroborate the story, suggesting
Will return the next day.

The following morning Will was again in Bates' office
where, to his surprise, the executive offered four thousand
dollars for the land grants, payable without interest at four
hundred dollars a year for the next ten years. Bates spoke
very little and never mentioned the journal.

Will returned to Gunnison with the first installment and
the brothers couldn't wait to tell their father of their success. But learning they had discovered the box, and before

Will could explain about the yearly payments, Tom Brannigan flew into a rage and ordered his sons to never discuss what they found. It wasn't until receipt of a second and third installment that Will decided he needed to tell his father—it was difficult to hide a thousand dollars in the ranch's general account. Two days ago, while driving in the buckboard with his father to Crested Butte with a load of supplies, Will explained about the sale of the papers.

⚜

The cloudless April sky was deceiving. The air was dry and cold, the temperature well below freezing. Silas Kindred stopped to pull his coat collar and scarf tighter around his neck. He stepped off the sidewalk and waited for a wagon to rumble by before crossing Elk Avenue. At the door to the saloon he paused to peer through the window at the crowd— a habit developed when he was a lawman.

One vacant lot removed from the corner of Second Street, Brannigan's was a large building by Crested Butte standards. Because of the vacant lot—which Tom Brannigan owned and on which he someday intended to build a fine hotel—the saloon dominated the surrounding establishments. The downstairs was one large open area except for a storeroom built into the corner down from the long bar. Tables with chairs were spread about the middle of the room, with poker, roulette, and faro tables lining the far wall. The obligatory upright piano, nestled in the corner by a window, was in use every night of the week, joined by a banjo player and a fiddler on weekends. There were strategically placed spittoons to keep a sense of cleanliness, although the floor around them was often wet with tobacco juice and other oral expellants. Interspersed between the spittoons were piss buckets for the serious drinker who didn't feel he had the time or inclination to use the outhouse located in the alley. Upstairs were five rooms that were rented out by the hour to aid the hostesses in their pursuit of any miner whose luck had arrived. These rooms had caused consternation with the owners and madams of the various whorehouses in Crested Butte, but Brannigan pointed out that this portion of his business was small, relative to theirs, and that there were enough men with money for all.

Kindred resembled the Texas cowboy he once was. He was slight in stature and slender in build, and walked as if he had just stepped off his horse after a long trail ride. His unlined face made him appear younger than his age and his light brown hair was kept short and neat. He no longer wore a holster on his hip, but Kindred did carry a short-barreled .22-caliber pistol in his boot beneath the rolled cuff of his denim jeans.

In 1884, at the age of twelve, Kindred left the family ranch in San Antonio to work on the great cattle trails. For the next thirteen years, he worked on cattle drives, and spent time as a deputy sheriff in Santa Fe, before giving it up to drive a stagecoach between Santa Fe and Tucson for an additional fifty dollars a month. After a third robbery attempt left him beaten and nearly dead on the side of the trail, Kindred left Santa Fe and headed to Colorado to try his hand searching for gold.

Having come up empty, Kindred pointed his horse and mule in the direction of Crested Butte. Arriving on a crisp fall day with only a few dollars in his pocket, he did what most would do: he tied his stock to the hitching post of Brannigan's, the first saloon he came across. Kindred stepped up to the bar and ordered whiskey while he pondered his situation. Before he finished his first drink, a town bully demanded that Kindred buy a round or be run out of town.

Kindred handled the situation in workmanlike fashion. He pulled his gun and smashed it into the bully's face in one swift motion made smooth by many such encounters. Kindred finished the job with his fists, then drug the unconscious man to the sidewalk and left him in a heap. This did two things for the young cowboy: it established he wasn't a man to be trifled with, and it got the attention of Tom Brannigan, who offered him a job.

Fourteen years as bartender, manager, and now part owner of Brannigans, Kindred surveyed the saloon patrons through the window. Even with the door closed tight to prevent the cold from seeping in, the noise was loud. He couldn't see Brannigan, but knew he was waiting. Kindred had been asleep when Brannigan sent for him. The wall of noise rocked him back on his heels as he pulled open the door. The noise level briefly subsided as the numerous bar patrons, poker players, and whores turned to see who had disturbed their merriment. Kindred was popular with the clientele, and attention quickly turned back to individual pursuits of happiness. At the bar, one of the bartenders had a mug and a shot waiting. "Evening, Silas," he said. "Didn't expect to see you again tonight."

"Where's Tom?" asked Kindred, nodding his thanks at the beer, which he picked up and drained. The bartender tilted his head in the direction of the back room. Kindred polished off the shot, waited for his beer glass to be topped off, and walked to the door that separated the saloon from the storeroom. Brannigan sat on a wooden crate staring at his boots. Kindred pulled another crate from the corner and sat.

Brannigan was stocky with a barrel chest and muscular arms, his short beard and thick brown hair were flecked with gray. He wore a collarless white shirt, cord pants that stacked over his worn boots and an old vest that he was rarely seen without. Unlike Kindred, the years outdoors had turned his lined face into leather. Brannigan waited until Kindred had finished his beer before breaking the silence. "Thanks for coming back."

"What's so bad ya'd send the boy fer me?" asked Kindred in his Texas drawl that was so slow half the townspeople had trouble understanding him. The other half didn't bother to try.

A smile slowly creased Brannigan's face. "I believe I need your help."

"Ya know yawl got it," Kindred said.

"After you hear what I've got to say, you might not be offering." He reached for a bottle of whiskey and offered it to his friend. Kindred took a pull and handed it back. Brannigan drank deeply, wiped his mouth with the back of his hand, and then said, "My name isn't Brannigan."

"Ain't the first ta be changin' his name." He gestured at the door. "Buncha them ole boys out there got new 'uns."

Brannigan grinned. "I believe you're right. But in any case, I changed my name a long time ago...after I came out west. Just so you know, my family was from Missouri." He took his time. "As a matter of fact, that's where the boys were born." He looked into Kindred's eyes. "I got a past, and some of it isn't so good."

Kindred reached for the whisky.

"You might say I hooked up with the wrong folks," said Brannigan. "You might even say it was them others who made me do some bad things. Course, if you did, you'd be wrong." As his strong hands rubbed his forehead for a moment, he added in a muffled voice, "Dead wrong."

"Ain't my place ta say," said Kindred.

Brannigan continued, eager to get the worst out. "You ever hear of the Hole in the Wall Gang?" He smiled at Kindred. "Course you have. What you don't know is who was in the gang." There was another long pause. "But I know." Kindred looked at the floor as Brannigan said, "I guess you should know I'm trusting you with my life and the lives of some good friends."

"Figure ya must gotta reason," said Kindred. After a moment, he said, "But ta tell ya the truth, Tom, ah don't see why this be of importance. Ain't been nobody lookin' for tha' gang since ole Butch and Sundance lit out. Hell, musta been since '99."

"Yeah, but—"

Kindred interrupted: "An' hell...if ah recollect, there was the story they'd been kilt. Shot by the Mesican army."

"Bolivian."

"Ah guess. So ifen them boys be dead, and the rest of the gang got shot up by them...uh...Pinkermans, what's this gotta do with yawl?"

"Ever hear talk there was a member of the gang that nobody knew?" Brannigan asked. "Course, that really means that it was one member nobody could recognize."

Kindred shook his head, and Brannigan continued, "Well, you'd best believe it when I tell you there was. He wasn't known because he didn't get in that picture that the gang had taken...the one the railroad men used when they were hunting them down." He shrugged and then laughed out loud. After taking another sip of whiskey to wet his throat, he said, "The reason that boy didn't get his picture took was because he had run off to look for gold. Didn't even know about the picture until Butch showed him."

After a time, Kindred said, "Sounds like yawl knowed the boy."

"Well enough. And, so do you."

The silence amplified the noise from the saloon. Kindred took his time as he thought about what Brannigan had just said. Finally, he reached for the bottle. "Mebbe ya oughta tell the whole story," he suggested.

"Not much to it," said Brannigan. "Back in '89—only been out west a coupla years—I drifted into a fella up in Wyoming. It was February, the dead of winter, and he had just gotten out of jail for horse thieving. He said his name was Longabaugh, but he was changing it in honor of the town that jailed him." Brannigan stared at the ceiling as he thought.

"The town was Sundance," he said. "Harry Longabaugh from then on was known as the Sundance Kid. Sundance didn't like working for a living, so we headed to Utah, where Hole in the Wall was located as a hideout for outlaws. We figured it'd be easy to hook up with an outlaw band and make some money. That's how we met Butch Cassidy. We all became friends, and it was shortly after that Longabaugh killed a man who was gunning for Butch."

"What caused ya ta take up with Longabaugh?" asked Kindred.

"Damned if I know," he admitted. "Harry wasn't the most sociable of men, and his prospects were iffy, but I was young and near broke and didn't have another plan. Course it turned out real good when I met Butch. Even then Butch had a reputation of taking care of his men. Smart enough to keep 'em out of jail too." He paused in thought, before going on, "First thing Butch said was to change my name. I was amenable to that, 'cause we might be doing some bad things. I figured if nobody knew who I was, I might be able to get out of trouble."

"With Butch in charge, we started running together. At first, we rustled cattle and horses, but later turned to banks." Brannigan grinned at the thought, and said, "When bankers got tired of being robbed and hired security men known to be deadly guns, we turned to trains. Eventually, E. H. Harriman decided enough was enough and put together a group of Pinkerton agents and retired lawmen whose job was to kill us."

Kindred again interrupted. "Ah 'member readin' 'bout that. That'd be when ole Butch an' Sundance lit out."

"Yeah," agreed Brannigan. "But what you don't know is that they had a plan to come back. Course they didn't think it was gonna take ten years."

"Are yawl sayin' they made it back? Don't seem right. All them newspapers said they was kilt."

"Sundance had a woman name of Etta Place," said Brannigan. "Not her real name, of course. But Etta was educated—schoolteacher, as a matter of fact. She came back from South America in aught-seven. Sundance brought her back because she was supposedly real sick. Put her in a hospital and then took off for South America the day after. It was kind of hard for Sundance. He and Etta had quite a romance going. They really liked each other." He took his time in describing the relationship between the couple.

"What happened ta her?" asked Kindred. Brannigan paused for a sip of the whiskey, then offered the bottle to Kindred. Immersed in the story, he waved it away.

"She supposedly died," said Brannigan. "The story is she was in a hospital and wasn't expected to live. But that very night, she disappeared and nobody's heard of her since."

Kindred thought for a minute. "Sounds like ya got an idee of what happened to her."

"Just might," admitted Brannigan. "What happened to her started years before, around '94. Butch had put together the gang just right. Everybody was makin' good money and living more or less like we wanted. But Butch was looking out for what would come if the Union Pacific caught up with us."

Brannigan was weary. Thinking back over a life will do that, but he picked up the story.

"After a few years of non-stop thieving, and after a good take, Butch wanted a break. He told us to meet up in Denver when spring rolled around, about three months out, I recall." He grinned. "For some reason, I wasn't interested in going back to Missouri. Probably because I'd heard of a mining town near Gunnison, where men were striking it rich. Before I left, I mentioned it to Butch that I'd go try my luck. And that got Butch to thinking, so he pulled me aside for a talk."

During their time together, Cassidy had been impressed with Brannigan's courage and ability with a gun. With the exception of Sundance, Cassidy had never seen a draw as quick as Brannigan's. Realizing Brannigan had some education and a head for business, Cassidy decided he could be of great help once their outlaw days were over.

"Butch wanted something legit," said Brannigan. "Something nobody could take away from him. You might say something for old age, but no one was bettin' on any us getting there. So my idea of mining struck a fancy with him. He figured we could get rich by kicking over the right rock."

Kindred chuckled. "I 'member those days. I had the same notion."

Brannigan picked up the story. Cassidy gave him a saddlebag full of stolen railroad money and instructions to set up a legitimate business. Something that would provide an income when the train robbing had run its course. Even though Cassidy was thinking of the future, it hadn't dawned on him that Harriman would take such serious offense at the gang's continued harassment of his railroad. When Brannigan arrived in Gunnison, it took only a few conversations with former miners to convince him that mining wouldn't pay out for a steady income unless a fellow was mighty lucky. And relying on luck left a man nowhere except his own spot at the bar with the other men who thought they had heard Lady Luck's whispers. On the other hand, there were always drinkers ready to hand over money. He'd buy a saloon, or possibly a whorehouse.

He also discovered that to add another saloon or house of ill repute in Gunnison, a town in which one-half of the establishments were one or the other, was futile. So he rode north to Crested Butte. It only took a week to decide a saloon had the best chance for success. The whorehouses made money but created a different set of worries. The employee problems with a saloon, to say nothing of cash management, were far easier to handle.

Brannigan convinced the owner of the second-largest mercantile store in town to sell, and within three weeks the saloon was open for business. A month later, it was the busiest establishment in town. The enormous popularity was due in part to Brannigan's heavy-handed response when a competitor sent a couple of his gunslingers to start a fight and put the new saloon out of business.

When the two toughs confronted Brannigan, he threw off his apron and dared them to draw. The tied-down holster should have tipped them off, but they were too arrogant to notice. When the first man reached for his gun, Brannigan placed a shot in the center of his chest. He was dead before he hit the floor. The other tough never cleared leather before the second bullet ripped through his forehead.

The townspeople of Crested Butte decided Brannigan's saloon was the safest in which to enjoy themselves when not tending to their daily duties. The next time he was tested, it was with fists. But the results were the same; the altercation always ended with the new owner tossing the challenger out of the establishment. By the time Brannigan rode off to rejoin Cassidy, he was able to leave his saloon in the capable hands of a retired Nebraska sheriff who had concluded working for Brannigan was more rewarding than digging for gold.

While Brannigan was in Crested Butte, Cassidy was also busy. Due to a tip he had received from a friendly telegraph operator while he and his family were in Denver, he visited

the library and the newspaper office to find out more about
E. H. Harriman. It didn't take long for Cassidy to discover
that Harriman was more than unhappy about the train robberies. Harriman had telegraphs sent to each of his train sta-
tions announcing he planned to put a stop to the practice. In
the telegraphs, Harriman specifically mentioned Cassidy and
his gang.

Cassidy wasn't particularly insulted. He viewed his mana-
gerial and planning skills equal to Harriman's. Like Harriman,
he always had an eye to the future.

Brannigan met the gang in Denver, and in a private
meeting with Cassidy described the new business. Later that
night, Butch announced that Brannigan was leaving the
gang so that he could be available to provide assistance,
should any of the members need it. Giving Brannigan
another sack of cash and suggesting that he look for other
opportunities, Cassidy told Brannigan to run it himself.
Cassidy periodically sent funds to be set aside for future use.
Brannigan eventually sent for his family in Missouri, settling them on the Gunnison ranch.

After an hour, Brannigan's voice trailed off. Kindred
again reached for the bottle; but before setting it down, he
said, "That'd be sum story."

"There's more, but nothing of real importance," he
replied. "Other than what you already know. Butch and
Sundance took off after Harriman's men shot up the gang.
Hell, they ran for a couple of days before they finally shook
'em. Butch even told me they jumped off a cliff into some
river, but I don't know if I'd believe that part. Anyway, they
made it back to Etta's, and everybody thinks they took off
for New York—"

"Where'd they go?" interrupted Kindred.

He laughed again. "They did go to New York, of course,"
he said. "But before they got there, I met 'em in Missouri. It's
where we cooked up the story."

"Had yawl been back ta Missou' before?"

"A few times," said Brannigan. "But in this case, there
was a good reason. My family was still there, and I figured

nobody would know Butch and Sundance. Plus, I had a sister who'd got married to a river man. He was so good he was offered a job up in New York guiding them big boats into the harbors, and they'd moved there. Because business here was good, I'd been sending my sis money...for her, and to hold for me." He looked up at Kindred and said, "You know, in case somebody showed up in New York needing money."

"Yawl planned this?"

"Butch mostly. But Etta and me refined it as we went along. Sundance didn't much care what we did as long as it got them out of Harriman's range. Anyway, Butch figured if they took off for Bolivia for a few years, interest would die down and they could come back. But I guess the boys got restless after a while and they started robbing again down there. That's why the army was after them."

"But they didn't git 'em, did they?"

"Depends on how you look at it. According to the newspapers, they got killed in a gun battle and was burned up. It isn't important now, but someday I'll tell you what they did." He picked up the whiskey bottle and replaced the cork. He faced Kindred. "I got to ask," he said. "Knowing what I told you, will you help me?"

"Could ah go ta jail?" Kindred asked. "Ah ain't worried, but ah'd jest like ta know."

"You won't be breaking any laws," he promised. "All I want you to do is take a little trip. At the same time, I'll be going on one myself."

"Where yawl want me ta go?" he asked.

"I thought it'd be good if you took the train back east."

<hr />

The following day, just as the two brothers were finishing the afternoon chores, they heard the sound of horses. "Probably Pa," said Will as he tossed the currycomb onto a shelf in the stall.

"Want me to do the talking?" asked Josh. He followed his brother to the door. "Pa might simmer down if I tell him it's my fault. He'll figure I was too young to know any better."

Ignoring him, Will greeted his father. Looking past Brannigan, he nodded and said, "Afternoon, Silas."

"Will," replied Kindred. He climbed off his horse and rubbed his stiff thighs before tossing Will the reins. "Ah don't do as much ridin' as ah used ta."

"You boys bed down the horses," Brannigan said to his sons as he dismounted. "After supper we'll talk. Don't dawdle."

The brothers led the horses into separate stalls. As Josh was lifting Kindred's saddle onto a wooden bracket he said, "Pa's still mad."

"I don't understand it," the older brother replied. "Maybe it's something other than those papers."

Brannigan led Kindred through the back porch into the kitchen where Molly bent over a dough bowl with a little cloud of white dust rising from her busy hands. She paused to receive Brannigan's gentle kiss. When Kindred stepped out of the house to take his saddlebag to the bunkhouse, Brannigan turned to Molly, "Me, Silas, and the boys have to talk after supper. I'd like you to sit in."

"If you want me there," she said. She watched him pour a cup of coffee before she added, "Daddy Tom, the boys are wondering what they did wrong."

Brannigan set the cup down and sighed. "It's not what they did. It's what I did." He reached up to the shelf over the sink and pulled a bottle and two glasses down and started to the dining room. "The boys opened up an old wound, and we're gonna have to fix it. I should have told them about my past, but the truth is I was hoping it would never come up. That it was behind me forever."

They ate dinner in glum silence, then Molly cleared the table and joined the men in the parlor. Brannigan shortened the story he had told Kindred the night before. When the tale was told, Will was the first to speak, "Pa, it's my fault. What if I return the money and we just forget about it?"

"Not that easy," he said. "A trail from the journal to me to other people that nobody needs to know about is laid out. As a matter of fact, I'm surprised nobody's been here asking questions."

"Maybe the journal doesn't have anything to do with it," said Josh. "Maybe Bates didn't want any trouble from the land grants."

V

Harriman Building—New York City

Kotkin acknowledged Bates with an absentminded glance then returned to the papers scattered on the large desk that had been his father's. Bates sat in a chair and patiently waited for Kotkin to finish before asking the question that burned his throat, "Have you news?"

"Possibly…concerning Etta Place," said Kotkin.

Bates was astonished. "You found her already?"

"Found her isn't quite accurate. According to Father, she left the hospital under mysterious circumstances and disappeared. Pinkerton scoured the hospitals, even contacted the local cemeteries for burial records at that time, but they found nothing." Kotkin pulled out more papers. "I've gone a step further in that I requested they investigate doctors in the area who might have provided treatment for a young woman the night she disappeared. Another ten-year dead end."

"I'm confused," said Bates. "You're telling me there's nothing new, but—"

"Not exactly," interrupted Kotkin. "By expanding our search, we've proven two things: Miss Place does not appear to have received medical assistance, which indicates she wasn't dying. Or for that matter, sick."

"And the second?"

"According to the medical records—scant as they are—she did not leave on her own. She had to have had help," said Kotkin. "Her disappearance indicates Miss Place wasn't as ill as the doctors thought. And, because of my time spent in that cursed jungle, I suspect she might have used potions that could feign a deadly illness unknown to physicians in the United States. Do you recall my face before I used the salve?" Kotkin looked down again at the papers on his desk.

Exasperated, Bates rose and began to pace. "Have you, or
have you not, found Miss Place?"

For the first time Kotkin smiled. "I believe we're nar-
rowing it down," he said. "In the beginning, the Pinkerton
detectives acted under the assumption that Miss Place was
infirmed, even dying, and that it would be necessary to
investigate under the belief she would have had medical
attention. I changed the hypothesis by accepting she had
help in leaving, and by assuming she had not been seriously ill. In the last year I've instructed the detectives who were
working on the case to look for a woman who is alive and
well. And, I believe, living in New York City."

"Why New York?" interrupted Bates.

"The little knowledge that we have of Miss Place—and
Harry Longabaugh—indicates they were originally from
the East and—"

Bates again interrupted. "But logic would dictate they
wouldn't stay in the area where they might be recognized?"

"Recognized? By whom?" countered Kotkin. "It's been
ten years since Longabaugh and Parker left the United
States—besides us, I doubt anyone is looking for a couple of
outlaws no one's heard of in years. Besides, anyone who was
interested had been reassured by the press that they were
dead." He went on, "The only known picture of Longabaugh
shows a man with a thick mustache, long hair and a deep
tan. Don't you think it would be easy for Longabaugh to
change his appearance?" Kotkin slid the picture across the
desk for Bates to better contemplate the answer. After a
glance, Bates gestured to continue.

"The only Pinkerton description of Etta Place tells me
that she is of medium height, had dark hair, and was a
comely woman. Before she took up with Longabaugh somewhere in Wyoming or Colorado, she'd been a schoolteacher.
I sent detectives to the small towns where Longabaugh and
Parker were known to have operated and may have lived.
The Pinkerton men were thorough, as you know. They
searched through the sparse municipal records, also visited
schools and talked to as many of the locals as possible."

"In Greeley, Colorado, they got a lead that Miss Place was indeed attractive, and she was an independent woman periodically seen with a handsome man assumed to be her husband. She taught from 1895 until 1899 when she suddenly announced she was returning to her parent's home in the East. Another piece of information was that Miss Place was surprisingly adept with a pistol and rifle—she once won a ladies shooting contest at the fair."

Bates reclaimed his chair and sat with crossed arms. "So what does all this mean for today—for our search?" he asked.

"Most people who wish to change their appearance do so by becoming the opposite," he said. "For example, Miss Place may now have shorter light-colored hair, and because of the cooler weather in the East, she would probably have fairer skin. Longabaugh, on the other hand, would also shorten his hair, maybe even change the color, although I doubt that, and he might have shaved the facial hair." He continued, "I think they would have stayed in the New York area because they rightfully assume that they would not be recognized. However, having said all that, it's possible I'm entirely wrong," he said and smiled.

Bates was now clearly impatient. "All you have to do is look for a man and a woman who possess the characteristics you've just described. There can't be more than fifty thousand couples like that in New York alone."

"Probably more," admitted Kotkin. Raising his hand, he quelled Bates' mild outburst. "Longabaugh was originally from New Jersey and still has family there. Unfortunately, no one with the Longabaugh name will admit to even knowing him, much less claim him as a relative. Quite frankly, the Pinkerton investigation hasn't found anyone who will even talk about the infamous Sundance Kid. If you think about it, this in itself is significant. If he's dead, why wouldn't someone be willing to talk about him?"

Kotkin had ordered Pinkerton agents to expand their search. He suggested that the agency use its formidable reputation to check with banks for any large deposits made by a single woman. He also wanted them to contact hotels for purchases of apartments from 1907 to 1909. And, assuming there weren't unlimited funds to live on, schools that might have employed Miss Place while she waited for Longabaugh's return. The Pinkertons expanded the investigation to businesses that were similar to work performed by Longabaugh, other than thieving, while he was out West—anything related to horses, such as livery stables. So far, nothing had shown up.

Bates pulled an expensive timepiece out of the front of his vest. "I don't have much time. Do you, or do you not, know the whereabouts of these people?"

Kotkin ignored the question. Instead, he rose and walked to the window. As he stared down at the street, he asked, "What are you doing about the Brannigan situation?"

Surprised, Bates hesitated, and then said, "I've just recently authorized another installment on the agreement. Why?"

Turning back to face him, Kotkin repeated, "Why?" He shook his head before saying, "Because it is possible that young man is related to this story."

"Brannigan's not old enough to be involved; he can't be more than twenty-five."

"Perhaps there's an older Mr. Brannigan."

"Meaning?"

"According to LeFors, it's possible there were other members of Parker's gang," he said. "After all, no one knew for sure how many were involved, and perhaps young Brannigan has knowledge of other people in the gang." He returned to his chair, and as he sat, reached for a thin file. He was quiet for so long that Bates took another look at his watch and rose to leave. His mouth was forming a goodbye when Kotkin said flatly, "It's something I've decided to look into personally."

Bates stared at him. "If you're sure the situation warrants your personal involvement, by all means," he said. "But if you plan to handle the matter in the way you were trained, it's imperative you also obtain the journal."

This time it was Kotkin who looked up. "Do you know its contents?" he curiously asked. "Father never revealed the specifics, other than the event. That, in itself, would be damaging."

"I have knowledge," admitted Bates. After a moment of thought, he went on, "Pardon me, Elias, I'm not being forthcoming. It's obvious that I never saw the document young Mr. Brannigan alluded to. But when Mr. Harriman enlisted my services to deal with this issue, he went into depth as to the problem, subsequently relating the significance of the journal. Suffice it to say your father was correct in his assessment: this book could bring down not only the business, but also the entire family." Before closing the door, he said, "Equally important, this is also a political issue. There could be enough of a public outcry that other companies could be destroyed. Therefore, only when it's time, will I reveal the contents to you."

Kotkin stared at the door for some time. He wondered how possession of an article that could be so devastating as to be able to shake the Harriman empire, was allowed to go unchecked for as long as it had. With a sigh, he turned his attention to the file.

As usual, the Pinkerton detectives had been thorough in their search for Miss Place, even in the absence of solid clues. After adopting the theory that she hadn't been ill and was the front for the eventual return of Parker and Longabaugh, the agents had searched for property transfers. In addition, they contacted building owners for evidence of a single woman renting or buying a home. This would have stood out. Given the difficulty of a woman buying property, she could have had a proxy—perhaps someone in Longabaugh's family—purchase a dwelling for her. The investigation was made more difficult by the lack of sales records.

However, Kotkin had insisted the detectives pursue this line of thinking. He'd decided that if Longabaugh returned to the United States—and assuming the outlaw wasn't planning on resuming his criminal career—he would hide in plain view. He'd become a businessman with unshakable credentials, lost in New York City.

While in Bolivia, Kotkin had discovered just how successful Parker and Longabaugh had been in their bank robbing escapades. Not only had they robbed most of the banks in several countries, but they had managed to rob the same bank more than once—one bank had been driven out of business after it had been hit for the third time. With a bit of luck, Kotkin had discovered a remarkable piece of information while interviewing the colonel whose army had spent the better part of three years chasing the bandits.

In early 1907, prior to the return of Etta Place to America, the outlaws hired out as security guards for the richest gold-mining outfit in the country. Their job was to go with the owner to the city to bring back the payroll for his employees. Kotkin had been incredulous at the idea of the two robbers being given the job of guarding the very thing they were constantly stealing. However, the owner of the mine was an American, and perhaps he thought he'd have better luck with his own countrymen. His trust was short-lived. After withdrawing thousands of dollars in gold coin from a bank Parker and Longabaugh had already robbed, the owner's body had been found on the trail back to the mine. No sign of the payroll.

That scenario did not surprise Kotkin. However, the colonel added a twist to the story: the bodies of five men, with a few gold coins scattered about, were found less than a mile away—all of whom had been shot. The colonel theorized that the murdered men were accomplices, and that the *Bandidos Yanquis* had killed them to avoid splitting up the money. The colonel admitted he was surprised that all had been shot from the front while standing. He assumed that the *bandidos* would have killed the men by sneaking from behind and shooting them in the back.

Kotkin doubted this. In the eight years Parker and Longabaugh had been in Bolivia, never once had there been any indication that Butch and Sundance had a gang.

Witnesses had described a third person minding the horses as a small man, but his face was always hidden. Kotkin had no doubt this person was Etta Place.

If Parker and Longabaugh had helped themselves to the payroll, it would have been enough to allow their return to America. Robbing banks was profitable for someone willing to remain in a backwater country. It would never have provided enough funds for the two outlaws, one with a woman, to return and live without returning to their old ways. *No, thought Kotkin, the boys finally made a large score.*

The dates worked. Shortly after the payroll robbery, Etta Place and Longabaugh booked passage and showed up in New York. The only thing that bothered Kotkin was why Parker didn't return with the others and start over then. *What could cause Parker to remain behind? And why would Longabaugh go back to South America?*

At one time, the outlaws owned a ranch in Argentina. Perhaps Parker stayed there while waiting for Longabaugh's return from New York. Kotkin turned and surveyed the room. And then it hit him: the outlaws were shaken by the posse that Harriman had sent to kill them. If they were gone long enough, no one would give them a thought. *Was it entirely possible they decided to simply wait?* According to the colonel, after the payroll robbery, the bandidos disappeared and there were no further robberies. *Until that day they were spotted in that café by an observant waiter who quickly informed the local police,* Kotkin reminded himself.

He sat at his desk and pulled out another file with the names of the members of the posse. Legendary lawman Joe LeFors headed the posse and had selected each member, including an Indian tracker they called Lord Baltimore. After Parker and Longabaugh disappeared, LeFors returned to Oklahoma and eventually left public life. The Indian was never heard from again.

Suddenly inspired, Kotkin tossed the file back on the desk and hurried down the hall to Charles Bates' office. He entered without knocking. "When did Father find out he was ill?" Bates didn't seem surprised by the intrusion.

"Nineteen-eight," Bates calmly answered. "Near the end of the year…in fact, he told me right before Christmas."

"Did it become public knowledge then?"

Bates shook his head. "No. But it wasn't long before it did. Keep in mind your father was a well-known man and it was inevitable that rumors would get started. As his illness progressed, he stopped most public appearances. This caused friends and business associates to speculate on how sick he must be."

Kotkin inexplicably smiled. "It's beginning to make sense," he said. "The posse that Father put together was headed by—"

"LeFors," said Bates. "I know—"

Ignoring the interruption, Kotkin continued, "—LeFors. And by then, the Indian had disappeared and was probably dead, and the rest of the posse was scattered. Then in '08, Father's illness becomes known, or at least suspected. That's why Parker and Longabaugh waited…someone here in the States was tracking my father. And at some point, this person let them know he was dying. It wouldn't have been hard; as you said, Father was a public figure. So Parker and Longabaugh bided their time, planning on returning once he was dead."

Bates eyed him. "A little coincidental, don't you think?"

"Absolutely not," he replied. "It makes perfect sense. Unusual, I'd agree, but in my line of work, I've found that coincidences are usually not coincidences at all." He quickly related the payroll incident, before saying, "Don't you see? This makes perfect sense: Parker manages to secure enough funds for their return, he sends Miss Place and Longabaugh back with the money—or at least a portion of it—and, at the same time, while in the U.S., Longabaugh could find out if anyone was still after them."

"All right," conceded Bates. "Your theory does make sense."

"It does. And I must say, I admire their thinking," Kotkin smiled before turning serious, "With all this speculation comes a concerning thought."

"What's that?"

"They had help stateside," he said. "Someone had to be providing information. Young Brannigan could be the conduit to that person."

"If that's the case, what do you intend to do?"

In a voice that chilled the air between them, Kotkin replied, "Go to Colorado."

VI

T he train arrived at the New York Grand Central Station a few minutes ahead of time. The last passenger to disembark, satchel in hand, stepped down onto the concourse and looked around the massive building with awe. Even though on business for Tom Brannigan, Kindred had thoroughly enjoyed his first cross-country train ride. He'd slept little as the train moved on its seemingly endless journey across the country, not wanting to miss a minute of the ride.

Kindred wore the finest clothes he'd ever owned. He constantly ran a finger around his collar to escape the pressure of the heavily starched shirt. On the train this morning he had changed into the new clothes that Brannigan insisted he wear while in the city, explaining it was important not to stand out. For this reason, it was one of the few times in Kindred's life that he wasn't wearing his Stetson hat. Kindred walked through the gate where the impatient porter glared at the small man. "Didn't think you were ever getting off," the man said as he closed and locked the gate.

About to respond, Kindred's comment died in his throat when a slender young man stepped out of the shadows. "Mr. Silas Kindred?" he asked.

"Yessir," he replied, shifting his case to his left hand.

"I'm Randolph O'Toole," he said. "I've been sent to fetch you to my boss. And then take you to your hotel."

"Let's git goin'," Kindred said with a look at the porter.

O'Toole led Kindred to a side street where the wagon was waiting. He removed the feedbags he'd put on the horses to keep them quiet and climbed onto the seat as Kindred did the same from the opposite side. "Got a nice-lookin' team," he commented as the young man untied the reins and urged the animals into action. O'Toole nodded and was about to speak when Kindred asked, "How 'bout stoppin' at ma hotel fust fer me ta clean up a bit?"

Because it was his first time talking with someone who spoke with such a pronounced Texas drawl, it took a few seconds for O'Toole to respond. "Uh...all right. Your hotel's the Ludlow. It's small, but nice, and you'll be comfortable." If Kindred's Texas accent was hard for O'Toole to understand, the young man's clipped words were equally difficult for Kindred. He wasn't entirely sure what O'Toole had said, so he simply nodded.

It wasn't long before the wagon stopped and O'Toole pointed to a building across the street. "They'll have a key waiting. If you don't mind, I'll stay with the horses."

Kindred hopped off the wagon. He stepped into the street and was almost run over by a smoke-belching vehicle screeching around the corner at breakneck speed. Jumping back, he waited a few seconds; now cautious, Kindred looked in both directions before crossing to the hotel entrance. He paused for a look around the lobby and then walked to the front desk to be greeted by a bored clerk. Ten minutes later, minus his satchel, and with his collar wet from rinsing his face in the washbasin in his room, Kindred climbed back into the wagon.

The last part of the journey was accomplished in short order. As the wagon rounded a corner Kindred saw the sign that announced he had arrived at the warehouse and stable of the Longley Freight Company. An office fronted the warehouse, and to the side, large doors opened into a stable that housed numerous buckboards and wagons. He could hear the sounds of horses and guessed they were corralled in the back. *All in all, this has the makin's of a right fine outfit*, he thought as he hopped off the wagon.

A scowling, heavily-muscled black man wearing an impeccable white dress shirt under his workman's overalls emerged from the stable. His right eye was milky and never moved, giving him a menacing appearance. After appraising Kindred from head to toe, a friendly white-toothed grin softened his broad face, and in a deep baritone voice the man said, "Marcus Tyler, Mr. Longley's foreman." He didn't extend a hand. "He said for you to go on in the office." Tyler attached a rope to the bridle of the lead horse and, while O'Toole remained in the seat, led the wagon into the stable.

Kindred pushed the door open into a small office with rolltop desks in two of the corners, a wood-burning stove in the center of the room. He was wondering why there wasn't anyone to greet him, when the door in the back opened and a man stepped in. "Silas Kindred?" he asked.

"Yessir," replied Kindred. In spite of himself, he couldn't help staring. "Yawl must be Longley."

The man nodded and led Kindred down a hallway to a second office, where he pointed to a chair. Longley was just over six feet tall. He was wearing a business suit, his light-colored hair was short by current standards and he sported a well-trimmed mustache cut close over his lip. His eyes were a piercing blue, and Kindred had the feeling Longley was looking directly into his soul as he appraised the short cowboy. The man in front of him did not look anything like his picture, but Kindred knew he was sitting across from Harry Longabaugh. As he walked around the desk the man said, "I'm James Longley."

"Yessir," agreed Kindred. "Tom Brannigan sent me."

"We got his telegram," said Longley. "He said we could trust you. And that you had something to tell me."

"Nice 'a him ta say thet," said Kindred, a little embarrassed. "Ah'm much beholdin' ta Tom. He's a good 'un—and ah'm proud ta be his podner."

There was silence, until Longley spoke, "I guess you know the whole story."

Kindred hesitatingly said, "Tom was, uh, as truthful as he could be 'bout yore past."

"He's always been honest—and loyal," Longley said with a small smile. The smile faded, as he asked, "What's so important that he had to send you all the way from Colorado."

From his inside coat pocket, Kindred pulled out a thick envelope, handed it to Longley, and then sat back to wait.

The only sound in the room was the rustle of the stiff paper. Minutes passed before Longley said, "Tom's right."

"Ah don' know what he writ, but it seems like Tom's boys ain't been a big hep ta yawl," said Kindred. Choosing his words carefully, he continued in his slow drawl, "Course, they don't know no better, and ah'd hate ta see trouble comin' at 'em."

"I've never met the boys," admitted Longley. "But Tom said they didn't mean any harm, so that's good enough for me." He held up the letter and said, "He also says that Hattie and I ought to take a vacation, even suggested Denver was nice this time of year. It's been awhile since we've been out west. Maybe he's right."

"Yessir. Uh, is Hattie yore wife?" asked Kindred.

Before Longley could answer, the door swung open and a woman entered. As Kindred stood, she acknowledged him with a smile, before crossing behind the desk and kissing Longley on the cheek. "Forgive me for being late," she said.

"My wife," Longley said to Kindred. "Hattie, this is Tom Brannigan's partner, Silas Kindred." Turning back, he said, "Since you know most of the story, Silas, you might as well know she changed her name too."

"How do, ma'am," mumbled Kindred. Always shy with women, her appearance left him flustered and at a loss for words.

Hattie Longley was also slender and above average in height. Her thick hair was combed off her neck and, unlike her husband, was quite in style, although she did allow a wave of hair to flow over her forehead, softly framing her face. Pale perfect skin accented her brown eyes, full lips and a dimpled chin combined to present the impression of a woman both intelligent and beautiful. Kindred would have sworn Hattie Longley was still in her twenties, if he hadn't known that Etta Place was much older.

Longley handed her the letter. "You might want to look at this," he suggested. While Hattie was reading, he turned his attention back to Kindred. "Did Tom tell you what to do while you're here?"

"Well...ah guess ah'm ta wait 'til yawl tell me what ta take back ta him," he slowly replied. "Course, he's on a trip hisself." As an afterthought, Kindred added, "Ah guess ah could hep with the chores awhal am heah."

Looking up, Hattie asked, "Tom's in Oregon?"

"Yes ma'am," said Kindred. Shyly, he asked, "How'd ya know, ma'am?"

"Stop calling me 'ma'am'," she said. "From what Tom says, you're a member of his family, which makes you a friend of ours."

"Yes, ma'am."

"Call me Hattie." Gesturing at Longley, she said, "And call him James."

Brannigan's first thought was that the train station in Portland was considerably different than its counterpart in New York that he had visited long ago. Carrying his bag, he stepped into the light mist that made the morning pleasantly cool and followed the line of passengers to the station, but skirted the entrance and walked around the building to the street. Brannigan set his bag on the wooden sidewalk and watched the wagon traffic for a few minutes. "Excuse me," he asked a passing stranger. "Where would I find a livery stable?"

The man stopped, thought for a moment, and then said, "Best go to Orrin's around that corner." He pointed and added, "He hires out carriages and wagons." Brannigan nodded; he picked up his bag and started walking in the direction the passerby had indicated. To his surprise, the man fell in step with him. "If you don't mind my asking," he said. "Are you planning on renting a horse?"

"I am," said Brannigan.

"Tell him Rafe sent you—that's me," said the man. "Orrin's damned good about buying a man a drink for recommending his outfit." Rafe picked up his pace to match Brannigan's and asked, "You know where you're going?"

Brannigan stopped. After looking the man up and down,

he decided Rafe was harmless and resumed walking. "Carlisle Lumber Mill. I've been told it's on the river."

"Yep...the Columbia...the mill's about four miles east of town," said Rafe. "Orrin's place sits just up from the river and you can see the road to Carlisle's from his gate." He stopped, tipped his hat, and said, "I best get on to work, but don't forget to remind me to Orrin."

Brannigan walked three blocks before finding the gate that opened into a grassy area in front of the stable. As Rafe had promised, he could see the river at the end of the street. He walked through the open door and came face to face with an old man whose thatch of white hair perfectly matched his eyebrows. "You Orrin?" asked Brannigan.

"Yup," he said. "Who would you be?"

"Name's Brannigan and I need a horse. Could be for today, but I might be gone as long as two." As an afterthought he added, "Or maybe even three."

The old man carefully appraised Brannigan before he replied, "Well, you look like a man that knows which end goes forward. Can't be too careful these days—damned Eastern dandies come to town and try to ride. Half the time they end up getting throw'd, and half the time it's my animal that gets hurt." Orrin carefully spit tobacco juice away from Brannigan's boots.

Beginning to like the old man, he said, "I'm pretty sure I can avoid all that."

"Believe you can," he agreed. Once again he looked Brannigan over. "Well, I got a nice gelding. He's big and fast, but well broke. You can have him for seventy-five cents a day, but you got to feed and water him."

"Include tack?"

"Yup," said the old man. He pointed to a room and said, "You pick out a saddle and blanket while I run back and bring in Widowmaker."

Brannigan paused at the door of the tack room and reached in his pocket to pull out three dollars. "You can pay me back if I don't use it all. By the way, that's an interesting name for the horse. What's the story?"

The old man accepted the money and started for the back of the stable. He stopped and asked, "Why do you think he ain't a stallion no more?" He reached for a set of reins hanging on a post and headed to the back door. "The wife of the late previous owner named him—right after Widowmaker throw'd her man through the fence."

Ten minutes later, after saddling the big gray, Brannigan adjusted the stirrups before taking the reins. As he led the animal out of the stable, he said, "Seems well-mannered."

Orrin nodded in agreement. "That he is. Now, he might jump a bit at first, but that's just because he ain't been rode lately."

Brannigan separated the reins, tossing them around the gelding's neck. He briefly whispered to the horse before swinging himself up in the saddle—true to form, the gelding jumped and would have bolted had he not been shown firm hands. Orrin watched in satisfaction. "Thought you might do well with him." He set Brannigan's bag on the back of the saddle and tied it down.

"You do this for all your customers? Or just the ones that ride Widowmaker?"

"Nope," said the old man. "I generally don't let too many ride this fella."

Brannigan laughed. "I appreciate it," he said. "By the way, some fellow by the name of Rafe said I was supposed to tell you he sent me down here."

"Damn," swore Orrin. "If I'd known, I would have told you the price was eighty cents to help me cover his fill." Shaking his head, he looked up and asked, "You want to tell me where you're taking my animal? Just in case you don't come back, of course."

"The Carlisle place," he said. "I'm told it's a few miles east."

"That it is. Just follow the river," said Orrin. "You know Mr. Carlisle?" Brannigan's eyes darkened and the old man hurriedly said, "Even though Mr. Carlisle hasn't been in Portland all that long, he's well thought of."

"I'm a customer of the mill," said Brannigan. "Robert's expecting me."

The old man nodded. "Didn't mean to be nosy," he said. "If you don't mind, I have something Mr. Carlisle asked for. Would you take it?" Brannigan waited patiently as the old man hurried to the back of the stable, emerging with a newspaper-wrapped package. He tied it on top of the bag and stepped back. "It's a set of reins for the older son," said Orrin. "If it be a bother, I can have somebody else do it."

"No bother," said Brannigan. He touched the brim of his hat and lightly kicked Widowmaker. Urging the horse into a trot, it wasn't long before he reached the river and turned east. The rain had subsided and a bright sun was peeking through rapidly thinning gray clouds.

With better weather, the ride to the Carlisle Mill was both pleasant and entertaining. The Columbia River was heavy with fast-flowing water, the current creating rapids along the rock-laden banks of the river. The road was damp but there was no standing water. It wasn't long before Brannigan rounded a bend and discovered he'd arrived at the mill. His arrival had been anticipated, a man jumped down from the fence as Brannigan approached.

"Morning," he called. "I'm Lawrence. My father sent me to watch for you."

Brannigan stared at the young man whose image was that of a young Butch Cassidy. Lawrence possessed the same light-blue eyes, devilish grin, and easy-going air as his father. "I'm Brannigan," he said as he swung his leg over the saddle horn. "A friend of your father's."

"I know," said Lawrence. He shook Brannigan's hand.

"Where's your pa?"

"He's at the house. Pa thought you might want some dinner, and afterward he'll show you the mill. He figures you'll stay for supper and probably the night. We're all looking forward to talking with you."

Brannigan nodded, and asked, "How old are you?"

"Twenty-eight, a year younger than my brother," he said.

"My boys are twenty-three and twenty-six." After a pause he said, "My wife and daughter died a few years ago."

"I know that too," said Lawrence. "Pa's told us a lot since he came back." Turning, he said, "Let's walk on up to the house."

Although both were located on the river, the lumber mill hid the white clapboard house that sat a quarter mile up the river. Brannigan led his horse, following the young man as they walked the short distance. A boy was waiting by the front door, and as the two men approached, he took the reins, leading Widowmaker around the back of the house to the barn. "Make sure he gets water and feed," called Brannigan. "And mind that package for Mr. Carlisle." The boy glanced back and dipped his head before continuing on without a word.

"Don't worry about him, he'll take good care of your horse," said Lawrence. "He doesn't say much, but he's good with horses."

"That's an admirable thing," said Brannigan as he followed Lawrence up the steps into a foyer with a curved stairway leading up to bedrooms. They continued through the parlor into a dining room where two men sat at opposite ends of a large oak table. The older man at the far end rose. "How are you, Tom?" asked Robert Carlisle. "It's been a long time."

With a glance at the second man who could have been Lawrence's twin, Brannigan laughed aloud as Robert Leroy Parker bear hugged him while Lawrence and David looked on. Matching the embrace, Brannigan stepped back and asked, "Where's Kate?"

"You mean Theodora," Carlisle quickly said with a familiar grin. "Thea's in the kitchen." Turning to his sons, he said, "Go help your mother bring in dinner." The boys immediately left the room; seconds later, voices could be heard from behind the door.

"I wouldn't have recognized you," said Brannigan. It was true. Not as tall as Longabaugh by three inches, Carlisle was trim, and he looked like he could still ride any horse alive. The familiar grin was there—the one that made everyone around him feel at ease. Even so, to Brannigan, his old partner seemed remarkably different. After a minute, he grinned and said, "That beard. It changes your face."

"Yeah," agreed Carlisle, ruefully tugging at the trimmed gray hair that left only his lips exposed. "Took me some time to get used to it." He looked Brannigan over. "You look good," he said. "Haven't gone to fat."

"Not yet anyway," he agreed. "Lawrence says you and Thea told the boys all about the old days."

"I owed it to them." Carlisle led Brannigan over to a side table under the window, and as he poured the whiskey, gestured toward the kitchen with a nod of his head. "There's plenty of time to talk, so let's take it easy while we eat," he said. "And Thea's planning on putting you up in the guest bedroom, so I guess you should count on staying a few days." Carlisle walked backed to his chair and pointed across the table. "Sit and enjoy your drink."

Both men were getting comfortable when the door from the kitchen opened and Thea Carlisle walked in with a platter in each hand. Carlisle's wife was on the short side—just an inch or two over five feet tall. She had rosy cheeks, a lively smile, and curly brown hair that was just beginning to gray up. The apron she was wearing covered most of a neck-high yellow blouse that was tucked into her long black skirt. Realizing he had never met Butch's wife, Brannigan hurriedly stood as she set the platters down and turned to him, saying, "Robert's told me all about you." With a smile, she extended her hand, which Brannigan gently touched.

Brannigan resumed sitting. "You have a beautiful place here."

"It took some time to get settled," she said with a glance at her husband.

Lawrence and David came into the dining room and took their places. Thea offered a blessing and began passing dishes. As they ate, Brannigan glanced often at Robert Carlisle who was directing the conversation by making suggestions to his sons as to the milling schedule for the afternoon. For her part, Thea questioned Brannigan about Colorado, smiling at his descriptions of Crested Butte and the Rocky Mountains.

✦

After dinner, Carlisle gave his old friend a tour of the lumber mill. The size of the business and the number of men working impressed Brannigan. That evening they were met by Thea and the boys for a supper of cold beef, tomatoes, and vegetables from Thea's garden.

Later, as the men sat in front of the fire, Carlisle was the first to speak. "I'm glad you're here, Tom, but you said you have some news that might be troubling."

Brannigan reached into a canvas sack that he had brought from his room and removed a leather-bound book. "This is it," he said as he glanced at the two sons. "You might remember that we came into possession of this and other papers the next to the last time we hit the Union Pacific." He handed the book to Carlisle.

Turning the book in his hands, Carlisle examined the cover before opening it. "The famous journal," he said to himself. He looked up at Brannigan. "This could be more interesting than when we first got it. I never bothered to read it."

"Until you'd been gone, I didn't either," Brannigan said as he once again glanced at Carlisle's sons. After hesitating, he said to the boys, "I know your pa has told you everything, but if you don't mind, I need to talk to him alone. He'll tell you what you need to know later."

Carlisle searched Brannigan's eyes before turning to his sons. "I've known Tom for a long time, so let me find out what's going on," he said. "Why don't you go on up to bed? If there's something we need to talk about, we can do it tomorrow."

Hiding his disappointment, David stood and nudged his brother, "Come on, we have to get up early." Both men stopped to shake Brannigan's hand before climbing the stairs to the bedrooms above.

Brannigan waited until he heard the doors close. "I know you trust your sons, but it just hit me hard that we need to talk about this first." He rubbed his eyes before going on. "I think we've got a problem that could get out of hand. Did you ever think these railroad boys might have a reason to come looking for you?"

Holding up the book, Carlisle flashed his easy grin. "You must have found something in here," he said. "Something that's got you spooked."

"Why don't you start reading while I get us a refill?" By the time Brannigan returned with the whiskey bottle, Carlisle had read the first two pages. He barely glanced up as Brannigan set the glass on the table next to his chair, sat down, and took a sip of his drink.

Minutes later, Carlisle straightened. He quickly flipped through the remaining pages before saying, "This is going to take longer than I thought." In spite of his good humor, his voice had an edge.

"Take your time," said Brannigan. "I'm right comfortable. In fact, I might take me a little nap while you read."

From the Journal of E. H. Harriman

JUNE 1, 1864 — At last, I'm on my own. Completing my course of study in economics has already proved beneficial, and joining the brokerage house of Thomas and Bothefield here in Philadelphia was a wise move. In spite of this cursed War, I accepted their kind offer in lieu of a commission in the Union forces. It is clear to me that the North will put down the Southern Renegades and restore the Union to its former brilliance—and my battlefield heroics, or loss of my life, would not change the outcome whatsoever.

My rise to the position of personal assistant to Mr. Thomas lent a unique perspective.

At this time, Mr. Thomas is engaged in placing the Firm in a most advantageous position following the completion of the Insurrection. As such, he has ordered me to accept a temporary assignment with Mr. Covell Worthington, senior aide to Mr. Edwin Stanton, Secretary of War for our United States. My purpose is simple: become a confidant to those men who are charged with bringing this war to its successful conclusion, while at the same time exerting as much influence as possible to dissuade the President of his mild position on the Reconstruction of the South. There is much speculation that Mr. Lincoln's aides are engaged in developing plans that would allow the return of the South's agriculture production, restoring that part of our country to a position that could lead to another insurrection.

Mr. Thomas feels this would not be in the best interest of our firm. He wants to be in position to receive a full share from plundering what's left in the defeated South.

He is quite correct. As such, I have decided to keep this Record—believing that I am embarking on a journey that will lead me to my rightful place in life and in this firm.

To make certain that my mission will be a success, Mr. Thomas has shared secrets with me concerning certain business dealings between him and Mr. Worthington that emanated from the latter's position within the Government.

I am to use this knowledge at my own discretion.

One thing is clear: I must develop a relationship with Mr. Stanton—this comes on the advice from Mr. Thomas himself, who seems to know more about the Secretary than he is predisposed to say. It is also clear that I am placing myself in a tenuous position. Danger lurks at all times with Treasury agents' unending pursuit of spies and Confederate sympathizers. My future is mine to make, and that future holds great wealth. Barring foolish mistakes on my part, I will endeavor to listen, plan, and set myself on a path of my own determination.

JUNE 10, 1864 — On my arrival last week, I was met by Mr. Worthington himself.

A rotund man, Covell is constantly flushed of face, and as a result of not availing himself of a bath on a consistent basis, possesses a most unpleasant odor. I have subsequently discovered that this peculiar characteristic is not uncommon among those men who walk the Halls of our Government.

This journal will serve as a record of my personal activities, as well as a potential weapon against those who profess beliefs contrary to my own. I have already discovered there are numerous officials who seem to be in accord with Mr. Lincoln's soft plans.

JULY 5, 1864 — Yesterday was a day of celebration for us. Not only the joyousness of this great country's birth, but also the anniversary of our stupendous victory at Gettysburg, which took place last year from July 1st through July 3rd. Following the Grand Celebration, I must admit to being pleased at an invitation I received from Secretary Stanton. Apparently my work with Covell is already being considered, and the Secretary has suggested I join him and Covell for dinner at his home. I look forward to the meeting, and dedicate myself to pleasing any who can do so much for my future.

JULY 11, 1864 — Dinner with Mr. Stanton was highly successful. Covell has told me that the Secretary is impressed with my work and ideas, and he commanded a report from me concerning my firm's position on the question of resurrection of the South. The War is going quite well now, and our Forces are beginning to exert their will on the Confederates (no one here calls them Renegades). The North prevails and will soon be able to capture General Lee and imprison President Davis. There are no other Southern Leaders with whom we need trifle.

JULY 31, 1864 — Only two days after completing and submitting my report to Covell, I was summoned by the Secretary. Mr. Stanton was quite effusive in his praise and I admit to a feeling of great satisfaction, as I believe I have advanced the case against restoration of the South. Our nation would be best served by utilizing Southern resources for the advancement of our national treasury. Our win should enable the Government to set whatever punishments it deems necessary for the Confederates. It would be more than a bit ironic if the Government inflicted a form of slavery on the South. Ironic because slavery, while a contention, was not the primary cause of this conflict. If we could have control of the agriculture and shipping industries that have proven so successful for the Confederates, our country would surely become the most powerful in the world. Regardless what the British or other Europeans think, economic might is far superior to the number of soldiers, in spite of how well armed or well trained they might be. In re-reading my thoughts, I must laugh, I see I have strayed from relating the facts of my meeting with the Secretary.

In fact, Mr. Stanton seems of like mind. I say seems to because he is a politician and rarely expresses declarative positions; instead, he waltzes around issues, waiting to see which way the wind is blowing. Currently, in public at least, the Secretary reinforces his loyalty to Mr. Lincoln and endorses the same attitude toward Reconstruction as is being circulated by the President's aides.

In private, Mr. Stanton has indicated a far less generous attitude toward the enemy—today's meeting was singular for me in that the Secretary wanted to hear more of my
opinions on the absorption of the industries of the
Confederacy. I admit that I strenuously reiterated my firmly
held convictions. After a few minutes of consideration, the
Secretary asked me two rhetorical questions...or at least I
took them to be rhetorical.

How far am I willing to go to advance my ideas? What
price am I willing to pay?

AUGUST 18, 1864 — The War goes well. Union advances
have been steady.

General Sherman has begun to advance his march
through the South and now approaches Atlanta, vowing to
burn everything in his path. Having once met the General,
I do not doubt his resolve.

SEPTEMBER 3, 1864 — Early this morning, the Secretary
was summoned to a meeting with the President and other
Cabinet members. Upon his return, I joined Mr. Stanton in
his chambers where I learned that Atlanta had fallen, and
was indeed burning. The Secretary further informed me that
General Sherman was preparing to continue his march to
the sea, cutting through South Carolina and continuing the
destruction. The Secretary was agitated by this—clearly he
is concerned that the surrender of the South could come
soon. Mr. Stanton has a more far reaching interest than
simply defeating the enemy. I duly notified Mr. Thomas
by telegraph.

SEPTEMBER 29, 1864 — *My relationship with the Secretary has advanced considerably. He now seems to see me as more than a lowly aide. Covell was not asked to attend today's meeting, and as a result he has become quite short with me. Poor Covell. His life revolves around Mr. Stanton and it is apparent he now sees me as an adversary. I cannot afford to offend him at this time and will take appropriate action to make amends and re-establish the relationship.*

My meeting with the Secretary began with a discussion of Mr. Lincoln's policies regarding the South, but it did not take long before Mr. Stanton reached his main point. He wishes me to meet with a committee exploring ways to sway the President's position on Restoration. I admit to concern and trepidation over his request. Partly because before the Secretary discussed this issue he requested all others leave. This means these meetings are to be clandestine in nature. However, I see no alternative and at the Secretary's suggestion will meet with Sir Reginald Forrester of Rothschilds Bank, London.

This group's interest is not surprising—given that the European bankers have made no secret of their dissatisfaction of the policies of the President. Mr. Lincoln was rightly offended at the exorbitant interest rate under which these bankers were willing to fund the war. Thank God he was able to arrange other financing, albeit at the displeasure of the Europeans, especially the House of Rothschild. Now the Europeans see our conflict as a great opportunity for investment, and while I share in their zeal for increased profitability, I abhor the idea of this group buying my country at a bargain price. In answer to the questions Mr. Stanton asked some time ago, I am willing to go far and pay a great price to prevent foreign interlopers from making a puppet of my country.

OCTOBER 15, 1864 — Sir Reginald is a man of charm, possessing a quick wit and great intelligence. He expounded at length on the dilemma that arises if the question of leniency to the South is not resolved. I would be less than truthful if I did not admit to suspicions about European involvement; however, Sir Reginald has assured me that his Consortium is interested in the United States solely as a passive investment. He has full understanding of the potential value of the resources of the South and is specifically interested in textiles, agriculture, and shipping. Sir Reginald views the Southern ports as gateways to the West, which he perceives as a primary opportunity for this country's growth. He is quick to point out that railroads connecting the country would be an extremely valuable commodity. I could not agree more, having become fascinated with this line of thinking.

This evening, I joined Mr. Stanton for a dinner at the Willard Hotel. The Secretary enjoys strutting down the Promenade (the local people call it Peacock Alley) before sitting down to a sumptuous dinner in the main dining salon. It was evident as to the power and public popularity of the Secretary, as he was given his customary table next to the window overlooking the garden, with the neighboring tables left empty to afford Mr. Stanton and his guest privacy. These arrangements met my approval, for my report of today's meeting with Sir Reginald was certainly for his ears only. I would have been more comfortable meeting behind closed doors in Mr. Stanton's chambers and will insist upon this for future meetings. Perhaps the Secretary does not realize the potential danger I am opening myself to, and that care should be given to minimize pitfalls.

The dinner itself was grand. Over brandy and cigars, the Secretary asked for a full report on my meeting with Sir Reginald. Mr. Stanton is a surprisingly good listener. He is easy to talk to and rarely interrupts except when additional explanation is needed.

As I spoke, I could see he was in full agreement with
Sir Reginald. I could not help pointing out that it was my
opinion that the Europeans were untrustworthy.

At the completion of my dissertation, the Secretary agreed
and then suggested a meeting with a second committee (the
continued use of this word, for some reason, causes me
unease). He gave me a sealed envelope and contact information for a representative of a group that, relative to the
South Reconstruction, has an agenda in order to advance
their positions. However, it was what followed that not only
surprised me, but with further thought has me greatly concerned.

Before handing me another envelope—and suggesting
I wait to open it until I was home for the evening—the
Secretary remarked how pleased he was with the enthusi-
asm with which I pursue my duties. He further added that
he was particularly appreciative to see me adopt his beliefs
and policies in my planning.

Mr. Stanton has gone so far as to personally express his
pleasure to Jonathon Thomas. I confess to a feeling of
warmth and gratitude over his platitudes.

It wasn't until I reached my boarding house and locked
myself in for the night that I allowed myself to think that
a scheme is being hatched. What kind of scheme, I do not
know. But there leaves little doubt as to the magnitude of
its potential (leaving me to speculate and fear the outcome).

The second envelope contained $5,000, and a short note
that the money was to be used at my personal discretion.

For the second time, the clock on the mantle chimed. Carlisle looked up in surprise, noting it was already ten o'clock. He gently closed the journal and set it on the table next to his chair before leaning forward to shake Brannigan awake.

Brannigan stirred and coughed. "You finished?" he asked.

"Not yet, but I'm getting the point." He grinned, and then gestured at the journal. "Harriman was after more than just wanting us to stop train robbing. In fact, I'm beginning to wonder if he even cared about that."

"Probably did. After all, we were taking his money."

Carlisle stood and walked to the fireplace. He poked the fire back to life and returned to his chair. "I guess old habits don't go away. I can see making a profit if we were to play our cards right."

"I was afraid you were gonna say that," said Brannigan. "Fact is, you need to finish that journal and then decide if there's a profit." He continued in a low voice, "You aren't going to like it, but we're going to have to bring Sundance and Etta into this. I sent Silas to see them."

Seeing his old partner was deadly serious, Carlisle leaned forward again. "I was trying to be funny just then. For the life of me I can't see what's so damned important about Harriman's past. The man's dead, his family's famous and has got more money than he can shake a stick at, so why would they want anything to do with a couple of dead train robbers?"

"It's sitting right there," said Brannigan, pointing at the book on the table. He drained his whiskey. "I've never told you to do anything, or even offered you advice—I'd like to meet the cuss who could—but I'm saying now that this is bad business. Harriman's men will do anything to get their hands on that book. And truth be told, I'm fearful for my family right now. Will and Josh made a mistake. They didn't know it, but they opened a rotten barrel." He unconsciously began rubbing his arm, and then said, "Hell, the fault's mine. I should have done something with that book years ago. Should have burned it, or I should have sent it back to Harriman without him knowing where it come from."

"He'd have figured it out."

"Maybe," conceded Brannigan. "But it don't matter. I didn't even think about sending it back, even after I read in the newspaper that old Harriman had died. Hell, when Will and Josh told me what they'd done, I didn't give those papers any thought—other than those old land grants." He stretched and yawned. "Actually, that's what made me put it together. I always figured those things to be worthless, and it wasn't until Will showed me the money he'd gotten that I remembered that damned journal." He pulled himself out of the chair. "I'm going to bed." Brannigan walked toward the stairs, mumbling, "Shoulda burned every damned thing."

"Hold on there," called Carlisle. "Come on back, we need to talk." Brannigan hesitated with his hand on the banister, weighing fatigue against curiosity, then returned to his seat. After a moment Carlisle said, "Look here, Tom, what's done is done. As I see it, this may be bad or it may not. We don't know for sure if the Harriman family is really after the book, do we?" Brannigan didn't respond, so Carlisle continued. "It seems to me that if we light a fire under Sundance and Etta, it could be opening a door nobody was looking for. Like I said, who really gives a damn about us now?"

Brannigan took his time before speaking. "Well, you've got a point," he said. "But I've got to ask a question. If those land grants and rights-of-way were worthless, why did Bates give my son four thousand dollars?"

"Four thousand dollars? They gave—"

"Spread out over ten years," interrupted Brannigan. "Hell, even if they gave Will a hundred for his trouble and called it quits, it's a hundred more than I figured they're worth."

Carlisle sat back and thought. "I didn't know they'd paid that much."

"Figured it wasn't something I could discuss in the telegram."

"Yeah, that's reasonable," he agreed. "You got any ideas?"

"When I sent Silas to New York, I gave him a letter for Sundance. I wanted to let him and Etta know that I was coming out here...and that it might be time for a vacation. I suggested Denver," Brannigan said.

"Good place for a meeting," said Carlisle, grin now in place. "Thea would enjoy a trip. Did you know she's never met Etta?" He pulled on his beard as he thought, and then asked, "You got a time in mind?"

"I mentioned the end of July. Figured it would give Sundance and Etta enough time to find somebody to run their business. I figured the boys could take care of yours."

"Fair enough," said Carlisle as the clock chimed again. He stood and said, "It's late, so let's turn in. Tomorrow I'll finish the journal—"

Brannigan interrupted: "You only have to get to the middle. After that, it don't matter."

"All right. Once I get there, I'll talk to Thea and the boys about the whole situation," he said. "Although I have a pretty good idea of what they'll say."

"What's that?"

"I'm guessing they'll say I don't have a choice," he said. "Tomorrow we'll head into town to the telegraph office and wire Sundance." Carlisle blew out the lamp and climbed the stairs. His voice drifted down, "Denver sounds good, so why don't you come up with a date? Might as well plan for a couple of weeks and have some fun."

❦

Two days later a messenger delivered a telegram to the Longley Freight Company. Longley set down the currycomb, opened and read the note, before handing it to Kindred who had been repairing a set of reins. "Looks like we're going on a vacation after all," said Longley.

"Ah believe so," Kindred agreed, handing the telegram back. "Ah noticed Tom said the enda' July. That's a good idee cause there won't be many folks in town 'bout then, and the weather'll be nice."

Longley turned and started through the stable. When Kindred didn't follow, he stopped and asked, "You coming?"

"Yessir," he said, setting down the reins. "Ah'll finish these later." As they walked toward the office door, Kindred asked, "Whatta yawl plannin' on doin'?"

"Start making arrangements to get ourselves to Denver." He waved at O'Toole, who immediately came over. After a short conversation, Longley handed the young man a few bills with instructions to buy a ticket for Kindred's return to Colorado. After the young man hurried out the door, Longley said to Kindred, "Hattie wants you to take a letter to Tom." Kindred simply nodded.

Longley held open the door to the office and said, "We appreciate what you're doing, Silas. We think something bad can happen, and Hattie's made it clear that she's not going to be happy if we have to leave New York." He closed the door, and continued, "The business was bought through somebody else, but Hattie kept it going until I could get back to the U.S. If it wasn't for her, I'd have probably gone back to thieving again. Butch would say the same about Thea."

Ten minutes later the door opened and Hattie entered. "Morning, Silas," she said. Setting her parasol in the stand next to her desk, she asked her husband, "Have you heard from Oregon?" Longley silently passed her the telegram. She read it and turned to Silas. "When do you leave?"

"O'Toole went ta buy a ticket fer me, so ah'll be catchin' the train tomorra', ma'am," he said. Quickly adding, "Uh, ah mean, Hattie."

"Well, before you go, I need you to promise something," she said. Kindred sat up straight and was nodding even before she continued. "Tom's boy—maybe both of them— could be in trouble, so I want you to look after them when he's not around. If someone were serious about finding Butch, or us, that's where they'd start." With a look at her husband, she added, "That, and maybe searching for my whereabouts."

"Not much chance of finding you," said Longley. "You're dead."

"We're both dead, and have been for quite some time," she said. "That aside, if what Tom's saying is true, we could all be in bad shape. Maybe you ought to contact a certain person." With a look at Kindred, she smiled and said, "Forgive me. I don't want to mention a name. What you don't know, you can't be made to repeat."

"Ah understand, Hattie," he said, staring into her eyes. Longley watched the pair and grinned, knowing poor Silas had fallen for his wife. And Longley understood. His wife's beauty and intelligence was more than most men could withstand. If she'd asked, the cowboy would have caught a mustang with his bare hands.

"I knew you would," she said. "Also, I think it would be prudent to send a telegram letting Tom know you're going to watch over his sons until he returns home." She reached for Longley's hand. "Come, James," she said, urging him out of his chair. "Let's take Silas out on the town tonight. Give him a real send-off." As the three walked out of the office, Hattie asked, "Have you ever been to see Shakespeare?"

"He be a singa, or an acta?" asked Kindred. "Ain't nothin' but singas or actas what come visiting Gunnison's Opree House."

VII

Kindred tossed his bag over the side of the buckboard and climbed up to sit next to Will Brannigan. "You made it back before pa," the younger man said in greeting. "Pa sent a telegram. He's gonna be a few more days getting' home, maybe not before the end of the week."

"Goldammit," swore Kindred. He removed his hat and wiped the inside band. "Ah was plannin' on talkin' ta him." The look on Will's face caused him to add, "Simma down, there's plenty 'bout this story that ain't bin spoke yet."

"Yeah? Must be a pretty good yarn to take you all the way to New York City."

"Ifen yore pa wanted ya ta know, he'd tole ya," Kindred replied. "Listen here, boy, ah got ta git back ta Butte. An' yore goin' with me. Josh an' Molly kin mind the ranch, so yawl snap them reins."

Will immediately got the team moving. He remained quiet until they reached the outskirts of Gunnison, before asking, "Why do you need me to go?"

Studying the trees cut back from the dirt road, Kindred pondered the question as the team pulled the wagon. Young Brannigan knew better than to interrupt a cowboy when he's thinking, so he patiently waited until Kindred spoke: "Ah don' believe ah kin tell ya without talkin' ta yore pa. But ah want ya ta be mindful that they's things goin' that might git a bit unhealthy."

"You mean dangerous? Is Pa in trouble? What's going on? It's about that journal of the railroad man, isn't it?" Before Kindred could think of how to respond, Will exclaimed, "Damn it, I knew Pa wasn't telling us everything!"

"He cain't tell ya everythin' all at once," Kindred replied, his drawl helped to hide his frustration. "So jest bide yore time, boy." He pulled down the brim of his hat as he leaned back against the seat. Will leaned over to look the other man in the face. "Whatya lookin' at?" mumbled Kindred.

The younger man chuckled. "You damn cussed old fart," he said. "Better tell me, or when I own the saloon I'll fire that Texas ass of yours."

In spite of himself, Kindred grinned. "Ah believe ya would," he replied. "Course, ya'd be cuttin' yore own goldam throat cause ya don' know squat 'bout runnin' no bidness."

Their laughter evaporated into the thin mountain air, leaving each man to chew on his thoughts. By the time the wagon stopped in front of the barn, curiosity and frustration were building a volcano in Will. It took some effort to keep it from boiling over. Before Will hopped down, he asked with surprising calm, "You aren't going to tell me a thing, are you?"

"That be the first thin' ya got right all day. Ah'll mosey on up and git yore brother while yawl saddle the horses— Josh kin unload this here wagon." As Kindred started toward the house, he had a thought and stopped. "Ah did say problems could come 'bout," he said. "But ah don' think it'll involve yore brother and Molly as much as it might involve yawl."

At the house, Kindred knocked on the back door. He always knocked first but seldom waited for a response before walking into the kitchen. The warmth from the stove and the smell of overcooked coffee was comforting. It smelled like home. He helped himself to a cup of thick-as-mud coffee, and called out for Josh. Kindred peered into the mug wondering if he'd have to chew the coffee.

The muffled noise of scrambling feet reverberated from the ceiling above his head. Looking up, Kindred laughed— he was standing under the newlywed's bedroom. When Josh burst into the room, he was slightly out of breath and hurriedly tucking his shirt back into his pants as he said, "About time you got back."

"Glad ta see yawl're bein' watchful, like ya wuz told," said Kindred, sipping his coffee. He pointed and asked,

"Why ain't them buttoned?"

"I, uh, we, uh—ah shit, that's none of your business." Josh busied himself with the buttons of his trousers, and then looked up with a sheepish smile. "You want something, or are you just here to bother us?" he asked.

"Ah'm lettin' yawl know that me and Will is goin' up ta Butte," he replied. "Looks like yawl have ta take care of thins' on yore own." He pulled a chair out from the table, gesturing at the young man; Josh poured himself a cup of coffee before taking a seat across the table. "Ah got somethin' ta say, so yawl listen good," said Kindred. "Ah cain't tell ya much except that ah need ta get yore brother outa here. Yawl got ta keep yore mouths shut about this. An keep yore eyes open fer strangers—'specially strangers what might be askin' questions 'bout yore brother or yore pa. Yawl got that?"

"Yessir," said Josh. "But why them? What about me?"

"Ah don't believe a body knows yore alive, leastways fer now," he said. "Anyway, not as fer as this railroad thin' goes. An ah want yawl ta keep it that way."

Having been around Kindred since he was eight, Josh knew the cowboy was serious. It wasn't until he nodded, and the older man stood, that he realized Kindred's holster was tied down gunfighter-style on his leg. Pointing, he asked, "You aiming to use that gun?"

"Never know when a body might be runnin' across a mountain lion." After a thought, Kindred added, "Or a snake." He walked to the door of the porch. Looking back, he said, "There's a wagon ta be unloaded. Me and Will be leavin' right now, so yawl have to do it yoreself. Now be mindful of what ah told ya: keep yore mouth shut, and 'specially don't talk ta no strangers."

The gravity of Kindred's words left Josh perplexed. As he pondered the situation, he remained at the table and finished his coffee. A few minutes later, hearing the sound of the horses as they were led from the barn, he jumped up and hurried to the door in time to see Will mount and then wait for Kindred to hand him the rope of the pack mule. "Will!"

called Josh. When his brother turned, he said, "You take care. Don't let nothing happen to Pa and Silas—or yourself."

"I'll do that," said Will. He turned his horse and the pack mule in the direction of his brother, gave him a wave, and kicked his horse into a trot. After Will turned the corner of the barn, Kindred mounted his horse. He rode over to Josh and reined his horse to a stop. "'Member what ya bin told, boy," he admonished Josh. "This ain't no jokin' matter. Yore pa'll be back soon." Kindred tugged on the brim of his hat. "'Member to tell yore pa that Will's with me, an' he's ta come up ta the saloon raht quick," he said. "But, no matta what, yawl stay here with Molly."

"Yessir," he said. With a nod, Kindred turned his mount to follow Will. "I'll take care of everything," Josh called after him.

When Kindred caught up, Will asked, "What'd you tell him?"

"Ah didn't tell him nothin'."

"When are you going to let me in on what's going on?" he almost demanded. "Damn it, Silas, I'm old enough to handle whatever it is."

"Ifen it wuz me, ah'd tell ya," replied Kindred. "But ah gotta talk ta yore daddy first. Speakin' of, ah wonder where ole Tom is keepin' hisself?"

❧

At that moment, Tom Brannigan was on his way to Denver. He had left Oregon two days earlier, and stopped in Salt Lake City for a meeting with Trenton Carver, the son of an old friend. The train would arrive in the Colorado capital in a few hours. A train ride usually lulled him to sleep, but as he replayed the events of the last weeks, his mind refused him the luxury. For too many years Brannigan had carried the secret of the outlaws, terrified that one day he might be the one who slipped and blabbed about the real story of the deaths of Butch and Sundance. Of course, Brannigan never really believed he would. He'd sworn that even a gun to his head wouldn't make him talk.

But he never figured on someone putting a gun to the head of one of his sons. Now that possibility was his greatest concern. To his way of thinking, there was little doubt the Harriman organization was going to come for the journals, and what worried him most was why they hadn't up to now. Hattie's telegraph found him at Carlisle's but did little to ease his mind. Hattie let him know that Kindred was in full understanding of the predicament and was on his way to Colorado to watch over the boys until Brannigan could get back and make plans. Carlisle had agreed that Will would be the target of Harriman's henchmen, but if Kindred followed Longley's orders, the older of the Brannigan sons was removed from Gunnison, and the cowboy was not letting Will out of his sight. Unfortunately, Brannigan had no way to contact Kindred. Brannigan had complete confidence in Kindred and his ability to protect his son. When times were slow at the saloon, they would often ride into the woods and target shoot, practicing their draws even though they both knew they had little need for the old skill. Kindred possessed a steady eye and was as adept with a rifle as a handgun. Any altercations in the saloon could be handled by either, and they didn't mind resorting to fisticuffs. Disruptions to the drinking and gambling in the saloon were rare—the saloon's regular clientele had witnessed numerous examples of their lack of reluctance to establish order.

Brannigan took a deep breath, slowly letting it out as his mind wandered. This only served to make him irritable. He wanted to make arrangements for the Carlisles and Longleys in Denver as quickly as possible and return to Gunnison. He looked at his watch. Assuming the train was anywhere near on time, he'd soon be arriving in Denver.

At the same time Brannigan tucked his watch back into his vest pocket, the door to the Union Pacific Railroad office in Denver opened. Union Pacific District Manager Horace Akers didn't bother to look up from the papers scattered across his desk when the door creaked. He automatically asked, "May I help you?" When there was no response, Akers glanced up to find a tall stranger standing uncomfortably close. The cold eyes inches from his face caused Akers to involuntarily flinch to get away from the stare. The desk chair crashed into the wall behind as he jumped to his feet—hands at his side, Akers achieved a position of rigid attention, as if waiting for a blow.

The stranger was dressed in a long leather coat that all but covered his khaki shirt, military riding pants, and knee-high boots. When he spoke, his voice was calm and without inflection, "I believe you have been informed of my arrival." It was not a question.

Akers took a deep breath. "You must be Mr. Denard Kenney. I received a telegram from Mr. Bates' assistant yesterday." He came around the desk with his hand extended. "You're here to see about getting holdings into some of our more remote regions."

"That's correct," said Kenney. He ignored Akers' hand and walked around the desk, uprighted the chair and sat. "I will be starting my assignment by way of the southerly route through Colorado Springs and Pueblo—"

"But, sir, we already have…"

As if Akers hadn't spoken, Kenney continued, "—specifically searching for possibilities to the west, perhaps as far as Montrose. Mr. Bates and I wish to pursue railroad lines into mining regions that we believe will prove profitable." He paused.

Akers was about to say something when Kenney went on. "With an area as large as the western states, it becomes necessary to consolidate our travel and shipping potential. Round them up, so to speak. Mr. Bates is hopeful of gaining a larger share for the company in these areas." He paused again and then said, "Your expertise will be a help in making the expansion happen. Do you understand?"

"Yes sir," Akers said, wondering if he did understand. His face was flushed with excitement. Visions of traveling in a private car from city to city as an executive of the railroad quickly vanished when he realized Kenney was staring at him. Akers tried to guess what he should say. "Where would you like me to start?" was the best he could manage. He reached across the desk and pulled his pen out of its well, holding it poised over a blank piece of paper.

Kenney smiled—a smile as cold as his eyes. "It won't be difficult," he said. "Tomorrow morning, make arrangements for three seats on the first train to Pueblo—I'll be starting there—after which I intend to travel to Gunnison. From there, I'll travel west. I'll need horses and supplies for three men for ten days." He stopped to think, before adding, "Once I'm back from this trip, I'll notify you of my return to Denver in plenty of time to arrange my car." He added, "I've already taken the liberty of ordering it backed on to the siding."

Akers wrote the instructions, brow furrowing in confusion. He looked up and said, "But, sir, why wouldn't you take your private car to Pueblo? I can arrange for it to be added to tomorrow's train. It would be no—"

Kenney's raised hand silenced him. "Because I choose not to," he said. "I do not wish my presence known, nor my intent as to our future plans. If you want to profit from our expansion, you must understand the need for secrecy." He lowered his hand and stared at the other man. Chilled by the dark eyes that seemed drained of life, Akers immediately nodded.

"Excellent," said Kenney. "No one should know of my visit here. You may not speak of me to any of your acquaintances. There is to be no discussion with company employees, your wife, or anyone else." Kenney rose. He walked over to the window and stood staring out for some time. Akers felt a tremor of fear run through him before Kenney returned to the desk. Gesturing at Akers' chair, Kenney said, "Forgive me, I took your seat, and I had no right." Kenney sat in the chair across Akers' desk.

"Yes sir," said Akers. Relieved to be moving, he went around the desk and sat. His hand shook ever so slightly as he picked up his pen, and he could not help the rush in his voice when he said, "I do understand, Mr. Kenney, and I'll not speak of your visit."

"You're as fine a man as Mr. Bates has said." Kenney once again studied the man, whose forehead was now shiny with sweat before he added, "He's had his eye on you for some time. Now, as to my needs…" He spoke for some time, and as he did, Kenney inwardly smiled, momentarily wondering who would be replacing Akers.

When Kenney finished with his instructions, Akers looked carefully over his notes. "You can count on me. I'll make sure everything is taken care of." He was beginning to relax.

Kenney again rose, this time he extended his hand. "Thank you, Mr. Akers," he said. "While you're making the arrangements, I'll be in my car. One more thing: you will also make arrangements for the well-being of my crew while I'm gone. There are a total of five, however two will accompany me."

Akers nodded. "Uh, as to expenses, should I use railroad funds?" He stopped as Kenney reached into the inside pocket of his coat and pulled out a large bundle of bills.

"Put them up in a hotel. Or if they wish, make arrangements for a stay at a local sporting house. But, wherever they choose to stay, arrange to allow them credit for their food, baths, and other necessities," said Kenney. He tossed the bundle to Akers, who used both hands to catch it. "As to their personal entertainment, let them see to that on their own. Give them a daily stipend of five dollars."

"Five dollars!" exclaimed Akers. Then, more tentatively, he asked, "Isn't that a bit excessive?"

Kenney smiled ominously. "You would do well to understand that I demand—and therefore reward—complete loyalty and instant compliance to achieve success in my endeavors. And my personal well-being." He turned and went to the door. Akers stared as Kenney eyed the street through the window. As if coming out of a dream, it hit Akers that something was expected of him. He hurried to open the door, half bowing as Kenney stepped out onto the sidewalk. Behind the building, the afternoon train was arriving. The screeching and grinding of brakes forced Kenney to wait until the noise subsided.

Standing in the doorway, Akers asked, "Will there be anything else?"

"Yes," said Kenney. "While I'm gone, consider yourself a member of my staff and award yourself ten dollars a day in addition to your salary. And remember, no one is to know why I'm here or where I'm headed. Absolutely no one."

Before the train came to a stop, Brannigan jumped down and headed for the station office. As he rounded the corner, he nearly collided with a tall man leaving the office. "Excuse me," said Brannigan as he sidestepped and almost slipped off the edge of the wooden sidewalk.

The tall stranger shot him a glance and was about to say something, then he thought better of it. Tipping his hat, Kenney said, "My apologies." With that, he walked away.

Akers stepped onto the sidewalk. "Afternoon, Tom. How was your trip?"

"Can't complain." Gesturing at the disappearing man, Brannigan asked, "Somebody new in town?" He looked closer at the station manager. "You all right?"

"Yes, I'm quite well," said Akers. He quickly said, "That gentleman's a traveler who's interested in exploring some of the country. I doubt we'll be seeing him again."

"Been a lot of those folks around lately. When's the train leaving for Gunnison?"

Akers automatically replied. "Tomorrow morning at seven. Barring any misfortune, you'll be in Pueblo by eleven, spur route leaves for Gunnison at two." Producing a handkerchief from the inside pocket of his coat, he mopped his forehead and asked, "Care to step inside for a cup of coffee?"

"Sorry, I've got to send a telegram to the ranch—after that, I'll be at the hotel," replied Brannigan. He hoisted his bag and said, "But in the morning, I'll take you up on your offer."

VIII

Will hurried down the street toward the saloon with a folded paper clenched in his fist and a scowl on his face. Inside, he went to the storeroom door and knocked before entering. Once the door was closed, he said, "Telegraph boy tried to deliver this at the cabin." He handed it to Kindred. "What's the big secret? Damn kid said that only you get to read it."

Kindred used his hammer to point to an empty wooden keg. "Set while ah sees what 'tis." Will waited patiently, but his patience was not rewarded. The older man finished reading and simply folded the paper. Will watched it disappear into Kindred's pocket. "Yore daddy's in Denver, an' will be back ta Gunnison tomorra'," he said by way of explanation. "He'll be here the mornin' afta."

"That's all? There isn't more?"

"Yeah, but it ain't none of yore bidness," he said. Will was about to explain that his business extended a bit farther than he was given credit for, when Kindred said, "Awright, I'm lyin'. It's all 'bout ya—an' Josh."

"Let's hear it then."

Kindred turned his back and began prying the top off a case of whiskey. With a glance over his shoulder, he said, "If yore pa wanted ya ta know somethin', he wouldna sent it ta me. Now git busy behind the bar. Go hep Jimmy, it's his suppa time."

"But—"

"Git," ordered Kindred. Will didn't move; after a few minutes, Kindred sighed. "Yore beginnin' ta remine me of Tom," he said. "Now listen here, yore pa has somethin' he wants ta talk ta ya 'bout, then he's got somethin' fer the two of us ta do. Fact is, yore goin' up ta the mine an' git started openin' it."

"Which mine?" he demanded. When Kindred simply stared at the young man, Will asked, "You don't mean the Sadie Mae, do you?"

Kindred was hard-pressed not to laugh, but he didn't. He knew Will was already furious. "Ah guess yore daddy is thinkin' of lookin' fer gold or somethin'," he said. "Now listen here, ah know it seems kinda strange, but he's got his reasons, so 'nough of this shit. Do like ah tole ya an git yore sorry ass behind tha bar." Kindred's voice convinced the younger man he wouldn't be getting any more information and might as well do as he was told.

Will rose and left the room, closing the door behind him. The noise and heat of the saloon hit him full force as he walked to the bar. "Why don't you go ahead and get your supper," he said to Jimmy, the day bartender. "I'll watch over things."

Jimmy was a slight man with a swarthy complexion and rich handlebar mustache. Some customers called him "Greek." He had his apron off and under the bar before Will could change his mind. "All right by me," he said. "I'm going over to the boarding house; you want me to bring something back?"

"Piece of Miz Addie's pie wouldn't hurt," said Will. He reached into his pocket and pulled out a quarter. "While you're at it, get a slab for yourself."

Jimmy grabbed the coin in mid-air. "You're getting more like your pa all the time. 'Cept he'd get me two slabs," he said as he left.

An hour later the saloon tables were full of drinkers and poker players, and the faro tables were stacked three deep. Every space at the bar was filled. Men stood leaning against the walls, raising the noise level so loud it was impossible to speak in a normal voice. The piano player spotted Jimmy making his way to the bar holding a pie above his head and began banging out Jimmy's favorite rag. Jimmy pushed his way up to the bar and handed Will the pie. "Miz Addie sent the whole thing," he said. He smirked and said, "She said for you to come by and have a visit with Jenny."

Will looked at Jimmy and raised an eyebrow. Jenny was Addie's 22-year-old daughter whose lack of beauty started with her stringy brown hair and ended at remarkably crossed eyes that accented the hook of her nose. And unknown to her sainted mother, Jenny was the town's easiest woman. "I'd be smart to send this back," Will remarked as he accepted the pie.

As Silas had told Will he would, Brannigan rode into Crested Butte two days later. He stopped to toss his bag at the Maroon Avenue cabin he shared with Kindred when he was in town, and then went to the saloon. The trip from Denver had been pleasant enough. He noticed the tall stranger he had bumped into the day before was on the same train, but not having been properly introduced, Brannigan didn't feel good manners required him to speak.

The weather was unseasonably warm for June, the doors and windows of the saloon were open to catch any breeze that might be passing through. A couple of the faro-playing prospectors greeted Brannigan and received a nod in return. He pulled himself a beer and then stood behind the dealer to catch up on the latest news in Crested Butte. It wasn't long before the back door opened and Kindred returned behind the bar from the back where he'd tossed out a bucket of sudsy water. "Afternoon, Tom," he called. "Figured yawl get here soon enough."

Brannigan nodded. "Train was on time out of Pueblo." Looking around he asked Kindred, "Where's Jimmy? Little late, ain't he?"

"Ah 'spect he'll show any tahm now."

"When he shows up, you and me need to talk." With that, Brannigan patted the dealer on the shoulder, wished the players luck, and headed for the storeroom. When Kindred joined him, he found his friend sitting on a chair, reading. Brannigan looked up and asked, "Is Will at the mine?" Kindred nodded. "Anybody besides you know?"

"Naw," he said. "Ah ain't talked ta a soul, an' ah told Will ta keep his mouth shut. So otha' than Jimmy, ah don't suppose there's nobody else Will woulda thought ta tell—Josh and Molly up ta the ranch an' all."

"Good. The Longleys sent a telegram saying everything went well with you in New York," said Brannigan. "And the others are in accordance with what we oughta do. By the way, their name is Carlisle—Robert and Theodora—and that's what we're to call them." Kindred nodded, and Brannigan continued: "The Carlisles and the Longleys are gonna meet in Denver in about a month. You and I'll both be going. But our bigger concern for now is that Robert's pretty much convinced there's a problem, judging from the way the railroad was so quick to pay Will. He says we need to keep the boy out of sight, and I tend to agree. That means Will's not going back to the ranch, and you're gonna have to keep a careful eye on him."

"Yessir, ah'll do ma best," promised Kindred. He thought for a moment and asked, "What'd yawl do with Harriman's book?"

"Robert has it. He and Thea read the whole thing—the important parts, anyway—and they think it's best if they keep it," he said. Kindred was surprised at the worry on his friend's face, as Brannigan added, "I got a real bad feeling about this. It's like something's about to happen."

"Seems ta me, ifen it was, it woulda been when Will went ta see them railroad folks. Leastways, the Longleys think it's likely they woulda done somethin' then."

"Yeah, that's what Robert said too. But I'm thinking that Bates might not have known exactly what Will had, so he gave him the money to find out where we live. But it don't seem likely a city man would be coming after us way out here."

Kindred agreed, and then asked, "Think they be hirin' somebody close ta us?"

"If it were me, that's how I'd play it," Brannigan said. He was quiet, and then he asked, "You tell Josh and Molly not to talk to strangers?" Once again Kindred nodded. "Thought so. But the problem is, we can't be everywhere, and we don't know for an absolute fact if there's even anything to worry about. Hell, it was too many years ago, right?"

"Sorry ta disagree. It's clear ta me theys trouble in the air," said Kindred. "Now that ah know the whole story."

Brannigan stood, he reached for a bottle on the top shelf and resumed sitting. "Ah, dammit, I gotta be honest and go along with you," he said. Pulling the cork, he handed the bottle to Kindred. "Wet your throat," he said. After Kindred handed the bottle back, Brannigan took a swig, and then wiped his mouth with the back of his hand. "At first, Robert didn't think so either," Brannigan said. In spite of the gravity of the situation, he chuckled. "He was trying to figure out an angle. Thought he'd find a way to turn a profit in this."

"Money the boys got change his mind?"

"It's not right for the railroad to be offering that much for worthless grants and rights-of-way. Will did say Bates didn't show much interest until the journal came up, so that's gotta be the answer. That damned Harriman got himself involved with the wrong people, and it will be hell to pay if his early dealings get out."

"So what we gonna do?"

Brannigan offered the bottle and waited for its return. He replaced the cork and set it back on the shelf. "Robert did send me another telegram. He figures we should be all right for now. Leastways until we can get together in Denver," he said. "Hattie's mighty worried about the boys and Molly, and so's Robert. That tells me that we gotta keep them close."

Kindred stood. "Ah did lahk ya said an sent Will up ta the Sadie Mae. Ah told him ta git it opened—that ya was thinkin' of lookin' fer gold again." He opened the door. "Maybe one of us oughta ride up there in the mornin'." He grinned and added, "He shore weren't happy 'bout it."

"He'll be all right for a few days," said Brannigan. "I'm gonna head back to the ranch tomorrow and have another talk with Josh and Molly—maybe I should send them over to her daddy's place. You wait until Sunday, and then go on up to the mine. I'll be back that afternoon, which gives us time to convince Will that he's got to stay out of sight. Like you say, he ain't gonna like any of this."

"Ah don 'spect he will," agreed Kindred. He paused, and then said, "What about tellin' Jimmy? He's gonna wonda where Will is."

"Just tell him he's doing work for me up at the mine," Brannigan said. "It's the truth, but make sure he knows to keep his mouth shut. And tell him to let us know if any strangers come around asking for Will or me." The door shut behind Kindred, but it was several minutes before Brannigan resumed reading.

Since it was still too early for much of a crowd, Kindred and Jimmy were able to talk privately. If Jimmy had a flaw, it was that he tended to believe the last person he'd talked to. That tendency and his slowness at putting two and two together often negated his loyalty. Kindred's admonition about strangers was quickly lost as the bar picked up and the saloon came to life.

While Jimmy and Kindred talked, a tall stranger ordered whiskey at the other end of the bar. Jimmy didn't pay much attention to him until Kindred had left for the evening. Soon, however, he was engrossed in conversation with the man whose clothes were cut too fine to brand him a local. It wasn't long before Denard Kenney mentioned that he represented an Eastern firm which had recently developed a process to make closed mines profitable through the use of steam. He was in the West looking to buy out a few dry holes for his company. Ever helpful, Jimmy told him without prompting that his boss owned the rights to several mines and might possibly be in the mood to sell—in fact his older son was at that moment at one of the more promising sites working to get it opened. Kenney expressed interest in meeting with Tom Brannigan but suggested that Jimmy might want to hold off on introductions until he'd completed his study. With that, Kenney paid for his drinks and, after inquiring about a suitable boarding house, left the saloon. Shortly after, two men left the other end of the bar and followed him out the door.

It wasn't until Jimmy was walking home that he remembered Kindred's warning about talking to strangers. He came to a stop and almost reversed direction to head back to tell Kindred about the stranger. But Jimmy figured the cowboy would be unsociable this time of night. Besides, tomorrow was Jimmy's day off and he intended to go fishing, taking along one of the two bottles of whiskey that was part of his pay. He'd tell Kindred the day after tomorrow. He was in sight of his cabin, when the sound of boots crunching on the gravel road caused him to turn. A whistling sound was followed by a dull thud. Jimmy was unconscious before he hit the ground.

Kenney didn't bother to look around as he slid the weapon back into his pocket. He'd followed the bartender from the saloon and had no particular need to choose his ambush spot carefully. Once Jimmy was away from the main streets of town, Kenney had been patient, guessing the other man was on his way home. At this time of night, it was unlikely the bartender was looking for company. Kenney was not squeamish by any stretch of the imagination, he simply viewed women and children as clutter that would have to be removed. Particularly when an interrogation was to proceed.

Kenney grasped the front of Jimmy's jacket, straightened the unconscious hulk, and effortlessly lifted him over his shoulder. He kicked open Jimmy's cabin door, allowing the moon to cast light into the one room—it was apparent the cabin was empty. Once Jimmy was deposited on the rumpled blankets, Kenney used pieces of rope from his coat pocket to truss the man. He then took his time looking around the cabin and found a coiled rope, which he put to use. Finished with the rope, Kenney picked up a water jug and went out to the stream that ran behind the cabin.

The icy-cold water splashed on Jimmy's face and in a few seconds he was awake. "Who the hell are you?" he gasped, water obscuring his vision. He stared in horror at Denard Kenney, struggling to make sense of why the stranger he'd met in the saloon was in his cabin, and why he meant him harm. Jimmy tried to lift himself off the bed and almost choked. He discovered he was spread-eagled on the bed with his hands and feet tied to the legs of the bed—more importantly, a rope was fastened around his neck. His horror was intensified as he realized the lump extending from under his chin was a hangman's noose. "What do you want!" he screamed and at the same time tried not to move.

Kenney leaned down and stared. To Jimmy, the black, unblinking eyes were the eyes of the devil. As Jimmy gathered himself to scream again, Kenney raised his hand; a movement that silenced the hog-tied man. The next sound was of a knife being drawn from a sheath, followed by a tugging that started from the crotch of Jimmy's pants and continued up to his throat. It wasn't long before the man's entire body was laid bare of clothing and Kenney resumed staring as he slowly replaced his knife.

When Kenney finally spoke, the venom of his voice caused Jimmy to lose control for the first time since he was a child. "You are going to tell me a story," said Kenney. The hoarse whisper was the voice from Hell, and it wasn't long before Jimmy lost control of other functions. Even with the stench, Kenney watched in satisfaction before speaking again, "Good, Jimmy—yes, I know your name—I know everything about you. And you will talk to me."

"What do you want?" Jimmy asked again with a trembling meekness. Again Kenney was silent before turning away from the bed to pick up a filthy cloth that he crammed into the groaning man's mouth. Reaching into his pocket, Kenney pulled out the weapon.

Jimmy was in no position to notice, but the weapon was over a foot in length—made of soft leather and two inches in diameter, it was heavy to the hand. Kenney held it in front of the helpless man. "This is a cosh, although you might call it a sap. I call it my friend. Beautiful, isn't it?" he asked. "I made it myself. It's of the finest Spanish leather from a fighting bull, and is filled with shot, a most efficient device." He stopped talking and gently slapped the sap against his hand. "Do you have any idea what I use this for?"

Jimmy was barely able to shake his head. "I thought not," said Kenney. "Perhaps an explanation is in order." The next movement was too quick to see. The sap landed on the bone of Jimmy's upper thigh with a muffled thump. It was as if he had been shot and pain exploded in all directions, the gag muffled his scream as his body elevated off the bed. Writhing in pain, Jimmy was unable to stop the tears from running down his face.

"Easy, Jimmy," whispered Kenney. "That was just a sample. You see, my friend is what I term a teaching aid." He lovingly repeated, "A teaching aid. And it's like this: should you become reluctant, or untruthful, he'll encourage you. Tell me if you understand."

Jimmy ignored the pull of the rope around his neck and nodded. Kenney then continued, "I must tell you that the shot and the leather work miracles. I can hit you as often and as hard as I want, but it won't kill you unless I want it to. Isn't that interesting?" Jimmy quickly nodded again. "Good. We're making progress." The leather sap flashed again, this time landing with force on Jimmy's shin, the third blow was against the point of his shoulder, the next on his wrist. Two of the strikes broke bones.

It took longer to wake the trussed man. After twice using water, Kenney was forced to slap Jimmy's cheeks before his eyes stayed open. "Ah, there you are," said Kenney. "I believe you're convinced, so we can begin."

He removed the gag and set it and the sap on the bed next to Jimmy's face. "I'll leave them there in the event of a memory lapse, or a decrease in cooperation," he said. He pulled a solitary three-legged stool next to the bed, sat down, and casually crossed his legs. "Now, where would I find the Sadie Mae mine?"

<hr />

Three days later, Kindred dismounted in front of the cabin. He had been waiting since three o'clock the previous afternoon for Jimmy to show up to work, and now was about as mad with him as he'd ever been. Every few months

Jimmy would go on a toot and miss a day—once even showing up still drunk—but he'd never been absent for more
than one day, even when sick. Kindred yelled at Jimmy's
open door, "Git yore ass out here!"

There was no response.

"Ah'm comin' in, an' if yore still drunk, ah'm gonna toss
ya in the crick." He tied the reins to one of the posts that
supported the roof over the porch and pushed open the door.
It was then he smelled it.

Being a cowboy, Kindred was—more or less—used to foul
smells. But considering that the Greek tended to be fastidious
about his clothes, even proclaiming that he bathed in the
creek at least three times a week, this odor was far different
from that of someone who didn't bother to clean themselves.
Stepping past the door, Kindred came face to face with a sight
that would be with him for the rest of his life.

Hanging from a beam by a noose around his neck,
buzzing flies almost hid Jimmy's purple tongue that pushed
between his swollen lips. He was naked, and underneath his
hanging body was a rumpled blanket on which the shit had
dried, a three-leg stool lay on its side next to the blanket.

"Goldammit, Jimmy," groaned Kindred. "What'd ya go
an' do this fer?" He pulled his handkerchief from around his
neck and tied it over his nose and mouth. He took out his
clasp knife and sawed through the rope tied to the beam.
With a thump, Greek landed in a heap on the soiled blankets. Kindred lifted his friend onto the bed, and gently
removed the noose before stepping back. "Ah'll be back," he
promised. As he started out the door, he stopped, looked
backed, and said in sorrow, "Why ever yawl did this, ah'll
make sure ya git a proper burial."

Brannigan had been back from his trip to the ranch less
than an hour before Kindred burst through the storeroom
door. Not long after, Brannigan and Kindred were back at
the cabin, Sheriff Royal Burnage in tow. They all dismounted. Burnage looked around and then told Brannigan and
Kindred to stay behind. He took a deep breath and went into
the cabin...he was back shortly. "Looks like he did himself

in, all right," he said, wiping his hands on his pants. "I can see the rope and the marks on the beam, even some scuffs on the wall where his feet must have hit." He added unnecessarily, "Guess he died slow." He motioned for Brannigan to follow him back inside.

Kindred waited while the others were in the cabin. It wasn't long before they returned and all three stepped away from the porch. Burnage spoke first: "Either of you have an idea as to why he'd do this?"

Brannigan said, "I can't think why any man would kill himself. But in Jimmy's case, I can think of even fewer reasons. He never bitched about nothing."

"An' he always tole me he was happy workin' fer Tom," said Kindred. "Said nobody was ever as fair. Hell, Tom used ta give him a coupla of bottles a week, on topa his pay."

"That right?" asked Burnage.

"Yeah. But Jimmy was no drunk. He did like a bender every once in awhile, like most men," said Brannigan. "But he had an account with the bank in Gunnison, and every month he had me take half his pay and put it in for him. Always said that if Silas and me ever wanted to sell the saloon, he find a way to buy us out. Don't seem to me that he had any reason to die."

Burnage tugged at his hat, thought for a moment, and then as they watched, began walking around the cabin, enlarging the circle until he reached the road. Coming back, he explained. "Thought I'd take a look and see if there was any tracks. But I'm damned if I can see anything but one set. 'Course, our horses messed it up, so it probably don't make a difference." He looked around again and then said, "Well, come on, let's get back. I'll send the mortician to get him."

On the ride back to town, Kindred said, "Sheriff, ah'd be obliged if ya'd tell Harley ah'll be payin' fer Jimmy's funeral. Tell him ta make it a good 'un." Burnage nodded.

"We'll both pay," interjected Brannigan. The men were silent until they stopped in front of the jail. "Thanks, Royal," said Brannigan. "I guess we're never gonna know what happened."

"Hell, I know what happened," he said. "Jimmy killed himself. Case closed." He stepped around the hitching post and disappeared into his office.

Brannigan turned his horse in the direction of the saloon, Kindred followed. Halfway up the street, he asked, "You think that's what happened?"

"No sir," replied Kindred. Suddenly he sat up in his saddle and grabbed Brannigan's arm. "We'd best git ta the Sadie Mae!"

IX

Carlisle lingered at the supper table, watching the sun disappear over the tree-shaded river and listening to the sounds coming from the kitchen. He felt the special peace that always came over him when he heard Thea humming as she cleaned up after a meal. It was quite some time before he shook himself out of his reverie and moved to his favorite chair in the parlor. As he had often done in the past few days, Carlisle picked up the journal and flipped through the pages, searching for words that weren't there, or meaning that had eluded him in previous readings.

When Thea joined him, she brought a basket filled with thatches of yarn. Sitting on an ottoman near his chair, she pulled out a thatch and said, "Do you mind?" Carlisle set the journal on the table and obligingly held up both hands for his wife to wind the yarn into a ball. Thea glanced at the book. "Have you been reading it again?" she asked.

"Yes. But I don't know why. The more I read it, the worse I feel."

"Then perhaps you should put it away until we go to Denver," she suggested, deftly rolling the yarn.

Carlisle cast another look at the journal. "I wish I could," he said. Resting his elbows on the arms of his chair, he grinned and said, "It does makes for interesting reading."

"In that case, perhaps you need more excitement in your life."

"My life is fine," he said with a laugh. "And working with David and Lawrence and the mill, there's plenty of excitement."

"Only because of the boys and the mill?" she teased.

"Yeah, Thea, only because of that," he said, laughing again. "Of course, it helps when I remind myself where the boys came from."

She finished winding the yarn and placed it in the basket and motioned for Carlisle to hold another thatch. For a
while he watched Thea's quick hands, but she soon realized
he was staring at the journal again. "Robert," she said.
Carlisle looked up, "do you wish to tell me something?"

"You've read it, so I doubt if there's anything I could tell
that you don't already know," he said.

Thea worked quietly while she thought about what she
might or might now know. Ten minutes later, she set the
basket on the floor and moved the ottoman opposite her husband. "Perhaps you could tell me exactly what's troubling
you," she said.

"What's to tell? You know about Harriman, and you
know he paid men to track us down and kill us. The way
this is going, his family could be trying to kill us all over
again." He laughed. "Who goes to the trouble of trying to
kill a couple of dead guys?" He became more serious. "Sorry,
Thea," he said. "I don't mean to make light of this, but the
fact is, we could be in Harriman's sights again. Even though
he's been dead for all these years, if I'm right, they got a
direct bead on Tom's boy—his trip to New York accidentally
showed the Harrimans that the journal still exists. And
based on what's in that journal, I believe they are gonna try
to kill us."

"Tom can take care of Will," Thea said. "You said yourself
that, besides Sundance, there's no one you trust more than
Tom." Carlisle rose and walked to the sideboard. Cut-crystal
glasses surrounded two decanters, and even though he was-
n't fond of sherry, he knew Thea was and poured one for her,
and then one for himself. "Sherry?" she asked, accepting
her glass, "You *are* upset."

Carlisle laughed. Making himself comfortable in his
chair again, he sipped the sweet liquor like a child who had
been coaxed into medicine. His silence made the clock tick
seem louder. After a time, he looked up at Thea. "When we
go to Denver, James and I will have to make a decision about
how to handle this—" He would have gone on except his wife
raised her hand.

"That's not entirely true," she said. "You've already reached a decision. It's quite simple: neither you nor James will tolerate any interference with your lives, and neither of you will let anything happen to your families." She lifted her sherry in a silent toast.

Carlisle set his glass on the table and reached for the journal once again. He looked at his wife. "You're right," he admitted. "And God forbid anything happens to Tom or his family."

⁕⁕⁕⁕⁕

The ride to the Sadie Mae mine took less than an hour. Both horses were well lathered by the time Brannigan jumped off and raced to the shack. "Will!" he yelled. Shoving the door aside, he pulled his pistol and stepped inside.

Kindred tied the reins of both horses. Brannigan reappeared and said, "Supplies are all here but no sign of Will."

Pointing to the small corral next to the outhouse, Kindred said, "Team's put up. An' it's early, so mebbe he's still in the mine."

The mine was up the side of the hill, a short hike across the creek that flowed behind the shack. As they walked, Brannigan took the lead at the incline. The high altitude left both breathing hard by the time they reached the entrance where Brannigan was almost brought to his knees with relief. The boards that covered the opening were neatly stacked to the side, along with a pile of tools. "Will," he called again. "It's Pa. Come on out."

The only sounds were the water flowing over the stones in the creek and the cry of a hawk that circled overhead. Kindred took a deep breath and said, "Could be he's down one of them shafts."

Brannigan entered the mine and stopped. Two tunnels ran into the mountain; one was a half-mile deep, the other no more than a quarter-mile. The tunnel to the left had a vertical shaft that ran down fifteen feet to a lower tunnel. He turned to Kindred, pointed at the tunnel on the right and said, "You go down that one, I'll go down the other."

Kindred picked up two kerosene lanterns sitting next to the tools, lighting the first and handing it to Brannigan, before lighting his own. "Mind that shaft," he cautioned. "Yawl keep yore eye down so's ya don't wanda 'bout an' slip." He was still adjusting the wick when Brannigan turned and started down the second tunnel.

The vertical shaft was dug out of the floor on the left side of the tunnel, about two hundred paces from the opening. Brannigan heeded Kindred's advice and moved slowly, keeping his eyes down and his footsteps within the forward glow of the lantern. Even moving carefully, he reached the opening on the floor of the tunnel in short order and, leaning precariously over the hole, peered down into the darkness. "Will!" he yelled. "Are you down there?! Will?!" But there was no reply.

A wooden ladder was inches from his hand; he reached out and steadied himself before stretching his upper body over the shaft. The light from the lantern wasn't strong enough for him to see the bottom so he pulled back and took a step toward the front of the tunnel. "Silas!" he yelled. Waiting a minute, he yelled again, this time he could hear the growing panic in his own voice. "Silas! You hear me?"

"Ah'm comin'!" Kindred yelled back. Shortly he was standing next to his partner, breathing heavily. "Air's thin, makes it hard fer a body ta breathe."

"You find anything?"

"No sir," replied Kindred. He peered over the ladder and asked, "Ya ain't been down there yet? Think he's sumwheres down there?"

"Must be," said Brannigan. "Hold the ladder, I'm going down." He handed Kindred his lantern and swung one leg over the ladder before he held out his hand for the lantern. He climbed down the first two rungs. Wrapping his arm around the side of the ladder, he leaned over and peered through the glow of the dim light. Something was out of place on the floor. A shape that should not have been there. "Will!" he yelled. "Will!" He loosened his grip and stepped down.

Crack! The rung snapped beneath him.

With only one hand holding on the ladder, Brannigan could easily have fallen. But like a rattlesnake strike, Kindred's hand snatched Brannigan by the collar. "Ladder's broke," gasped Brannigan. He held on to the lantern, and with Kindred's help hoisted himself to the top. "Will's down there...he's down there," said Brannigan. He looked into the blackness and yelled, "Will! It's Pa! Can you talk, boy?" There was no reply.

"Ah'll git sum rope," said Kindred. He disappeared in the direction of the mine opening.

Kindred moved quickly down the side of the mountain to the horses and grabbed a rope from his saddle. As an afterthought, he stepped into the cabin and picked up the blanket folded neatly at the end of the bed. Desperation overcame the altitude. He made it back to the vertical shaft in a short time, and handed the rope to Brannigan, who quickly fashioned a loop. "You can't support me, so you're going to have to get him, Silas," he said. "Once you're down, I'll drop the light to you."

Kindred tied the rope around his waist and waited until Brannigan looped his end around a boulder and braced himself. Using the ladder as a support, he draped the rope over the top rung and, placing a boot on each side, inched his way down the hole. Brannigan eased the line until Kindred hit the bottom where darkness surrounded him—the only light came from the lantern that hung over the top of the ladder. Kindred called, "Send 'er down." He was afraid to move about in the darkness. Even though he knew Will was only a step away, he still couldn't see the young man.

Once he had the lantern, Kindred dropped to his knees next to Will. He gently turned Will over and sat back on his heels looking into the still face. For the first time in years, a sudden thought of his own long-gone home sent him close to tears. Brannigan's voice from the top brought Kindred back to the duty at hand. "How is he?" Brannigan's voice was urgent and at the same time reluctant for the answer. When there was no reply, he repeated, "How's Will?"

Kindred rose. He stepped to the ladder and managed two words, "Will's dead."

It was a long time before Brannigan spoke. "Tie the rope around him and guide him up," was all he said. Kindred did as ordered, making sure the rope was secure before calling to pull. He guided the body by pushing on Will's legs as it slowly rose alongside the ladder and disappeared over the top. He stood still and listened to Brannigan's sobs, feeling as lonesome and empty as the tunnel he stood in. Before long the rope was lowered again, and Brannigan hoisted him up to face what must be faced. Kindred slowly coiled the rope and looked around in all directions except down at Will. When he felt he had a grip on himself and his friend's sobs had turned to short gasps, he put a hand on Brannigan's shoulder. "Best we take him out," he said gently.

Wiping the tears from his face, Brannigan stood and allowed Kindred to wrap the blanket around the body. Kindred moved to Will's feet and said, "Yawl take the shoulders, ah'll back out." Together they carried Will out of the mine and down the mountain.

At the shack, Brannigan wet a rag from the bucket hanging by the fireplace and tenderly wiped the dirt from Will's face. Unable to watch, Kindred went outside and hitched the team to the supply wagon. He tied their horses to the back of the wagon and took his time before going back inside. Kindred waited until his partner looked up. "Ah got the wagon ready," he said. "We'd best put Will in the back an' take him home."

Kindred wasn't surprised when Brannigan climbed into the wagon bed and crouched beside Will. Neither spoke until they were almost in Crested Butte. "Did he fall?" Brannigan asked, his voice low and hoarse.

"Looked lahk his neck was broke," said Kindred. Misery made his drawl even slower. "There was 'nother busted rung a ways down, so it looks lahk he jest fell."

Brannigan took a shuddering breath. "The ladder was worn out." Seconds later he cried, "Goddammit! Goddammit! Goddammit! It's my fault!"

Kindred could do nothing for his friend. But as he guided the wagon into town, a thought ran over and over in his mind. *It's them damn Harrimans.*

***

Three weeks later, Longley sat waiting for his wife to return to the office. His handsome face was pale with anger as he repeatedly pulled the watch from his vest pocket. When fury finally got the best of him, his chair crashed against the wall. Striding to the safe in the corner, he spun the dial before yanking the handle, the numerous ledgers and files that covered the locked wooden box spilled across the floor. Longley again pulled out his watch, this time also pulling out a small key that was attached to the end of the chain that rested in the other pocket. He inserted the key and unlocked the box.

Minutes later, Longley was pacing the office, stopping periodically to whip the pistol from his tied-down holster. He sighted and dry-fired the empty gun at different targets, practicing from various angles, both high and low. As he drew and whirled to face the door, gun held at his hip, the door opened and Hattie entered. Luckily, her scream was low and was not heard in the stables. It was a credit to Longley's anger and concentration that he ignored his wife and continued with his practice.

Hattie stepped behind the desk and righted the chair. As she did, she noticed the telegram on the desk and sat down to read it. Long after Hattie had set the paper back on the desk, Longley finished and sat across from her. "Poor Tom," said Hattie. Longley's only response was to nod as he continued to pull back the hammer of the gun and then thumb it forward. The incessant clicking annoyed Hattie. "Could you stop?" she finally demanded.

Longley stood, and before holstering his weapon, loaded a round in each of the six chambers. "We're going for a ride in the park," he said. Her husband was a quiet man who rarely showed emotion. Hattie read the anger and concern on his face and moved to pick up her hat. "Marcus has the carriage waiting," he said.

After Longley helped his wife into the carriage, Hattie waited until he snapped the reins. "Is there a chance Will's death was an accident?" she asked. When he didn't answer, she added, "I don't think so either." She thought again. "If Tom believes the Union Pacific Railroad had anything to do with this, I doubt he'd be forthcoming in the telegraph."

At the entrance to Central Park, Longley turned the carriage down the graveled path toward the lake. At this time of the morning there were few people out—mostly walkers, who ignored the Longleys as they drove by. Rounding a curve, he pulled the carriage to the side and tied the reins before hurrying around to help Hattie down. As they were crossing the path, an automobile came into view, belching smoke out the back. Hattie waited until the noise from machine had passed before she said, "I dread the thought of those filthy things replacing the horse."

"Well, they're going to," he said. "And if we're to stay in business, we'll have to get used to them." Longley directed his wife to a wooden bench near the lake's edge. He pulled a second telegram from his pocket and handed it to Hattie. "Robert doesn't think Tom's boy died accidentally," he said. "He said the death was unexpected. He would have said it was unavoidable if he thought it was an accident."

A breeze came up, causing Hattie to place a hand on her hat. "If this is a sinister act, and assuming it's emanating from the Harriman organization, there's the possibility they could be getting close to us. Unlikely, but it's still a possibility."

"How?" asked Longley. He reached over and pushed a lock of hair from her face.

"I have no idea," she admitted. "I don't see how anyone could know about us. But, having said that, I suppose if someone was tenacious enough, our business dealings could be discovered." She looked up at the sky as she thought.

Longley stood and walked to the water's edge. A few yards away, a pair of ducks paddled by, their ducklings in a line between them. He watched until the birds disappeared around the bend before turning back. "We'd better plan on leaving sooner than we thought," he said. "Will's death wasn't an accident. And I don't have to tell you that this shows the danger we might be in."

"Maybe we're all right. According to Silas, Tom didn't tell his sons who we are, or where we are," Hattie pointed out. She joined her husband and slipped her hand under his arm. "All Will knew was that there was a journal that had something to do with a couple of long-forgotten outlaws." After a time she seemed to arrive at a conclusion. "However, I see your point. Perhaps we should leave right away." Hattie tugged on her husband's arm and said, "Let's get back to the livery. You set things up for Marcus to take over, while I get started packing." As an afterthought, she went on, "And once you're finished, you should send a message to Robert, to let him know our change in plans."

He smiled for the first time. "Besides getting out of town in a hurry, just what are the plans?"

She glanced down at the holster. "Well, you could perfect some necessary skills." Hattie touched a finger to her lip; after a short time, she said, "And, of course, we'll have a short stay along the Mississippi."

Three days later, the Longleys boarded a train west.

X

T he sound of the door opening made Horace Akers look up to check the time on the Union Pacific station clock. Six-thirty. No trains were due until after midnight and not many of the town folk dropped by at supper time. He squinted and tried to make out the silhouette in the door-way. Akers rose and stepped toward the shadow, and then he stopped. "Oh. Well...good evening, sir," he stammered. "How was—"

"Sit down," Denard Kenney commanded. He moved toward Akers, forcing him to bump into his desk and knock his inkwell to the floor. Without thinking, Akers picked up the well. The ink ran over his hands and pooled on the floor like black blood. "Attend to yourself," Kenney said. It sounded like an order. He stepped around Akers and sat in the lone seat reserved for office visitors.

The station manager was still wiping the residue off his hands when he returned to his desk and took his chair. With an embarrassed look at Kenney, he tossed the ink-stained rag into a waste can. Kenney watched in amusement until Akers asked, "What can I do for you, sir?"

"Have you spoken to anyone of my presence?"

"No sir," he said. "Not even to my wife."

"Any inquiries concerning my car?"

"No sir," he repeated. "I made it clear it was no one's busi-ness." Kenney was silent for so long that Akers felt obligat-ed to ask, "Did your study go well, sir? Did you visit the mines you were interested in?"

"In fact, it was excellent," he said. "Very illuminating." Kenney's expression became peaceful as he spoke of his travels for some time, as if he remembered the past days fondly. At the end of his story, his features hardened, and he said, "I assume you received my directive that I wish to depart early in the morning."

"Your car will be added to the train that's arriving from Salt Lake later tonight," said Akers. "The schedule directs that the train depart at six-fifteen tomorrow. Does that meet with your approval...sir?"

The tall man smiled—or at least his lips moved; the eyes were lifeless. "I have great latitude within the company," said Kenney. "But reconfiguring the schedule is something even I cannot do." Standing, the smile left his face, and he asked again, "You're sure no one knows of my being here?"

"Absolutely sure," Akers replied. "As I said, I spoke to no one of your activities, not even the members of your crew. After all, I didn't know if you had informed them of your itinerary." Even in the cool of the evening, sweat added a sheen to Akers' brow.

"Fine job," said Kenney. "Of the funds I left with you, are any remaining?"

The station manager turned to the safe behind his desk and spun the dial. He pulled out a thick envelope and handed it across the desk, but Kenney shook his head. "No," he said. "The balance is for you. Perhaps your family can make use of it."

"But there's over three hundred dollars here."

"Good-bye, Mr. Akers," the tall man said and turned to leave. He stopped halfway and said, "Remember, you do not know me, nor will you ever speak of me."

Akers didn't have a chance to reply before Kenney stepped through the door and closed it without a sound. He wiped his sleeve across his forehead and breathed his first easy breath since Kenney had walked through the door. Akers couldn't quite put his finger on it, but somewhere in his very soul he knew Denard Kenney was the most dangerous man he'd ever met.

The clock chimed seven, three hours before the night manager would come on duty. Akers started to wipe his forehead again when he realized he was clutching the money in his fist. He recounted the bills and thought of a house that was not more than four blocks away. A fine house rumored to be available. It was just the right size for a family of five.

⚬ ⚬ ⚬

Night manager Floyd Braselton walked across the street to the train station. As was his custom, he was early. But tonight he had a reason. He was hoping to talk to Akers about a job opening in Colorado Springs. Braselton was a bachelor and had been an employee of the Union Pacific Railroad for six years. Thanks to Akers, his prospects for a major promotion were good.

The light shining through the station house window was dim, causing Braselton to wonder if Akers hadn't bothered to return from supper. The manager often took a break at eight o'clock and, on occasion, if things were slow, would simply leave a note. As the young man opened the door, the dead silence of the station gave him a chill. He stopped and called out, "Horace? Are you still here?" When there was no answer, Braselton stepped over the threshold and tried again. "Horace? You here?"

No answer. Just the heavy quiet that made Braselton tiptoe. Braselton shrugged. Akers must have already left for the night. He bent over the lamp and adjusted the wick. The light illuminated the room and the body lying on the floor. Braselton took in everything with a one-second sweep of the room. Akers' bloody remains were behind the desk, the safe stood open, and the door to the back of the station was ajar.

Braselton wanted to run. He'd never seen a dead body except in a funeral parlor, but it was too late to spare himself the sight of blood and brains leaking from the split skull. He turned and ran for the door, barely making it to the sidewalk before vomiting, mostly into his boots.

A reveler from the saloon a block away stopped to watch Braselton retch and spit. After a moment, the man asked, "You off your feed? Want me to fetch the doc?"

"No. Get the chief," groaned Braselton. He turned away and vomited again. He caught his breath and blurted,

"Horace Akers is dead. He's been murdered."

The man took off in a sprint to the constable's office around the corner and returned with not one but three men. Police Chief Jed Russell merely glanced at Braselton before he shoved the door open and rushed in. He was back in seconds and stationed one deputy outside the door to keep anyone from entering. The other deputy was sent around back to keep guard there. Russell dismissed the drunken messenger with a gruff, "Be on your way now," and pulled Braselton inside the station.

The following morning, Chief Russell announced that Horace Akers had been murdered during a robbery. The safe had been cleaned out and, according to Braselton, being that it was Thursday evening, and it was Akers' practice to make a weekly bank deposit on Friday, over a thousand dollars was missing.

The following week, Floyd Braselton received notice from New York that he was to assume the responsibilities of station manager.

❦

"Was this necessary?" Bates demanded. It had been over a week since Kotkin returned to New York, and this was his first meeting with Bates, who himself had just returned from a business trip. With a controlled effort at calm, Bates closed the door and tossed a piece of paper on the desk. He took a seat across from Kotkin.

Kotkin glanced briefly at the letter, noting the date. "News travels fast. This information is only two weeks old," he said with studied casualness. He slid the letter back across the desk unconcerned. Holding up a file, he asked, "Do you know what's in here?"

"Please answer my question," said Bates. "Robbing the station, murdering a respected employee—a father of three. Was this necessary?" Kotkin locked eyes with Bates who was forced to look away before adding, "I don't wish to tell you how to handle your affairs, but the welfare of the railroad is my responsibility."

In a deadly voice, Kotkin asked, "What makes you think I had anything to do with Mr. Akers' death?"

"Well, it seems quite obvious—." Once more Kotkin's gaze into the other man's eyes caused Bates to hesitate, before he went on, "I'm sure you had your reasons, but isn't this something you should have discussed with me?"

Kotkin now smiled. "Perhaps," he agreed in a friendlier tone. "On the other hand, it's difficult to discuss strategy when we're thousands of miles apart. But did it occur to you that poor Akers simply was the victim of bad luck?"

"Quite frankly, no."

"Well spoken," Kotkin said, his smile widening. "Think about it. Akers had met me and could therefore have imparted information to the wrong people. I couldn't have that, could I?" Before Bates could answer, Kotkin continued, "Of course not. So in this case, the end justifies the means, if I'm to achieve Father's goals, or should I say the goals that have been set for William."

"I'm not at all sure this is what your father meant."

"You know as well as I that my job is to remove obstacles," he replied. He again picked up the file. "Enough about Akers. Do you wish to know what I discovered?"

Bates stood and walked to the window, his hands clasped behind his back. After a time, he returned to his chair and said, "Forgive me, Elias. It's true that you have complete discretion in handling your affairs, and I'll try not to meddle again. Now, what is so important about that file?"

Kotkin began by explaining his trip to find Will Brannigan.

"Upon my arrival in Gunnison, it had been easy to get an old bartender in a local saloon to talk about the Brannigan family. With little effort I learned the location of the ranch and that it was the two sons who ran it."

Kotkin could see Bates wanted the story to go faster, but he was enjoying the telling. "The following morning, I rode out to the Brannigan ranch where I introduced myself to Molly, the pretty wife of the younger son. By posing as a representative of a company interested in land speculation,

I gained Molly's trust and before long we were sitting on the front porch chatting. Damned inconvenient for me that Josh had left the day before on a horse-buying trip, not to return until the end of the week.

"I used my charm and not a little guile to learn the whereabouts of the older brother," continued Kotkin. "He was in Crested Butte with his father. I left soon after, knowing that Molly's untimely death would be suspicious."

Bates couldn't believe he had heard the words, but he tried to make sense of yet another planned murder. "She could have identified you, no doubt."

"Yes. But my business was to take care of Will Brannigan, and I couldn't call that much attention to myself or the other Brannigans. So I took my leave of the ranch."

"I suppose there's more," Bates sighed.

"Oh, yes. Once in Crested Butte, Brannigan's bartender—you knew Tom Brannigan owned a salon there, didn't you?—was quite talkative. But not as talkative as when we were alone, and he was in great pain."

Bates grimaced, but Kotkin didn't slow down. He was tempted to give Bates details beyond Bates' wildest imagination, just to watch him squirm. "After some convincing, I gained the directions to the Sadie Mae mine where I'd find Will. I disposed of the bartender, and set up a scene to convince any lawman with more than a passing curiosity that the bartender had hanged himself.

"Will had been prepared for an unscheduled visit, but unfortunately for him, not for my level of expertise. Subduing him required no particular skill. Just surprise. We had our chat in the mineshaft. Brannigan held on for quite a lengthy time before telling me what we need to know."

Bates was offended by the use of *we*, but Kotkin took no notice. Kotkin concluded that he had extracted what information he could and then tossed Will through the lower mine shaft opening. "Don't worry," Kotkin added. "I made sure he was dead and gave plausibility to the scene by breaking a rung in the ladder."

Bates wasn't worried. He was slightly ill. He had been

watching as well as listening, and couldn't help noticing the light that flashed through Kotkin's eyes as he described interrogating the bartender and the young man. Bates wanted the interview over and asked rather briskly, "What did you learn from Brannigan?"

"As we suspected. Actually, as we know," Kotkin replied. "Parker and Longabaugh are alive, as is Miss Place. I have to admit to a partial failure on my part; I was unable to gather as complete information as I would have liked." Bates was unsure whether this was said in chastisement of himself or in admiration for Will. Kotkin continued, "I was unable to discover their aliases, or their specific whereabouts. Given what he was going through, I have to believe young Brannigan did not know."

Bates was astounded. "Are you saying you killed three people and have nothing to show for it?"

The dark eyes turned flat again. "You would do well to soften your remarks." The room was quiet.

"Of course. I apologize. If I appear short, it's because I want this business concluded." Bates thought he'd never uttered truer words.

Kotkin pushed back his chair. "Charles, in my line of work, everything comes in good time," he said. "For example, while I did not obtain all the information I wished, I did discover three things. One, Parker lives somewhere in the Pacific Northwest. Two, Longabaugh does indeed live in a large city in the East." He smiled and then went on, "Most likely New York, based on the fact he was originally from across the river."

"The third?"

"Tom Brannigan was once a member of Parker's gang," said Kotkin. "I'll grant you, this was speculation on young Brannigan's part. After all, he was in great duress. But, I'm convinced Will thought his father was part of the gang." He gestured at the file, as he said, "I think Tom Brannigan may have been Parker and Longabaugh's conduit to America—it was he who most likely made the arrangements for them. I also think that Miss Place had much to do with this scheme, and possibly even Parker's wife and sons were involved."

"Do I take it that you intend to interrogate Tom Brannigan?" asked Bates. Never in his wildest dreams did he think that consequences such as were evolving could be possible. As Kotkin paused, Bates reached into his coat pocket and fished out a spotless handkerchief.

Kotkin finally spoke. "If possible, I would have already done so," he said. "But in matters such as this, one must follow a certain...well, perhaps the best way to say this is that one must follow what is presented. It would have been extremely difficult to get close to Tom. And until I talked to the daughter-in-law and the bartender, I wasn't *absolutely* sure who my target was."

"I see," said Bates. "But—"

Kotkin didn't care to hear anymore from Bates. "As I said, all things in good time. Rest assured, Charles, I'll do what must be done, and you'll not be a part of it." He smiled and said, "Unless something goes dreadfully wrong."

Bates found the fortitude to ask, "And what does that mean?"

Kotkin picked up a gold letter-opener and tossed it from hand to hand, higher and higher. With a slight twist of his wrist, the opener came down point first and stuck into the wood an inch from edge of the desk. Kotkin gestured and said, "It means that someone could come for you, should they manage to get by me."

Bates rose and tried not to look at the quivering opener as he walked to the door. Stopping with his hand on the door knob, he asked, "And how remote a possibility would that be?"

"Very remote," said Kotkin. He pulled the opener from the wood. "Bordering on impossible."

The iron wheels turned endlessly in a mesmerizing beat. Longley leaned forward to peer out the window. As usual, he had the feeling the city was moving and the train was stationary. Soon drab St. Louis gave way to green hills as the tracks led the train across the Mississippi River and into the heartland of Missouri. He had sat motionless with chin in his hand so long that Hattie reached out and gently placed her hand on his shoulder. Conscious of other passengers, she said in a low voice, "You had better move. It looks like you're asleep."

Knowing how quiet her husband could be, Hattie reached across the seat and pulled a notebook out of her carpetbag. She untied the ribbon and turned to a page that was covered with her delicate handwriting. Within minutes, Hattie was engrossed in the notes she had taken during last night's discussion with Sophie.

Longley suddenly stood. He pulled down a bag from above. Hattie was about to say something, but one look from her husband made her decide that protest would not deter him. After he removed his gun, he set the bag on the empty seat across from him and proceeded to clean and oil the weapon. Perhaps because of the stylish clothes they wore, their fellow passengers decided there was no danger, and the novelty of watching an expert clean a gun soon wore off.

Hattie returned to her notebook. It wasn't until Longley replaced the satchel that she looked up from her reading and asked in the same low voice, "Do you feel better?" There was no answer, so she set down her book, and tried again. "Perhaps you can tell me when you'll be yourself."

Longley looked around. "I don't like this," he said, also in a low voice. "You don't believe in coincidence, anymore than I do."

"I know," she said. "Even if I thought Will's death could have been an accident, once Tom sent the telegraph about the robbery and murder at the train station in Denver—then on top of that, the death of his bartender—I do not think anything but murder now." Before he could speak, she went on. "And it's becoming clear that people are being killed so that someone can get at you and Robert. And, to a lesser extent, me."

"Through Tom."

Nodding, Hattie held up her notes. "According to what Sophie had to say, there's not much doubt about where the threat is coming from." She slowly closed the notebook and said, "If it's what we think, we're lucky her son is in New York."

XI

Although it was late July in the Queen City of the Plains, a cool breeze welcomed Carlisle and Thea to Denver. As they stepped out of Union Station, Carlisle was taken with the automobiles in the streets. He pointed and told Thea, "I believe that one's a Cadillac. And those two over there are Tin Lizzies." Thea gave him a singular look that made him laugh. "Can't help it," he said. "The boys are always talking about automobiles. They've got me interested."

"For all you really know, that ugly monster could be any number of automobiles," she said, indicating the Cadillac. The breeze caused her to reach up and steady her hat.

At the hotel, a bell hop pulled a handcart toward the couple. Carlisle handed him a coin and said, "The name is Carlisle."

"I believe Mr. Tom Brannigan has taken care of your registration," the doorman replied. Carlisle turned to his wife and said, "I thought Tom would meet us."

"Actually, sir, Mr. Brannigan is on the verandah in the back of the hotel," replied the young man. "My name's Alfred. Call me Alf. I'll be happy to retrieve your room key and take your bags to your room. If that meets with your approval, proceed through the lobby and take the hallway next to the main salon. You'll find Mr. Brannigan at a table between the bar and the lawn." The young man turned and started unloading the numerous bags out of the back of the carriage.

Carlisle guided his wife up the steps, glanced back at the bellman, and then said, "In a way, I dread seeing Tom." Thea stopped and waited for him to continue. "I'm sure he wants to tear the throat out of somebody. But he doesn't know who; and besides, now's not the time. His patience has gotta be wearing thin."

Thea sighed and simply nodded, thinking of how her husband would react if one of his own boys had met a fate such as Will's.

Thea preceded her husband through the double doors to the main foyer. The Colorado Grand Hotel was the premier Denver hotel. Only four years old, it featured electricity and the latest in other modern innovations—including individual washrooms with running water in the bottom-floor suites. These suites were the rage of the gentry and generally available only through a recommendation from a valued guest, such as Tom Brannigan. "Do you think we should freshen up before meeting Tom?" asked Thea.

Carlisle shook his head and directed her up to the promenade level and down the hallway to the back lawn. Thea smiled when her husband tipped his hat to the ladies in the hallway. "My, but you're the gentleman," she chided him.

"It's a gentlemanly lesson learned at the knee of my dear departed mother," said Carlisle. They pushed open the enormous glass door and stepped onto the terrace surrounded by a finished-oak railing inset in carved rocks, which turned into a magnificent rock staircase leading to well-spaced tables on the lawn. Beyond the lawn were a river and a bank of trees with walking paths interspersed to allow an afternoon or evening stroll. Beyond the trees was a panoramic view of the Rocky Mountains' eastern slope. All in all it was a place to linger and be reassured of the beauty and orderliness of the world. *Perhaps this is why Tom chose the hotel,* Thea thought.

"We're with Mr. Brannigan," Carlisle told a waiter at the top of the staircase. The waiter led down the stairs to Brannigan's table. Brannigan stood as the Carlisles approached. Thea gave Brannigan a brief hug. His face was pale and his voice softer than when they had met in Oregon. "How was your trip?"

"We had a pleasant journey," she said. "Please, do sit." Brannigan smiled at Thea and turned to his old friend with a look that reminded Carlisle of a man who was short of water in the desert. The men shook hands and all three arranged themselves around the table.

With a look at her husband, Thea said, "Why don't you remove your hat, dear?" In spite of himself, Brannigan smiled.

Carlisle set his hat on the table and said, "Tom, you've paid a helluva price for being our friend. There's no way to repay what its cost you."

"It wasn't your fault that Will was murdered. He was a damn fool to go to New York," said Brannigan. His eyes showed life for the first time. They were bright with anger. "The fault was mine for not getting rid of those papers." Brannigan stopped talking as the waiter set a bottle of whiskey and a glass in front of Carlisle and opened a bottle of champagne and poured a glass for Thea. She thanked the waiter with a smile that was as bubbly as the champagne. The men picked up their glasses and drained the whiskey.

Once they were alone again, Brannigan continued as if he hadn't been interrupted. "You got my telegram about my bartender hanging from the rafters of his cabin, and the Union Pacific station manager getting killed here in Denver." They nodded. "Will didn't fall down that mine shaft. He was thrown. This is the work of Harriman's people, and I owe it to Jimmy and Akers —but mostly to Will— to find the son of a bitch that Harriman's people sent to do all this." Looking beyond the Carlisles toward the mountains, he fell silent. His anger spent, he looked back at them with a smile fixed in place. "Say, how about something to eat? They got good food here."

Carlisle ignored the offer. Sitting this close to his friend and seeing the suffering first hand, made Carlisle itch for revenge. "Once the Longleys get here, we'll figure how we're gonna find the bastard." He heard the rage in his voice and changed to a softer tone and subject. "And while I'm coming up with a plan, Thea wants to see something of Denver." His grin faded and he asked, "I know the answer, but do you have anybody covering our backs?"

Brannigan shrugged and, with a gesture in the direction of the bar, said, "Silas Kindred. Not very big, but he's as tough as they come. And he don't stand out in a crowd."

Carlisle casually turned, as if inspecting the hotel, and noted a small man nursing a glass of beer at the bar. "I wouldn't have noticed," he admitted.

"Nor I," agreed Thea, as she gazed over Brannigan's shoulder. "Wasn't it Silas who went to New York?"

"He did."

Carlisle leaned closer to Brannigan and asked, "Speaking of New York, when are James and Hattie getting here?"

"Tomorrow morning," replied Brannigan. "They made a stop along the Mississippi."

"Your sister's still in St. Louis?" asked Carlisle.

"You got a good memory. Sophie's husband got killed a few years ago while they were living in New York," said Brannigan. "She never did like the East and went back to Missouri. Only bad part was her son had a good job, so he stayed."

"Is that right," said Carlisle. The waiter stopped at their table to replenish their glasses, so Carlisle waited to ask, "What does your nephew do?"

For the first time Brannigan laughed. "You aren't going to believe it when I tell you." He lowered his voice, "He's some sort of lawman."

Thea, who had spent years looking over her shoulder for the law, froze. But Carlisle immediately saw the humor and laughed so long that Thea eventually smiled too. Carlisle finally stopped and dabbed his eyes with a napkin. "A lawman related to you? He wasn't part of LeFors' posse, was he?" He started laughing again.

Thea put a hand on his arm. "Calm yourself. Not everything is a laughing matter."

"Nah, it's all right," said Brannigan. "The fact is, he didn't have anything to do with us. He's too young to even know about all that." He grinned and said, "Guess you could say he got there a little too late to get in on all the fun."

Thea gave the couple at the next table an apologetic look. "Perhaps a change of subject would be appropriate. We really don't wish to draw attention to ourselves."

Carlisle said, "Little late for that." He raised his glass. "Here's to the future." All three drank, but the mood turned serious again.

Brannigan set his glass down. "I know you been thinking about all this. You got anything in mind that you might be willing to share?"

Carlisle twirled his hat on his index finger. "I've got an idea or two, but it's best to wait until James gets here. That way I only have to listen to Thea's screaming once."

"Robert—" began his wife in a warning tone.

He interrupted, "Don't worry about a thing, Thea. You're not going to be in on it."

"If you're in, I'm in. Whatever it is."

"I can't chance it," he said as he took her hand. "And the same goes for Hattie, except for the planning. She's pretty good at giving me ideas."

"How do you know I wouldn't be?" Thea asked, a bit testily. "I have spent the best part of my life in your shadow, Robert Carlisle, and I will no longer be put aside." Her green eyes flashed.

In the silence, Carlisle reflected that he'd never seen Thea so resolute. But it was Brannigan who spoke first, when he said to Carlisle, "It would be best if you changed your thinking."

"I guess so," agreed Carlisle. He then said to his wife, "But you might hear things you aren't going to like."

"I'll chance that," she said. "So, do you have a plan?"

Carlisle leaned forward. "Of course I have a plan. What if we robbed the Union Pacific Flyer?"

⚬⚬⚬

The following day, the Carlisles and the Longleys met in the dining room without Brannigan. He begged off, knowing the two couples would better enjoy their first visit in years without a grieving father to accommodate. He and

Kindred would eat in a nearby dining house that advertised genuine sipping whiskey along with the finest beefsteaks in Colorado.

The Carlisles arrived first and were directed to a secluded table in the corner where the floor-to-ceiling windows gave an unobstructed view of the mountains. After they were seated, Thea admitted to a growing fondness for sparkling wine, and Carlisle ordered a bottle of the champagne she'd enjoyed the previous afternoon. Her anxiety over meeting the Longleys—whom she knew only through Robert's letters to her and the boys—was matched by his impatience as they waited.

The bottle was half-empty before the maître'd ushered the Longleys to the table. Carlisle stood and hugged Hattie warmly before reaching around to shake hands with his former partner. Remembering his wife, he turned and made the introductions.

"I would have recognized you anywhere," Carlisle lied to Longley after they were seated.

"I'll bet," he said. He smiled at Thea. "Any reason I start believing him now?"

"None that I know of," she cheerfully replied. Turning to Hattie, she said, "You're more beautiful than Robert ever said, and I'm glad to finally meet you. He rarely speaks of James; but, of course, talks incessantly of you."

Hattie laughed. "In that case, you should believe every word," she said. The ice was broken and within minutes the two women were chatting as if they had known each other all their lives. Hattie was particularly interested in the Carlisle boys and wanted details of how they ran the mill.

"Guess the women have hit it off," said Longley. Holding up the delicate champagne glass he asked, "What is this?"

"What'd you expect?" asked Carlisle. "I've always said you've got to change with the world. You can't drink rotgut all the time."

"Why not?" Waving his hand at the headwaiter, Longley ordered a Tennessee whiskey, which to his surprise, the hotel stocked. He looked around the dining room, finding it little different from the better restaurants he and Hattie frequented in New York except the view was much better. The waiter returned with the bottle and poured two glasses. As their wives continued to talk, Longley tilted his head at Carlisle and said, "We have to do something about Tom's situation."

"I figure that's why we're here. It makes me sick to think about Will."

"Forget about Will," Longley replied. "Think about Will's murderer. Tom seems to think you have a plan." He paused for a moment. "I hope it's better than the last one."

"What was wrong with that one? You have to admit your life's a lot better than in Bolivia," said Carlisle. Longley thoughtfully looked around when Robert dropped the word *Bolivia*. Carlisle grinned and picked up his whiskey. "Here's to old friends."

Longley lifted his glass and asked, "What's the plan?"

"Boy, some things never change. We'll talk about it with Tom and his man—"

"Silas," said Longley. "A good man."

Carlisle nodded. "That's what Tom says. Anyway, why don't we visit with our wives and enjoy our dinner? We'll get together tomorrow. Besides, you and Hattie have some reading to do before we talk."

Longley's blue eyes clouded over before he asked, "Why don't we send that damn journal back? Isn't that all they want?"

"You'd think so," said Carlisle. His smile disappeared. He stared out the window at the mountains before saying, "But there's more. Whoever is behind this probably thinks we could ruin things for them just by what we know. And the problem is, we could." He turned and waved at the waiter.

The evening passed pleasantly as the couples enjoyed a fine dinner. As they made their way out of the dining room two hours later, Carlisle suggested a nightcap by the fireplace in the main lobby. The ladies arranged themselves on the sofa as Carlisle and Longley sat across from each other in leather chairs, all four ignored the two men who sat together at the end of the bar nursing drinks. While they were waiting for their brandy, Carlisle went to his room and returned with the journal. When he gave it to Longley, Hattie immediately reached for it. She noted the ribbons between the pages and asked Thea, "Is it necessary to read the entire manuscript?"

"I'd suggest you skip everything but what's marked," she replied. "Most of it is irrelevant and dull as a school lesson. The second passage is the most difficult and constitutes the threat. You'll understand once you've read it."

Hattie opened the journal and she and Thea leaned together. In a quiet voice, Carlisle spoke to Longley, "According to Tom, there were no suspects in Jimmy's death, but to his way of thinking, it was clear that the man had been murdered. As to Will, there was no reason for him to be in the lower level of the mine at all since it had flooded years ago and was inaccessible beyond a hundred feet from the ladder. The real kicker is that both the bartender and Will had several broken bones. Jimmy's shoulder and shinbone—and six fingers—were shattered, not just broken."

"Maybe he changed his mind after he jumped off the table," suggested Longley.

"I suppose that's possible," said Carlisle. "But it's strange he'd break fingers trying to stop from strangling." After some thought, he added, "Hell, I don't know. Maybe he did kill himself. But Tom's right. There was no way for Will to break both legs and crack his skull." He took a drink, set the glass down, and then went on, "If the boy landed that hard on his legs, it would have broken his fall and his head shouldn't have gotten smacked."

Longley considered this for a minute. "I guess you're right," he admitted.

"Yeah. But on the other hand, the sheriff still thinks it was an accident."

Longley interrupted, "And in the same week, the railroad guy just up and gets killed, too."

"To me, the really strange one is the railroad fellow," said Carlisle. "It seems a real stretch that a Union Pacific employee, who just happened to be a friend of Tom's, gets robbed and murdered a few days after Will dies. And only a couple of days after Tom's bartender kills himself for no reason." After a moment, he continued, "I think whoever did this was after Will. He used the bartender to find out where the boy was and then went and got him." He shook his head in exasperation. "If Tom hadn't contacted us about Will's trip to New York, none of these things would be questioned."

"Dammit, everything was good until this," Longley said. "Anything else?"

"Just this: the widow of the railroad man—his name was Akers—said her husband had come home for dinner with a fistful of cash, but it wasn't money from the safe. According to Tom, Akers told his wife that it was a bonus from a big man in the company, but he couldn't tell her anything about it. Anyway, after supper, he went back to the station and that was the last anybody saw of him." He reached inside his coat pocket and extracted a case. After offering it to Longley, who declined with a wave of his hand, Carlisle scratched a match on the bottom of his shoe and lit his cigar.

Longley waited until Carlisle was contentedly puffing before he said, "So tell me what we're going to do. You're the brains of this operation."

"I'm surprised you'd say that," he said, eyes crinkling over his beard. "You always bitched about my ideas."

"Only when they didn't work, which was most of the time."

Carlisle couldn't argue. "The fellow who killed the bartender also killed Will, and then went back and killed the station manager to shut him up," said Carlisle. He flicked the ash of his cigar into a brass urn. "Whoever this guy is, he's good. He sets up his work to look like anything but murder, and so far hasn't left any witnesses."

The look on Longley's face changed from curiosity to concern. "He had to get Will to get to us. What did he get from Will?"

"That's the part I don't know," admitted Carlisle. He looked into his glass and then said, "I've got some ideas—so does Tom—but we're going to have to think on it some more." He stood abruptly. "Why don't we turn in? It's getting late, and if I know Hattie, she's gonna want to read the whole damn journal tonight."

XII

From the Journal of E. H. Harriman

OCTOBER 24, 1864 — *I have locked my door and pulled the shades before sitting down to scribe this entry. Having just returned from a meeting and sworn to total secrecy, it is with great difficulty that I am able to quell the pounding of my heart. I fear I have ventured into treacherous waters and it is imperative that I control myself or, failing that, take leave of the City, never to return.*

The three gentlemen with whom I met are plotting a nefarious scheme to foster beliefs to which I confess to heartily subscribe. Now I'm being drawn into playing a part in the scheme. If I am in agreement with the cause of these gentlemen, what is the basis for my fear? Is it because I doubt the potential for success? On the contrary, I see the scheme as relatively simple to accomplish. The end result is virtually assured, and quite frankly, my participation—or lack of—will not change the outcome. Do I fear being implicated? Might I face execution? Or perhaps a lifetime of incarceration? Yes, all this frightens me, but my distress also arises in part to the possibility of the direction that the Country may turn, due to pressure brought by Foreign Powers. Yet, I cannot help but admit a fascination with the fiscal potential that will arise, should the scheme come to fruition.

In spite of my consternation, I refuse to give in to fear. Perhaps in honesty I should add that a sip of brandy has helped calm my nerves and strengthened my resolve. I freely admit that I know what I want in life—and am prepared to do whatever will advance my standing. Reflecting on my life and ambitions, I know what my true course must be.

The success of this plan could be a step forward in the attainment of my life's work.

But my speculations belittle my actions. I would be remiss if I did not acknowledge that I am immersed in the plans of men who plan beyond my ability to see. I have completed Mr. Stanton's wishes and delivered funds entrusted to me by him. Tonight I met a man who introduced himself as Mr. Herold. He readily professed to a shortage of cash for his small group of patriots. I handed over the money Mr. Stanton left in my care and thereby I have become a courier between the Secretary of War and these gentlemen.

NOVEMBER 2, 1864 — This evening was the second meeting with the men who will become the arms and legs of any scheme developed by Mr. Stanton and his friends. Three days prior, I met with the Secretary and conveyed the results of the meeting of October 24 with Mr. Herold's men. Mr. Stanton was quite pleased, and even though I am unaware of the exact events that are about to transpire, I expressed my willingness to be of further service. Thus far, my involvement only goes so far as to gather information and serve as a courier. Mr. Stanton and I have an agreement that at no time will I engage either in planning or in the operation of the plan itself. He has assured me that there is no need for any action beyond that of delivering funds and information as needed. This pleases me. The information I will be privy to should give me advance knowledge for judicious investments.

This evening's meeting reinforced my impression of Mr. David Herold. He is not of upper class, nor is he of higher education. He dresses well and carries himself as a gentleman, but it is readily apparent this is the result of training and not the happenstance of birth. Herold has a trace of a Southern accent that is not always apparent in his speech. Politically, he is of the opinion that President Lincoln and the Reconstructionists are a danger. Although I understand that Herold is, in a sense, also a courier, there is little doubt he has attachment to the operational side of the scheme. Once again I admonish myself to use caution in dealing with Herold and his cohorts.

Again tonight I delivered funds to the group. This time in the amount of $3,000. Secretary Stanton had also given me four envelopes to deliver—three of which were sealed. I confess to satisfying my curiosity by reading the contents of the fourth. The envelope contained a set of maps of the Virginia, Maryland and Pennsylvania countryside surrounding the Capital. The envelope also contained itineraries and public schedules for a number of dignitaries, including President Lincoln, Vice-President Johnson, Secretary of State Seward and, most surprisingly, General Grant. I was kept ignorant of the contents of the sealed envelopes.

I am uncomfortable with these recent developments. It strikes me that if this journal were to fall into the wrong hands, some might question my activities. This being the case, I will make sure to keep my journal with me at all times.

By the chime of the hall clock, it is two o'clock in the morning. I shall pause here and continue this narrative following a third meeting with Herold in one week.

NOVEMBER 9, 1864 — Unsettling events threaten to take their toll on the country, and on me. Tonight I have learned the plans of Herold and his group. The pen shakes as I write. The plan is to simultaneously kidnap Mr. Lincoln, Mr. Johnson, and Mr. Seward. General Grant is out of Washington and apparently will be for the duration of the War. It is the plan of these low-bred idiots to take these gentlemen by force, remove them to the South, and use them to negotiate for favorable surrender terms. This is predicated on the probability of the War ending soon with the defeat of the South. This ill-conceived plan could work against the position I have advocated. Should something adverse happen to Mr. Lincoln, the response of the government might well be to obliterate the South, destroying any assets that could be used for future growth, and at the same time, eliminate any chance of a future Reconciliation on our terms. Tomorrow, I will meet with the Secretary and express my fear over this scheme. There is only a small chance of success and virtually no hope of the desired results being achieved.

DECEMBER 2, 1864 — The Secretary has assured me that the moronic scheme of David Herold has been abolished. In fact, I have been informed that my work for Mr. Stanton was to allow Agents to infiltrate the bands of anti-Reconstruction groups that have threatened the Union victory in the War. I am greatly relieved.

As a result of my success, the Secretary has offered my services to an agent who requires my help in suppressing threats against the very same dignitaries. I am happy to oblige—it puts me in close proximity to the very workings of the Government, guarantees opportunities for advancing my position.

DECEMBER 21, 1864 — The Secretary invited me to an evening of entertainment at Ford's. A Shakespearean troupe presented a series of scenes from the Bard's plays, followed by a singing of Christmas Carols. All in all, a superbly entertaining evening.

One event struck me as odd. At the reception following the entertainment, Mr. Stanton took great pains to introduce one of the troupe's more famous actors, Mr. John Wilkes Booth. I profess to not being a student of the theater and am only vaguely familiar with the work of Mr. Booth. I have been told he is an actor of some note. Later, the Secretary explained that, although Booth was born in the South, he was actually an agent working on our behalf.

JANUARY 14, 1865 — My first entry in the New Year. The
Holidays in the Capital were merrier than in past years.
Many of our elected officials remained in Washington as the
war is winding down and there is much to do. The South is
failing and many monumental decisions will soon force
themselves on the legislators.

My services as a courier were called upon again the
evening before last. Mr. Stanton directed me to deliver
additional money to a tavern in a Maryland boardinghouse
run by Mrs. Surratt. Mrs. Surratt—a rather unpleasant
woman—led me into a back room where to my surprise
John Wilkes Booth met me. He accepted my package without acknowledging we had met. Apparently, Booth is acting
as a subterfuge to a group with conspiracy plans of their
own.

As I was leaving, Booth stepped out of the tavern and
asked me to join him in the stable. Mr. Booth admits to
a close relationship with the Secretary and expressed Mr.
Stanton's pleasure of my work for the War effort. I was
pleased, of course, but waited patiently until Mr. Booth
expressed the true nature for detaining me.

In the near future, Mr. Booth will need my services to
meet either himself or an associate in the Pennsylvania
countryside where I will be obliged to deliver a package from
the Secretary. He impressed upon me the need for secrecy,
and I assured him of my trustworthiness.

MARCH 2, 1865 — Something is surely amiss. I was contacted yesterday by a man acting on behalf of Secretary
Stanton. This man, who used the name George Atzerodt,
indicated that it was acceptable for me to speak to the
Secretary. In the process, Atzerodt suggested that an important event was nearing and that my meeting in the countryside would soon be at hand. I immediately contacted Mr.
Stanton in his private office. He claimed no knowledge of
what I was talking about, underscoring in my mind the seri-
ousness of events to come.

Regardless of Mr. Stanton's contradictory claims to have no knowledge of any plot and to be acting well within the scope of his duties as Secretary of War, whatever happens with Mr. Booth's plans, it is clearly with the understanding and cooperation of the Secretary.

I have come too far to worry about the ins and outs of some minor event of political scheming. My life will soon take on a proportion beyond that which I have ever dreamed. This cursed War will be ending soon, prosperity will be restored to my Great Country, and I will play a large part in developing that prosperity.

MARCH 17, 1865 — My unknown assignment is nearing. Yesterday morning, I was summoned into the Secretary's office where Mr. Stanton suggested I go to the Willard Hotel for a meeting with Sir Reginald Forrester of the Rothschilds Bank.

When Sir Reginald handed me a heavy leather bag, there was no question as to the contents. He told me the gold coins were payment for Mr. Booth to stop a last attempt of a major insurrection directed at the Capital in general, and Mr. Lincoln in particular. I will be contacted the day of the scheme and given specific directions as to my participation. Once I'm finished, Sir Reginald cautioned me to return to Washington before daylight and to speak of the assignment to no one.

I confess to the curiosity of using a Foreign Agent for such an important event, but realize as I write this entry that it makes sense. Sir Reginald has already indicated his bank's desire and willingness to work for the Reconstruction of the South, if terms are satisfactory.

APRIL 11, 1865 — God in Heaven! Can it be? Lee has surrendered to General Grant. Finally this cursed War is at an end! The long healing process begins.

This Country will grow and take its rightful place in the world. Now is the time.

The President delivered a short but heartfelt speech from the second story window of the north portico of the White House. I was pleased to be invited by the Secretary to stand with other Cabinet officers behind the President. Seeing Mr. Lincoln up close, I was struck by the sadness in his very being. I fear the weight of this strife has robbed him of his health. His words, measured as always, conveyed hope for our Nation; however, the President suggested certain rights be granted to the Negro. This was a cause for concern. If the President is leaning in that direction, it is clear he will continue his soft stance on the South in general.

Oddly, I glimpsed John Wilkes Booth standing off to the side of the gathered crowd and at one point, I felt his eyes boring into mine.

APRIL 14, 1865 — The excitement permeating the Department of War is exhilarating. Several times today, I found myself caught up in the continuing celebration.

Tonight is the night. When I entered my office this morning, I found George Atzerodt waiting. He tersely explained that threats on the lives of some of our great leaders were imminent. I was to leave Washington on horseback no later than nine o'clock this night, bring my package, and be waiting at Sharon's Crossing in Pennsylvania.

It is now early evening and after a supper in my boardinghouse, I will saddle my horse without awakening the groom. Whatever this insurrection is, I have no doubt that our secret agents (Atzerodt and Booth among them) have the situation well in hand.

With this, I end tonight's entry.

MAY 5, 1865 — My life is in ruins! I have been a pawn in the assassination of President Lincoln! How can this be? How could I have been so naïve to the chain of events? Booth murdered the President at Ford's Theatre; he was tracked for two weeks and killed. David Herold, George Atzerodt, Mrs. Surratt, and others have been captured. I have not returned to the Capital because of the surety that I will soon meet with my own capture.

When Booth and Atzerodt failed to meet me, I started my return to Washington, only to be met by soldiers, led by a Major Williamson. Because of the genuine shock I displayed when told of the assassination, and the fact that I was not in the city, the Major was convinced I played no part. As a result, once the militia had left, I retired to a tavern not far from my appointment location with Mr. Booth, and here I have remained under an assumed name.

Because I know I will be implicated in this horrible deed, I have been entering my final thoughts. Under any circumstance, it is poor judgment to continue this journal. I should destroy it, but to what end? My death warrant is signed, and they will soon come. I will remain at Fielder's Tavern until they do.

JUNE 4, 1865 — It is quite clear that I am still alive, and once again scribing my thoughts. So much has passed in such a short time. I have removed myself from Washington and established myself in New York City. With the gold I was to pass on to Booth and Atzerodt, I have in essence created a new life for myself.

For although I have come to believe that no one is searching for me, I have taken steps to thwart anyone who tries to discover who I am. My real name is no longer of importance. I have adopted a new name with the move to New York.

I have always considered that it was a mark against me that my Philadelphia family was not renowned, and on occasion, I have regretted that I am an only child of deceased parents. Now it appears these circumstances work in my favor. Cyrus Hardeman Jamison no longer exists, assumed to be just another victim of the war.

In the Capital, the call to punish the South is the order of the day, and Secretary Stanton, while not under direct investigation, is certainly being looked at in a less-than-favorable light. There are so many conspirators who have been accused, I know I should be safe. Frankly, I wonder if I was the only courier who was set along a road to aid the assassin. It seems to me that I was either used as a decoy or was posted at a secondary escape route.

The only person who directly knows of my part in this scheme is Sir Reginald Forrester. This is most fortuitous for me. Under no circumstances would Forrester, or the Rothschilds Bank, admit involvement in the Assassination of the President.

I intend to chronicle my life, for my ambitions will make it a life worthy of recording. Sir Reginald has left me with the notion and desire to link this country through a railroad system, and I intend to do so.

From these days forward, these journals shall record the advancement of Edward H. Harriman.

Hattie slowly closed the book, leaving it in her lap as she sat back in the chair. Her husband, sitting on the bed, waited until she looked at him. "Quite a story," Hattie said.

She picked up the book and returned to the last page. "Cyrus Jamison became E. H. Harriman," she said, "Who would have believed it?"

Earlier, while Hattie read aloud, Longley had sprawled on the bed, pillows propped behind his head. It hadn't taken him long to sit up and listen to every word. "It's more damning than we thought."

"The Harriman Company, not just his family, is in trouble if this ever comes to light," said Hattie. "To say nothing of the threat to the banks that have been, or are currently doing business with the Rothschilds Bank. If Rothschilds were to fail, they would bring down numerous others, maybe even damage the economies of some countries."

"Why would Rothschilds fail?"

"I'm not sure they would in Europe, but our government couldn't allow them to operate here," she explained. "It's because of the newspapers. The Lincoln assassination has remained a point of speculation, and the newspapers would like nothing better than to expose the scandal."

"So what do we do?" Longley asked. Having already removed his coat, tie and boots, he had lain back down and was now staring at the ceiling.

Placing the journal on the table, Hattie said, "It's after midnight. Let's go to bed. In the morning we'll all get together and discuss the situation." As she was removing her dress, a thought forced her to pause. "Whatever Robert's plan is, it needs to be a good one," she said.

Longley groaned aloud. "I'm too old for whatever it is he comes up with."

⚜

After breakfast on the terrace, the Longleys and Carlisles joined Brannigan waiting in the driver's seat of a carriage at the front of the hotel. Unnoticed by the concierge and doorman, as the carriage pulled out into the circular drive, a solitary horseman waited until it turned, then followed. Having received directions from the stablehand, Brannigan easily found the road leading to the South Platte River where the young man had assured him there were excellent shaded areas along the water.

Even though it was early, the sun was already burning the cool of the morning out of the cloudless sky. No one had spoken of Harriman's journal, but all knew it would be the topic of the day. For a time, Brannigan looked back, but after seeing nothing, he relaxed and listened to the conversation between Thea and Hattie who were sitting behind him, facing their husbands. For their part, Carlisle and Longley rarely spoke.

After a short drive, the carriage rounded a bend where a green meadow with the river running behind it came into view. There were no other adventurers so Brannigan pulled through the long grass to get close to the water before setting the brake and jumping to the ground. Carlisle assisted the ladies, and Longley strolled off in the direction of the surrounding stand of trees to make sure no strangers had followed. The length of his coat, which might have been termed out of style, hid his holster. Early that morning he and Brannigan had been out to the hotel's shooting range for target practice.

As the ladies spread the tablecloths provided by the dining room along with their lunch, Carlisle helped Brannigan lift a wicker basket from the back of the carriage. Inside were bottles of whiskey and wine, and several smaller brown bottles. With a grunt, Carlisle set his end down. "You sure you brought enough?"

Brannigan grinned. "Never know who might be joining us," he said with a glance at the road.

A quarter of a mile back in the trees, standing next to the road, Longley stood hidden by the trunk of a magnificent cottonwood tree. However, it wasn't the tree that interested him, and his patience was rewarded when the rider who had followed the carriage appeared. Longley silently drew his gun and waited. As the rider approached, his face became visible through the shafts of sunlight that filtered between the trees. Longley holstered his weapon, stepped out on the road, and grabbed the bridle. "Took your time, didn't you?" he asked the rider.

"Didn't know there were a time," said Kindred. "Yawl kin let go of ma hoss now." The small man swung his leg over the saddlehorn and dismounted. "Nice ta see ya 'gain," he said, as he and Longley shook hands. Stetson centered low over his forehead, Kindred was dressed in Levi Strauss jeans and a long-sleeve tan shirt. His pistol was in plain sight, the holster tied down around his leg. The two men walked together, with Kindred leading his horse, as Longley showed the way to the picnic area. As they approached the meadow, Hattie rose to greet them. "I wondered when we would see you again," Hattie said, as she leaned down and kissed his cheek.

Blushing furiously, the small man had to take a breath before he could speak. "Yeah, uh, ma'am...uh, sorry...Hattie. Ah wuz wonderin' the same." Brannigan introduced his partner to the Carlisles, grinning at Kindred's embarrassment at being singled out. Taking pity, he reached into the hamper and handed Kindred a bottle of beer. It was the first time Kindred had seen beer in a bottle. "Kinda small, ain't it?" he asked.

"Old man Coors is selling them in the general stores nowadays," said Brannigan. "He thinks it'll keep better than a bucket. Be easier for a man to take home." He took the bottle from Silas and pulled the cork. Kindred watched the beer spill over the top of the bottle and wondered who in the world would prefer a half-empty bottle to a full bucket of beer. Handing the beer to Kindred, Brannigan speculated, "We might even start selling them at our place."

After a taste, Kindred allowed the beer was acceptable and sat down on the grass at the edge of the blanket. Carlisle retrieved his own bottle, and after pulling the cork, sat next to the small man. "Thanks for helping out, Silas," he said.

"Yessir," the cowboy replied, once again embarrassed. "Ah'm pleased to." He pulled his hat lower and looked at his boots.

Carlisle laughed and said, "Maybe everybody ought to sit so we can talk." His first question was for Hattie. "Did you read the journal?"

"From a historical standpoint, it's a remarkable document," she said. "James and I discussed it briefly last night, and we're of the opinion that it's as dangerous as Thea has said." She glanced at Kindred, adding, "Silas, perhaps if we have some time this afternoon, I'll explain it to you."

"Ah already read it, ma'am, uh, Hattie" he slowly replied, head still down. "Ah read it 'while back and ah kin see what the problem is. Them Harriman folks would give everythin' ta git it." The front of the Stetson rose as Kindred straightened up and said, "But, truth be told, ah don't see why we cain't jist send it back. Seems like once them folks git the book, they'd let thins' be."

Carlisle shook his head. "We can't send it back because we know what's in it, and that makes us a threat. The way I see it, we need to send a message that we got it, and that we might use it. We propose they send the killer to us, and we'll give him the journal."

"Robert is right," said Hattie. "There's too much for them to lose if the information becomes public. Quite frankly, the best solution would be to give the journal to a newspaper and let them expose Harriman, but that would expose us too." She looked at Brannigan. "I'm sorry, but we all know that Will was murdered because of the journal. So was your man, and so was the railroad man." She turned back to Carlisle, "This is indicative that someone is desperate to recover the journal. And whoever that person is—as you've said—he's very good."

"These people will stop at nothing," interjected Thea. She looked at her husband. "So what's your plan?"

"Rob the Union Pacific," said Carlisle. The only noise was the birds in the trees.

"That's your plan?" Longley demanded.

Carlisle leaned back and admired the sky. "It's the only way I can get the killer to come to us." After more silence, he added, "Well, I didn't say it was the best plan. But it's a start."

XIII

New York City

"**D**amn it to hell! This is not possible. It defies plausibility!" Kotkin stormed toward his office, cursing at no one and everyone. "What the bloody hell are we getting for our money?" No one dared answer his rhetorical question. His ways were his own and his concerns not known to many in the firm. Throwing himself into his chair, he picked up Pinkerton's report and then threw it down again. *Idiots. No leads. No sightings. Nothing.* Sometimes he wondered why they bothered to report at all. Then he remembered: they wanted to get paid.

An entire year of searching New York City for evidence that Etta Place had purchased property, or a business, had turned up nothing. The agents had started by searching hospitals and cemeteries, and then expanded to real estate transactions between the years 1907 and 1909. Kotkin knew that property purchases weren't always duly recorded, making the job even more difficult.

The latest report contained nothing new, and reading it again would not make the answers appear. If the world famous Pinkerton National Detective Agency could not come up with the next move, Kotkin would have to do it himself. *How hard could it be?* A half-hour later, when his secretary knocked and announced that George Nelson of the Pinkerton Agency had arrived, Kotkin still had no answers, but plenty of frustration.

George Nelson tipped the scales at three-hundred-ten pounds. Despite his bulk, he was nattily dressed and carried himself with an aristocratic bearing. Nelson had impressed Kotkin with his mental acumen. He had started with the agency in 1892 as a strikebreaker during the Homestead

Strike, and had worked his way to second-in-command and was now the chief of administration. Nelson's job was to develop and retain clientele, and thanks primarily to Kotkin, the Harriman organization was his most important customer. It was a profitable relationship he planned to hold on to.

Nelson made it a point to never be intimidated by a customer, but in the case of Elias Kotkin he had trouble keeping that resolve. The Harriman executive made him uneasy—perhaps it was the demands that Kotkin made, or the way Kotkin offered advice, just to show that he was one step ahead of the agency. Nelson was not used to being ordered about, nor did he like it. He squeezed his wide body between the arms of the chair across from Kotkin's desk and held a steady gaze on his client.

"I'm not pleased," Kotkin said, as he fixed his visitor with a stare.

Nelson smiled. "I didn't think you would be," he replied. "That is why I am here personally. I want to give you what I think is good news. But given your current displeasure, I'm not sure you'll agree."

"Don't play games," snarled Kotkin. He seemed more tense than usual, like a cat ready to pounce.

"I'll get to the point," Nelson hastily replied. "One of my men recently uncovered a possible lead." In September of 1907, a freight company near Central Park was purchased for cash. This information turned up quite by chance when the original owner died, and his youngest son filed a motion contesting the bequests of the estate. The son questioned the source of his father's wealth. The matter was investigated, and even though the owner never properly recorded a deed of sale, the transaction was judged to be legal and binding, and ultimately a deed of trust was awarded. Nelson ended his story by unnecessarily adding, "The unfortunate son received nothing."

"Was the purchase made by a woman?"

"It's not that simple," he answered, raising a hand to stem off Kotkin's outburst. "Shortly after the freight company changed hands, it was clear the place was run by a woman. The purchaser was an out-of-town gentleman content to own the business from afar. At some point he either sold or turned over the business to the lady." Kotkin sat back and waited. "However," continued Nelson, "based on our current investigation, there's a husband in the picture now. It was in his name that a deed of trust was issued. The primary business is freight, but the company has numerous contracts with the city to move or store documents."

"Documents?" Kotkin's curiosity momentarily eclipsed his anger.

Nelson explained that several such businesses had sprung up due to the size of city government and number of large businesses in the city. New York City was constantly running out of storage space for its paperwork. Millions of files, journal records, receipts—just about anything one could imagine—all that had to be maintained for a prescribed number of years. "The company stores the paper for a monthly fee. However, the true backbone of their business remains delivery of just about everything, but food. Delivery of food creates special storage problems, unlike storing papers, I guess."

Nelson watched Kotkin swivel his chair and look at the painting of his father hanging on the wall behind his desk. He turned back and asked, "Is there more? I don't see why this would interest me."

"Since you haven't told me the true nature of what you're looking for, I'm not sure," Nelson admitted. "Thanks to a bit of luck, we managed to discover the name of the man who purchased the business in nineteen-seven. His name is Tom Brannigan."

Late that afternoon, Kotkin stood across the street from the Longley Freight Company. The shade of a tree was a godsend, providing protection and camouflage as he waited. His patience had been stretched beyond his usual time limit by the time the last wagon arrived and the horses were unhitched. When the stable doors closed for the evening, he concluded it was unlikely that either the owner or his wife were present. Kotkin was turning to leave when two men came out the office door, locked it, and walked down the gravel driveway. At the corner, the black man turned north, and with a wave the other man headed downtown.

Kotkin tailed the second man to a saloon not far from the stable, but he didn't enter. The saloon was filled with men dressed in denims or dungarees. Dressed as the successful businessman he was, Kotkin would have stood out. Much safer, he decided, to have Nelson put his men on the job. They could find out who the employees were and the current whereabouts of the owner and his wife.

⌑

At the sound of the train whistle, Hattie held tighter to her husband. "It's time," she said. Longley pulled her close and delivered a robust kiss. The small group around them looked away.

"Really, James!" Hattie said as she pulled away. "You'd think we were never to see each other."

He kissed her again, but this time gently on the cheek. "Don't go anywhere without Randolph or Marcus. Make sure they follow you home and check the house before you go in. And get up to Connecticut as quick as you can. Tell your father the story; he'll know what to do."

Hattie smiled and turned to face the Carlisles, who were standing with Brannigan and Kindred. "Are you sure this is your best plan, Robert?" she asked.

"I tell you it's a fine one, now that Thea's finally gotten rid of the notion of waiting for us here in Denver," said Carlisle. "I can see that you're a bit skeptical, but that probably comes from listening to James all these years."

"Skeptical with good reason," said Hattie. She turned to Thea. "Once this is over, I'm looking forward to visiting you in Oregon."

"I wish you'd reconsider and come with me," Thea said. "Back in New York, you're too close to the Harrimans."

"I'll be fine," Hattie promised. She was about to say more when the whistle sounded again. "You had all better get aboard." Brannigan punched Kindred on the shoulder before going up the three steps and disappearing inside the railroad car. Thea hugged Hattie and followed.

Carlisle waited until his wife was on board before turning back to the Longleys. "Hattie, we can't keep them from coming after you, so you've got to watch out for yourself, for our sake as well as your own," he said. "The idea here is to get whoever it is that's after us, and that's going to be a lot harder if something happens to you."

She gave Carlisle a push in the direction of the train. "You mustn't worry. I'll be at my family's farm within a week. In the meantime, the entire city will be gossiping about the handsome young men escorting me about town."

"That's my girl," said Carlisle. He said to Longley, "Train leaves in a couple of minutes." He turned and took the steps in one stride.

Longley pulled his wife close before saying in a voice muffled by her thick hair, "Didn't count on us being be apart again. This will be the first time since South America." The whistle blew for the last time, and with a groaning sound the brakes were released and the train slowly began to move. He let go of her and said, "Just for once, do like we say."

"I'll be in the city long enough to get things in order," said Hattie. "After the end of the week, send the telegrams to Stamford." Longley stepped backward in time to grasp the iron rail and pull himself up and onto the steps of the moving car. She answered his wave with one of her own and watched as he stepped inside.

Kindred waited patiently for her to turn. "Don't yawl be worryin' none, Hattie," he said. "Ah'll take care of everythin'."

As they walked to the front of the station, she said, "I know you will. But the most important thing is for you to be at the pass before the twenty-fifth. If you don't make it, we'll have lost before we even got started." She stopped to look back at the train, watching it disappear around a bend. She was surprised there were tears on her cheeks.

Carlisle, Longley, and Brannigan wasted no time once

the train picked up speed, thundering west toward the mountains. Thea was already busy with her knitting as all three hunched over the map spread across Carlisle's knees. The cattlemen at the far end of the car were too interested in the bottle they were sharing to wonder why there was so much interest in a map. "See this?" Carlisle asked. He pointed to the map. "Loveland Pass. That's where we do it."

Longley grabbed the map from Carlisle's lap and held it up, staring at it and frowning as if the English had been replaced with hieroglyphics. "What do we need the map for?" he demanded. "Let's do it like before."

"If I remember correctly, it's been fifteen years since you jumped on a moving train," said Carlisle. "At your age, you most likely would miss the whole train."

Longley handed the map back to Carlisle, as Brannigan hid a smile. "What's so hard about jumping a train?" Longley grumbled. "I always did it. Right, Tom?"

"Well, yeah, but that was a few years ago."

The noise from the wheels grew louder as the train picked up speed. Carlisle stuck his head out the window and watched Denver fade in the distance. "Engineer's already trying to gather speed to get up the mountain," he said. "When we get to the highest part of the pass, this train will be moving at its slowest. Slow enough for us to pull this off."

Brannigan sat back. "Will it be as slow on the return trip?"

Carlisle pointed at the map again. "I found this in my son's surveying book. This line says it's going downhill from there, so you need to be watching. When we cross over the pass, the speed will pick up. When you feel that, you need to find a landmark that you can remember." He sat back and folded the map. "And then we have to wire Silas and let him know the exact point where he's gonna meet us."

***

The following morning Kindred carried Hattie's bag on to the train and set it on the shelf above her seat. The first whistle had sounded, and he knew there wasn't much time. "Ah still don't like the idee of yer goin' back ta New York by ya self," he said. "It woulda bin better ifen yawl had gone with Thea—thet fella what kilt Will and Jimmy is loco, an' there ain't no sayin' what he'll do next."

"Whoever it is, he doesn't know who James and I are, so you don't have to worry," said Hattie. "There aren't any records of us, and we don't look like we did in 1899."

"Mebbe. But liken ah said, this fella is loco," said Kindred. "Thas bad enough, 'cause it means he don't give no shi...don't care 'bout nothin'. The otha thin' is he's smart an' lucky."

Hattie touched the small man on the cheek. "I'm aware of the danger, and will take every step to avoid trouble. Besides, the men at the livery will protect me."

"Ah guess." The whistle sounded and steam billowed. "Well, ah'd best go," Kindred said. He shyly removed his hat. "Yawl take care."

Hattie was touched by the cowboy's affection and concern. She stepped close and kissed his cheek. "I'll see you in the city," she said. "You come back with James when this is done, and we'll go see more Shakespeare."

<hr />

Bates arrived so early that his appearance in the doorway of his office suite caught his assistant by surprise. "Good morning, sir. You're early," said Phillips. Morning edition of *The New York Post* in hand, Bates barely acknowledged Phillips as he walked past the man's desk into his private office. As the door closed, Bates' voice drifted back, "I'm not to be disturbed."

"Yes sir," Phillips murmured at the door. Unperturbed, he returned to his job of collating the weekly freight receipts.

Bates tossed the newspaper onto his desk and sat in his leather chair. It was part of his daily routine to buy a newspaper and read the headlines as he walked to his office. Today, the front page headlines promised all the details of the most recent of "the Central Park Murders." The grisly murders had sold a lot of newspapers in the last two years as the city grew more and more fascinated with the mysterious homicides.

Bates read the full account of the latest killing. The murders were being compared to London's infamous Jack the Ripper murders. Of course, he reminded himself, in the London murders the victims were prostitutes who worked the poor sections of the city. All the New York victims were men—men who worked for financial institutions in the city.

The story had fascinated Bates from the beginning. He had more important things to attend to, but Bates often found himself mulling over the various newspaper reports, often rummaging from newspaper to newspaper for details of the murders. He knew that all the victims had bones broken by a savage beating before dying of strangulation. Bates belonged to the same gentleman's club as the police commissioner and often discussed the investigation with him, keeping up-to-date with the latest information. The most shocking was that the victims had been sexually invaded. So far this tidbit had not been reported by the newspapers. In spite of never having been remotely interested in the daily criminal events that took place in a city the size of New York, Bates was becoming concerned over his inability to ignore incidents that should have made absolutely no difference to him.

He moved to deposit the *Post* in the wastebasket and once again read the headline: 'CENTRAL PARK MURDERER STRIKES AGAIN.' The victim was found in the park early Sunday morning and turned out to be a long-time executive of the J. P. Morgan Company. Married and the father of two daughters, he had been reported missing Saturday night when he did not return from his evening walk following dinner with his family.

Bates ordered himself to put the story out of his mind and get to work. He had been successful in doing just that when half an hour later there was a tentative knock and Phillips stuck his head around the door. "It's time for your meeting with Mr. Kotkin," he said.

Bates glanced at the clock in the corner and said, "Is he in the boardroom?"

"I would imagine," Phillips said. "He walked by a few minutes ago."

Bates closed the file he'd been working on. His eyes fell on the newspaper in the waste bin. He wanted to retrieve it for another reading, but ignored the impulse. As Bates was leaving, Phillips asked, "Will you be back here before your luncheon appointment with Mr. Lowenstein."

"I'll go directly to the club," said Bates. He was halfway to the boardroom when a strange but sure thought hit with such force it brought him to a halt. He stood as still as a hunted deer and felt a long-denied realization take over first his stomach and then his lungs, forcing him to simultaneously concentrate on keeping his breakfast where it belonged and sucking air into his lungs. He couldn't believe what he was thinking. The blood returned to his head, and he told himself it was ludicrous to think of the Central Park killer and Kotkin in the same thought. *No. Not even Kotkin would. . . Still?. . .No. Not even Kotkin.* Bates' reassured himself. *It can't be true. I am not a person who associates with murderers.* One foot followed the other down the hall to the ornate door of the boardroom.

A massive table surrounded by twenty chairs dominated the room. The walls were paneled in dark wood—each panel containing a painting of incalculable value. Under each painting was a hand-carved side-table with a decorative lamp that served to set off the beauty of the artwork. Three exquisite chandeliers stretched the length of the table, the crystal shimmering in the light from the windows that looked over Madison Avenue.

Kotkin sat at the head of the table, either deep in study over a sheaf of papers or pretending to be in order to let Bates know his presence was not as important as what he was reading. Bates heart still pounded, yet he was irritated by being kept waiting and that Kotkin was sitting in the chair normally reserved for Bates himself. He was about to ask for his seat, when Kotkin looked up and took in Bates. "Sit down," he ordered.

A change in leadership had just occurred.

For a moment resentment welled up, but with a second look at the dead eyes, Bates swallowed his resentment and took the chair on the right. Old habits die hard, and he couldn't refrain from asking, "What's so important it couldn't wait?"

Kotkin answered without emotion, "I've found Etta Place and Harry Longabaugh."

Bates took the news without too much surprise. He knew that Kotkin would eventually get what he sought. "What do you intend to do?" The lines that appeared around Kotkin's eyes bothered Bates. He seemed to be enjoying the moment, as if in anticipation of pleasure.

"Perhaps I should be more specific," Kotkin replied. "I've found a couple named James and Hattie Longley. They are the owners of a freight company near the park, coincidentally not far from this office. Due to some excellent work by the Pinkerton Agency, I've been able to observe their business." Bates didn't respond. "The Longleys appear to be out of town at the moment, but I'm quite sure they're who we're looking for."

"I'm confused," said Bates. "If they're not here, then how do you know who they are?"

Kotkin smiled. "Because I know. Their absence would be a concern if it wasn't for the fact I've discovered they're on some sort of holiday." He couldn't resist adding, "Although, I've never thought of a funeral as a holiday."

"A funeral?" repeated Bates. "What are you talking about?"

Kotkin said, "I have the Brannigan family tied to the Longleys. It was Tom Brannigan—father of the late Will— who purchased the freight company in aught-seven within six months of the return and subsequently assumed death of Miss Place. In any case, I have concluded that the Longleys have traveled west—probably to Colorado—where out of respect for a dear friend they would have attended the young man's funeral."

"Inconvenient for you that they're out of town."

Kotkin absentmindedly turned his gaze back to his papers as he murmured, "Yes, I suppose so." As the tone of the words sunk in, he looked up. "Do I detect a note of squeamishness on your part?"

"Does murder have to play such a part of this?" Bates asked before he could restrain himself. "I can't imagine your father ordering you to do these things." Growing bolder, he said, "Don't you see what's happening? One murder leads to another. You'd think you enjoy this."

Kotkin laughed. "Ludicrous."

Perhaps. Bates thought to himself, but then said aloud, "After considerable time reviewing our options, I've reached the conclusion that it would be better if we simply negotiate with these people and retrieve the journal. After all, once it's in our hands, they can do no harm."

Kotkin's face darkened and the lines around his eyes disappeared as he contradicted Bates. "Don't be naïve. These people will try to extort us for as long as they can. And then they'll attempt to profit in another manner."

"How? We're the ones paying them."

"Think, Charles. Don't you imagine the newspapers would pay handsomely for the journal's contents?" he asked. "That is the true value to Parker and Longabaugh. But as Father pointed out, the mere hint of a scandal could damage the company, and something this big could ruin it. Our so-called friends would desert us like rats leaving a sinking ship." He watched the other man for a moment, before going on, "We have to look to the future. William must always be unencumbered by scandal—his political life will be a springboard for this company, and I intend to make sure nothing interferes with his rise." He stood. "With you, Charles—or without you."

Except for the ticking clock, the large room was ominously silent. Long after the door closed behind Kotkin, his parting words continued to echo.

XIV

Loveland Pass, Colorado—Union Pacific RR

"Everyone got this straight?" Carlisle glanced at Longley who sat next to him, then at Brannigan and a third man who sat facing them. All three nodded at Carlisle. They had spent the last two days in Salt Lake City going over the plan while they waited for the train on its way from San Francisco to Denver. If they didn't know the plan now, it was too late to turn back. The Union Pacific Flyer was approaching the long grade that would lead over Loveland Pass and down to Denver.

The third man, Trenton Carver, spit on the floor and grunted. "I got it. The train stops and anybody in this car gets any notions, they answer to me."

Carlisle ignored the bravado. "Tom has the second car, and I'll handle this last one." He turned to Longley. "You sure you won't have any problem getting to the engine?"

"Just keep the passengers quiet." He stood. "Give me five minutes, and when the whistle blows, you'll know." Longley left through the forward door.

The train engine pulled a coal car, followed by passenger, mail, and freight cars, with the customary caboose at the end. The plan was for Longley to climb over the coal car and jump down into the engine compartment, taking the engineer and fireman by surprise.

Using the ladder, Longley eased himself onto the coal car. Carlisle and Brannigan were right about one thing—it had been a lot of years since he had climbed on top of a moving train lurching from side to side. His balance held out until he was about half way over the piled coal. When the train hit a bump, he was thrown face first into the coal. Spitting dust, and working to free himself from the shifting coal, he clambered to his feet, only to lose his balance again.

This time he fell backwards. Struggling to his feet again, he widened his steps. His movements were measured and more deliberate as he waddled to the end of the car.

Longley fished through his pockets for a second bandana to wipe his eyes. Streaks of sweat-mixed, blue-gray dust turned his face a macabre mask and the coal had colored his entire body a deep black. The swath of red cloth tied around his lower face was sweat-soaked.

The fireman, Claude Goodfellow, was unprepared for the black apparition that landed before him. Before he could scream, Longley gave him a smack with the barrel of his pistol and motioned for him to sit. Goodfellow threw himself into the corner with a wail and pulled both arms over his face.

Longley turned to the engineer. "Stop this train," he snarled. Engineer Terrence Walcott never took his eyes off the tracks in front of the engine until Longley lightly jabbed him in the back. Walcott turned and met two eyes and a patch of red atop a gray and black form—and the form was pointing a gun. Longley caught the engineer as he fainted and fell forward. He had used up extra time extricating himself from the coal car. Longley jerked the terrified Goodfellow to his feet. "You better know how to slow down this train, or you're dead." The fireman looked at the gun and turned to take hold of the brake lever. "Stop it when I tell you," ordered Longley

Goodfellow's hands shook, but he managed to slow the train. Longley peered out the window and spotted the clump of trees where he hoped Kindred was waiting. He grabbed the whistle cord and gave three short pulls and then waved the gun in Goodfellow's direction. "Stop the train."

During the time the fireman had been in the process of slowing the train, he realized that Longley was nothing more than a man—albeit a filthy one—and not a particularly dangerous man in spite of the blow Longley had given him. Instead of complying, he pushed the handle forward.

"Go to hell," he retorted. "You ain't gonna kill me."

Longley didn't hesitate. He fired at Goodfellow's leg, and a combination of events resulted in what he was to later claim was one of the great shots of his career. As he pulled the trigger, the train lurched again, throwing his shooting hand far enough to the side that when the gun discharged, the bullet hit the steel floor. It then pinged off the open door of the firebox causing it to ricochet once again—this time an inch above the unconscious Walcott—finally coming to rest in the calf muscle of Goodfellow's left leg. Other than the fact Longley was aiming for the right leg, it was miraculous sharpshooting.

Now that he had the man's full attention, Longley shoved the gun against Goodfellow's temple. Goodfellow yanked the handle backwards, and the train gradually slowed to a rest. With a glance out the window Longley could see that the train had come to a stop fifty feet beyond the clump of trees. "Shut down the steam," he ordered.

It took Goodfellow a very short time to decide that he wasn't paid enough to die for the Union Pacific and, despite being dazed and in pain, did as ordered. Steam billowed as the engine shut down.

"Nice work," Longley commented and gestured at Walcott. "Help your partner out of the car." As he jumped from the engine, he saw Brannigan and Carver emerge from their respective cars. Carlisle was nowhere to be seen. He yelled to Carver, "Keep those people from sticking their heads out!" Carver fired a shot in the air and eighteen faces disappeared back into the train.

Longley pulled the bandanna from around Walcott's neck and used it to stop the bleeding from Goodfellow's leg. Walcott was still out, but as Longley walked away, Goodfellow could have sworn he heard him ask one of the other men, "Where's Butch?" as he hurried to the mail car where Brannigan was pounding on the door.

"You in there?" Brannigan called toward the reinforced walls of the car.

A muffled voiced answered, "Give me a minute." Shortly, the door opened, and Carlisle and a railroad employee jumped down to the track, losing their balance and rolling in the dirt. Springing to his feet, Carlisle yelled, "Get back, the fuse is lit." A minute later a muffled explosion rocked the car as smoke poured out the new hole in the roof. Satisfied with the explosion, Carlisle looked Longley up and down. "What happened to you?"

"Just get the money, Butch," snarled Longley. By now, passengers' faces were reappearing in the windows. The passengers who had heard Longley, began whispering.

Carlisle pulled himself back into the car where Brannigan was already stuffing bills into a black satchel. "Take only what we talked about," he said.

"Each bundle is five hundred," Brannigan said. He held up the bag. "I got ten."

"Let's go then." As Brannigan stepped around him, Carlisle looked at the remaining money. "First time I've ever robbed a train without actually robbing the train. How much do you figure we're leaving?" he asked. With a sigh, he placed an envelope on top of the undisturbed bundles of money and followed Brannigan out the car with a hard thump as he hit the ground. All four turned toward the stand of trees.

"Counting the gold coin?" asked Brannigan. "Hell, I don't know. Maybe $75,000."

"There was gold?" asked Longley. Not waiting for an answer, he stopped and called to Goodfellow, "Wake up your partner and fire up that engine."

The fireman gave Walcott a couple of slaps. He couldn't wait for the engineer to open his eyes before he asked, "You know who just robbed us?"

Walcott sat up. "I been mostly playing possum," he said. "That must have been Sundance himself who scared the shit out of me when he jumped out of the coal car." He pushed himself up from the ground. "Didn't think he'd shoot. Maybe you shoulda done what he told you."

"I ain't bad hurt," said Goodfellow with a glance at the bandanna tied around his calf. "Think about it, we got robbed by Butch and Sundance," Goodfellow marveled, as they climbed aboard. After a moment, he added, "Wait a minute, that couldn't of been them. They're dead." Later, as they were waiting for the engine heat to come up, Goodfellow said, "Folks will think we're loco, so I ain't gonna say nothing about this except to Braselton. Let him be the one to notify the company."

Walking into the clump of trees, Carlisle came to a halt—Kindred was nowhere in sight. A low whistle sounded. "Sure hope that's Silas," Carlisle said. "Otherwise, we're in trouble." As they walked toward the sound, he looked back at Longley. "You never did tell me what happened."

No answer.

Kindred was waiting with five saddled horses and a pack mule. "Everythin' work out?" he asked. "Ah was gittin' a might worried when the train didn't stop." After a look at Longley, he asked, "Why yawl covered in soot?"

"It's not important," he replied.

Swinging into his saddle, Carlisle reached for the reins. "If I didn't know better," he said to Longley, "I'd say you fell in the coal."

<hr />

Two days later the weather turned cold. Longley took a pull on the whiskey before replacing the cork and tossing the bottle at the motionless form lying against a saddle. Brannigan's thick leather gloves made it hard to catch the bottle. Carlisle watched the bottle go around the campfire, but the cold weather got to him and he hopped up to throw more wood on the fire. He stamped his feet and said, "I'd forgotten what it's like out camping."

"You're getting soft," said Brannigan.

"Must be," he admitted. "I swear, tonight is downright frigid." He poked the fire with a branch, and held his hands toward the flames. "Let me have another shot of that whiskey." Unlike Brannigan, Carlisle had no trouble catching the bottle, and after a drink, said, "Silas, you want a touch?" He would have asked Carver, but he had already pulled his blanket over his head and was asleep.

Since dinner of biscuits and tinned beef warmed in a Dutch oven, Kindred had barely said a word. The cowboy was unaware he was being spoken to until Carlisle stepped over and lightly kicked his boot. "Drink?" he repeated.

"Uh...shore." Kindred accepted the bottle and then sat staring at it.

Carlisle hunkered down next to him. "Something on your mind?"

When there was no response, Longley and Brannigan looked over at the cowboy. Brannigan asked, "What's wrong?"

Kindred sat up. "Ah been thinkin'," he said. "Ya know ah was at the ranch 'afore comin' ta meet yawl with the hosses. Did some talkin' with Josh and Molly, and it's been botherin' me ever since. Ah ast' them ifen strangers had been sniffin' around, an' at first, both said nobody had. Then, just 'afore ah left, Molly kinda mentioned there'd been a fella, but she didn't think anythin' 'bout it 'cause he was an educated gentleman." He looked over at Brannigan. "Sorry, Tom," he said in an apologetic voice. "Ah don't mean no disrespect ta yore daughta, but Molly was a might slow in her thinkin'."

"What'd she mean by an educated gentleman?" asked Longley. He and Carlisle exchanged a look across the campfire.

"Ah believe Molly meant he was finely-dressed, an' well-spoke. She said the fella was tall an' real polite."

Longley asked, "That's the way she described him?"

"Yep. Jist the way ah told ya," he replied.

"Too bad," said Carlisle. "If this fellow had something to do with this, it would have been good if she could have given us an idea of who we're up against."

Brannigan tossed his blanket aside and stepped to the fire. He added more wood before turning back to the others. "Couldn't of been the fella who killed Will. He'd have done something to Molly. Or Josh, if he had been there."

For a time the only sounds were those of the night: the cry of a wolf echoing through the canyon, the whistling wind, the crackling of the fire. Carlisle spoke up, "You gotta be right, Tom. If it was the man who killed the others, he'd have killed Molly too." He thought for a minute, then went on, "Unless, of course, he was looking for your boy, and when Josh wasn't there figured he could always come back."

"Then the killer made a mistake," said Longley.

Carlisle looked across the fire. "You think this fellow was the one?" he asked.

Reaching for the whiskey, Longley didn't answer. But a few minutes later, as if talking to himself, Kindred softly said, "Ah 'member sumthin' else. Molly said the fella's skin was dark-complected."

No one spoke until Carlisle asked, "An Indian maybe? That would be something. No Indians I've known are what you'd call tall."

Rewrapping the blanket around his shoulders, it took some time before Kindred's comment penetrated. When it did, Brannigan whirled and demanded, "He was tall, you say?"

"Yessir," said Kindred.

"I'll be damned," said Brannigan as he slowly sat. "I know who this fella is, and he's no Indian." There was exasperated anger in his voice. "I damn near ran into him at the Denver Station when he was talking to Akers. And then, on the train to Gunnison the next day, he was sitting in the front of the car I was riding in." He thought for a moment, and then asked Kindred, "Didn't you say Jimmy was talking to some stranger a couple days before you found him?" After he nodded, Brannigan asked, "You didn't get a look at him, did you?"

Kindred took his time. "Ah recollect that me an' Will had been in the storeroom," he said. "It was when yawl sent me tha' telegram 'bout us comin' ta Denver for this here meetin'. Afta ah talked ta him 'bout what needed ta be done, ah sent the boy out ta spell Jimmy." He stared at the stars for awhile, and then said, "When Jimmy come back, Will left early 'cause he was headin' up ta the mine the next mornin'. It strikes me now thet mebbe he tole Jimmy where he was goin'. Later tha' night ah talked ta Jimmy an' tole him to be on the lookout fer strangers. Thet he was ta let me know— especially them what asked fer Will." Kindred sadly added, "But Jimmy never said nothin'."

Brannigan tossed a rock at the fire. "That's the bastard that killed my boy."

"Hold on there, Tom, we don't know anything for sure," said Carlisle. He looked at Longley again. "What do you think?" he asked.

"Possible," he said. "But there's a lot of people traveling out west these days."

"Yeah," agreed Carlisle. "But except for Tom's daughter-in-law, everybody who's been around this tall fellow seems to be dead. That makes it more than a coincidence to my way of thinking." He said to Brannigan, "Especially considering what happened to Will."

Brannigan lifted his head. He had unholstered his pistol and placed it in his lap. "Yeah. He went through an awful lot."

The wind whistled through the trees. "It's gonna snow," said Kindred. As if in answer, the wind gathered intensity and began to howl. "Best bring them ponchos an' git ourselves up by them rocks." He gently kicked Carver's blanket, causing the young man to sit up in confusion.

Later, as they huddled under an outcropping of rock, Longley asked Carlisle, "How are we going to find out who this tall stranger is?"

"We already know he's a railroad man," he said. "He's worse than the others that were after us because it looks like he hurts people before he kills them. But we do know a couple of things. We know that Will went to New York, and we know he talked to somebody important."

"Charles Bates," interjected Brannigan.

"Right," agreed Carlisle. "So Bates must be the big man in the company. Which means in the next couple of days when we leave the other message, it's just for him. If I'm right, this tall killer could be working for Bates, so maybe we can sucker both of them." He lay back against his saddle and pulled the poncho over his blanket for protection against the snow. "It makes me wonder if Bates is the one who's upset over the journal, now that Harriman's dead," said Carlisle. "If so, whoever wants it, he'll be doing anything to get it back." With that, he pulled his hat over his face and went to sleep.

❦

It was neither cold nor raining in New York. Kotkin stood in the shadows across the street from the brownstone building. It was not the first time he had waited for the woman to return home. Since Hattie Longley had reappeared, he had spent much time waiting for her. Sometimes he waited near her business and watched with amusement as she was escorted at all times by two men, regardless of where she was going. Having followed her for most of last week, Kotkin was not surprised when she came around the corner arm in arm with two men. Kotkin knew the tall black man was named Marcus, and that the younger man was O'Toole. Two nights previously, Kotkin had followed O'Toole to his favorite saloon and sat nearby as O'Toole drank his fill. But, much to Kotkin's disappointment, O'Toole had never once said anything about his employers, much less their whereabouts.

The only significant thing Kotkin knew about Marcus was that at one time he had been a bare-knuckle fighter who had to give it up after an injury blinded one eye. To anyone else, credentials such as this might cause hesitation at the thought of a personal confrontation, but to Kotkin the black man's physical prowess was a challenge. He was certain that within a short time he would learn once and for all where the Harriman journal was and how to get his hands on it. And, then, well, there remained the job of eliminating all those cursed with knowledge of the document.

Kotkin noticed that it was always O'Toole who took the key from Hattie and entered the home. Marcus waited next to her with his back to the building and watched for anyone approaching. As the black man's gaze swung from side to side, Kotkin held his breath even though he knew his dark clothing blended with the bushes around him. While he watched, he listened in fascination as Hattie kept up a running conversation, seemingly unconcerned over her own welfare. Tonight she was discussing the prospect of the freight company eventually having to turn to motorcars and delivery trucks as a means to modernization. It was clear she was worried about her horses.

It didn't take long before O'Toole reappeared, his voice carrying in the night air as he handed her the key. "Everything's in order, Hattie."

Turning, Marcus asked, "You check the upstairs?"

"Yes," said the young man. "And the cellar."

Hattie laughed. "You're overdoing it, don't you think?" She took her parasol from Marcus and patted his massive shoulder. "Not that I'm offended," she said. "After all, who gets escorted around the city by two handsome men?"

"It's no laughing matter," said Marcus. Originally from Boston, his deep voice conveyed his New England accent, and the extent of his education. Like O'Toole, he was intensely loyal to the Longleys. It was James who not only gave him a job, but also the position of foreman; and as far as Marcus was concerned, woe be it to the unfortunate man who strayed too close to James Longley's wife. For her part, Hattie treated Marcus as an equal, often verbally sparring with the well-read man over interpretation of various novels they mutually enjoyed.

"You shouldn't worry," said Hattie. "I'll be joining my parents at their farm shortly. Besides, we haven't seen anyone who even looks suspicious."

"It's never the one you see," said Marcus. He looked up at the star-lit sky. "I'll be glad when James is back."

She laughed again. "Perhaps tomorrow we can have another discussion of Poe's work."

"What's poor work?" asked O'Toole.

"Edgar Allen Poe, a writer of macabre works of fiction," said Marcus. He smiled at the look of confusion, before saying, "Good night, Hattie. We'll be back to fetch you in the morning."

"Just as long as you don't sit here all night. Good night, gentlemen." Hattie went up the steps, making sure to lock the door behind her as she entered her home. She hung her parasol on the hall tree before waving to her protectors through the side window. Because it was late, Hattie decided to forgo dinner in favor of a cup of tea and a slice of homemade bread with a dollop of jam, a gift from a neighbor.

Across the street, Kotkin watched as the lights the young man had left on now were extinguished. Having broken into the apartment two previous times, he knew that the small kitchen was located in the back, along with a second set of stairs that led up to the bedrooms. It was a credit to his concentration that he was no longer focusing on the two bodyguards who had started back down the street. If another man hadn't greeted them, he'd have missed the exchange. As it was, at the sound of the voices, he turned his attention back to the corner where four men now stood. Even though he couldn't hear what was said, the intent of the meeting was clear. This was a new turn of events, the previous nights there hadn't been additional guards.

Money was passed from the black man to the newcomers, who stuffed the bills into their pants pockets. The taller of the two lifted his coat and moonlight glinted off the handle of a pistol. The other man followed suit and showed his weapon, laughing as he did. Kotkin smiled to himself as he realized that there was to be more to this endeavor than he had anticipated. As he watched the taller man disappear back around the corner—obviously he was to guard the alleyway behind the building—the second man took his place on the steps of the Longley's brownstone.

Kotkin nodded in satisfaction. It was clear that Hattie didn't believe enough of a threat existed to warrant nighttime guards, or the men would have been waiting for her return. The night guards had been hired without her knowledge. He had little hope Marcus would become lax and remove the guards before he had a chance to act.

Turning his attention back to the windows, Kotkin waited until all the lights were extinguished except for the one shining through the upstairs front window. He knew this was the Longley's bedroom—quite modern in the fact that the couple shared the same room.

Upstairs, Hattie set her cup on the bedside table and turned back the quilt. Even though it wasn't cold now, she knew the temperature would drop during the night and the morning would be chilly. She walked into her dressing room to remove her clothes; setting them aside, her day-maid would pick them up and, if need be, have them cleaned at her uncle's laundry. She paused for a moment to look in the mirror. Hattie was quite proud of her slim body highlighted by perfect breasts that fascinated her husband. She pulled a silk nightgown off its hanger and sliding the sheer material over her head. The feel of the silk caused an immediate reaction and she was momentarily shocked at the intensity. She missed James more than she anticipated; this was the first time they'd been apart since he had returned from Bolivia.

Hattie smiled at her reflection and turned away. She pulled the pins from her hair and gave a shake, the thick hair cascaded to her shoulders as she reached for the brush. Minutes later, hair shining, she set the brush back on the dresser and returned to the bedroom. Prior to turning the light switch on the wall next to the door, she lit a single candle and carried it to the bed, setting it on the stand before sliding under the covers. She smoothed the quilt around her, and sipped her tea before unfolding the sheet of paper that had been delivered to the stable in the afternoon. Marcus had also read the telegram—it was the reason why he had employed the night guards without bothering to inform Hattie.

She set the telegram on the bedstand next to the candle and reflected aloud, "Robert's plan seems to be working...of course, they always work in the beginning." Hattie finished her tea and blew out the candle.

When the light went out, Kotkin noted the time. He turned his attention to the guard sitting on the top of the steps leading up to the Longley's front door. The man had pulled out his pocket knife and was cleaning his nails by the light of the streetlamp. Kotkin inched around the bushes and silently moved down the street toward the opposite corner, taking care to keep to the shadows that lined the street. He decided that this night would be the last chance to reconnoiter his prey.

An hour later, sitting comfortably on the couch in his bedroom, Kotkin contemplated his plan. He was confident that the information he had long sought was well within his grasp and that he would soon be traveling to Colorado. *Even if Hattie Longley was in possession of the Harriman journal*, he thought. And then quickly reminded himself, *That's ridiculous...Cassidy wouldn't be stupid*. Kotkin knew the need to eliminate anyone with knowledge of its contents was paramount. In fact, once he set his plan in motion, removing Carlisle, Longley and Brannigan—and the remainder of Brannigan's family—was an absolute.

Kotkin decided that tomorrow's first order of business was to summon George Nelson from Pinkerton. He'd soon need a personal bodyguard to accompany him on his travels. It would have to be a man who possessed three attributes: a physical specimen who was also well versed in weaponry; total loyalty to Kotkin; and most importantly, amenable to the opportunity to earn a great sum of money. Of course, Kotkin reminded himself, the possibility existed that whoever was picked would have little chance of spending his reward.

XV

Bates looked up from the rather dull report of the freight activity for the previous month as Phillips peeked into the office. "Excuse me, sir. Sorry to interrupt, but Mr. Caudill needs to see you. He says the matter is urgent."

Herman Caudill was the director of line security for the Union Pacific Railroad, a position he had held for more than twenty years. E. H. Harriman had relied heavily on him—in fact, it was Caudill who hired Joe LeFors to go after the Hole in the Wall Gang. Bates knew that Caudill would not have asked for a meeting if it weren't a matter of great importance. "Tell him to come in," Bates said, as he set the papers aside.

"He's requested that you meet him at the terminal," Phillips said. Holding up an envelope, he quickly added, "He had one of the boys deliver this."

"Is the telephone not working?" Bates asked. He looked at the instrument on his desk and once again marveled that so many of his business associates refused to use it. *Handiest thing since the typewriter, and it's virtually unused,* he thought, as he opened the letter and pulled out a single sheet of paper.

Phillips watched his boss's face turn bright red then back to chalky white as he read, re-read, and then carefully placed the letter in his coat pocket. Without so much as a word to Phillips, Bates ran down the stairs to the street where he ordered the doorman to hail a hansom cab. As he waited for the cab, Bates occasionally looked up to the corner window of the top floor.

"Something was bound to happen," he told himself, not for the first time. "That damn Kotkin." He glanced up at Kotkin's office again and tried to calm himself, but his anger accelerated and soon he was slapping his leg in frustration. The cab arrived, and Bates ordered the driver to take him to the Union Pacific freight office at Grand Central Station.

Bates' mind raced as the cab crawled across Manhattan. The drive seemed an eternity by the time Bates jumped out of the carriage. He dodged passengers as he hurried to the far corner of the building where a young woman wearing octagon-shaped glasses looked up in surprise as Bates burst through the office door. "Where's Caudill?" he demanded.

"Waiting for you in the counting room," she calmly replied.

When Bates reached the room, the steel door was bolted and he was forced to knock. "Charles?" asked a voice from the inside.

"Open the damn door."

At the sound of the heavy bolt releasing, Bates shoved the door aside and stepped into the secure room. In this room, bank, mining, and investment officials met to count and claim funds or valuables that had been shipped by the railroad. Inside, Herman Caudill, a short, heavy-set man with a thick mustache that extended over his lower lip, respectfully moved aside. Breathing deeply, Bates took a moment to gather himself before asking, "What's the meaning of this?"

"You'd better take a look," said Caudill. As he led the way to the center table he said, "I take it you're unaware of the recent robberies."

Bates stopped. "Robberies?"

Caudill pointed to an opened lockbox. A brown envelope sat on top of the bundled money. "It would be best if you read the letter. And before you ask, no one other than me has seen its contents."

With a sense of dread, Bates opened the envelope. The letter was addressed to him.

Charles Bates
Union Pacific Railroad
New York City, New York

Dear Charles,

We've never met, but our adversarial relationship began years ago when I was in the habit of lightening the load of Union Pacific rail cars.

Largely due to your personal intervention, your rail lines have enjoyed safe passage without the scourge of constant robberies. That could all change, for now it seems you are once again determined to arrange my murder, and the murders of my associates. How strange that after all these years, you would stoop to these desperate actions.

Perhaps it is because you desire the return of the journal of E. H. Harriman, or more accurately, that of Cyrus Jamison. Several deaths can already be laid at the feet of your great desire to retrieve this damning chronicle. For these deaths, I admit to a desire for revenge. Therefore, I have a proposal for your consideration.

Send your killer for the journal. If he is as skilled at his trade as he seems to be, he will retrieve your journal and your quest will be over. Your company will once again be safe to exploit the nation in any manner it can get by with. If, however, your associate is not equal to the trust you apparently put in him, we will give him an appropriate burial, which is not to say a Christian burial. I will know your answer when your associate shows up at a saloon already familiar to him in Crested Butte, Colorado.

By now I am sure you are aware of my recent activities in relation to your trains. As I have no need for Union Pacific money, I enclose the funds we appropriated on two occasions.

Bates stopped reading. He opened the box and peered inside at the neatly stacked bundles. "How much?" he asked Caudill.

"In the two robberies, ten thousand dollars," he replied. Pointing at the bundles, he said, "It's all there." Bates returned his attention to the letter:

Of course, harassment of your railroad will continue and escalate, if that is your desire. With every passing day, you run the risk that the newspapers will find the journal before you do. Please be aware that I too am acquainted with thugs and assassins. These 'hired hands' can be dispatched to your home and family with one telegram, and not a second thought. I trust you will send your killer, and our relationship can at long last come to an end. Send your killer back to where he has killed before.

I promise that after I have dealt with him, the journal will be returned to you and forgotten here. Furthermore, I will forswear vengeance against you personally.

I remain your ever constant adversary,

B.C.

Bates was baffled. Butch Cassidy seemed to be demanding a showdown with Kotkin. *But how did this petty criminal connect Kotkin's notorious deeds with me?* His hands shook, not so much at Cassidy's threats but at being tied to Kotkin's murders. It was the first time Bates had thought of the killings as murders, and possible imprisonment and execution was not a comfortable feeling. The not-so-veiled threat to attack his family was not an issue—Bates had no family—but the threat to turn over the journal to the newspapers couldn't be taken lightly. *Still, Cassidy did return the money.*

Bates looked up at Caudill and demanded, "What do you know about this? What aren't you telling me?"

"Well, Charles—" the security chief began, then hesitated. "I only know that the Flyer was hit between Salt Lake City and Denver. Then, four days later on the return trip, it was hit again."

"Why wasn't I told?"

"I was going to," said Caudill. "But somehow Mr. Kotkin got wind of the situation and told me that he was in charge." He looked at the floor, but decided the two knot holes were not large enough for him to disappear through. "He said he was personally handling this incident and that I wasn't to concern myself, nor you. Mr. Kotkin was downright rude. And, quite unnecessarily, he threatened me with the loss of my position, among other things."

"Why are you telling me now?"

Caudill used the sweat that had broken out on his forehead to slick back his hair before saying, "When the box was opened this morning, my clerk saw the letter. It was brought to me because we have never received railroad correspondence like this before. The letter was unsealed, and I felt obligated to inform you immediately." Now he was angry. "I read it because I didn't care for Mr. Kotkin's demeanor, and I was worried for you."

Bates thought for a moment. "Herman, you've done the right thing, and I greatly appreciate your loyalty," he said. "However, as difficult and confusing as this may seem, Mr. Kotkin is correct in that he needs to handle this situation himself. This matter is, of course, in no way a reflection on your competency, nor your abilities as a valued manager." He pointed at the box. "Since the funds have been returned— and are the property of the company—deposit them with the bank." Bates turned, but stopped at the door. "How long have you been with the company?" he asked, knowing the answer.

"Thirty-four years," Caudill answered promptly.

"And when was your last raise in pay?"

"Three years ago."

"Herman, I must apologize. I'm afraid I've been less than attentive to you," said Bates. "When I return to my office, I will inform the treasurer that your salary has been doubled. Rest assured that your position with the company is secure."

"Charles, I'm appreciative, but it's not necessary. Quite frankly, I didn't act as I should have, and it distresses me that—"

"You are a most loyal associate, and I may need your help in the coming months," interrupted Bates. "I fear these incidents are a sign of impending trouble." He opened the door, hesitated, and then asked, "I trust I can count on you?"

"Of course," Caudill hurriedly said. "But, Charles, please wait. What's going on?"

Bates paused again. "Perhaps nothing, but we must be prepared for any situation," he said. "In spite of Mr. Kotkin being in charge, let me know of any further incidents, or communications. Keep this between you and me—let me be the judge as far as bringing in Mr. Kotkin." The steel door closed, leaving behind a perplexed Herman Caudill.

The ride back to the office gave Bates time to prepare for a meeting with Kotkin. What he wanted to say was not what he would say. He did not want Kotkin to know that he had an informant in Caudill. Upon returning to his office, Bates told his assistant to find Kotkin and arrange a meeting. The *Post* lay where he had dropped it hours ago. Bates picked up the newspaper and the headline, 'Fire Ravages Local Business!', jumped out at him.

He scanned the story. *Not so unusual*, he thought. Minutes later he folded the paper and set it on the desk. The report had been unusually graphic in describing the burned-beyond-recognition remains of two unfortunate souls who had perished in the fire not far from the Harriman Building.

The fire was burning out of control before the fire company could respond. Also of question was the discovery of two bodies lying outside against the wall of the stable. The bodies on the inside were thought to be employees: Randolph O'Toole, was described as a young man employed as a driver and stable helper; the second was the foreman of the company, a Negro named Marcus Tyler.

There was something familiar about the story that caused Bates to wonder. *Had the Harriman organization used this company in the past?* Then it hit him: *Longley Freight Company.* Kotkin had said that he was confident that James and Hattie Longley were actually Harry Longabaugh and Etta Place. Bates knew then that the fire was no accident, and Kotkin was the perpetrator of the scheme. "Damn that man," he said aloud. "His murderous ways will bring this company to its knees. Who is he? What is he? He's become an animal."

Bates had been a part of the Harriman organization too long to be naïve that the disappearance of a competitor or ruination of a competing business was happenstance. He had always considered it a part of doing business, or simply another way to insure company growth, and looked the other way.

But this was going too far. Four people had died in the freight company fire. Regardless of Kotkin's promise to Mr. Harriman on his deathbed, surely, as in the past, a compromise could be worked out. Or at least Bates had believed so. Mr. Harriman never let matters escalate to the point of turning deadly unless the competing company refused to cooperate. *After all*, Bates reasoned as he looked out his window, *this is a legitimate business—we're not the Black Hand or the Sons of Italy.*

Bates pulled out scissors and cut out the account of the incident before removing a small lockbox from his lower desk drawer. It held an impressive number of clippings, all detailing unsolved murders over the last three years. Bates was still thinking about the fire when there was a knock at the door. Assuming it was Kotkin—but surprised that he would knock—Bates hurriedly replaced the box in the drawer before calling, "Come in, Elias."

"Sorry, sir," said Phillips. "Mr. Kotkin is ill and home in bed. His aide suggested that you pay a call at the end of the week." Handing him a letter, Phillips continued, "He sent this."

Bates took the envelope but put it down immediately. "I'll go to Mr. Kotkin's when it's convenient," he said. "Now, if there is nothing else, I'm not to be disturbed." The young man returned to his desk leaving Bates to wonder with growing anxiety what Kotkin was planning next.

⟡

At the same moment, Kotkin was in his suite at the Waldorf-Astoria reading the same newspaper article, although for a different reason. For the last two days, Kotkin had refused entry to anyone other than his maid—a Portuguese woman who spoke virtually no English. His nose was swollen and discolored as a result of a vicious hook by Marcus Tyler, and he didn't want anyone asking him how it happened. Nor did he want anyone asking about the welts on his cheek that resulted from a stinging blow from a set of reins swung by O'Toole, whom Kotkin had assumed was unconscious.

From time to time, he gently rubbed the bridge of his nose where the break was already healing. The night of the fire, he had inserted a wooden dowel into his nostril and forced the cartilage into place, all the time staring in the mirror. The welts on his cheeks had been more upsetting; the unpleasant discoloration limited his nightly study of his face. His only regret was that he hadn't been able to punish O'Toole for his temerity. When O'Toole struck him, he had lashed out and crushed the man's windpipe with a single blow.

Tyler had given him the challenge he wanted. He was a skilled boxer and extraordinarily strong. Too bad he'd walked in just as Kotkin was rendering O'Toole unconscious by pinching his carotid artery in a stranglehold. Tyler's intervention was why the smaller man was able to swing the reins. The black man had jumped on Kotkin and wrapped his forearms around Kotkin's throat, causing him to release O'Toole who had grabbed the set of reins and swung them in a desperate attempt to aid Tyler. After delivering the death-blow to O'Toole, Kotkin dropped to one knee and pulled the big man over his head, slamming his body on the dirt.

Tyler might have had a sporting chance—after all, he was very strong—had Kotkin not gained a psychological advantage when he said he had Hattie restrained in the back of the stable. The black man seemed to go insane. Forgetting all his pugilistic skills, he attempted to pummel Kotkin into submission by using only his strength advantage. Kotkin was able to misdirect the swings, other than an occasional deflected punch to his body, and at the same time delivered his own debilitating blows. A left thrown by Tyler met its mark, breaking Kotkin's nose and causing a copious amount of blood to be expelled and cover both men. Thoroughly angered at this unseemly event, Kotkin jammed his fingers into Tyler's eyes and forced Tyler to the ground. In a practiced move, he placed a knee in the man's lower back and snapped his neck.

The chime of the great clock caused Kotkin to come out of his reverie. Realizing it was still early, he decided that a soaking bath would give him ample time to contemplate his up-to-now highly successful interrogation of the woman. And, more importantly, the next round of questioning.

◆～⧉⧉⧉～◆

Carlisle tossed his cards on the table. "You're too good for me, boys," he said to the other players as he picked up his remaining bills and pushed back from the poker table.

"Don't be no stranger," said the skinny miner who had just beaten Carlisle's flush with a kings-over full house. "I can dig my claim any time."

At the bar, Kindred set a mug in front of Carlisle. "Yawl lose 'gain?"

"Can't help myself. I tried mining once, so I must feel sorry for these boys." He drank his beer. As Kindred refilled the glass, Carlisle asked, "You seen Longley?"

Kindred went back to wiping the bar. "Telegraph office. James tole me yestaday he wired Hattie's pa cause she ain't sent no word one way or 'nother 'bout where she be. So he's waitin' fer a answer."

"Yeah, he mentioned that to me too," said Carlisle. He sucked the foam off the beer. "But Hattie's smart. She won't take chances, so she should be all right."

Kindred nodded in agreement before hustling to the end of the bar where two men had bellied up, each waving a leather sack. "The way yore behavin', ah guess ya struck pay dirt," he said to the larger of the bearded brothers.

"Goddamn right!" the miner yelled in response. He turned to the other customers. "Me and my little brother just found us a vein, and we're buying the house!" With a roar, the men crowded the bar, causing Kindred to be hard put to deliver the orders that were shouted at him. After watching him struggle, Carlisle set his glass down and went around and started filling mugs while Kindred poured whiskey into shot glasses lining the bar. "Drink up!" yelled the miner. "We're buying 'til this is gone!"

It was over an hour before Longley pushed the swinging doors aside, the excitement was over and half the customers were asleep with their heads on the tables. He signaled to Carlisle and then headed for the storeroom at the back of the saloon. Carlisle joined Longley and Brannigan, who had been counting his inventory. After turning the bar over to Jimmy's replacement, who had arrived during the miner's buying spree, Kindred was behind him. "Find out anything," asked Carlisle as he eased down on an up-turned keg.

"Hattie's father hasn't heard from her since last week," said Longley. He held up a telegram. "She wrote him a letter saying that she'd be coming as soon as the company affairs were in order. And about a week later, he got a telegram that she'd been delayed." There was a long, ponderous silence before Longley went on, "But she still hasn't shown up, so I'd better get back. If she's in trouble, I'm doing her no good out here."

Carlisle held up his hand. "What does Marcus say?"

"That's another reason I got to get back," said Longley. "It's been at least a week since I've heard from Marcus or Randolph. They'd been watching Hattie, even bringing in a couple of boys for the nights. The last time Marcus sent a telegram, things were going fine."

Brannigan stirred. In the past weeks, he had grown quiet and more introspective, often disappearing for days at a time. Kindred knew he was riding back to Gunnison to check on Josh and Molly. Looking at Carlisle, Brannigan said, "Only problem is that if something's gone wrong, there isn't a hell of a lot anyone can do."

"That's a fact," agreed Carlisle. He pulled on his beard with one hand and said, "Look here, even with the telegraph, we all know how long it takes for Hattie to get a message out. Maybe she's hiding and will get word to you when she can."

"Maybe," conceded Longley. "But I'm not sitting here and doing nothing."

Carlisle thought again. Turning to Brannigan, he asked, "What about that fellow you know in the city?" he asked.

"Maybe we could wire him. Ask for information about James and Hattie's livery. Because if there were a problem, I figure that's where it would come from."

"I'll do that right now," Brannigan said. He started out of the room, and then added, "We could have an answer in a couple days."

After the door closed, Longley said to Kindred, "What do you think?"

"Ah dunno," he said. "Seems ta me Hattie coulda took care of herself. Plus she's got a coupla good boys watchin' over her. Ah don't know 'bout that young feller, but Marcus strikes me as a man who coulda taken right proper care of hisself."

"Yeah," interjected Carlisle. "From what you've told me, a man would have to be a fool to take him on."

"With fists," Longley said. "But Marcus doesn't know anything about guns."

Carlisle hopped off the keg. "There's nothing we can do for now," he said. "Silas, let's get the horses and ride out to the mine."

An hour later, as Carlisle led on the trail to the Sadie Mae, Kindred caught up with him and asked, "Yawl think we got problems?"

Carlisle glanced back at Longley before answering. "I don't know for sure. But my gut says something isn't right."

XVI

New York City

The following day, George Nelson, Pinkerton head of administration, was summoned to the Kotkin's suite in the Waldorf-Astoria. He was greeted at the door not by Kotkin, but by a swarthy stranger who acknowledged his presence without a word and led him down the hall. At the double doors to a bedroom, the man knocked and then stepped aside. The heavy drapes blocked out much of the sunlight, but Nelson could make out a form on the bed by the flickering light of a small candle on the sideboard under the window overlooking Park Avenue and 49th Street. As the door closed, the light from the hall dwindled and vanished, causing Nelson to put out his hand as he walked toward the bed. "Are you ill?" he asked.

"I've been under the weather," said Kotkin. There was a rustling of sheets. "I apologize for my appearance, but I'm afraid I'm the victim of an unspecified illness that has made bright light temporarily excruciating for me. Step to your left, there's a chair."

Nelson found the back of the wingback chair and eased into it as he searched for Kotkin's face in the shadows. His eyes were becoming accustomed to the dim light, and although Kotkin gradually came into view, his features remained indecipherable. "Is this a serious ailment?" asked Nelson.

"When I was in South America, I contracted some sort of malady that periodically reappears. It's not serious, only annoying," he replied.

Nelson settled into the comfortable chair. "As long as you recover," he said. "Now, what can I do for you?"

"I have need of a personal bodyguard," said Kotkin.

Nelson was surprised and immediately suspicious. His

face remained impassive even as he thought, *Kotkin? Kotkin needs a bodyguard? Better be careful until I know what he really wants.*

Kotkin sensed Nelson's momentary concern, so he quickly explained. "Rest assured it's not the sort of investigative job that you are most familiar with. I need a trusted man who will work directly for me, and who must be able to travel on short notice, although probably not for a long period of time."

"Are there particulars?" asked Nelson.

"This man must be physically fit, an expert with firearms, and preferably up-to-date on the latest fighting techniques. He is to be of the highest intelligence and compliant to the point of absolute loyalty. Furthermore, there are additional requirements..."

When Kotkin finished, Nelson gave a short laugh. "That's all?" he asked. "You don't want much."

Kotkin continued as if Nelson had not spoken, "He may come from the ranks of the Pinkerton Agency, should he possess the attributes I have described. Furthermore, he must be apprised that there is an element of danger involved. In fact, he could be injured, or even killed." Almost as an afterthought, he said, "Although, that's quite unlikely."

"May I ask the nature of this assignment?"

"You may not," said Kotkin. "Suffice it to say that if your candidate is currently employed with Pinkerton, he would be required to immediately submit his resignation to work exclusively for me."

"If he doesn't work for the company, what would be in it for me?"

"Employee or not, you'll receive a significant fee for your recommendation. In addition, of course, your company's relationship with the Union Pacific, and other Harriman enterprises, will continue to grow."

"I might know of such a man. Maybe more than one," said Nelson. The ensuing silence made it easy for the detective to contemplate various candidates. Unfortunately, most of these men possessed only a few of the attributes demanded by

Kotkin. "I'm in a quandary," said Nelson. "Perhaps you could give me some time to consider the problem."

"Certainly," said Kotkin. "I'm sure you will come up with someone soon." The stiffly starched sheets rustled again and Nelson realized the meeting was over. He struggled out of the chair and shuffled to the door without a word. Kotkin pushed himself into a sitting position and turned up the lamp next to the bed.

Two days later Nelson was back in the darkened bedroom. He groped his way to the chair and said without preamble, "Andrew Reilly."

"Explain."

"He's college educated, unmarried, and there's no immediate family, which means he should have no ties that would hinder him traveling on short notice. You'll be pleased to know that Andrew is considered the finest shot in the agency, and the current boxing and wrestling champion," said Nelson. "However, there is a problem in that he won't be available for at least two weeks."

"Why is that?"

"He's recovering from a bullet wound sustained while he was aiding in the arrest of the notorious bank-robber-turned-killer, Davis Van Houghton," he said. "It was reported in all the newspapers."

"I read the story," said Kotkin. "I believe Van Houghton was being trailed by your operatives; one of your men tried to corner him and was overpowered. Another agent risked his life to free your man. I hope you're not saying the hostage was Reilly."

Nelson smiled. "On the contrary, Reilly was the man who freed the hostage. At great risk, he broke down the door and charged Van Houghton, who was ready to kill our agent. He took a bullet in the shoulder but still managed to return fire and killed Van Houghton with a well-placed shot through the eye."

"And your other man?"

"Physically unharmed," said Nelson. "Unfortunately the experience was more than the poor man could bear and we've had to pension him off. The trauma of impending death—Van Houghton apparently had the weapon to his head—was too much."

Kotkin was silent. After a moment's reflection, he asked, "Do you believe Reilly would be interested in my proposal? I would like to have an interview but without him knowing the specifics."

Nelson hesitated. "I think he might be interested," he said. "Reilly is a serious young man who entertains notions of going far within the company. Unfortunately, at his age, he might not be willing to stand the test of time for Pinkerton. We have a tendency to promote based on longevity, so it's quite possible he would consider your offer." Trying to get comfortable, he shifted his considerable bulk in the chair and said, "You mentioned a fee."

"If you could use your persuasive powers to convince the young man to agree to a meeting. Assuming he's what I need, would a personal stipend of a thousand dollars allow you to see your way clear into releasing him from any further company obligations?"

"Why, yes, I believe it would," he said.

"Excellent," said Kotkin. "Make arrangements for a dinner meeting at Le Meritage one week from tonight and tell him to dress appropriately. Explain as little as possible. For your part, you need not attend. If the man is acceptable, you may collect your fee here the next day. Agreed?"

"Yes."

"Now if you'll excuse me, I have another meeting," he said. "Forgive me for not showing you to the door, but my man will take care of you."

Once Nelson was gone, Kotkin turned up the lamp on the stand next to the bed and reached for a small mirror. The redness on the side of his face was barely discernible, but the swelling on his nose was still visible. "Two more days," he concluded aloud. "Two more days, and I'll have all the pieces to the puzzle."

Kotkin set down the mirror and pushed his blankets aside. Stepping to the armoire, he opened the door and reached inside the inner pocket of a leather coat and removed a ring. The gold band gleamed in the lamplight as he raised the ring to examine it in detail. *The woman had certainly been reluctant to surrender her symbol of fidelity. However, as with all things I want, it hadn't taken long last night to achieve this goal either.* In his silent reverie, he failed to hear the knock on the bedroom door. It wasn't until his man knocked again and announced his next appointment, that he put the ring back. Sliding into bed, he pulled the blankets under his chin and turned down the lamp before calling, "Come in."

In the dim light, Kotkin watched Bates step into the room. "Charles, so good of you to call on me in my moment of weakness."

<hr/>

The big bay had been run hard; when he was reined to a stop, his breath came fast and white in the chilly air. Carlisle, who was lounging in a chair with his feet on the rail, offered no greeting as he watched Longley jump out of the saddle and lead the horse to the corral where he unsaddled the exhausted animal. The door of the shack opened, and Brannigan stepped out. He leaned against the rough wood and noted Longley's arrival. "That animal's been worked hard," he said without judgment.

"James always had that habit," Carlisle said indifferently. "Comes on when he's upset about something and wants to think."

"How can he think when the horse is running?"

"Don't know," he admitted. "But it's the way he is." Carlisle let the chair fall back on all four legs and went back to watching his partner, who was watering the horse after finishing the rubdown and combing. "I don't think the news is good," said Carlisle. After a few more minutes of watching, he stood. Indicating that Brannigan should stay on the porch, Carlisle walked up the path.

Longley looked over the top of the bay and said, "She hasn't been heard from." Carlisle groaned and then waited until Longley wanted to go on.

Longley had been in Crested Butte two days. He sent three telegrams: one to Hattie's father, the second to the livery in care of Randolph O'Toole, and the third to be delivered to Marcus Tyler. Two of the responses had been eerily similar. Hattie's father hadn't heard from her, and Marcus' brother, who lived with the big foreman, had not heard from him either. The third reply was equally disturbing. Devlin Hamm, the Longley's lawyer, had sent a telegram detailing the disaster at the stable.

Finished with the bay, Longley slapped the horse on its rump and walked over to the fence. "Maybe she's hiding," said Carlisle. "It was always a possibility."

"Maybe," he conceded. "Although, I can't come up with any reason Hattie would fire the place before she left."

"Son of a bitch. Your house was burned?"

"No. Just the stable. All the boys showed up for work the next morning except Marcus and Randolph."

Carlisle climbed up to sit on the top rail. "Well, that's your answer then," he said. "If Marcus and Randolph weren't there, that means they're with Hattie and probably have her hid somewhere. You know, like the time—"

"Marcus and Randolph are dead," Longley interjected. "Their bodies were found in the fire, along with a couple others."

After a minute, Carlisle asked, "Any chance one of them was Hattie?"

"It was two men. Marcus had wired me that he had a couple of boys show up after he and Randolph walked Hattie home. They always made sure everything was all right at the house." After a moment, Longley said, "Why in God's hell didn't she do what we told her?"

Casting a shadow, a cloud passed in front of the rising sun, making it seem colder. Carlisle looked up at the sky and said, "She could still be alive."

"I suppose," Longley agreed. He hoisted himself up on the fence next to Carlisle. "But I'm not counting on it. If this killer murdered Randolph and Marcus, he probably got his hands on Hattie." After another pause, he added almost to himself, "Unless he was shot, I can't imagine anyone getting the best of Marcus. The killer would have had to get him straight up; otherwise Marcus would have gotten his hands around the bastard's throat." Longley unconsciously rubbed his hand against his holstered gun.

Brannigan and Kindred joined them. "Bad news?" asked Brannigan. Kindred pulled a log from the pile by the corral and sat to listen as Longley repeated the contents of the telegrams. As Longley spoke, Carlisle watched Kindred's face turn pale.

Brannigan waited until the story was finished. "We don't know for sure if Hattie's in trouble," he said to Longley. "I know it don't look good, but she's always been careful. And I always thought she could see through anybody who tried to get close. She's too smart to get finagled."

It was as if Longley hadn't heard Brannigan's weak reassurances. He continued to stare across the corral, and then asked Brannigan, "How long would it take to get to New York?"

No one argued. Brannigan took out his watch and said, "If we left within the hour we could make it to Gunnison by four, and if I remember right—and assuming it's on time— the east bound leaves about seven. In Denver, Floyd Braselton will be able to set us straight on whichever is the fastest route. But you'd better count on not getting there for at least four days. Hell, maybe more, what with track delays and such."

"What day is this?" Longley lifted his feet over the rail and jumped to the ground. His pistol, which hadn't been tied down, popped out of the holster. Almost too quick to see, his left hand flashed down and picked the gun out of the air. He twirled it twice before slipping it back in the holster. The other men watched without comment.

"Tuesdee," said Kindred. He pointed at Longley's hip and said, "Best ta set the tie. Ya don't wanna lose it 'gain."

Slipping the rawhide tie over the hammer of his gun, Longley said, "Then I can make it back to New York by Friday or Saturday."

Brannigan nodded. "Most likely," he said. "But thinking about it, maybe it would be better if one of us went with you."

"One of us has to go with him," said Carlisle. He jumped off the fence and said, "It's gonna be me." His words indicated he'd made a decision.

Brannigan was furious. He faced Carlisle, "I'm the one to go. If this killer is who I think it is, than I can point him out—" Brannigan took a deep breath to calm himself. "Except for Molly, I'm the only one who's seen him. I'll talk to her and get his features fixed in my head. Hell, maybe she can come up with a picture. She's always drawing flowers."

Longley stepped between Carlisle and Brannigan and said, "Nobody's going but me."

Brannigan turned to Longley. "He killed my boy," he said. The shorter man leaned forward until his chest was almost touching Longley. "That means I got as much right to cut the bastard's throat as you. Besides, you don't know if Hattie's dead, but I know for a fact Will is."

Longley tried to intimidate him by staring him down. But after a time, he realized he didn't have the right to deny Brannigan the chance to avenge his son's death and said, "Let's get our things."

"Ah'll saddle the hosses," said Kindred. "Ya best take mine, James. Yawl wore the bay out, an' it'll kill him ridin' lahk thet 'gain."

Twenty minutes later, gear tied behind the saddle, Brannigan swung up. He leaned over and said to Kindred, "If I don't make it home, take care of Josh and Molly."

"Ah, jist don't take no shit from them city folk," he said. "Yawl be mighty careful, an' remember ta watch James' back, he'll be watchin' yore's." He turned and called to Longley on the porch, "Best be gittin' along."

Longley waved back at the cowboy to indicate he was coming. He looked at Carlisle. "If everything goes right, we can be back in a couple weeks, three at the longest."

"If everything goes right, you won't have to," he said. "Now listen here, I don't want you or Tom doing anything stupid. You go in there, get Hattie, and if you can, leave a few more crumbs where that killer can find them. We want him here, there's no real chance of getting him in his territory." Longley looked up at the mine entrance and gave a short snort. "Laugh if you like," said Carlisle. "I know how good you are, but this guy's convinced me he's better than LeFors, Wild Bill, and John Hardin all rolled into one. He'll kill you and Tom for sport and brag about it at dinner."

Longley nodded and said, "Time to go." As they walked toward the horses, he suddenly stopped. "You remember when you fought Harvey?"

"Kind of hard to forget. What's your point?"

"You told me if you lost to kill him," Longley said as he started toward the corral. He stopped again, this time facing his friend. "Seemed like a good idea, and I would have done it," he said. "So the point is, if something happens, you got to promise to kill the bastard that killed me." He grinned and walked toward his horse.

"Love to," said Carlisle as he followed. "That's what I remember you promising me."

Kindred shook hands with Longley. "Yawl do what Robert says. An' ya take care of ma podner here."

"I'll do it," said Longley as he swung into the saddle. He leaned down, offered his hand, and said to Carlisle, "You're the best friend a man ever had."

XVII

New York City

Kotkin stepped out of the Waldorf-Astoria into fall weather. It had been summer when he had closed the doors to his suite to heal after Longley's man had landed a punch that broke his nose. Since that unfortunate night, he had left his hotel only for after-midnight visits to a small house he'd rented on the New Jersey shore. He gratefully took a deep, refreshing breath through tender nostrils. It was good to be out of his self-imposed confinement.

Kotkin had not been completely out of touch during the three weeks. He had twice summoned Bates for discussions on events at Harriman, and through Bates had managed to keep up with the investigation of the fire at the Longley Freight Company. At Kotkin's urging, Bates had used his relationship with the police commissioner to gather information.

The deaths of the two men inside the building had been ruled an unfortunate accident. Wrong place, wrong time, case closed. The investigating police officer accounted the fire itself to an explosion after the discovery of several cans of a common solvent used to clean the wagons and gear, making a plausible case for spontaneous ignition.

The commissioner assigned Samuel Morrison, a respected homicide detective who dabbled in the new science of criminal forensics, to investigate the scene outside the stable where two more bodies were found. The identity of these victims posed a challenge because they were burned beyond recognition. Morrison hated these cases. Even if someone came forward, perhaps a family member, it was unlikely the identification would be of any help in determining why the men were outside Longley's freight company that night, and the trauma to the family members would be harrowing.

As a result of a heavy caseload, and despite pressure from the commissioner, Morrison concluded there was little chance of learning just what had happened without days of investigation. He decided there was no point in finding the exact cause of the fire—even if four men had perished in it. To save time, he wrote his report stating that the men outside the building had set the fire for reasons unknown. The solvent had exploded, trapping O'Toole and Tyler. The same explosion killed the two arsonists who perished in the backlash of their own fire.

Morrison was satisfied the facts would substantiate his summation. His report duly noted that the owner and his wife were absent from New York, but a stable employee had provided the name Devlin Hamm, Esquire, attorney to the Longleys. Hamm verified that Mr. Longley was on a business trip, and that Mrs. Longley was on holiday at her parent's home. It was now Hamm's job to contact the Longleys and take responsibility of the company financial matters. By the end of the week following the fire, Hamm had authorized rebuilding the stable and offices, ordered new wagons and additional horses, and seen to it that on-going freight contracts were honored. He also arranged for an interim foreman to oversee the daily running of the business.

The case was closed.

As Kotkin continued to enjoy the fresh air, his satisfaction grew. Based on Bates' review of the situation, it was unlikely anything would come of the investigation. Yes, Kotkin was quite pleased. Even though he had not orchestrated the scene at Longley's, the results couldn't have been better than if he had written the script himself. Had he been the sort of man who hums or whistles, music would have accompanied him as he walked the seven blocks to Le Meritage, to meet with the young Pinkerton agent, Andrew Reilly.

Le Meritage was located on the ground floor of a seventeen-story building that was home to the city's largest insurance company. The entrance to the restaurant was around the corner from the building's main lobby. The seven brick steps led to hand-carved walnut doors, inlaid with beveled glass. Inside, warm walnut walls provided the perfect backdrop for French tapestries offering an elegant welcome to the wealthy as they stepped into the foyer. The lucky among the restaurant clientele were shown to their table by proprietor Henri Richleau. It was Henri's closely guarded secret that his country of origin was not *la belle* France, but *la belle* Brooklyn. Somehow, Hank Richland did not convey enough importance for the owner of one of the city's most elegant dining establishments, and with the change of name had come a change of identity.

Kotkin was greeted by Henri, who immediately relieved him of his coat. Henri handed it to one of the numerous waiters who passed it down to a busboy who delivered it to the coatroom, ten feet away. "Elias, my good friend, where have you been keeping yourself?" Henri asked in his practiced and almost perfect French accent, unaware that Kotkin knew his background. "Have you, perhaps, been ill?"

Kotkin was always amused at Henri's mannerisms. "A slight reoccurring malady." Looking around, he asked, "Has my guest arrived?"

"*Oui,*" said Henri. "Already Mr. Reilly is situated in your salon. The young gentleman was offered one of the wines from your approved list, but he insisted on waiting for your arrival." He snapped his fingers to summon a team of waiters.

Following the three men wearing white aprons, Kotkin walked alongside Henri. "I assume Andrew is dressed to your standards," Kotkin said. Henri insisted on a strict dress code and kept to it fastidiously.

"*Oui,* and quite so," he replied. "Ahh, the young. A new set of clothes is hardly needed. *Non?*" The waiters reached the door at the end of the hall and stepped aside to allow Henri and Kotkin to enter.

Andrew Reilly rose as the men entered. "Good evening, Mr. Kotkin," he said. The evening clothes gave Reilly a sophisticated appearance, yet he was not totally at ease as he stood to shake Kotkin's hand.

"Evening," said Kotkin. He extended his hand with a smile and said, "But let's dispense with formality. You must call me Elias, and I shall call you Andrew. Now, let's sit and have an enjoyable evening."

Reilly smiled in return. As he took his chair, he said, "Never having had the privilege of dining at Le Meritage, I've been looking forward to this evening."

Kotkin turned to Henri. "The preparations?"

"We will be achieving perfection," he promised. "I've taken the liberty of ordering your favorite merlot. And, it is my pleasure to assure you that your *heure du diner* will surpass your expectations. Now, if you'll pardon me, I must attend to details." Crooking a finger at Marcel, the headwaiter, Henri whispered briefly in the man's ear before leaving the room.

Reilly watched as Marcel expertly cut the wax from the neck of the bottle, and with a practiced twist of the wrist, removed the cork without a drop lost. Once the tasting ritual was complete and both gentlemen's glasses filled, Marcel led his assistants from the room.

Kotkin watched his guest sip his wine. Reilly no longer appeared nervous; in fact, the young man seemed to be quite at ease. Setting down his own glass, Kotkin said, "I'm glad you've come, I've wanted to meet you for some time."

Reilly let a sip of wine linger in his mouth for a few seconds. "My pleasure. The wine is better than I'm accustomed to. It has a crispness, which I like."

"Oh. You are a connoisseur?"

Reilly smiled at the notion. "I've experienced more wine that I've disliked, than liked. But my aunt's husband is Italian, and he's trying his best to educate me. I admit I'm not putting up much resistance. The more I know, the more I enjoy it."

"Interesting," said Kotkin. He lifted his glass in a toast. "To knowledge." Daubing his mouth with his napkin, he said, "Now, perhaps a little business." Reilly set his glass on the table and leaned forward, as Kotkin asked, "What has Nelson told you?"

"Very little," he admitted. "Only that you might offer an opportunity by which I might advance myself. That it could entail my resignation from the agency—a prospect that on the surface I don't find particularly appealing—and that there was some danger involved."

"You wouldn't leave Pinkerton?" asked Kotkin, momentarily perturbed. "Under any circumstance?"

"I didn't mean to imply that. My career has been paramount in my life. However, I consider myself a man with an open mind and am willing to listen to any proposal."

"And the possibility of danger?"

Reilly laughed. "I won't deny it. My life could use some excitement. As much as I enjoy my position, the majority of my tasks are mundane, if not downright boring." He played with the stem of his glass before adding, "But in the long run, Pinkerton does offer a rewarding career."

"Well spoken," said Kotkin. "If you'll permit me the liberty, I'd like you to first tell me about yourself. If I like what I hear, I'll explain in detail what I have in mind."

"Not too much to tell that you probably don't already know. I was born in 1884, and grew up in New Jersey as an only child. I finished high school at sixteen and attended the College of William and Mary in Virginia. I'd known for some time that I wanted to be a Pinkerton agent, but I was too young when I graduated. As soon as I turned twenty, I was hired and have been an agent for seven years."

At the time of his employment, Reilly was six feet and weighed one-hundred ninety pounds. The physical training had been easy for him, and as a result of the habits he developed in college, the scholastic portion even easier.

"I've enjoyed some success on the shooting range and in the gymnasium. The recent Davis Van Houghton affair made me a bit of a hero, in my small circle, at least. And, I imagine that series of events is why I am dining with you this evening."

Kotkin was more generous than usual with the young man. "Nelson says it wasn't the first time you've shown your mettle. He was also quick to say you are not a thrill-seeker, and that your courage and loyalty are unquestioned."

Nelson had provided a full dossier detailing the young man's experience, including periodic evaluations and supervisory comments. The dossier had contained much more than the young man disclosed and yet he did not seem falsely modest. Kotkin replenished their wine and said, "You are to be complimented on your success for such a young man. Nelson has told me something of your recent injury. Have you fully recovered?"

With a gesture at his left shoulder, Reilly explained, "The bullet didn't find any bone, and the tissue has healed nicely."

"I understand you risked your life for an associate."

"Not much of a risk," Reilly conceded. "There was no doubt that Van Houghton was going to kill him. Upon reflection, I might have been premature, but I believe the fact that both of us are alive vindicates my impetuous actions."

"And Van Houghton is dead," said Kotkin. "How did that come about? For example, how much luck was involved?"

"Very little," he responded. Realizing he may have sounded arrogant, Reilly quickly offered an explanation. "Perhaps I should put it this way: I deduced Van Houghton had nothing to lose—that he was going to kill Harold, my associate, no matter what I did or did not do—therefore, I went through the door with one goal. I had no option."

"You went into the room knowing you were going to kill him?"

The young man repeated, "No option. It wasn't a matter of bravery, or of being foolhardy. In the end, it was Harold's only chance, and the only risk was my life. I had the element of surprise, and it seemed logical that I could get Van Houghton to remove the gun from Harold's head and fire at me. Had I failed, it's possible both of us would be dead. But, in that case, Van Houghton would no longer have a hostage, and my fellow agents would have taken him." Again he repeated, "There was no option."

They stared at each other across the table. Kotkin said,

"I am in need of a special assistant. You seem to be a good match to the needs of the job." Reilly listened, expression unchanged, as Kotkin went on, "There is a conspiracy to undermine the Union Pacific Railroad, and broadly, the entire Harriman organization. The president of the company and I believe we're under siege from scoundrels who will stop at nothing."

"I know Mr. Bates," Reilly volunteered. "Or, I used to."

"Oh? How is that?"

"Actually, I met you and Mr. Bates when I was assigned to guard Mr. Harriman during his last days."

Kotkin studied the young man before it came to him. "That's correct," he said. "I remember. You were at the front door on the night I discovered Mr. Harriman was my father." Lifting his glass, he said, "I apologize for not recognizing you. However, the trauma of his impending death left me out of sorts, and I'm afraid I wasn't paying as close attention as I should have."

"No apology necessary," Reilly replied quickly. He reached for his glass and was about to speak, when the door opened and Marcel preceded the two waiters carrying dishes.

"*Monsieur* Henri has directed me to deliver the first course," he said.

Kotkin waved the men away. "We haven't concluded our business yet." As they were leaving, he said to the headwaiter, "Bring a second bottle. And periodically check on us. We're not on any schedule."

"*Oui, monsieur.*"

Reilly hid his disappointment as seeing the enticing dishes whisked away. "You were saying that the company is threatened?"

"In a manner of speaking. There's a valuable article that belonged to my father that is in the possession of blackmailers. This article can cause great damage to the company and ruin the Harriman family."

When Kotkin went no further, Reilly asked, "At the risk of sounding mercenary, if the job is retrieving a single item, what reason would there be for me to give up my career with the agency?"

Kotkin didn't hesitate. "Wealth," he said. "More wealth than you can imagine." He held up a finger. "Perhaps money isn't important to you, so I offer far more if you meet my expectations. I think you'll be eager to work for the country's most respected company. You will have responsibilities that will fulfill your ambitions, and a title as vice-president in charge of a new department I'm calling Special Projects. This will be a position of importance, and represents a great opportunity." He then added, "And lastly, I can offer the advantage of working directly with me, and to a lesser extent, Charles Bates."

The young man leaned back in his chair. Kotkin could see he was conflicted, so he waited patiently for the first question. Reilly asked, "Exactly what would be expected of me?"

"For now, you will be my personal bodyguard...as I will be yours. I am seen as a threat to those individuals in possession of the aforementioned article. Suffice it to say, they would like me out of the picture. That in itself would generally not be a problem, but there are more of them than there are of me," said Kotkin and smiled. "You must understand that each of us will become a target. Me, because of my knowledge; you, because of your relationship with me." He looked down at his hands.

"I would expect as much," said Reilly.

"There's the possibility—no, that's not right—there's the likelihood, that we will be forced to defend ourselves in a lethal manner. You must be prepared to kill." The young man waved a hand indicating this wasn't a problem. "I thought not," continued Kotkin. "Still, it's a possibility." The door opened and the wine steward presented a second bottle of wine. "Open it and leave," directed Kotkin. "And you may tell Marcel to begin serving in ten minutes."

The interruption gave Reilly time to think. Once they were alone again he said, "You mentioned wealth. From a monetary standpoint, what are you offering?"

"Three thousand dollars immediately—a bonus in consideration of your transition from Pinkerton," Kotkin said. "A suitable apartment at company expense and a salary of five hundred dollars a month." Reilly was speechless. Just as Kotkin had said, it was wealth beyond his wildest dreams. Kotkin continued, "Of course, your resignation from Pinkerton must take place upon any agreement between us. And, there are a few additional considerations."

"Such as?"

"You cannot speak of our arrangement to anyone," said Kotkin. "For protection, during the transition from Pinkerton to the Harriman Company, it's possible your employment will be kept secret. Quite frankly, Charles and I are suspicious of the infiltration in the company, so we are playing this close to the vest. When we deem it suitable, your appointment will be duly announced." He sipped his wine, then continued, "You must be available at all times, day and night. And you must be able to leave the city at a moment's notice. I would suggest you keep a bag packed and on hand."

After a time, Reilly asked, "Anything else?"

"Yes. I must have your answer tonight."

Reilly rose and walked to the window. Pulling the drape aside, he stared down at the sidewalk, now busy with pedestrians. In the cold air, the gaslights sparkled, mirroring an excitement Reilly was trying to hide as he weighed the pros and cons of Kotkin's offer. It took only a minute. "You have a deal." He crossed back to the table and extended his hand.

Henri never spoke truer words—their dinner exceeded all expectations.

<hr>

Brannigan peered out the window at the moving landscape, then pulled his watch from his pocket. "How soon?" he asked.

"Half an hour," replied Longley without looking up. In the four days they'd been on the train, he had spoken little and getting closer to New York had made him even more reticent. He had telegraphed Hattie's father on the morning of their departure from Denver and received the answer at the Chicago train station—Hattie had not been heard from.

Brannigan stood, stretched, and reached for the satchel on the shelf above his seat. He rummaged through the clothing looking for his holster and gun wrapped in a pair of long johns. Without leaving his seat again, he belted the weapon around his waist. Like Longley, he would wear an overcoat that would hide the tied-down holster.

Longley had not bothered to remove his gun during the trip. He ignored Brannigan's preparations for arrival in New York until Brannigan returned the satchel to the overhead shelf and sat down. "Expecting trouble?" Longley asked.

"Never know," he replied. He looked down at his holster. "Listen, it's time we had a talk. We still don't know for sure what's doing with Hattie. Hell, she could be holed up at your house and not letting anybody know she's even there. She could be damn near anywhere, waiting for you to get back."

"Maybe." Longley continued staring out the window.

"We need to do what Butch says." Longley never looked up. Exasperated, Brannigan went on, "Let's feel our way around these fellows. After all, we don't know for sure if the killer even works for Bates. The killer could be anybody in the organization." Still no response from Longley. "Dammit, are you listening to me?" Brannigan demanded.

Longley slowly lifted his eyes. "I'm listening," was all he said.

"I think Butch's idea to stay separate as much as possible is what we should do," said Brannigan. "It gives each of us a chance to scout around and see if we can find anything. In fact, maybe you ought to head up to see Hattie's parents."

"She hasn't shown up, so there's nothing to be done there."

"All right," he conceded after a moment. "Then what will you do?"

Longley glanced around before saying, "I'm going to the stable and talk to the boys. After that, I'm going home. But

Hattie isn't going to be there because she'd have found a way
to get word to me."

Brannigan disagreed. "Not with Marcus and Randolph
dead. If she's spooked, she might have barricaded herself in
there. You got one of them telephones yet? Maybe you could
get hold of her that way."

"No. I didn't think they'd catch on," said Longley. "Hattie
wanted to, but she said we'd wait until it wasn't so hard to
get someone on the other end." He added, "She said the same
thing for the business."

"I don't know much about them," admitted Brannigan.
"Only what I read in those slicks that Molly gets. Anyway,
like I said, Hattie could be there behind locked doors."

As the train slowed, the wail of the whistle indicated
their journey was coming to an end. Longley sighed, and
then said, "You're right. We'll split up. So let's do it before we
get off. Go up to the next car and use the door at the far end,
I'll do the same here. You remember the name of the place
you stayed the other time you were here?"

"The Ludlow."

"Hire a cab and go there," he said. "About three blocks in
the direction of the stable is a place called Wilson's—you
should be able to find it, but just in case, you can ask the
clerk at Ludlow's. It's like your place in Crested Butte.
Starting tomorrow, you go there every day at noon. If I don't
show up within an hour, you come to the stable. And if I'm
not there, and the boys don't know where I am, you come to
my house. If you do have to come, come armed and come
careful. You remember how to get there from the stable?"

It was the most words Brannigan had ever heard from
Longley, and it rattled him. He looked into hard eyes before
saying, "Yeah, I remember." He paused, and then added, "I'll
do exactly like you say."

"Good," said Longley. "By noon tomorrow, I should know
if something's happened to Hattie. And if something happens to me, you get out of town without looking back." After
a moment his eyes twinkled, before a small smile appeared.
"Of course, that's after you deliver the message," Longley

said as he reached into his pants pocket and produced a key. "This will get you in the back door. Front door has a different lock."

Brannigan snatched the key in mid air. "Is there something you know that I don't?"

"Nothing in particular. But right now I'm not feeling good about this, so I'm taking Butch's advice."

In spite of his misgivings, Brannigan smiled. "Some of the time it's good."

"Some of the time."

The train pulled into the station, grinding its brakes and blowing steam. Longley reached for Brannigan's bag and handed it to him. "I'll see you at Wilson's."

"Be careful," said Brannigan as he walked toward the next car.

⁕

Half an hour later, Longley climbed down from the hansom cab and walked up the gravel drive to the building. He was both surprised and pleased. Expecting a burned-out shell of a stable, he was amazed at the fresh wood of the exposed framing that seemed to rise from the ground, and the roof was already in place. He could hear the nickering of horses from the corrals in back, and even though there was still an empty space where the office had been, a stack of lumber left him to think it was next for framing.

A shadow moved from under a tree singed by the fire. "State your business," said a voice, followed by the click of a hammer being thumbed back.

"Put that down before you hurt somebody," Longley said as he walked. The progress of the restoration had lifted his spirits—he was sure Hattie had a hand in it.

"Welcome back, Mr. Longley," said the young man. The voice belonged to fifteen-year-old Nathan Schock, one of several stablehands.

"Where's Hattie?"

Pointing the cocked pistol at the ground, the boy said, "At her parent's house."

Longley came to a stop. "When did she leave?'"

"The day after the fire, I guess. She sent a note to Mr. Hamm saying she was too upset about Marcus and Randolph getting killed to deal with fixing this place up. Said that Mr. Hamm was to take care of everything and that you'd be back soon."

The heaviness in his chest returned. Longley reached out and gingerly took the pistol from the boy's hand before lowering the hammer. He handed it back and said, "You're doing a fine job. Why don't you go back to guarding the place while I look around?"

"Yes sir," he said. "Did you know about the others?"

"I heard," said Longley. "I don't suppose anybody's figured out who they were?"

"The detective said it was the fellows who started the fire," said Nathan. "He said they got killed perpetrating a crime...that's what he said...perpetrating a crime. I guess that means they did it." He stopped, and then as if he suddenly remembered, added, "The detective, his name is Mr. Morrison, said that when you got back, he'd be available to speak to you at your earliest convenience."

Longley looked around again, "First thing in the morning."

⌖

Kotkin climbed down from the saddle and took a moment to stretch his stiff legs. The midnight trips to the house on the New Jersey shore—the only times he'd dared to leave the Waldorf-Astoria—had become as intoxicating as they had been uncomfortable, but he was quite willing to overlook the discomfort. After tying the reins to the post, he untied the package on the back of the saddle, and slung a canteen over his shoulder. He avoided the sandy mud by stepping directly onto the small porch that jutted out from the door. He had to shift the package he was carrying from one arm to the other as he dug into his pocket for the key. Inserting it into the padlock hanging from the brass hasps, he turned the lock and quietly entered the house.

At the first sound, she'd sat up, causing the chains to rattle and rub against the bloody abrasions circling each ankle. She watched as the reflection from the moon high-lighted the silhouette—a continuing prelude that changed her fear to out-and-out terror. Hattie held her breath and once again fruitlessly searched for a weapon. For the three weeks she had been a prisoner, the instinct to protect herself had never left her, even after she had accepted that escape was impossible.

Kotkin set his parcel on the table next to the bar-covered window, lighting a lamp before turning to ask, "How are we feeling tonight?" When Hattie did not answer, he laughed and said, "Now, you know that won't work." He stepped toward the bed and rubbed his hard hands together as he allowed his gaze to run up and down his prisoner. Hattie's once-flawless body was covered by bruises varying in color from black to yellow-green, depending on how long it had been since the blow was delivered. On and below each breast were a number of parallel lines of scabs resulting from slid-ing a scalpel across the skin—each stroke meticulously delivered in a motion designed to cause maximum pain with a minimum amount of blood loss. Identical lines ran verti-cally the length of each thigh.

After a minute, Kotkin set a chair next to the bed. "You know we don't have to do this." Hattie tried to scrunch back against the wall, but her restraints allowed only the slight-est movement. As if in understanding, Kotkin nodded, before stepping back to the table; opening the package he had brought, he removed a clean towel before picking up a pan and splashing some water from the canteen into it. He placed both articles on the chair and rinsed the towel in the water and began gently washing the urine and sweat from Hattie's body. Later, he unlocked one chain and moved her to the chair while he changed the bedding before laying her back on the bed and relocking the restraint.

When he finished, he sat in the chair, before asking, "Don't you feel better?"

In spite of her fear, Hattie shook her head no. When she

spoke, it was in a voice that was hoarse from screaming. "Why..." she croaked. "Why...are you...doing—" She painfully coughed, unable to go on.

He leaned forward. "You know why," he reminded her. "I have to have the information before I can let you go." Kotkin reached for a metal cup and filled it from the canteen. "Drink this," he ordered as he held it to her mouth, "it will help you to talk."

Taking small sips, Hattie gratefully swallowed the water. She watched Kotkin refill the cup and pull meat and bread from the package. She devoured the sandwich, aided by Kotkin periodically pressing the cup to her lips. When she had finished her first meal in three days, and drank her fill, Hattie was able to say in a normal voice, "You have all the information."

"Perhaps," he agreed. "On the other hand, I don't know if you're telling the truth. After all, you're a remarkable woman—one, I believe, who is fully capable of withholding facts."

"I was sent back to New York, so I don't know what Butch and Sundance have planned," she protested. "As you say, I'm only a woman. Why would they tell me anything?"

It was the wrong thing to say. Kotkin reached down and grabbed her breast, twisting brutally. Hattie gasped and writhed, the blood from the cuts began to seep on the clean linen. "Haven't you suffered enough to know better than to think of me as stupid?" he demanded. Once he released his grip, he wiped the sweat from her face before saying, "You've been involved in all aspects. In fact, I suspect you have aided Cassidy in his planning all along. You should take that as a compliment. I imagine I'm not the only man to admire your intellect and courage."

"I've told you all I know," she repeated, tears running down her face. "Please believe—" She involuntarily gasped when her tormentor suddenly rose and stalked to the door.

With his back to her, Kotkin asked, "Have you asked yourself why I haven't taken advantage of you as a woman?"

"Do you mean do I wonder why you haven't raped me?"

she asked. In their previous conversations, the idea of trying to survive this nightmare had relieved her of any fear of sexual violation. She assumed it was inevitable.

"Yes," he answered. When she didn't say anything, he said, "It's not because you're unattractive to me." He returned to his chair. "Quite frankly, I've discovered I'm blessed with a curious affliction. Would you like to know what it is?"

"Not unless you're planning to let me live," she said.

Kotkin went on as if she hadn't spoken. "Originally, when I was ordered by my superiors to remove obstacles in the way of the growth of their companies, I did so with a minimum of effort. But now, I find myself more and more fascinated with the means rather than the results. It is far more entertaining to find what information I can derive from my victims, and most importantly, extend the length of time I can pleasure myself in the extraction of that information. Subsequently, I have found that normal relieving of sexual tension takes away from the purer satisfaction of extracting what my prisoner does not wish to tell me. Unless, of course, I'm relieving those sexual tensions with my victim. So far, we haven't arrived at that point yet. Whether that is fortunate or unfortunate for you, you will have to decide." He was quiet, and then amused at his own observation, adding, "I fear I'm becoming deranged."

"Your sexual tensions are of no interest to me. I'm dead either way. Why don't you just kill me now and be done with it? You have all the information."

"Perhaps. But I find that there is always the possibility of going that one step further in sparking terror."

Hattie stared at him, realizing it was true. She cared less and less about his plans or his twisted proclivities. "Besides rape, what can you do to me that hasn't already been done?"

"Give you some news," said Kotkin. Leaning back in his chair, he took a long time to study her still-beautiful face framed by filthy hair. He let the moment linger as he watched Hattie's eyes draw inward, as if to ward off a blow.

"Your husband has arrived in New York."

Later, in the early morning hours as he rode away, Kotkin reflected that the scream at the news of her husband's return had been her best.

XVIII

When the train screeched to a stop in Denver, Carlisle was ready. His boots hit the ground before the conductor could set out the step. He turned and gestured to Kindred. "Let's get going." Carlisle was almost at the station office before Kindred caught up.

"Best let me do the talkin' at the start 'cause of Tom's cattle bidness, I know Braselton right well." Carlisle nodded. Kindred pushed open the door and stepped in ahead of Carlisle. From the middle of the room, station manager, Floyd Braselton rose from behind the new four-foot stub wall that had been built after Horace Akers's death. Braselton extended his hand, which Kindred declined, saying, "We ain't here on no social visit."

Braselton sat down and moved some papers to a corner of his desk. "Then what can I do for you?" he asked. "I have a very busy day, so whatever your business is, I hope it won't take long."

"Yawl still lookin' ta find the man who kilt Horace Akers?"

Braselton was surprised. He took a deep breath and said, "The railroad has offered a substantial reward, so I guess more than a few folks are interested." With a disdainful glance at Carlisle, he addressed his question to Kindred, "Why would this be of interest to you?"

"Because we know who the killer is." Carlisle had been quiet for as long as he could bear. "And we also know there's not a hell of a lot anyone in this organization is gonna do about it."

Braselton ignored the insult. "I don't believe we've been introduced," he said to Carlisle.

"That's not important," said Carlisle. "And Horace Akers'

murder is important to me only because Tom Brannigan is a friend. You do know that Tom's son was murdered in the same week?"

Braselton took in Carlisle's attitude and the well-worn holster that hung low on his hip. "Who are you? You're too young for Dodge City or Tombstone." Carlisle casually moved his hand from his belt buckle and rested it on the butt of his gun. Braselton's mouth went dry; he swallowed before adding, "Meaning no offense, of course."

"None taken," said Carlisle, but he left his hand on the butt. "Anyway, the killer might have headed back this way. In fact, I'm pretty sure Colorado is in his plans."

"How does this involve me?" Braselton's attitude had changed considerably. He'd slid out of his chair and was now standing at attention.

"You're gonna let me and my friend Silas here know when the killer arrives in Denver. Believe me, you're gonna want to help."

"Well, of course, I'd do anything to solve—"

Carlisle interrupted, "Because none of us are interested in that reward—neither Tom, nor Silas, and especially not me."

"Are you saying—"

"It's all yours," he said. "Every penny. How much did you say it was?"

"Three thousand dollars," said Braselton with a wink. "Setting a reward that size makes it unlikely the railroad's planning to pay off."

Carlisle frowned. "Seems kind of small for such a valued employee, but that's not my concern. We'll pay off if the railroad can't see their way clear to the three thousand," he said. "You in?"

Braselton returned to his chair. "What is it you want me to do?" he asked. "I'm no good with a gun."

Kindred spoke up, "Yawl don't do nothin' but wire us as soon this killer hits town. There's a coupla other things, but they be right small, an' won't be no bother ta ya."

"What other things?"

"You tell us when he's planning on leaving Denver and where he's headed," said Carlisle. "And how many men—if any—he's got with him. Wouldn't hurt if you were able to describe them."

Braselton thought for a moment. "I guess I could do that," he said.

"There's something else you might want to know," said Carlisle.

"What's that?"

"There's a good chance the killer works for the Union Pacific Railroad," said Carlisle, closely watching Braselton. "That could be a problem for you. Especially if he shows up in a private car—makes him an important man."

"What makes you think that?" he asked.

It was Kindred who answered. "Tha' don' matta none."

Braselton looked around the room, weighing the likelihood that he'd be discovered as the informant against the desire for the reward. It wasn't hard for Carlisle and Kindred to guess what he was thinking. The man's annual salary was less than a thousand dollars. With the reward money, a man could straighten out any financial difficulties, get married, or start a new life. It opened up a whole can of daydreams. The lure of the money won out, and Braselton said in a pious voice, "It crosses my mind that I could help the widow and her children, so I'll do whatever it takes to help you find Horace's killer."

"Good thought," said Carlisle. He pulled papers from his pocket and handed them across the desk. "In a couple of weeks or so, maybe as long as a month, a man looking like that drawing will come through that door. He's gonna have you arrange supplies for a trip out of Gunnison. You do whatever he wants, just make damn sure you get a wire out to Brannigan's ranch, and one to his saloon in Crested Butte. By the way, if I were you, I'd keep in mind that the last time this bastard came through, Akers helped him and got killed for his trouble."

"I was the one that found Horace. It's not something I'm going to forget," said Braselton. Focusing on the drawing, he asked, "But what happens if this fellow doesn't make it to Denver?"

"If taking care of Akers' widow is as important as you say, you gotta hope this man comes through here," said Carlisle. "If not, someone else is gonna get rich."

Braselton straightened in his chair. "You can count on me," he said. His voice became stronger. "Quite often, I get word when a private car is attached to a train. Do you want me to let you know then?" As an afterthought, he asked, "How am I going to get credit for the reward?"

"Leave that to me," said Carlisle. He gestured to Kindred, and they started toward the door. "You'll just have to do your job, and you'll get your money. And I never lie," he said over his shoulder.

The door hadn't quite closed behind them, when Kindred said, "Never lie, huh?"

Carlisle grinned. "Well, hardly ever." He looked at his watch. "Go on over to the hotel. I'm going next door to the telegraph office, and when I'm done I'll meet you. Maybe there's news."

When Carlisle joined Kindred at a table in the corner of the Denver Grand Hotel lobby, his face was grim. Kindred pushed a chair in his direction and said, "Ah kin tell somethin' didn't go raht."

Carlisle looked around to make sure no one could hear them. "There were a couple of telegrams," he said. "Longley's stable was burnt to the ground, but that's not the worst. The really bad news is Hattie's missing and hasn't been heard from."

"How 'bout her ma an' pa?"

"They haven't heard anything, so her pa's pretty upset," he said. "He came to New York and told James they expected her a couple of weeks ago, but she never showed up." Kindred straightened in his chair, he pulled off his Stetson and wiped the headband with a napkin. "This could change things for us," Carlisle said. "If Hattie's dead, James won't stop at nothing to get the man who did it."

"Tom git aholt of his pal?"

"Yeah, but right at the moment there's nothing his friend can do. It's a problem, because for now, according to Tom, there's no reason to think there's been trouble. The traveling clothes Hattie would have taken are gone; the day before she told Marcus she was leaving, she withdrew money from the bank, about what she would need to go visit her folks. Maybe something did spook her and she went into hiding."

"Wouldna she left word?"

"You'd think so. But if she was real scared, she might have feared for her parents and be trying to keep them out of it," said Carlisle. "I sent that thought back, so maybe it'll keep James calm." He abruptly stood. "Let's get out of here. We need to find Carver and make some travel arrangements." As they walked, he said, "I hope James is following the plan. Because if he isn't, our lives won't be worth squat."

❦

Fifteen hundred miles away, Longley sat on a plank supported by two stumps, and watched four teams of workmen lift and stand the framing for the new office. One man from each team quickly nailed down a cross brace to hold the walls into place, as other men joined the corners together. The lack of expression in Longley's face hid his anxiety as he waited for the stable boy to return. Longley spotted Nathan as he rounded the corner and started up the drive. He met him halfway, hand extended.

"He didn't give me nothing, just said to meet him in the park by the lake."

"All right," said Longley. "You take over supervising here." The young man watched his employer walk to the horse tied to the stable fence and vault into the saddle. Having been born and raised in New York, Nathan was fascinated by the western saddles that Mr. and Mrs. Longley insisted on whenever they rode.

Longley dug the point of his boot into the side of the stallion and sat easy as the large horse broke into a trot. In the street, he used the barest of pressure on the reins to guide the stallion toward Central Park. Because the brush was allowed to grow unchecked, it was difficult to find the trail that lead back toward the lake. He located a second path and rode the short distance into the clearing where a man waited.

The man turned as Longley rode up. Lifting a finger to his lips, he pointed at the lake where a rowboat was moving slowly along the shoreline—a lady serenely sat under her parasol while her sweating suitor pulled hard on the oars. Longley dismounted and tied the reins to a small tree. Once the boat was out of sight, he almost whispered, "You find out anything?"

"No," the man said. "And I've been asking."

Longley tapped the breast pocket of his coat and said, "She sent me a letter saying she was in hiding and wasn't coming out until the killer was found." He stared at the water.

"You're not pleased. Why?"

"Letter's not real."

Silence. "Well, you would be the one to know," he said. "What is it that made you think the letter was fake?"

"She wrote with her left hand," Longley said. When the other man looked surprised, he went on, "Hattie can write with both, but she's naturally right-handed. I can tell the difference."

"I see," he said. After a moment he went on, "I have two questions: when did you receive this communication, and do you have any idea of her whereabouts?"

Longley turned and walked to the water's edge, the other man followed. Longley spit in the lake before saying, "The letter arrived yesterday at my home. A messenger said a lady who could barely speak English gave it to him, along with five dollars. I couldn't tell if he was lying, but right at the moment there wasn't a hell of a lot I could do."

"What makes you think the messenger was lying?"

"Hattie wouldn't have given the letter to a kid," said Longley. "And I know she wouldn't have depended on another woman to do it, especially one that didn't speak English. My guess is whoever has Hattie paid some woman to get it to me." He faced the man. "Can you find out anything about this?"

More silence. "For now, probably nothing," the man admitted. He thought again, and then asked, "Have you contacted the authorities? Let them know your wife is missing?"

"No," said Longley. "Two reasons: Hattie's letter told me not to."

"And the second?"

"It's not important. Find out what you can."

"I'll try," said the man. He walked back to the clearing and untied Longley's horse. "Why don't you leave first? If I uncover anything in the next couple of days, I'll find you and let you know." As Longley turned the horse toward the path, the man had a thought. "Do you have someone watching your back?" When no answer came, he nodded thoughtfully, and walked in the opposite direction.

As he rode away, Longley swiveled once in the saddle, but the other man was already out of sight. He kicked the stallion into a full gallop. At the entrance of the park, he slowed the horse to a trot and arrived back at the stable where all activity had come to a halt. Nathan caught the reins as Longley said, "After you put him up, call it a day. Tomorrow, I'm going to be late, so I'm depending on you to get the men started."

"Yes sir," said Nathan. "Uh, while you were gone, Mr. Hamm came by and asked if you'd come to his office sometime soon."

"He say what he wanted?"

"No sir. I didn't ask."

Longley left the young man holding the reins. He walked down the drive to the street, turning toward Wilson's Saloon. Once there, he didn't enter. A man at the bar turned and looked toward the street. Longley started walking.

Brannigan finished his beer and tossed some coins on the bar. Hurrying, he caught up with Longley, and as they walked, it took two blocks for Longley to bring him up to date on the supposed communication from Hattie. The shorter man stopped to light a cigar, and then asked, "What's next?"

Longley stopped. "I thought all along the killer had got her, so I figured she was already dead. I could maybe live with that. But now it's worse. That's Hattie's writing, which means she's alive. He's got her someplace."

"That letter could have been written anytime."

"There was no way of knowing when I'd get here. Or if I was even coming."

Brannigan considered this, then agreed. "Assuming he already got the information he wanted, why would he hang on to Hattie?"

"Let's go back to Wilson's," said Longley. They turned and began retracing their steps. "Doesn't matter if anybody sees us together now." He began walking faster. "The killer's got a plan to trap us. I figure the only thing to do is for me to be the bait."

"Hold on there," Brannigan protested, pulling Longley to a stop. "You don't know what his plan is. Hell, you don't even know if Hattie's—"

"She's dead," he interrupted. "Maybe not at the moment, but she's dead anyway you put it. This fellow isn't going to let her live. Nor me, if he can help it." Longley added, "Or you."

Brannigan planted himself in front of Longley. "Goddammit, you start thinking right! We can get the killer here in New York—dammit, he killed my boy, and don't you forget that. We can get Hattie back. We can—"

Longley stepped around his friend. "We can't take the chance." He started walking. "Butch's plan is to get the killer to Colorado. But if the killer gets both of us, he'll light out after Butch and Silas on his own. And then he'll be after your kids."

At the mention of Josh and Molly, Brannigan calmed down. "All right," he conceded. "We'll do what it takes."

"There's something else," said Longley. "This guy is good, but I'll bet he's not working alone. So when I become the bait, you're gonna have to watch my back and your own."

They stepped into Wilson's and took a corner table with their backs to the wall. Longley waited until the bottle and two glasses were on the table before speaking again.

XIX

Reilly ignored the lift and took the stairs to his seventh floor office. In the weeks since he had joined the Harriman firm, he'd spent most of the time with Kotkin, who tutored him on his duties as head of special projects. To date, the primary duty was to act as Kotkin's personal bodyguard, both in the city and when he traveled. Therefore, when Reilly arrived at his office he was surprised to find Charles Bates waiting for him.

"Good morning," said Reilly. Unsure of what warranted the head of the company to wait for him, he assumed an air of nonchalance and tossed his newspaper on the desk. Reilly took a seat across from Bates, who was sitting behind Reilly's desk.

Bates left off the usual courtesies and asked, "What have you been told about your duties?"

Reilly crossed his arms. "I'm not at liberty to discuss this issue," he said. "Mr. Kotkin has instructed me to refrain from discussing either the nature of my position or the position itself. Because he hired me, and because I work directly for him, I feel it's only proper to accede to his wishes."

"Work for him? Are you aware of my position as chief officer?"

"I'm quite aware," he replied. "At the same time, I'd be remiss, not to mention ungrateful, if I ignored the instructions of Mr. Kotkin."

"And if I ordered you to tell me?"

Without hesitation, Reilly said, "I'd refuse."

Bates sat back with a smile. "Excellent," he said. "Forgive me, but I wanted to make sure you truly understand the special nature of your position here at Harriman. Elias and I discussed your appointment, and I will tell you that I heartily approved. Although, it never occurred to me that Elias would require assistance." He steepled his fingers before adding, "Particularly in his line of work."

"Yes sir." Reilly wondered what he didn't know about Kotkin's particular line of work. "What is your opinion of our dilemma?" asked Bates as he carefully watched the young man. "After all, you are now aware of the problem."

Reilly looked at the floor as he thought. "As far as I can tell from the files, failure to recover the item would result in a horrendous situation. But Mr. Kotkin thinks it won't be much longer before we have the last bit of information that will allow us to retrieve it."

"And you're prepared to do whatever it takes?"

"Yes sir," he replied. "In the short time I've been associated with the company, I've come to appreciate the opportunity for advancement that has been afforded me. One, I might add, that I would never have realized with my previous employer."

Bates rose and walked to the window where he stood with hands clasped behind his back. "Your assessment of the opportunity is correct," he said. Reilly waited as he stared down, seemingly fascinated by the busy street. After a time, Bates turned. "If something goes wrong—and I believe it's a possibility—there may come a time when you'll have to rely on *my* judgment. That is, assuming some misfortune by chance incapacitated Elias." Reilly remained silent. "You must understand that whatever adventure is in store for you in the field, should you come back without Elias, you'll be dependent on me," continued Bates. "This is our way at the company and I'm prepared, should it become necessary."

"That's very generous, Mr. Bates—"

"Charles."

"Charles," he agreed. "As I was saying, that's very generous of you. However, I don't foresee Mr. Kotkin succumbing to an unknown peril. You obviously know that right now my primary job is to protect him, and, rest assured, I will do so to the utmost of my ability, regardless of the consequence."

"Good," said Bates. "I don't know what we'd do without Elias. We view him as an invaluable facilitator." At the look of confusion on Reilly's face, he elaborated, "He gets things done. For example, if we're negotiating with a competitor who's having a problem seeing things our way, Elias is often able to bring that person, or persons, around to agreeing with our proposition. Do you understand?"

"I think so," Reilly said. His face indicated he wasn't so sure.

Bates read his expression and added, "In actuality, he specializes in removing obstacles to our future success. It's my hope that your talents will blend with and compliment his—after all, the company cannot have too many loyal employees." He left, closing the door quietly behind him.

Alone, Reilly sat for some time before moving behind his desk.

❦

By the early afternoon, Longley had grown tired of watching the workmen and frustrated by the waiting. He removed his coat and began nailing boards to the outside of the newly framed office. After days of inactivity, the physical labor felt good, and the effort calmed him. When the foreman of the construction company sent his crew home, Longley worked until the night grew too dark, and he was forced to stop. He was wiping his hands when he saw a figure step from behind a tree.

Longley finished wiping his hands and wadded the towel into a ball in his right hand. He whirled and threw the towel at the figure, and at the same instant whipped his gun from the holster. The man ignored the towel and stood with both hands out in front of him. "Nice throw," said Brannigan as he lowered his arms. "But you let me get too close, I could have back-shot you."

"Maybe," said Longley. "How long you been there?"

"Not long." Inspecting the building, Brannigan said, "You do fine work. Ever considered doing this for a living?"

"Don't like it."

"Yeah, I figured that," he said. "Well, if you're done for the night, what do you say we get something to eat?"

"All right," agreed Longley. He stooped to pick up the towel and rubbed the inside of his holster before twirling his gun home. "You talk to your friend?"

"He has some news, but he didn't want to tell me," Brannigan said.

Longley stopped walking. "Where do I find him?"

"Right now, I don't know. He plays it close to the vest. He said he'll get hold of you direct."

<hr />

It was almost midnight before Longley climbed the steps to his home and unlocked the door. He hung his coat and gun belt on the hall tree. The complete silence exacerbated his loneliness. And not for the first time he stood in the foyer waiting for something, anything, to stir in the house. The smells that made the house familiar—the scent of her perfumes and soaps—had long dissipated. It was as if Hattie had never lived there. The heaviness in his chest was at its worst when he first came through the door. But it helped to move his thoughts, imagining what he'd do to the tall killer. After a time, he climbed the stairs. He removed his shirt and was about to toss it in the corner, when he heard a rustling in the bushes. Something wasn't right.

Seconds later, he heard the noise. *Tap. Tap.*

He dove across the bed, and in one motion grabbed for the pistol hidden under the bed. Holding his breath, he waited and listened. The tapping began again; the sound was coming from the back stoop.

Unless he's a damn fool, it's not the killer, Longley thought. *If someone's coming to get me, he isn't going to knock.* He removed his boots and descended the back stairs, stepping on the sides of the steps to minimize the creaking he'd intended to repair for months. In the kitchen, he looked out the back window. In spite of himself, he was disappointed to see a man. Feeling foolish over his hope, he stepped to the door and barked, "What do you want?"

"Brannigan sent me," answered the man.

Longley unlocked the door and took two steps back, but he kept the gun leveled as he waited for the stranger. The man showed both hands, then lifted his coat to show Longley he wasn't armed. "Sorry to disturb you," he said. It was the man Longley had met in the park.

Longley led the way into the front parlor in the dark. He didn't turn on the light as he gestured at a chair. The men were silent until Longley asked, "You going to tell me your name?"

"Not important you know my name," he said. "The name you want is Elias Kotkin, the bastard son of E. H. Harriman."

"How did—?"

The man wasn't taking questions. "I took Brannigan's drawing and stood in front of the Harriman building. It didn't take long, and out came the tall man. Then, I followed him to a dinner house. I talked to a waiter, and for a couple of dollars got Kotkin's name." He waited for a reaction, but Longley was impassive. "I talked to some business friends of mine. Consensus is that people are uncomfortable around Kotkin."

"What's he do for Harriman?"

"No one would say for sure, but apparently he's the man that makes sure the deals go through. The story is that if a party to a deal balks, Kotkin goes in. After his particular *negotiations* are over, the Harriman Company gets what it wants. Others have said he's not someone to fool with, got a temper and a nasty streak. But I guess you know that. Folks at Harriman are scared shitless of him. He's likely having you followed, so I took care when I came here." He pulled his watch from his vest, thought for a moment, and then said, "Although if I had to guess, at the moment I'd say he's not...even so, I was careful and checked."

Longley pushed back his chair and they both stood. "Kotkin took my wife," he said quietly. It wasn't a question.

The man shrugged. "Probably, but I don't know for sure." They walked back through the kitchen to the door, and Longley followed Brannigan's friend to the fence separating the small yard from the alleyway. "I'm not sure that I can find out if he's got your wife." He added some parting words of advice, "I've been told Kotkin can sense things. That he's a sadistic animal that needs to be put down. One way or another he's coming for you, and he's a hard man to get the drop on. So be careful." Longley watched the figure disappear down the alley.

⸎

The following morning Andrew Reilly arrived in his office to find a message ordering him to meet Kotkin at eleven o'clock at the Waldorf. Having anticipated a day filled with paperwork and training, he was relieved to get out of the office. Reilly left the building with ample time to enjoy a morning walk. But it wasn't long before the gray low-hanging clouds and dread about how the meeting with Kotkin would go, changed his mood. He was unsure about what he should say about his recent independent activities. Kotkin might be pleased, or he might not, either way Reilly would have a hard time keeping anything from him.

Reilly quickened his pace and arrived at the Waldorf with twenty minutes to spare. He decided to continue walking farther to give himself more time to think before returning to take the lift to the top floor. It had been five years since he'd been to Kotkin's home. Then it had been the home of E. H. Harriman. For some reason he expected everything to be different.

As he stepped out of the elevator, Kotkin's personal aide, an Italian named Simonini set his dime novel on the floor next to his chair. "At least you ona time," he said in a thick accent.

"Good to know you can tell time," Reilly responded. Simonini brought out the worst in him. On introduction, he'd formed an aversion to the man, realizing that the aide's mental acumen was severely lacking. Reilly assumed the Italian was too stupid to take a bath or wash his teeth. In a closed surrounding Simonini's stench was overpowering.

He put the Italian firmly in his place by bypassing him. "Don't get up, I'm expected." Simonini mumbled in his home dialect, but Reilly ignored him and dropped the ornate door-knocker once before entering the apartment.

From the parlor off the entry, Kotkin called, "In here." As Reilly was making himself comfortable in a chair next to his mentor, Kotkin said, "Do try to get along with Angelo. After all, he might save your life one day."

"Little chance of that," said Reilly. He crossed his legs. "I admit I do dislike the man. His personal hygiene is atrocious."

"He serves a purpose," Kotkin said. Dismissing the thought of Simonini with a wave of his hand, he asked, "Now, would you care for tea, or perhaps a coffee?" After the maid had delivered the tray, Kotkin lifted his cup and asked, "What have you learned?"

"Longley is deeply upset over his missing wife," said Reilly. "In fact, he's deadset on revenge."

"Not surprising," conceded Kotkin. "Were I married I'd be revengeful too." He paused, and then asked, "If you don't mind my asking, how did you discover—?" Suddenly realiz-ing the significance of Reilly's comment, he demanded, "How would Longley know anything about me?"

"I told him last night that you probably had his wife, and it was evident he's distraught," said the young man. Reilly reached for his cup and made a point of calmly taking a sip before saying, "Actually, last night was the second time I've met with Longley. The first was in Central Park."

Kotkin was not often caught off guard, but this infor-mation caused a visceral reaction. He sat perfectly still until he was able to ask in a steady voice that conveyed to Reilly that he might not see the other side of the study door. "What caused you to arrange these meetings?" His fury swelled again, and he stood and stepped toward Reilly.

The young man remained seated, waiting for Kotkin to regain control and ready to spring if he didn't. Unconsciously clenching and unclenching his fists, Kotkin stared at his reflection in the mirror over the fireplace. "What did you think you were doing?"

"I didn't arrange the meetings," Reilly said. "Unaware of my current position, a former Pinkerton associate was approached by a man who professed to be a friend of the Longleys. Because of George Nelson's secret recommendation of me to you, Pinkerton cannot be involved in this affair. It seems that many of my previous colleagues at Pinkerton are under the impression I've formed my own agency, so my associate referred me to Longley's friend. Ironically, this man wanted to retain my services for a job similar to the one you've provided—although on the other side of the fence." Kotkin turned and stared at Reilly, who immediately lost his grin and became serious. "Longley's friend was very forthcoming. We now know their plans, and, with luck, we can trap both Longley and his friend."

<hr />

Arriving in Gunnison, Carlisle and Kindred pushed past the throng of people waiting for arriving passengers or saying good-bye to those departing. They walked the short distance to the livery stable and picked up their horses. The stable hand said he'd saddle them, and if they hurried, there would be enough time for breakfast at the café down the street.

An hour later, Carlisle took the lead and turned his horse in the direction of Brannigan's ranch. Josh and Molly were expecting them. Patches of snow spotted the road, causing Kindred to urge his horse even with Carlisle's. "Winter's comin' on. Might this be upsettin' to our plans?"

"I don't see why." Carlisle swiveled in the saddle and looked at the surrounding mountains whose peaks were covered in snow. In spite of the blue sky, the air was cold, and both men rode with scarves bundled around their necks. "It might be a problem if there were a bad storm on the day we get him," he said. Carlisle leaned over and patted the neck of his horse.

Kindred grinned and said, "These ole boys need a run." He snapped the reins and prodded the mare's ribs with his boot bringing the horse to a full gallop in less than ten yards. With a curse, Carlisle slapped the neck of his horse and was soon close behind. Two miles down the road, the cowboy reined the mare to a trot and waited until Carlisle's horse pulled even before slowing to a walk.

"I tell you, Silas, I need to get my ass on a horse more often." Carlisle was clearly exhilarated by the exercise and the brightening day.

As the Brannigan ranch came into sight, Kindred pulled up and pointed in the direction of the road. "Ah'll be dammed, Josh took ma advice an' gated the ranch." He lifted himself in the stirrups, cupped his hands around his eyes, and peered at the house. "Everythin' else looks fine, so we kin go on in."

"How do you know?"

"Fore we left ah tole Josh ta keep a fire goin' all the time. If ya notice, there's smoke comin' out of both them stacks," he said. "He musta remembered in spite of him and Molly actin' like a coupla new marrieds."

Carlisle loosened the reins to let his horse begin walking up the road. "Just because they're young doesn't mean they can't enjoy themselves," he said. "You ever been married?"

"Nah," said the cowboy. "Had me plenty 'a women in ma time, but none that were a keeper. Nowadays, if ah git lonely, ah jist stroll over ta one of the houses in Butte." He paused for a moment. "Course, that don' mean ah'm agin marriage. So far ah jist ain't found the raht one."

Carlisle laughed. At the ranch road he dismounted and looked at the gate. "What good is this going to do? It's not locked."

"Look at the back 'a them boards," suggested Kindred. "Ah told the kid that ifen he ever got around ta buildin' it, he should nail on some ole cans an' fill 'em with rocks an' glass. Go ahead an' open it. Should be enough noise ta let them kids know we're here." He added, "Let's see ifen it works."

Carlisle did as directed, and the clinking sounded through the frigid air. There was an immediate reaction. The howling of the dogs was followed by a shot that rang

out just after the bullet pinged off the post inches away
from Carlisle. As the echo of the ricochet disappeared,
Carlisle looked from the pile of muddy snow where he'd
taken cover, and said, "It works."

Kindred stood in the stirrups again and yelled, "Josh!
Put down tha goldam gun!"

"That you, Silas?" came a feminine voice. "Hope I didn't
hit nobody."

From the ground, Carlisle asked, "She that good, or that
bad?"

"What was ya aiming at, girl?!"

Molly appeared on the front porch, with the rifle pointed
at the sky. "It was just a warning shot. I made sure to fire
over your heads.

"Bad," he said to Carlisle. "Yawl can get up now." He
turned back to Molly and called, "Best ta put tha rifle away,
'afore ya hurt somebody."

Later that evening, Molly was apprehensive as she
washed the supper dishes. For one of the few times since she
had known the laconic cowboy, Kindred was angry. Unable
to withstand his silent disapproval, she turned and said,
"I'm sorry about Josh. I tried to talk him out of it, but you
know how he is."

"Yeah, gal, ah know." Kindred's frustration was evident.
"But, goldammit, the two of ya ain't been thinkin' raht. Yawl
know there be a killer out there...an' it could be yore husband who's next."

When the tears began falling down her face, Carlisle
rose. He took the dishtowel and gently wiped her cheeks.
"Forget it, Molly," he said. "We'll leave early in the morning,
and we'll get him. But for now, you need to pack a bag so we
can take you to your daddy's farm."

"Why can't I go with you?" She went over to Kindred and
put her arms around his neck as he sat staring at the table.
"I told you I'm sorry. And besides, I'm a good shot, so I could
help," she said. "I shouldn't have let Josh go, but he can get
me to agree to anything. I didn't think he'd be in danger
helping out at the saloon. So I'm going with you to Butte."

"No ya ain't," said Kindred. Then he smiled. "Now listen here. Yawl's too important ta me ta let ya git in the way. So, gal, yawl gonna do what yore tole. Git up them stairs an' pack a bag."

"But...what about the—"

"Ah said do what yore tole," repeated Kindred. He stood and said, "Go on now, git that bag. Yore pa'll send yore brothas ta tend the spread."

"And you being with your pa, we'll know you're safe," said Carlisle, urging Molly out of the room with a push. "Hurry, we need to get going before it gets any colder."

After she left, he asked Kindred, "You think Josh is in trouble?"

"Dunno," he admitted. "But with everythin' else goin' on, ah don't see no reason ta take no chances. Fact is, Josh should be safe ifen he's at the saloon. 'Fore the reunion in Denver, Tom hired a coupla boys ta watch over everythin' until we got back. Course, we didn't think it would come ta this."

"That's a fact," Carlisle agreed. Picking up his glass, and before taking a drink, he said, "There wasn't any way of telling." He reached for the bottle and asked, "You want some to keep you warm for the ride?"

"What's the next step?" asked Kindred, pushing his glass across the table.

"Well, I'm not sure. I've been concerned over Hattie miss-ing; I've been getting more concerned about our partners being in New York; and until we know for sure that Josh's all right, I've got something else to be concerned about." Carlisle tossed off the whiskey, coughed, and went on, "So until we know the killer's here in Colorado, I guess we don't have one hell of a lot to do."

"Tha last telegram seem ta say thin's was lookin' up," said Kindred. "Tom's got that fella workin' from the inside; and James be holdin' hisself together, so we should be get-tin' thins' lined up real soon. Fust thin', let's get Molly over ta her pa's." Hearing her footsteps, they said no more.

Carlisle and Kindred rode into Crested Butte just as the rising sun was peeking over the mountains. Their faces were rubbed raw by the wind, and their coats and gloves had done little to stop the cold. Carlisle tied his reins to the hitching rail and said, "First, let's get Josh. Then we'll head down to the café, get something to eat, and try to talk some sense into him."

"Molly ain't 'round, so mebbe he'll be thinkin' clear," said Kindred. He stepped aside to let Carlisle enter the saloon first.

One step inside, both men were stunned. Every table and chair was overturned, broken glass from smashed bottles covered the floor, and there was a powerful smell of whiskey and beer. Gloves came off simultaneously as each man pushed his coat aside for quick access to his gun. Someone moaned from behind a table. Carlisle stepped around to see who or what could sound so miserable. "You know this fellow, Silas?"

Kindred's looked over the top of the table. "Yeah. One of them boys Tom hired ta watch over the place. Useless sons 'a bitches."

Carlisle hoisted the man into a chair and gave him a couple of quick slaps. A few mumbled words escaped his swollen mouth before his chin dropped to his chest. "Well, he's just drunk." He let the man slide to the floor and back into unconsciousness.

Kindred relaxed. "Means there were a fight last night." He surveyed the ruins. "Musta been a good 'un."

"Happen often?"

"Only when Tom or me ain't here." Kindred looked around and said, "Ah wonder where the boy could be."

As if in answer, the door behind the bar opened, and Josh walked in with a bucket and mop. "About time somebody showed up to help with the mess. There was a little altercation last night."

"Tha' so," said Kindred. "What got 'em started?"

"Ah...the usual. Couple of miners got into it over cards, then one thing led to another, and before I knew it everybody joined in. It was kind of fun for a while." Josh rubbed his face and winced when he touched the cut on his cheek.

"Anybody get hurt?" asked Carlisle.

"No worse than usual. But it was late, so after I got it straightened out, I told the boys the night was over." He looked around and laughed. "Didn't look so bad last night."

"We be hepin' ya clean up," said Kindred. He began setting up tables and chairs. "Afta that, yore goin' back to Gunnison."

"The hell I am," said Josh. "If we're getting whoever killed Will, I'm in on it. I'm not leaving until we string up my brother's killer."

"Nope," said Carlisle. "I'm not saying you can't handle yourself when we find him. I know you can. But Tom's lost one son, and there's no use taking a chance on losing the only son he's got left. Besides, I've got plans for you, and being up here isn't one of them. You got Molly to think about."

Josh stared into Carlisle's eyes for a moment. "I guess I shouldn't have left her at the ranch, but a couple of her brothers have been riding over during the day." He took a breath. "What do you want me to do?"

"Glad you asked," Carlisle said. He set up a table and turned three chairs upright. "Let's talk about killing a killer."

XX

Brannigan waited next to the streetlight. He shuffled and stamped his feet to keep warm, but the bitter cold that had arrived the previous week was slicing right through his coat and he stood shivering. Not for the first time, Brannigan wished he could wear both gloves. But knowing that Longley—and to a lesser extent himself—were under constant threat, he couldn't afford the luxury of two warm hands. In the event of a direct confrontation, their only hope against the killer was a fast and steady hand.

To keep moving, Brannigan walked in the direction of the far corner. He was halfway down the block when ahead he saw a door open and Longley step onto the porch. Longley looked in both directions before proceeding down the steps and turning in the direction of the livery. If he saw Brannigan he gave no indication.

Brannigan continued to the corner and waited to cross the street. It wasn't until Longley had turned the corner that Brannigan saw another man stand, shake himself to restore circulation to frozen limbs, and then fall in behind Longley. The man, sitting on the step of a brownstone across the street, hidden in the shadow of the porch roof, had gone unnoticed.

Brannigan was frustrated. In spite of all their careful planning, they were at a disadvantage against Kotkin who had unlimited resources, and access to any number of back-ups to act as bird dogs. Brannigan followed the man tailing Longley; his concern gradually gave way to a hardened resolve as he reminded himself that Longley had been in tough situations before. Brannigan had no doubts about his own skill in handling a gun, and, as good as he was, Longley was better—much better. He also knew that neither would hesitate to draw and shoot—a decided advantage in New York where a gunfight was rare.

Of course, Brannigan reminded himself, *gunplay only works when you've got your target in front of you. A fast draw don't do much good if someone sneaks up from behind.* Ahead, he saw Longley stop at a corner newsstand to buy a paper, the man following also stopped and leaned casually against a fence. *This boy ain't too bright*, thought Brannigan as he crossed the street in order to walk parallel with the follower. Even from this distance, Brannigan could see the man was not overly tall, but was well-built—his dark complexion reminded him of Jimmy. Once Longley resumed his walk, the man fell in behind again.

Brannigan let the dark stranger get ahead before crossing the street to cut down the distance to be closer in case something happened. The man walked faster and was soon within ten feet of Longley, who had not glanced back. *James had to have heard the man by now*, Brannigan thought as he moved his gun to the outside pocket of the greatcoat. He cocked the gun, and was closing the gap between them when Longley turned into the gravel road that led to the stable. *Right about now*, thought Brannigan.

The swarthy man called out to Longley, who turned and faced him as the man spoke. Brannigan couldn't make out the words, but Longley stood still and stared at the man. His coat was now open and pushed behind the holster as his left hand rested on the butt. Longley said nothing and his expression never changed. The man took a step back—he then heard Brannigan and turned to face him.

Brannigan tensed and increased the pressure on the trigger. Even though he'd be firing through the pocket of his coat, he knew the muzzle was aimed at the man's heart. For a second the man simply stared at Brannigan, before he made out the shape of the gun muzzle. "*Escuzi*," mumbled the man. He rattled off a string of unintelligible words before turning and walking away. Brannigan watched the man disappear around the corner. He released the breath he'd held for the last minute and eased the hammer down.

"Had him all the way," Longley said.

"He was on your tail as soon as you came outside," said Brannigan. He grinned and slipped his gun back to its holster. "Must be some kind of foreigner. Said 'excusy' instead of 'excuse me'. What do you think he wanted?"

Longley shrugged. "Only word I got was 'job', so I think he was asking for one. He was probably Italian. They've been coming over here faster than the Irish. You notice anything else?"

"He needed a bath something fierce," he replied. "Let's get inside. I'm colder than hell, and we need to talk."

They met in the stable—the office still wasn't completed. Brannigan warmed his hands over the fire in the steel barrel that the stable boys used to keep the horses warm during the winter months. Longley dragged chairs from the corner, placing them close to the warmth before lighting a cheroot and asking, "So what's on your mind this early?"

"Forget Butch's plan. We should kill Kotkin here and now," said Brannigan. "As far as I can tell he's only got one man on the street watching his back. At least that's all that I can spot." He thought for a moment. "Unfortunately, we'd probably have to kill the bodyguard too."

"Seems kind of drastic."

Brannigan's face hardened. "I dreamed about Will last night," he said. "I don't know how much longer I can wait. And you know he has probably killed Hattie too. So what damned difference does it make whether it's drastic or not?"

"Take it easy," cautioned Longley. He had picked up a set of reins and was examining the brass rivets. Satisfied, he set them down and then asked, "You ever kill anybody?"

Brannigan hesitated before answering the question truthfully, "It was at my place. I killed two gunmen that were gonna kill me." As he stared at the fire, his anger diminished somewhat before he went on, "Other than that, I don't know. But it don't make no difference as far as Kotkin's concerned."

Longley rubbed his chin. "All right," he agreed. "But Kotkin might not be the only one. What if there are others and they keep coming? Sooner or later, they could make it back and go after the rest of your family—and that includes Silas—to say nothing of Butch and his family. And, as good as it sounds to kill the son of a bitch, I don't want to spend the rest of my life rotting in some jail. I know you don't either." He leaned back in his chair. "There's something else. Butch hasn't said too much about this Bates fellow, but I get the feeling he could be the brains of the operation. Butch telegraphed me that he got a letter back from Bates through Carver in Salt Lake."

Brannigan smiled at the mentioned of the Carver name, remembering old times. "Trenton's a chip off the old man's block."

"News was a friend," Longley simply said. He then went on, "That's another reason we've got to do what Butch says. Bates might have had a hand in all this from the beginning, in which case he caused the death of some good men." Brannigan was quiet for so long that Longley finally said, "We've got to follow Butch's plan."

"I suppose," he said. Holding his hands close to the fire again, he asked, "What about you? I got the feeling you've got something planned on your own."

"No," he said. "No, I'm going to do it the way Butch laid it out."

Brannigan rose and walked over to an unfinished horse stall. He rummaged through a pile of firewood and pulled out two small logs and tossed them in the barrel. "So what do we do next? Nothing?" he asked Longley.

"You're talking to your friend this morning, aren't you?" Brannigan nodded. "He came to see me last night," said Longley. He described the conversation. "What you need to do is see if he can get Kotkin to agree to a meeting. Tell your friend to use the story Butch came up with—we've got the journal and are willing to deal, but only if he'll come to Colorado to get it."

"He's too smart for that."

"Yeah. But Butch thinks Kotkin will look at this as a challenge," he said. The first of the construction crew came into the stable and Longley stood. "Time for me to hammer some nails."

Later that morning Brannigan sat waiting in a corner at

Wilson's Saloon. He didn't have to wait long. "Is Longley being followed?" Reilly asked as he took a chair.

"What makes you ask that?" Brannigan began to reconsider the encounter with the job hunter this morning. He briefly related the morning's activities, ending with a description of the foreigner who had followed Longley.

Reilly listened without comment, then said, "He's an Italian named Simonini, and he works for Kotkin. I know, because I've bribed the sister of Kotkin's maid. She says Simonini is a cowardly brute who's known to have a predilection for hurting people, even women if he gets the chance. The sister said he's not welcome even in the lowliest of the Chinese brothels."

"Why does Kotkin have someone like him?" asked Brannigan.

"Simonini is a moron, but he's a loyal moron. No one else would hire him. Simonini gets an income for hanging around the Waldorf to run Kotkin's errands, guard his apartment, that sort of thing. I am a bit puzzled by his following Longley." Reilly paused. "Nevertheless, the moron does what Kotkin wants, so he's a force to be reckoned with. As cowardly as Simonini is, he's still dangerous."

"They're the worst kind. I was thinking this morning that we'd have problems if Kotkin's got a back-shooter."

"Kotkin's a killer. Chances are you'll never see him until it's too late," said Reilly.

Brannigan looked across the room at nothing. "Yeah," he agreed. "That was clear with Will."

"And you'd do well to put your son out of your mind for now," said Reilly. He had met with Bates the previous afternoon. Bates gave him a whitewashed version of Kotkin's history with the Harriman organization, including the trip to Colorado but without all the details. "Now, what do you want me to do?"

Brannigan spelled out Carlisle's plan for getting Kotkin to Colorado. "We think the only way Kotkin will take the bait is if he hears directly from one of us. It doesn't seem likely he'll believe anyone but Longley."

Reilly agreed. "The problem is that Kotkin just might go ahead and kill your friend for the fun of it. And then come for you."

"We got a plan for that."

"I hope so. But what happens if Kotkin tells Longley he's holding his wife?"

Brannigan flinched. "Is he?"

"No way to know, but you can't ignore the possibility. If Kotkin has her—and so far there's no proof that he does—he'll use that against Longley." Reilly looked at the floor, then met Brannigan's eyes. "On the other hand, from what you said, Kotkin kills quickly. I doubt if anyone, much less a woman, could stand up to his tactics for long. And your guess is she's been gone for some time."

Brannigan looked around; the previously empty saloon was filling with a lunch crowd of tradesmen from neighborhood businesses. He focused on Reilly and then said, "You're probably right. Truth be told, I think Longley's already got that in his mind."

"How good is Longley?"

Hesitating for only a moment, Brannigan said, "Best I've ever seen. He's the only man I know that could force a stone-killer gunfighter to walk without making a play. Most amazing thing I ever saw, and I saw it more than once. In those days, no one in their right mind, or not liquored up, would fool with him. A couple of old-timers, who knew some of the frontier lawmen and gunfighters, said Longley was faster and deadlier than any of them. They said he had what made the great ones great—he had no fear of dying."

"That was a long time ago," the other man reminded Brannigan. He rose and said, "I'll use all my sources to get information to Kotkin, although I can't promise anything." Before Reilly turned to leave, he added, "I'll do what I can." He pushed through the crowd, glancing back once.

Brannigan suddenly felt very tired and sat until the waiter noticed his empty glass and hurried over with the bottle. It was a credit to Brannigan's concentration that he ignored a second man who had been sitting at the table near them. Had he been paying attention, he might have noticed the man follow Reilly out the door. He might have even seen the two men meet on the sidewalk and speak briefly before separating and walking in opposite directions.

It wasn't until early evening that Reilly was able to meet with Kotkin. Upon returning to his office, he had been summoned for another lengthy meeting with Charles Bates which, as with other meetings before, amounted to Bates probing for information concerning Kotkin's current activities. Reilly tried to give information without really giving information.

Arriving at the hotel, Reilly was surprised to find his mentor waiting in the lobby. Kotkin greeted him and then suggested a walk would do both of them some good. The doorman at the Waldorf opened the door and tipped his hat as they started up the busy street. Kotkin was silent as they walked the two blocks to a nearby park. They sat on an iron bench, and to Reilly's amusement, Kotkin pulled seed out of his pocket and fed the ducks brave enough to chance surviving the winter in New York.

After a few minutes of watching the ducks fight for the seed, Kotkin wiped his hands on his silk handkerchief then tossed it in the general direction of a waste can. "What news do you have for me?" he asked.

"Brannigan suggested that a meeting between you and Longley would be in order," said Reilly, a smile briefly appearing. "He's under the impression you wouldn't be interested in anyone other than Longley."

"True."

"I must tell you that Brannigan has a high opinion of the abilities of Longley. He makes a good case that no one has a chance against him if gunplay is involved."

Kotkin lifted his head and stared, his lifeless eyes caused Reilly to shudder involuntarily. "In a gunfight, that's true," he said. "On the other hand, in another method of combat, Longley would be the one at a decided disadvantage." The cold words caused another shiver to run through Reilly. For a time Kotkin looked away, and then asked, "Is Longley left-handed?"

Reilly hesitated. "Well," he said, "I believe so, but it's not something I know for sure."

"You must find out," said Kotkin. "In the one photograph that I've seen, his holster was hidden. Although, according to LeFors' report, the Sundance Kid was left-handed." Kotkin closed his eyes and said, "Give me a moment."

As Reilly sat in silence he wondered if he might be in over his head in this relationship. It was growing dark in the park. The sun was a pale orange ball sinking fast and casting long shadows across the two men, but Reilly would have sworn he saw a flash of light. There in the flash was the certainty that not only his future employment with the Harriman organization, but his very life, were at the mercy of Kotkin's slightest whim. And mercy was not a term Reilly associated with his mentor. Kotkin would eliminate him without hesitation. *Still,* he rationalized, *if Kotkin recovers the Harriman journal, I'd be in an advantageous financial position for the rest of my life.*

When Kotkin opened his eyes, he was smiling. "Andrew, I think it would be a wonderful idea to invite Mr. Longley to dinner." He paused and thought again before he said, "A dinner at Le Meritage. It will give me an excellent opportunity to size up my opponent."

"You do realize it could be dangerous."

"Nonsense. If either Longley or Brannigan wanted to eliminate me, they could have done so on numerous occasions, particularly after you were so generous with my identity. On reflection, a wise bit of thinking on your part."

Reilly nodded. "Once I saw Brannigan's drawing, I knew sooner or later they'd figure out who you were just by standing in front of the building," he said. "But with me and that idiot Simonini guarding you, it was unlikely they'd get close."

"You're not the only one watching my back," Kotkin said. He rose suddenly. "You possess great intuitive skills, Andrew. If you avail yourself of my training, you will go far in our world. Now, on our way back to the Waldorf, why don't you explain how you intend to convey my invitation to Longley."

As they walked, Reilly took time to think before he said, "I believe you should send an invitation, perhaps penning a personal note to indicate the evening should be considered a truce. After all, he's a killer in his own right, but not without honor, and the idea of a truce will help alleviate the notion of a trap."

❦

Three days later, Brannigan and Longley met again outside the Longley Freight Company. The barn, tack room, and corrals had been rebuilt, the office was not far behind. Longley sat on the fence stroking the nose of one of the horses when Brannigan walked up the driveway. He jumped down and led the way into the barn, taking one of the chairs near the fire.

Brannigan held his hands to the warmth. "You might as well start wearing both gloves," Longley said.

"Why's that?"

"Doesn't look like Kotkin's coming through the back door." He held up an envelope. "Take a look."

Brannigan read the note, then handed it back to Longley. "Nice handwriting. You figure on going?"

"Why not? Kotkin said it was under a white flag," Longley replied. Stretching out his legs, he smiled. "No reason I shouldn't believe him."

"No reason other than he's a merciless son of a bitch, who's not only good at what he does, but seems to enjoy it too," said Brannigan. He pointed at Longley's gun. "And you? What's to stop you from drawing down on the son of a bitch and killing his sorry ass?"

Longley grinned and said, "In spite of Kotkin's promises, he's going to be well protected. And the fact is, I don't know for sure that Hattie's dead." He held up a hand to stop Brannigan from contradicting. "Besides, we still don't know if Bates is really the brains behind this affair, and you and

Butch can't get all of the Harriman men before they get you or one of your kids. We can't risk it."

"Why bother with dinner then? Why don't we hightail it out of town and force him to follow?" Brannigan grabbed a stump sitting between their chairs and tossed it on the fire. "Why the hell do I have to be the one to keep it warm in here?" he asked. Flames soon rose over the top, casting a glow on the unpainted timbers.

"You're the only one who gets cold," said Longley. Unconsciously running his hand down his holster, he said, "Getting back to Kotkin. I figure by meeting with him, I could get a few things. Maybe if he hasn't killed Hattie, I can find out where he's got her."

"You think he's gonna just up and tell you?"

"It would probably please him to agitate me. No doubt he thinks he can force me to do something stupid," said Longley. "And besides," he went on, "if she's in hiding—who knows, maybe she is—then agitating me gives him cause for concern. If he doesn't have her, then he doesn't have any idea where the journal is." He watched the fire for a time, before adding, "That means he won't have a hell of a lot of choice about going to Colorado. Especially since I'm going to convince him it's the only way he's getting his hands on the journal."

Brannigan didn't like the sound of that. "How you gonna do that?" he asked. But Longley didn't answer. "Why don't we do the smart thing and have me get to Bates," continued Brannigan.

"Forget it. I'm going. I've already sent Nathan with my answer."

Brannigan stood. "I'm not gonna let you handle this alone," he said not without anger. "We agreed to stick together on this."

"I'm not doing it alone," interrupted Longley. "You're going to be watching me, and so is Nathan." He rubbed his hands together. "Just not from inside the restaurant. No one will recognize the boy on the street, and we'll have to take a chance that somebody might know you."

Brannigan thought about protesting the arrangements, but the set of Longley's jaw caused him to keep his thoughts to himself. "When's all this gonna happen?" he asked.

"Saturday evening," Longley replied. "Seven-thirty at Le Meritage."

"You know the place?"

"It's Hattie's favorite."

XXI

The snow that had fallen all day showed no sign of letting up as early evening set in. Carlisle stood at the window staring into the twilight and listening to the wind. The snow muffled every sound and covered the surface with a layer of loneliness. All day he'd been looking for Kindred to ride up, but if the cowboy had any sense, he was in Crested Butte waiting out the storm.

Carlisle had returned to the Brannigan ranch two days earlier after shepherding Josh into the care of his father-in-law. Max Hutchinson was a quiet man whose demeanor belied a strong will and attention to detail. He was not alarmed when Carlisle explained that Molly and Josh could be targets of the man who had killed Will. Max had assumed the take-care-of-business attitude that permeated the management of the ranch, and he assured Carlisle that Josh would stay put even if he had to hogtie him in the barn.

Two days at the ranch were just about two too many. *Well, at least Josh and Molly are safe...safer,* he thought. A gust of wind dropped a curtain of white outside the window, causing Carlisle to admire the sturdy construction of the Brannigan house. After another look toward where the road was buried in snow, he left the window and walked into the kitchen where it was warmer and the fire added some cheer to the darkening house. Maybe it was too early to drink on a clear day when there were chores to be done and daylight left, but it was not too early when the light is going and there's nothing to do but move from window to window. He found Brannigan's bottle on the shelf above the table and decided to savor re-reading Thea's letter while he savored Brannigan's whiskey.

Thea's familiar handwriting filled the pages, and he smiled at the news from Portland. The boys were chafing at being excluded from what they considered their pa's Colorado adventure, but they were keeping the mill running. Thea didn't like that the boys were vowing to join the expeditionary forces in Europe if it came to war—but Thea knew her boys and felt most of Lawrence and David's talk amounted to posturing. Besides, Lawrence had a good reason for staying home. His ongoing courtship with Portland debutante Sara Milligan seemed headed to a spring proposal.

As for herself, Thea wrote that she was fine but missed her husband. In the years since his return from South America, they had seldom been apart. Near the end of the letter, she'd expressed hope that this would be the final chapter for Butch Cassidy and the Sundance Kid.

Carlisle couldn't have agreed more. He had no stomach for the fight. It had taken over far more of his life than he wanted. Brannigan's most recent telegram hadn't eased his mind. As soon as he'd read of Longley's meeting with Kotkin, he'd not been able to shake a sense of dread.

The only good part of the meeting was that Longley wasn't going in with his gun blazing—in fact, he was insistent on going unarmed. Carlisle knew Longley's reasoning and concurred. The likelihood of Hattie being under Kotkin's control meant that he didn't dare kill the man without knowing for sure.

Still Carlisle was worried. "Damn, I never used to mope like this," he grumbled to himself. "Tom's right, I am getting old." He rose and took his whiskey back to the parlor and stoked the fire. He felt cold, but it wasn't the weather; he knew Longley was in trouble and there wasn't a thing he could do about it. And in spite of Hattie, Longley might just haul off and kill Kotkin. Even though he swore to Brannigan he wasn't going to.

"If James thinks Hattie's dead—," Carlisle mumbled to himself. He read the telegram again. "Dammit, that's what he thinks. If she's gone, he doesn't care anymore. And if James kills Kotkin in New York, that would unleash the newspapers, to say nothing of other Harriman killers. Son of a bitch, he's gonna kill him."

Carlisle was helpless, there was no way to contact Longley or Brannigan. The meeting might already be over for all he knew. "Son of a bitch," he swore again. "If Kotkin kills Sundance, I'll kill him myself. Then I'll kill Bates, and then I'll kill every other bastard who's got anything to do with this." Only the sound of stomping on the kitchen porch kept Carlisle from vowing to kill half of the male population of New York City.

He picked up his gun from the chair near the door where he had left it and made his way through the kitchen to the porch. Carlisle peeked around the doorframe, and came face to face with Kindred, looking like a ghost in a cowboy hat. Stepping into the kitchen, Kindred glanced at the gun and said, "Guess ah shoulda yelled out."

Carlisle asked, "How the hell did you make it back?"

The cowboy removed his heavy poncho and hung it on a hook. "Ah'm pretty thick, ah guess," he said. "'Sides, it weren't all thet bad when ah started out from Butte this marnin'. Got a lot worse 'bout halfway down the trail." He looked down at the snow melting off his boots. "Molly's gonna raise hell ifen I don' get outta these. Feet are 'bout half-froze, but they'll be fine when ah get 'em up ta the fire."

Carlisle looked down. "Yeah, get over to the stove. I'll heat up some coffee."

An hour later, Kindred was thoroughly thawed and heard Carlisle's news and worries. He refilled his coffee mug, added a little whiskey, and said, "Only thin' ta do is wait."

"I know, but—"

"James' a man," he interrupted. "He'll be doin' what he thinks best. Ain't a damn thin' we kin do fer now." Kindred tossed down the contents of his mug before again reaching for the bottle. "Yawl know it," he continued with a shake of his head. "An' ah know it. So we don't do nothin' but wait fer this here storm ta blow ova and 'nother telegram from Tom."

They studied the fire as intently as if it were one of the masterpieces on Kotkin's office wall. Kindred broke the mood and the silence. "Since we got nothin' better ta do, why don' ya tell me how ya got outa tha mess in Bolivia?"

Another gust of wind caused the windows to rattle. "All right," said Carlisle. He waved at the window. "This storm is like the one that caught up on me and Sundance after we got out of that shit-hole village in Bolivia." Carlisle stared into the fire. "Of course, that wasn't until we were in the pass." The memories flooded back.

"Once we got away from the village, Sundance was barely conscious. But we had a cave in the pass that we used as a hideout," said Carlisle. "Even had rations. Anyway, I used water and whiskey and cleaned Sundance's wound as best I could, then lit up the powder." Carlisle grinned. "It helped that Sundance had already passed out. I bandaged him up and then tended my wounds."

"How long ya stay in the cave?" asked Kindred.

"Three days," said Carlisle. He went on, "And then it took a couple of days to cross from Bolivia into Argentina. I used back trails to get to our ranch in Patagonia." He sipped his whiskey and took his time. "I knew we had to get out of Argentina, so I left Sundance with a neighbor—told him I'd give him our ranch if Sundance was alive when I got back."

"Where'd ya go?" asked Kindred. He was fascinated by the tale.

"Well, back to the mountains where we'd hid money. Gold coin we took from bandits," said Carlisle. "Not all of it though. Etta had already brought some back." Carlisle continued, "I got the money, gave the ranch to our neighbor, and hitched a team for the coast. It was another two-day trip. When we got to San Marcos, I booked passage for San Francisco. The ship didn't leave for ten days, so we had time to change our appearance. Damn near had to knock Sundance cold when I wanted to shave his mustache." He pulled on his beard. "That's when I grew this...had it ever since. It took two-weeks to get to Frisco, so Sundance had plenty of time to heal. After we got there, we parted ways. You know everything else."

Upon entering the private dining room Longley opened his coat, turning and lifting the back to show he wasn't armed. "That's not necessary," said Kotkin. But in return, he rose and opened his own coat. He extended his hand, but Longley turned away and looked over the room. Kotkin smiled. "All things considered, I'm surprised you accepted my invitation."

"Did my wife tell you about this place?"

"Your wife? Pardon me, Mr. Longley, but you have me at a disadvantage," said Kotkin. "Please sit down. I don't believe I've had the privilege of meeting your wife. Is she in the city? I should have included her in the invitation."

"Wouldn't think so," was all Longley said.

They stared at each other. "Your look is rather accusatory, Mr. Longley. Do I take your sullen expression to mean that you believe I have something to do with the disappearance of Mrs. Longley?" Kotkin asked.

"How'd you know she was missing?"

Kotkin took a sip of wine to recover. He placed his glass carefully on the white linen. "All right, Mr. Longley. You're aware that I've had you followed. My men report that your wife has not been seen for weeks. I assume she's in hiding. Quite likely, considering your respective backgrounds. I find it hard to believe she's come to any harm."

"Why are you so interested in Hattie and me?" asked Longley. He reached for his wine with a look that made Kotkin think he might bite through the glass.

Kotkin ignored the question. "Your devotion is commendable. If I were in your position, I'd wonder if I'd feel the same."

"What could you possibly know about my position?" Longley threw the wine glass across the room at the fireplace. The wine sizzled and dampened a flame.

Kotkin mentally stepped back and for the first time wondered if being in the same room with Longabaugh was prudent. The very thought of his own discomfort quickly became a source of amusement to him. "Rest assured that if I had plans for you, or your wife, there would be little you could do to interrupt those plans."

"That right?" Longley replied with a pause to regret not bringing his gun.

"Yes, Mr. Longley," Kotkin assured him. "I know you've killed in the past, but you must believe me when I say that my career in that area has far surpassed yours. You are an innocent compared to me."

Longley smirked at the boldface arrogance of the coward. "That right? You ever face a man straight up?"

"I never thought it necessary." Kotkin met the smirk with a cool stare. "My activities are simply a means to an end. What purpose would be served to allow a target an edge?"

If silence were the measure of whether Longley or Kotkin was dominating the meeting, Longley was clearly winning. And Kotkin was finding that the other man's reticence irritating. There was testiness to his voice when he continued. "You come from a time and place where a code of honor governed behavior in settling disputes. Meeting an adversary at high noon in the middle of Main Street is a foolish concept I long ago transcended. Why leave success to chance?"

This was not going the way Kotkin planned, once again he was forced to continue in the face of Longley's silence. "And I can't be goaded into a fight before I'm ready, even by a thrown wine glass. But, we have no need to talk of this. For the first time in my years in the Harriman firm, I'm not in charge. I've been instructed that it is in our best interest to negotiate."

"That must have come from Bates. What does he think we have to negotiate?"

"Mr. Bates is the president of the company and my employer," he replied. "Let me be frank. You are in possession of an article we want. In fact, we are the rightful owners. You and your associates appropriated it some years ago and, as you have now become respectable members of society, we believe you should want to return it. Surely you can understand our position."

The door opened and the maître d' entered, followed by two waiters carrying trays. The smell of rich food filled the room. Kotkin was about to order them out, but thought better of it and nodded for them to serve. Longley sat silently until the waiters finished serving. "You were talking about your position."

"Yes, but for now let's enjoy dinner. We'll continue our discussion over cigars," Kotkin said, in an attempt to regain control of the evening.

"No need," said Longley. "Being close to you kills my appetite."

Kotkin hesitated, and then said, "Very well. You'll excuse me if I enjoy my dinner. As I stated, we have a problem. The article, as you know, is Mr. Harriman's personal journal—"

"Before he became Harriman," interrupted Longley. He tossed his napkin over the plate of food in front of him. "Good food wasted."

"Uh, yes, it's quite good," said Kotkin. His inability to manage the conversation made him impatient. "As I was saying, the journal is invaluable to us, and we must have it back." He swallowed and then added, "Regardless of the consequences."

"You saying you want to buy it?"

"The mere fact that you and Cassidy have read the contents makes that option unlikely."

"Say we have Harriman's journal, what makes you think we won't turn it over to the authorities, or the newspapers?"

Kotkin licked his fork and placed it alongside his clean plate. "Because," he said, now thoroughly angry, "if you do, you're putting your life and Cassidy's at risk. To say nothing of any others who have had the misfortune to read it. I don't think you want that to happen."

Longley responded with a blank stare that warned Kotkin that it was dangerous to try to guess what Longley did or did not want to happen.

Kotkin took a breath and held it briefly before continuing, "You're beginning to disappoint me, Mr. Longley. Perhaps I have too much admiration for you and your partner—" He stopped, gathered himself again, and then went on, "You don't dare use the information because your life would be over in more ways than one." Again no flinch, no blink, no response or reaction, except the same cold stare from Longley. "Don't you understand that even if you got lucky, there are others like myself who could not let you live if this story became public," he said. "There are other companies that—"

"Rothschilds Bank?"

Silence.

"I commend you, " Kotkin said, lifting his glass in salute. "Rothschilds is certainly one. But there are numerous entities that can ill afford to be involved in a scandal of this magnitude. Because that is the case, I've been chosen to pursue an understanding, so to speak, in order to secure the return of the article."

Longley asked, "By *understanding*, do you mean killing a few people along the way?"

Kotkin rose and poured more wine into his own glass, before resuming. "This is going nowhere." Again there was silence. "All right, what is it you want?" he asked.

"You come get it."

"So you and Cassidy can kill me?" Kotkin relaxed and smiled. "Come now, Mr. Longley, surely you don't think I'm that naive."

"How bad do you want the journal?"

Kotkin suddenly felt back in control. "Your negotiation skills could stand refinement. It's best to recognize that give and take is always part of negotiation." He absentmindedly played with a butter knife. "On the other hand, I relish a challenge," he said. "When you say come get it, what exactly do you have in mind?"

"I've told you. Come out to Colorado and take your chances. Butch said your pride would make you come."

"Did he now?" Kotkin put down the knife and drained

his wine before saying, "Perhaps your Mr. Cassidy is right." He held up the empty bottle and pressed the button on the floor. Henri himself instantly appeared. "Henri, please send in another bottle and bring a glass for Mr. Longley."

Minutes later, after the owner of the restaurant closed the door, Kotkin raised his glass. "All right, I accept your challenge. Shall we toast the beauty of negotiation?" After drinking, he set his glass on the table and raised his napkin. The wine dribbled out of his mouth and was absorbed in the folded linen.

Kotkin watched as Longley took another drink before returning his glass to the table. "Do you enjoy wine?" he asked.

"Not as much as whiskey," said Longley.

"That's understandable, your past would be an impediment to a distinguishing palate," he said. Leaning back, Kotkin folded his arms across his chest and watched the other man like a cat watches a tormented mouse. "I must confess to something," he said. "In fact, I have had the pleasure of meeting your wife."

This silence was like waiting for a dynamite charge to go off. Kotkin's eyes narrowed as Longley fought the impulse to launch himself across the table. "Explain yourself." Longley clenched and unclenched his left hand as he waited.

"With all due modesty, I admit to having many discussions with Hattie in which she exhibited great interest in everything I had to say," said Kotkin. "She's quite a remarkable woman." He looked at Longley's face and read murder. "Violence, Mr. Longley, will get you nowhere. Only I know her whereabouts. If you kill me, you would be killing her."

Now it was Longley who had to breathe deeply. "I already figured she was dead. And even though you tell me you've got her, I'm not sure she isn't. So there's not a whole hell of a lot that's holding me back."

"Do you want to see her?"

Taken back, Longley all but shouted, "Where do you have her? She'd better not be hurt."

"One cannot have everything one wants," Kotkin said. "Calm yourself. It won't be long before you're united." Longley's face was beginning to freeze in place. He found it hard to blink or move his mouth to form words. "Rest assured," continued Kotkin, "that your wife is in no pain, and at the moment she's not far from here. You should know everything in a few minutes."

"What...are...you...talking about?" asked Longley. He was unaware that his speech was slowing and didn't know what to make of the blur on the other side of the table. "What...uh ...where...is she?" Longley's chin dropped to his chest.

Kotkin stirred and pushed the button twice. The door opened and Angelo Simonini entered followed by a tall Scandinavian named Jorgenson carrying Longley's hat and coat. Simonini looked at Longley in satisfaction and said, "I told you that Chinese stuff would work. You don't swallow any? It don't take much to knock you out."

Ignoring the question, Kotkin asked Jorgenson, "Do you know what is required of you?" After the Swede nodded, Kotkin said to Simonini, "And Andrew. Where is he?"

"He's following the one who carries the gun on his hip," said the Italian.

"Is the woman where I told you to take her?" asked Kotkin. When Simonini did not immediately respond, he turned and said, "Did you get the woman back?"

"Uh, yeah...yeah," he mumbled.

Kotkin snatched the lapels of Simonini's cheap suit and said, "I told you not to touch her. I'm going to assume what little brain you have convinced you to control yourself." He moved a hand to Simonini's throat and squeezed until the Italian's eyes began to bulge. Having made his point, Kotkin released his grip and asked, "Did you touch her?"

"No, boss," he gasped. "Uh, well, I mighta grabbed her tits a little." Quickly adding, "Only when I was carrying her." He backed away from Kotkin and said, "I swear I didn't do nothing else. Just like you said."

At that moment, Kotkin decided that Simonini's use-fulness had come to an end, along with his life span.

"Very well, I'll take you at your word," he said. Looking around the room, Kotkin said, "Angelo, take Mr. Longley out the back. You know what to do." Grabbing Longley by his suit coat, Simonini effortlessly tossed the unconscious man over his shoulder and disappeared through the door to the kitchen. Kotkin pointed to a chair and ordered Jorgenson to sit.

An hour later, Kotkin said, "It's time." Jorgenson stood and put on Longley's coat and hat. Buttoning his overcoat, Kotkin left the room with the Swede. They walked down the corridor to the entry past the desk where Henri was making a studious attempt to ignore them. Once out the door, Kotkin followed Jorgenson down the steps to the street. They stopped to shake hands as he said, "I'm pleased we could come to an agreement, Mr. Longley. I'll be in Colorado before the month's end, and then we'll see this to its outcome." The two men then walked in opposite directions.

Across the street, Brannigan leaned against a streetlight close enough to hear Kotkin, relieved that the killer had taken the bait. As Longley walked away in the dim light, Brannigan saw the blond hair beneath the back of his hat and followed, keeping a safe distance behind. But before Longley could turn the corner, a figure in a tan straw hat stepped out from an adjacent building and set out after Longley. Brannigan quickened his pace to close the gap, and when he reached the corner he was only a few feet behind the man. Brannigan decided enough was enough and pulled his gun from the holster and moved it to the outside pocket of his coat. Moving to within an arm's length, he waited until they were in the shadow between the streetlights before he made his move. "Say, mister," he called. "Can you help me?"

The man turned in surprise. Brannigan stepped close and with his left hand cupped the man behind his neck, pulling his head down. Simultaneously, he yanked the gun out of his pocket and slammed the butt of the gun into his captive's head. He dragged the unconscious man to a stairwell and lowered the body onto the steps. Sliding the gun back into his holster, Brannigan returned the fallen straw hat to the unconscious man's head and after a quick glance in both directions, hurried up the street in pursuit of Longley.

Longley had disappeared. Brannigan was about to start running in hopes of catching up when it hit him that Longley was headed in the opposite direction of his home. He figured Longley must be headed to Wilson's, less than a mile away. With a sigh of relief, he slowed his pace.

⸱⸱⸱⸱⸱⸱⸱

Simonini struggled and stopped to catch his breath. Longley's limp body was dead weight, and carrying the unconscious man up the narrow stairwell was more difficult than he anticipated. Realizing Kotkin would show up any time, he renewed his efforts and dragged and pulled Longley into the bedroom. In spite of Kotkin's admonition, the Italian stepped over Longley and pulled down the quilt. He stared at the naked woman, all the time trying to figure if Kotkin would know if he took advantage.

Kotkin had told Longley the truth, Hattie was not in pain. She was conscious, but confused and unable to move, her mouth was bound with a gag, making it difficult to breathe. Before being moved from the seaside house, she had been forced to drink water laced with another herbal powder, and now she could do nothing but stare at the ceiling of the bedroom in her own home. She heard Simonini struggling up the stairs, but could only watch from the corner of her eye as he dragged in a body. The clothing said it was James, and Hattie assumed he was dead. A tear rolled down her cheek.

Simonini leered over her, his hands roaming over her body; but his natural cowardice, and fear of Kotkin, got the better of him and he turned away. He had one more task to perform. In the corner by the solitary window was the sledgehammer he had left earlier. His heart pounded in anticipation. He hefted the sledgehammer and walked back to Longley.

Following Kotkin's explicit directions, the man turned Longley on his back. He stretched out the unconscious man's left arm and secured it by placing his foot on the forearm. With one powerful blow, he crushed Longley's left hand. No sound came from Longley. Simonini rolled Longley over and delivered a second blow, making sure every bone was broken. Blood seeped from the tips of each finger.

A sound from the bed broke Simonini's admiration of his own work. Hattie was slowly moving her head from side to side, moaning. "Looks like the potion is wearing off, missy," he said to himself. In spite of Kotkin, he again stepped close, reaching for the buttons of his trousers. As he bent over her body, the retching stopped him cold. The gag caused the vomit to come through her nose and cut off her air. Simonini pulled the gag off in a panic. If the woman died, Kotkin would surely kill him. He cleaned her mouth and let her get some choking breaths before the gag went back in place. Shaking at the close call, he turned his attention back to Longley.

Simonini lifted the unconscious man and stretched him out on the bed next to his wife. He then went downstairs to the kitchen, and returned shortly with a pitcher of water and a twist of paper containing a powder. He mixed the herb and the water and then pulled Longley into a sitting position. Simonini could see that Hattie's eyes were filled with pity and helplessness as she watched him force the potion down Longley's throat. The Italian laid Longley back on the bed. He'd done all that Kotkin told him to and went downstairs to wait.

Kotkin came through the parlor door. "Did you do as I instructed?"

"Yeah," Simonini replied. "He not gonna be using his hand no more. And he drunk all the powder." As an afterthought, he added, "I don't touch the woman."

"Wait outside on the steps, interfere here only if someone comes," said Kotkin. "I'll call when I need you." Eyes narrowed, he watched Simonini close the door. There was a muffled sound, so he turned his attention back to upstairs and was soon standing over the bed. "Good evening, Hattie." Kotkin smiled at her expression. "Are you pleased that I've reunited you with your husband?" He removed the gag.

"...why?" Hattie croaked. She moved her lips, but no other words came out.

"Because I have to make sure," he said. "Besides, we had an enjoyable supper, or at least I did. As one gentleman to another, I'm going to give him a fair fight. But first, let me get you some water, it will help in our discussion as we wait for James to awaken."

As before, Kotkin was gentle as he aided her to drink and it wasn't long before she could speak, albeit in a hoarse voice. All hope gone, Hattie felt something like peace. It almost seemed a victory to die with her husband, to not die alone in that seaside house. "A fair fight?" she asked, voice strengthening. "A coward such as you would never allow that."

"Come now, Hattie. You're expressing the same sentiment as your husband," said Kotkin. He leaned over to look at Longley, who was beginning to move as the potion drew him toward consciousness. "The fact is, he's no different than me. He's killed before, numerous times."

"Never by maiming anyone first," she said. The water helped her hoarseness. "And never in cold blood."

"In my opinion, a grievous mistake." Kotkin slapped Longley's cheeks and tossed water on his face. "Never give your opponent a chance. If his fate is determined, why risk the results being altered by some stroke of luck." He watched Longley open and close his eyes. It wouldn't be long before he could talk, although talking might be difficult. The ruined hand would cause an intolerable amount of pain, or so Kotkin hoped.

"Why don't you just kill us and be done with it?" Hattie spat the words at him. She was beginning to gain feeling in her body but was careful not to show it.

Kotkin nodded. "All things in good time."

"Then why not kill us now?" she asked. "You already know Butch's plan. There's nothing else to be learned from us." A spasm of pain shot through her body as the potion she'd been given continued to wear off.

Her question went unanswered. Longley's return to consciousness was as Kotkin hoped; the shattered bones and crushed nerves caused him to writhe in agony. Kotkin tossed more water in his face and slapped him hard. "Wake up. We have much to talk about, and I don't have all night." Longley struggled, but the pain blocked everything. He couldn't struggle beyond it.

Then, from somewhere far away, Hattie's voice called his name, "James." The sound did what Kotkin's potion and slaps could not. Longley turned his head toward her. "James," she repeated. "I'm here."

Longley's eyes met his wife's, inches away. He wanted to grin. He wanted to touch her beautiful face. In spite of the pain and the certainty of death, he wanted to be here beside Hattie. "Hattie...are you...?"

There was a whistling sound, followed by a second. The leather cosh had slammed down on Longley's knees, cracking his kneecaps. Longley bit through his lower lip, but to Kotkin's disappointment he made no sound. His small store of energy and dwindling focus were reserved for Hattie. Through blood-covered teeth, he croaked, "He's...a piece...of shit."

Hattie smiled through her tears. "Yes," she agreed. "Worse than that cowardly colonel in South America."

"Butch...and the boys...are going...to cut...off his balls." Longley gasped for air. "If he has balls."

Kotkin set the cosh on the floor and resumed his seat. "Enough," he said. "I admire your courage, but unfortunately we don't have much time." He said to Longley, "Your wife has been quite forthcoming in telling me about Cassidy's plan."

Longley gathered his remaining strength. When he spoke, his voice was still a whisper, "You go out west and take your chance on getting the journal back." Sweat poured from his face, and it took all of Hattie's remaining self-control to avoid reaching out to him. She had been wiggling her fingers and knew movement had returned to her.

"I'm afraid you'll have to be more specific," said Kotkin. He thought for a moment, and then added in a jovial voice, "But not too specific. After all, I enjoy a challenge."

Longley waited for a spasm of pain to pass then realized with some clarity the spasm would be followed by another and another and another. He forced out, "Get to Crested Butte. From there...make it to Brannigan's...meet Butch. He'll...he'll fill...fill you in...after...that."

"Who are you accustomed to dealing with?" Kotkin asked. "Why would anyone be so gullible as to follow those instructions?" He tapped the cosh against his hand. "I'm beginning to lose patience." When Longley's eyes rolled back, Kotkin set down the cosh and tossed the remaining water in his face.

Longley gasped. He blinked to clear the water out of his eyes, even this little movement ratcheted up the pain. "Butch will...give you a hostage," he was finally able to say. "Anybody you want. If you...don't make it...make it...back...your boys...can kill the hostage." It took a great effort for him to thrust out the words.

"Why should I care if your hostage dies?"

"Because we have one of yours," interjected Hattie. Kotkin turned his dead eyes in her direction.

Kotkin shook his head. "A flawed plan," he said. "There's no one I care enough about to be concerned over their situation." He reached for his cosh.

"How about Charles Bates?" When Kotkin didn't respond, Hattie asked, "If Bates is gone, who will believe your claim to be Harriman's son? And to his estate?"

"How do you know about me?" he demanded. The tapping of the cosh was increasing and Hattie knew from experience that the taps were the precursor of a painful strike.

There was silence, and then Longley again spoke in a surprisingly normal voice. "We don't know how, but Butch does. You can't get what you want from us." His body involuntarily stiffened. He gasped, "You might as well kill us." Blood trickled down his chin onto the sheets.

Kotkin stood and stared at the couple. He quickly ran through the facts, and realized that for once in his life he was in a precarious position. He didn't care whether Bates lived or died, but with him dead who could confirm Kotkin's birthright? Without Bates' support, even his position within the Harriman Company would be tenuous. Before he had finished sorting out all the implications of Bates' demise, Hattie asked, "Where is Bates? Have you seen him in the last week?"

Such was Kotkin's concern that he didn't respond with a lethal blow. Instead, he tried to remember the last time he'd seen Charles. He had been informed by Bates' personal assistant that Charles would soon be out of the office for a month. Kotkin had thought little of it. Bates often left for extended periods to inspect the railroad. But when had he left? He decided that Bates had been gone for a week and raised the cosh again. "Tell me where Charles is." His victims were past caring and neither registered fear. He lowered the cosh. "Then let us proceed," he said. Kotkin reached in his pocket for a pistol, and at the same time pulled a second gun from the holster under his arm.

Longley faced his wife and tried to grin through the red haze and dripping sweat. With their agony about to end, she smiled and said, "I wouldn't change a thing."

Kotkin set the pistol near Longley's right hand. Pointing at it, he asked, "Are you by any chance ambidextrous?" When he didn't answer, Kotkin said, "I would hope so. After all, I promised you a fair fight."

"Fair?" gasped Longley as he forced his body into a sitting position. The weapon sat no more than an inch from his hand.

"Certainly," said Kotkin. He was watching Longley like a snake. He was also watching Hattie who was clearly drawing herself together to make some sort of feeble strike. "I will allow you to choose whichever hand you wish me to use." He set his gun at the end of the bed, away from Longley's foot and stood poised.

Longley's old gunfighter reflexes came back, and he calculated the odds. Calm replaced the pain. Without moving his head, his eyes moved down to the gun sitting inches from his hand. At that moment his pain didn't exist. He turned to his wife and said in a strong voice, "He ate his dinner right-handed but drank with his left hand."

"Does it matter?" she asked. She sucked in her breath and kicked at the gun lying in front of Kotkin.

The quickness of both men was almost too fast for the naked eye. In less than a blink, Longley had the gun in his hand. Kotkin also used his right hand and leveled the barrel.

Two shots rang out.

There was surprisingly little noise, and for a long time there was no movement. Then Kotkin stepped to the bed to examine his work. Both shots were delivered to the head, killing instantaneously. Longley had fallen back against the pillows and lay with blood running between his eyes. Hattie had thrown herself sideways and died falling across her husband, a bullet behind her right ear.

Kotkin holstered his gun. He was breathing hard, but from anger not fear. Longley hadn't bothered to pull the trigger, instead he had simply pointed the weapon and waited. Longley had actually beaten him to the draw and could have killed him. But the gunfighter had been too smart, perhaps guessing his gun wasn't loaded.

Kotkin was disappointed as well as angry. It hadn't turned out as he'd planned, but he reminded himself that the success of the operation was far more important than personal pleasure. And, there was still one more task. He walked to the head of the stairs and called for Simonini, who, surprisingly, was awake.

The third shot of the evening was the end of Simonini. Kotkin fired the bullet with unerring accuracy in the center of the Italian's chest, then placed one gun in Simonini's hand, the other in Longley's. He pulled pieces of Hattie's jewelry from the box on the armoire and scattered money on the floor next to Simonini's body. He looked over the scene and decided that although there might be questions about Longley's injuries, if they were even noticed, it would appear to be a burglary gone bad. He picked up the sledgehammer, checked the room once again, and left.

When Brannigan had arrived at Wilson's, the Saturday night revue was on and every table was taken, customers were standing three and four deep against the wall as the orchestra played ragtime for the dancing girls. He decided it wasn't necessary to shove his way through the rowdy crowd to the bar where Longley was standing and waited until the show was over. Nearly an hour had passed before Brannigan pushed his way to the bar, but Longley was already gone. Drawing the attention of the proprietor, he asked Wilson if he had talked to Longley. Wilson shook his head, saying, "I haven't seen him tonight." Brannigan was stunned. "Wait a minute," said Wilson. He pointed toward the end of the bar. "You don't mean that tall fella that was standing over there, do you?"

Brannigan headed for the street without answering. As he pushed through the doors, he came face to face with Andrew Reilly. "What are you doing here?"

"I've been following you," replied Reilly. His agitation was evident in his voice when he said, "I think something might have gone wrong from my end. And if it has, I'm powerless to stop it." He looked around and asked, "Why isn't Longley here?"

"He's gotta be at the stable," said Brannigan, unwilling to admit his bewilderment. He wasn't thinking clearly. "Uh... meet me here. Noon, tomorrow."

"That may be too late," said Reilly. He whirled and was in a full sprint before he crossed the street.

Brannigan stared at the disappearing figure. *Too late? No, that's not right. James said if he wasn't here, he'd be at the stable.*

Brannigan walked the few blocks to the freight company. The door was locked. He lit a cigar and settled in to wait. It was over an hour before it dawned on him that Longley was taking too long.

Without thought, he ran to the Longley home. As he rounded the corner, Brannigan spotted someone sitting on the steps. He slowed and reached for his gun. "Mr. Brannigan? I just got here," Nathan called as Brannigan approached. "I followed that man, just like Mr. Longley told me. Once he went home, I came here."

"You haven't been inside?" he asked. The young man shook his head. Brannigan went up the steps, pulled his gun, and turned the knob on the front door. He cautiously pushed the door aside and entered. He turned back to Nathan. "If I'm not back in five minutes, you hightail it to the police station."

Brannigan was as quiet as possible as he made his way up the stairs, but in the back of his mind he knew it was too late for quiet. In the bedroom, he found the switch and turned on the light, not prepared for the tableau of death that greeted him. James and Hattie were dead, and there was nothing to be done. Brannigan backed into the hallway and had to open several doors before he found a linen closet. He pulled out identical sheets to cover his friends, the other body he left as he found it.

As he went down the stairs, Brannigan's fatalism took over, and he decided he wasn't surprised. All things considered, something like this was destined to happen; although he thought he would be the one who ended up dead. When he reached the street, he explained the tragedy to Nathan and ordered the young man to wake up Devlin Hamm and tell the attorney what had happened. "Tell him to get over here right now, " said Brannigan.

"Yes sir, I'll fetch Mr. Hamm," he said. "Will you be here when I get back?"

Brannigan thought for a moment and then said, "Yeah, I'll be here. I'm just gonna sit and contemplate why legends always come true—one way or another."

"What do you mean?" Nathan asked.

If Brannigan had an answer, he decided not to share it. "Just do as you're told," he said gruffly. Brannigan watched until Nathan was around the corner before his strength gave way and he had to sit. He removed his hat and laid it on the step below. Resting his arms on his knees, he let his head drop.

The following day's newspapers reported the murders of Mr. and Mrs. James Longley during a burglary. The Longleys were lauded for managing to kill the intruder.

XXII

As pressure from the steam built, the iron wheels gathered momentum and the engineer released the brakes. Like a living beast, the train heaved and groaned and moved out of Grand Central Station on the first leg of the journey to the other side of the country. Family and friends waved to loved ones hanging out windows of the passenger cars to call their last good-byes.

In the last passenger car no one waved or even acknowledged the parting scenes. The luxurious car was connected in front of a number of freight cars that carried merchandise for the new towns between Chicago and San Francisco. A second extra car hooked in front of the caboose was the property of a bank consortium. It was loaded with gold and silver, designated for transfer to the federal mint in Philadelphia, and then to Denver. The steel doors had small windows for venting, making the ride possible for the two heavily armed soldiers on guard in the car.

Several cars ahead in the private coach, Andrew Reilly sat in a leather chair against the wall that separated the sitting room from the two sleeping berths of Kotkin's private car. Across from him, Kotkin sipped a cocktail and lounged comfortably in an identical chair, his stocking feet propped on a pillow-covered footrest. He looked at his traveling companion and asked again, "You're absolutely sure?"

"When Brannigan boarded the train last week, he was alone," said Reilly. He added, "I think we should have persuaded him to travel with us."

Kotkin shook his head. "With the demise of the Longleys, it's imperative that Brannigan be the one to report to Cassidy. Are you sure he understood my plan?"

The younger man nodded. "When we met, I made it clear

that my sources had told me that your preparations to go West were underway, and that you'd already ordered your private car to be attached to this train. I've no doubt Brannigan understood you were going to Colorado to rescue Mr. Bates—and, of course, to retrieve the journal."

At the mention of Bates, Kotkin grimaced. "Damn him," he said. "If Charles had been more cautious, getting the journal would have been much easier. Now we'll have to play Cassidy's game."

"For a time," said Reilly.

Kotkin corrected the young man, "A short time." He rose and stepped to the window enjoying the feel of his stocking feet against the carpet. "Cassidy has me over a barrel. I can't act against him until I have Charles. However, once Charles is safe, I can and will dispose of Cassidy."

"I'm confused," said Reilly, sitting up straight as if anticipating a need to defend himself. "It's quite clear you have the highest-level status within the company, and you're independently wealthy. Given those facts, why bother with these has-beens? What possible harm can they do you? Or for that matter, to anyone?"

Kotkin returned to his chair. "I'm afraid, my young friend, that you're mistaken," he said. "Although, not entirely. It's true that I don't have a need for money. And while my paternal legacy is important, at this point a proper birthright isn't going to change my life, other than possibly improving my social standing. But there are other forces at work that make it imperative to keep my father's past a secret."

Reilly remained silent.

"The importance of the story is the company's continued relationship with Rothschilds Bank through Sir Reginald Forrester," said Kotkin. "Sir Reginald had a role in the Lincoln assassination. He acted as a banker for renegade groups, and he seduced Father into becoming involved in the scheme. This would be a forgotten bit of history if it were not for the fact that, one way or another, Rothschilds is aligned with significant financial organizations throughout the world. And if Rothschilds is shown to be part of the plot against Lincoln, it could be very detrimental to our monetary system and impact persons of wealth, both here and abroad."

"I'm afraid I don't understand the threat."

"The major banks of the United States and Europe are interrelated. But there's always been a dominate entity, a controlling force if you will. For some time, that controlling force has been Rothschilds. Always operating behind the scene but controlling everything. For now, as Rothschilds goes, so goes America," Kotkin said. "Think of New York's four-hundred families as a tangled web. All their wealth, in some form or another, is tied together." He paused and smiled. "My birthright, while still clearly an issue, isn't nearly as important now as when I started this endeavor to preserve Father's name."

After a moment, he asked, "Do you have any idea of my true vocation within the Harriman organization?" When Reilly didn't respond, Kotkin took some relish in explaining his background and training, omitting nothing from his past. When finished, he asked, "Don't you think that other businessmen employ people like me? As long as I retrieve the journal, and as long as knowledge of it remains a secret, it's unlikely someone would come after me. However, there is always that possibility."

"Who besides Cassidy and his associates could know about the journal?"

"Because of my father's continued relationship with Rothschilds, I have to assume that Sir Reginald is aware the journal exists," Kotkin replied. "And, even though he's now in his nineties and has little to do with the operations of Rothschilds, you can rest assured that someone within the bank is aware of the possible threat. There's little doubt Father would have used his knowledge of the bank's involvement in the assassination judiciously, but he nevertheless would have used it. For example, who do you think financed his railroads in the beginning? I'll grant you he had personal funds but not enough to achieve his dream." Kotkin

fell silent. He had given Reilly information that would elevate the younger man to a new position of trust in the company, and Kotkin wanted him to know this.

Reilly looked down at his hands. To change the subject,
he asked, "What are we to do about Mr. Bates?"

Kotkin came out of his reverie. "It's quite clear," he said.
"He's Cassidy's hostage, which means we must take care."

"So, our job is to extricate him?"

"Once we have the journal, Charles' situation no longer
matters." Kotkin averted his eyes. "However, rest assured
I'll do everything in my power to free him. I do wonder how
Cassidy managed to trick him into going to Colorado."

"I doubt he was tricked," said Reilly. "The lobby security
officer told me that the last time anyone at Harriman's saw
Mr. Bates he was leaving the building in the company of a
young stranger. My guess is that that he was forced to leave
with the stranger and was probably transported to Colorado
in a rail car like this."

Kotkin turned his gaze from the passing scenery. "What
makes you so sure Charles isn't awaiting us in Denver? He
could have come on his own to negotiate with Cassidy."

"Last week, I asked George Nelson to see if any of our
competitor's private cars-for-hire were unaccounted for,"
Reilly said. "George, of course, would be discreet—after all,
you and the Union Pacific are his best customer." He quickly went on before Kotkin could protest bringing Nelson
back into the picture. "He learned that the Baltimore and
Ohio dispatcher loaned a private car to the Harriman
Company two days before Mr. Bates was last seen. And the
arrangements were made by Bates' assistant, Thomas
Phillips."

"So what? Private cars are often borrowed by the company,"
Kotkin was quick to point out. "By many companies."

Reilly nodded. "Nelson was able to discover that this particular car, although final destination unknown, left
Philadelphia on the southern route and was scheduled to
switch tracks in New Mexico for a northern route. I think
Phillips was forced by Cassidy's men to do their bidding."

After a moment, he added, "Phillips has been missing since Mr. Bates left, so I'm assuming Cassidy had him killed."

Kotkin pursed his lips and asked, "Any chance the switch you mentioned was to our spur route that stops in Gunnison?"

Reilly grinned. "It's why I think Mr. Bates was kidnapped and is now in Cassidy's hands."

"Interesting. That means that once again Mr. Brannigan becomes a very important person in this little drama. Tell me, whose welfare do you think Cassidy will be more concerned about? His own? Brannigan's? Or perhaps this Kindred fellow that Mrs. Longley was so eager to tell me about?"

⚬⟊⟊⟊⟊⚬

While Bates' disappearance and future were being discussed on the train headed west, Bates was sitting in the front room of the Brannigan ranch house listening to Cassidy outline his own plan for Bates' immediate future. Because he'd been kept in isolation at the Colorado Grand Hotel for two weeks, the trip to Gunnison earlier in the evening was refreshing and exciting. Bates felt ready for whatever plan Cassidy had for him. He'd come this far and was prepared to see the conclusion of what he'd come to think of as 'this damn journal business.'

Across the room, Cassidy and Brannigan faced him from the couch. Kindred, his bodyguard for the last two weeks, slouched against the wall with his arms crossed. Bates listened patiently, holding his doubts until Cassidy finished. "You actually believe this plan has the slightest chance of working?" He directed the question to Cassidy.

Cassidy laughed aloud. "Well, I'll admit I've had my share go astray in the past," he said. "However, the boys and I think we've got the problems covered. Of course, any number of things can happen and make for trouble." He looked at Bates and said, "You don't seem too happy."

"I'm not," said Bates. "I don't think you fully realize what you're up against. Elias Kotkin has killed often, and most of these killings were without cause. He's devious and he enjoys his work. And he isn't a man to be trifled with. Elias is determined to end your life—on many occasions, he's told me he's looking forward to your demise."

Kindred straightened and said, "Ah wouldna be worryin' much. These boys been 'round a while an' they oughta be able ta handle thins'."

"I'm not in a position to dispute your confidence," Bates said. "But I'm afraid you fail to understand Kotkin's abilities." He waited, and when there was no response, said, "He killed Longley and his wife in cold blood and made it look like a burglary. Do you think you can do that? Killing him could leave you in the position of having your identities uncovered. And if that happens, you could all be brought to justice and likely be incarcerated."

The smile left Cassidy's face. "We're not particularly interested in justice. We'll settle for revenge," he said, his words dripping in anger at the reminder that they were all vulnerable to the long arm of the law. He walked heavily across the room and stood in front of Bates, who sat with expression unchanged. "And how do you figure you have any right to talk about justice, or even use the word?" He moved closer to Bates. "I haven't forgotten that you had almost as much to do with Hattie and James' murders as Kotkin. So don't get to feeling too good about yourself just because you suggested this little charade," said Cassidy. He drew his gun and cocked the hammer. "I'll put you out of your misery and feed your body to Brannigan's hogs."

From across the room Brannigan softly murmured, "Easy." Cassidy turned and winked. Facing Bates again, he released the hammer and slid the gun back into its holster before returning to his seat on the couch. If anyone had asked, Cassidy would have admitted he admired Bates' calm demeanor.

Brannigan turned to Bates, "I'd take his advice and go easy, Charlie. Don't forget it was your man that killed my boy."

"He's not my man," Bates protested. "I had no knowledge of his intentions, nor knowledge that Elias' plan was to kill innocent people. At least, to the extent he did." He held up both hands before going on, "I can't make it right. I can't bring back your son or the Longleys, or any of the others."

"Tha's a fact," mumbled Kindred from where he leaned against the wall.

Bates continued, "One thing I can do is tell you how he operates. He'll isolate you one by one and pick you off. And, I think you already know this, he doesn't fight fair. He has no code, and he's unpredictable. He doesn't think like normal people."

"Yeah, that we know," said Brannigan. "When I sent the boy for the police after I found James and Hattie, I sniffed the barrel of the gun next to James. There was an empty shell in one of the chambers, but the gun hadn't been fired. Course, nobody who came to see the bodies even thought that was strange."

Bates shook his head. "Elias has always been good at covering his tracks. He can make the scene—which is what he calls his kills—look like something else entirely happened. Sorry, Mr. Brannigan, but from what you told me about your son and your employee, he covered those killings pretty well, too." The clock chimed and he looked at the mantle over the fireplace. "It's late, what are the sleeping arrangements?"

"You're in my room down the hall," said Brannigan. He stood and nodded toward the hallway. "There's a lock on the door, and the key will be on the outside."

"I'd expect nothing less," said Bates. "In the event of a nocturnal emergency, I assume someone will be sleeping on this side of the door?"

"Me and ma pal," replied Kindred. He pulled out his gun and set it on the table next to the couch. "Mind ya knock ifen one of them 'mergencies come up."

No such emergencies came up and the following morning Bates waited to hear noise to indicate someone else was stirring before he rapped on the door. Kindred, who had been lying on the couch, called, "Yawl kin come out."

Bates turned the doorknob and smiled at human nature. "Let me guess, you figured out I wasn't going anywhere."

"Nah," said Kindred, tossing the blanket aside and standing. "The lock's been busted fer years, an' Tom ain't got 'round ta fixin' it."

In the kitchen, Cassidy and Brannigan were holding their coffee cups as though they were the anchors to the day. Bates preceded Kindred into the room. "Ya gotta piss?" Brannigan asked Bates in greeting.

"Now that you mentioned it."

"Out the porch, turn left...can't miss it."

"I didn't think I'd be roughing it so soon," said Bates. At the door, he asked, "What does one use for paper?"

"Paper's on the shelf. Contrary to your eastern notions, we're pretty modern out here," said Cassidy. "But just in case a bear or some other critter is indisposed, you might want to knock first."

After Bates closed the door, Cassidy chided Brannigan. "You never heard of running water or electricity? When are you gonna to fix up this place? I can't believe that half the year Molly's gotta go through the snow to use an outhouse."

"They say electric lights will make it out here within the year," said Brannigan. He blew on the steaming coffee. "Soon as they run the wire, we'll get set up. In the meantime, I guess I could get Josh to figuring out how to get the pipes to the house for the water."

Kindred was following the conversation from the stove, two eggs ready for the frying pan. "What are you waiting for?" Brannigan asked.

"How do that city fella like his eggs?" he asked.

"He don't get a vote. Just cook 'em."

The knock on the front door didn't surprise the men, although they exchanged a glance and Kindred put aside the eggs he had been about to crack. Brannigan stepped to the front room and peeked out the window before opening the door and letting the skinny teenager into the room. "Morning, Stevie," he said. Looking past the boy, he saw the horse was breathing heavily. "Looks like you rode old Gifford pretty hard."

"Yessir, but I've got a letter for you from the railroad

office in Denver," he said, handing Brannigan a sealed envelope. "Mr. Bellison said that it come up on last night's train. He said it was direct from Mr. Floyd Braselton and that ain't nobody else read it."

As he opened the letter, Brannigan asked, "You had your breakfast yet?"

"Yessir," he said. "Ma don't let me work until I eat good. But thank you just the same."

Brannigan smiled and handed Stevie a dollar. "You best mind your ma."

"Yessir. Do you have anything that needs to go back to town? Ma asked if there was any laundry—I could tote it back so Josh don't have to bring it to town," said the boy. "And if you want, I can take your letters to the post office."

"Josh and Molly are off on a trip, and I don't have anything for you," said Brannigan. He reached into his pocket again. "You give this to your ma, and tell her it's on account. We'll be having laundry next week." He put an arm around the boy's thin shoulders and walked him back to his horse. "You remember what you're supposed to do when that train arrives?"

"Yessir," said the boy. "I hightail my ass up here to let you or Mr. Silas know."

Brannigan held the reins until Stevie was in the saddle and then spoke in a low voice to the boy for some time. He turned to go into the house. "You walk Gifford to town. You'll bust his heart if you run him again."

Back in the kitchen, Bates and Kindred were eating fried eggs and bacon with homemade bread. "Floyd did his job," Brannigan announced to Cassidy. Handing him the letter he said, "There's a private car attached to the train that's arriving day after tomorrow. It came from New York."

Bates swallowed before saying, "It's Elias."

"No question about it," agreed Cassidy. He looked up from the letter and said, "Floyd wanted us to know the reward's been raised."

"That was my idea," said Bates. He ate a last bite of bacon and set his fork on the plate. "I did it before I knew you had a better plan for the reward." He continued in a tone that the men rightly heard as defensive. "It's not much, but under the circumstances, it was the best I could come up with." Cassidy was about to ask him what circumstances could possibly limit the reward, but he let Bates go on, "About the same time Elias returned from South America and started working for the company, a number of gruesome murders were carried out in the city. All of them unsolved, of course. I don't know for sure, but I believe Kotkin is the murderer. If not, then I'm convinced he'd like to be. I couldn't accuse him, but I could increase the reward in hopes that another of his crimes would come to light and stop him. Whatever is wrong with him, whatever his sickness, there's no cure."

"Worse than I thought," said Cassidy. He looked at Kindred and then at Brannigan. "I guess we don't need another reason to make sure we do this right. Kotkin has to be taken care of, personal feelings aside," he said. Turning back to Bates, he said, "Which brings us to you. Why should he even care about you? His birthright can't be that important, at least not anymore."

Bates sat staring at his plate for a long time. Without raising his head, he said, "In the beginning, the very beginning, when I went to work for Mr. Harriman, I felt noble. I was employed by a man who had done so much for this country and would do more." He looked up at Cassidy. "I doubt you believe this, but it's true. After all, he tried to eliminate you and the others who were stealing from his railroad. But Mr. Harriman linked the country together, and for the society he lived and worked in, he was honorable. Do you know that he started homes for orphans? Good homes, not those horrid hellholes. That he organized schools for poor children? That he arranged for his wealthy partners and friends to help out?"

No one spoke.

"Mr. Harriman wasn't perfect," continued Bates. "But I could live with it, even though he and his cohorts created people like Elias. I suppose Mr. Harriman lied and cheated as much as the next man, but at least he was charitable.

What if some other person had taken his place? Mr. Harriman was certainly not the worst thing to happen to this country. Believe me, I know many others who haven't done one-tenth of the good that he did."

"Next thing you'll be telling us E. H. was a saint," interjected Cassidy. "I'm not buying it."

Bates walked to the stove, picked up a towel and used it to lift the hot coffeepot. After filling each man's cup, he opened the lid and was amazed to see eggshells floating in the coffee. "Harriman wasn't a saint," he said as he returned to the table. "But he could have been much worse. And, I don't think he realized the full extent of what Elias was to become. In the past, the use of thugs and assassins to gain financial advantage was an accepted method of doing business. I'd be lying if I didn't say I was in full accord at the time. However, I no longer have the stomach for it." He was silent as he looked from face to face. "And that's why I'm here. I can't stop Elias by myself. And although I hope you can, I don't think you'll succeed."

Cassidy asked the question for all, "Why not?"

"You asked why Elias would care about me as a hostage," said Bates. "The answer is simple—he wouldn't. He could very well be planning to take your challenge, secure the journal, and then kill you. What does he really care if I'm dead?"

"He can't get us all," said Brannigan. "Just because we've included you this far, doesn't mean we've told you everything we have in mind."

Bates considered the point. "So you have others. Don't you think Elias does too? Do you think he's coming out here unprotected? I know for a fact he has a personal bodyguard of some reputation, a young man that is guaranteed great wealth if Elias succeeds in retrieving the journal."

"Andrew Reilly," said Brannigan.

Bates was stunned. "How do you know Reilly?"

"We know," said Cassidy. "We've been watching Kotkin and anybody who associates with him. We know that beside Reilly, there are three men—no, now there're only two—who tailed Tom in New York. Unfortunately, we couldn't get to them before Kotkin killed Sundance and Etta. But this time we will."

Bates was curious. "You started to make reference to three."

"Kotkin shot his own man and made it look like Sundance did it," Cassidy said. The chiming of the clock reminded him that time was passing. He looked at Bates' silk shirt and suit pants. "I hope you brought other duds." Cassidy suddenly remembered that they had ridden to the ranch in the wagon, and it gave him the sinking feeling he'd left a detail to chance. Ignoring his uneasiness, he asked, "Can you ride a horse?"

Bates snapped, "Of course I can ride. And as for clothes, I was informed by Mr. Brannigan that Levi Strauss and Company outfits most men in Colorado, so I've come prepared." He pushed back from the table and rose. "Since you didn't lock me in last night, may I assume you're not shackling me to my mount?"

"Not much sense in that," said Cassidy. "We'll leave as soon as you change your clothes. Bring all the cold-weather gear you've got. It will take the rest of the morning to get up there." Cassidy turned to Kindred. "Get the horses saddled but leave them inside. We'll be along shortly." Without a word, the cowboy grabbed his coat and left for the barn.

Brannigan said, "I've been thinking Silas ought to go with you."

Cassidy shook his head. "We're spread too thin as it is. There's no one to spare, so Silas has to stay here until Stevie gives him the word." He looked closely at Brannigan. "I know what you're thinking, but Trenton will take care of Josh. He won't let him do anything stupid. And besides, it keeps Josh out of the line of fire."

"I suppose," he said. "Hope nothing goes off too soon."

Cassidy gestured toward the coffee pot. As Brannigan refilled their cups, he and Cassidy spoke quietly until they heard the sound of Bates coming down the hall. Cassidy stood and then finished with, "...and just like Josh, make sure it's not you who does something stupid. If I've got Kotkin figured right, unless we change the odds—which the letter should do—the guard will kill you as soon as Kotkin's around the bend."

Bates entered the kitchen carrying a sailor's woolen watch cap and his sheepskin-lined coat over one arm. New blue jeans covered the tops of well-worn leather riding boots. Bates almost sheepishly produced a pistol from inside his coat and handed it to Cassidy. "This should show you where my loyalties are," he said. "I didn't have to give it up."

Cassidy weighed the weapon in his hand before snapping open the cylinder. "Thirty-eight caliber," he noted. After a moment, he tossed the gun to Bates. "Am I taking a chance giving that back to you?" he asked.

Bates put on his coat and returned the pistol to the inner pocket. "I've made the decision to trust you. Whether you trust me, well, that's up to you."

Cassidy led the way to the back porch and whistled for Kindred to bring the horses. "Go ahead and get mounted," he ordered Bates. After Bates was in the saddle, Kindred handed him the reins of both horses and joined the others on the stoop. "Everything's ready as it's going to be?" asked Cassidy.

"Yessir," said Kindred. "Ah'm headin' ta Butte the minute Kotkin gits here."

Brannigan was still worried. "You're sure Trenton and Josh know what to do?"

"Yessir," repeated Kindred. "Them boys will be ready. There ain't nothin' gittin' by 'em."

Cassidy shook hands first with Brannigan, then with Kindred. "Okay boys," he said. "Just follow the plan and we've got it covered." After a long look at Brannigan, he stepped to his horse, grabbed the saddle horn, and vaulted into the saddle. "Let's go, Charlie. It's time."

Brannigan and Kindred watched the two men turn their horses. Unknown to Bates, Cassidy didn't start out on the usual route to Crested Butte. Instead of taking the path past the barn to the main road, he turned toward the trail that led away from the house through the back pasture.

Bates found the ride easy going at first. But once the path left the stand of aspen trees and started climbing, he found himself grasping the unfamiliar pommel of his saddle as his horse changed his gait with the terrain. The longer they rode, the more confident he became in his mount and himself. As they climbed, he was awed by his surroundings. Bates had traveled extensively throughout the West, but his appreciation of the beauty of the rugged snow-capped mountains was always from the safe confine of his private railroad car. For the first time in his life he appreciated the raw power of his environment.

After two hours of riding, Cassidy led through the small pass at the crest of the mountain, down to a snowy meadow where the river had been reduced to a stream by thick ice on either side. Cassidy climbed down and stretched for a moment, then knelt by the stream, cupped a handful of water, and brought it to his mouth. The icy water was refreshing and shocking. "Better come get some," he suggested to Bates. "You've never had water like this."

After several gulps of the sweetest water he'd ever tasted, Bates asked, "How far to Crested Butte?"

"Well, as the crow flies, not far," Cassidy replied. "But as the horse walks, it's gonna take a few hours." He went on, "You might say we're taking the long way around."

"Why?"

Carlisle removed his hat and wiped the snow from the brim. He turned and looked up at the craggy peak of Mount Taylor before answering. "Can't say for sure. But it seems to me that there's no sense hurrying if the outcome might turn bad."

"I don't get it. Why would Kotkin take this trail?"

"Because he's going to be convinced it's the right one," said Cassidy. He replaced his hat and said, "Let's go."

Cassidy's horse took the lead. Bates was still perplexed and called to Cassidy's back. "But how are you going to get Kotkin to think this is the best way—he's already been to Crested Butte. He knows the way."

"Well, I admit it's a challenge, but Hattie's the one who said we couldn't miss." Cassidy swiveled in his saddle. "She said all Tom had to do was suggest the regular route and tell Kotkin he had nothing to worry about." He faced front, and then said over his shoulder, "So when Kotkin investigates and sees our tracks, he'll follow them thinking that I might be willing to sacrifice Tom by setting up an ambush on the road to Butte."

"What happens if Kotkin takes the main road after all?"

Cassidy turned again and grinned. "Well, that's not too likely. I guess I can tell you that our bets are hedged. Kotkin has hired himself a guide."

Now thoroughly confused, Bates said, "How do you know that?"

"You ought to pay your man in Denver more money. He's susceptible to a bribe," said Cassidy. "Anyway, he's let us know what arrangements Kotkin's been making. As a matter of fact, that kid—Reilly—is the one who's been handling the deal. He's hired an Indian by the name of G. C. Ontiveros. Actually, it's his ma that's Indian, his pa is Mexican. With a little convincing, G. C. agreed to guide Kotkin and his group once they leave Tom's ranch." Cassidy was forced to face front again when his horse shied away from a low-hanging branch. They had crossed the meadow and were climbing again as the wind picked up.

Ten minutes later the trail widened at the bottom of the hill and Bates urged his horse even with Cassidy's. "You said the Indian needed convincing," he said. "What convinced him? Money?"

"You might say it's a matter of family honor." Cassidy looked away, and then added, "His sister was married to Horace Akers."

Out of the blue, Bates asked, "What do the initials stand for?"

"His ma's got a sense of humor. G. C. stands for George Custer."

XXIII

Kotkin watched from the window as his private car was pushed onto the siding, parallel to and behind the station. Irritated, he snatched his watch from his vest pocket—Reilly was already a half-hour late. Kotkin was not a man to tolerate being kept waiting. He hated tardiness. Kotkin scowled and his burly companion could tell by the way the muscles in his jaw knotted and unknotted that Kotkin was grinding his teeth. From the corner chair, the big man gave some advice. "Take it easy, boss, he'll get here."

Kotkin threw him a look. He did not appreciate being told to take it easy by anyone, especially a hired thug like Hopkins. The gun hanging from Kotkin's shoulder holster looked somehow more menacing than the holstered sidearms of the men on Gunnison's streets. Glaring at Hopkins, he angrily said, "Get off your ass. Go see about the supplies."

"What about the—"

"Get out," snarled Kotkin. "Find Finley and make sure everything's ready." Hopkins noted his employer's pale face and set thin lips. He wisely decided not to test Kotkin's mood further, and set out to find the fourth member of their party. It wasn't hard. Jed Finley was bellied up to the bar in the saloon around the corner. As Hopkins was leaving, he saw Reilly walk around the corner of the train station and called back to Kotkin, "He's coming," and quickly closed the door.

Reilly met him on the siding. "Where are you going? I said to stick with him."

"He ain't in a great mood," said Hopkins. "He sent me to find Jed and check on the supplies."

Reilly was accustomed to Kotkin's orders superseding his own. He took the three steps in one stride and stepped into the railway car without knocking. Reilly had been around long enough to know that his mentor was furious. Hoping to stave off the verbal explosion that was sure to come, he reported on his morning's activities before he was asked. "I paid Ontiveros, and he's ready as soon as we are."

When Kotkin's entourage arrived in Gunnison, Reilly and Hopkins were dispatched to find G. C. Ontiveros, whose reputation was legendary as a guide and tracker. But Ontiveros had balked and convincing him took longer than Reilly expected. He sent Hopkins back to let Kotkin know that he was close to convincing the Indian to guide the party to Crested Butte.

"What was the problem?" Kotkin demanded.

Reilly was straightforward with his boss. "He wanted his fee up front, but wouldn't say so at first. Once I got that out of him, I gave him the two hundred and explained what we wanted. He'll be along shortly."

"That was all?" asked Kotkin.

"That was it."

Kotkin sat and gestured to the other chair. "There are a couple of things we need to settle." He leaned forward with his hands on his knees and said, "First, what's your opinion of Brannigan as our hostage?"

"It's a smart move. Brannigan's a longtime friend of Cassidy's, and his death would be a real loss," replied Reilly. He thought for a minute and then said, "There's no chance that Cassidy would have put up Brannigan's son as hostage, and Kindred was never part of their gang." After more thought, "Given the situation with Longley's wife, there is no possibility of Cassidy bringing the son's wife into the picture, so it had to be Tom."

Kotkin sat back in thought. Rubbing his finger along the bridge of his nose, he said, "And according to all reports, Tom Brannigan is an expert gunman, so why would we want him against us?" He rose and answered his own question. "By agreeing to Tom, we're removing one threat before the game begins."

Reilly moved on. "What was the second item you wanted to discuss?"

"Hopkins and Finley. We have to dispose of them as soon as we have the journal and have taken care of the others," said Kotkin. "They know too much, and that which they don't know, even these low-breds could figure out." He stood over Reilly and asked, "Is this a problem?"

"There's no other way," the young man answered without hesitation. "I don't like the idea of killing in cold blood, but as you said, we can hardly let them live." Glancing out the window, he pointed and said, "Speaking of the devil, here they come." After a moment, Reilly asked, "What about Ontiveros?"

Kotkin reached for his fur-lined coat. He was wearing a khaki hunting shirt and cord trousers that were neatly tucked in the tops of his boots, giving him a military appearance. He took a last look in the mirror before saying, "We'll have to see how much he learns, or guesses. When we leave here, I want no loose ends." He led the way out of the rail car and joined the men. "Where's the Indian?" he asked Finley.

"Waiting with the horses," he said. Jed Finley was as thin—almost to the point of stringy—as Luke Hopkins was thick and muscular. His straw-colored hair peeked out from under the brim of a bowler hat. He was dressed in cord pants and wearing a heavy plaid jacket over a thick sweater. He carried a pistol stuck in his belt, but Finley's true forte was his deadly precision with a knife. He had other talents as well. He had broken into some of the finest homes in New York. Kotkin had used Finley and Hopkins as a team when strong-arm tactics were called for.

Luke Hopkins was bullet-headed and tall—just a shade under six feet. He weighed close to two hundred and fifty pounds, of which little was fat. At ten, he was already working in the Pennsylvania coal mines. He was seventeen when he abandoned his widowed mother and seven younger siblings. In the mines, Hopkins had developed an expertise with dynamite. His training couldn't have come from a more informed source—his own father. But after Big Mike Hopkins disregarded the prescribed wait time for a hang-fire and was standing next to the charge when it exploded,

Luke decided it was time to get into a safer line of work. He arrived in New York a month later and met Finley, who was able to arrange work for the strong boy. It was through Finley that Kotkin met and eventually hired Hopkins for his own projects.

G. C. Ontiveros was waiting for the others in front of the station. He had checked each mount, making sure the saddles were tightly cinched and that the supplies were evenly distributed on the two pack mules. Thirty-six-year-old Ontiveros did not fit the image of an Indian held by many Easterners. He wore a Stetson, blue jeans, and a sheepskin coat, and when Ontiveros tipped his hat, Kotkin noticed that the Indian's short hair was neatly combed. "Ontiveros," the Indian said, leaning down and extending his callused hand. As he did, a boy riding a swayback horse cantered by. He waved at Ontiveros, who ignored the greeting.

Kotkin said, "I trust you understand that you are to take us to the Brannigan ranch and then to Crested Butte?"

Ontiveros spoke without a trace of an accent. "Yeah, although I don't see why you need a guide."

Reilly spoke as he mounted, "I thought I explained that. We have a situation that might cause someone to get antsy with a rifle. We want to make sure we can get through on back trails."

Shrugging, and without another word, Ontiveros turned his horse. Finley and Hopkins awkwardly swung up into the saddles and took charge of the mules. In single file, the five men started down the street. When they reached the corner, a woman stepped out of a house with a package. "G. C.," she called. "You forgot your other shirt."

Ontiveros reined in his horse and let the others pass. He took the bundle before swiveling in the saddle and pushing it into his saddlebag. "Thank you kindly," he said aloud. He spoke quietly with the woman for another moment before gently kicking his horse into a trot and taking his place in the front of the procession.

Leaving the outskirts of Gunnison, Kotkin caught up with Reilly and asked, "What was that all about?"

"That was Horace Akers' widow," he said. "She moved back to Gunnison with her children to be near her family." Adding, "She takes in laundry now."

Three miles out of town the young boy riding the sway-back at a walk passed the men on his return to Gunnison. This time Ontiveros nodded at the youngster, who grinned as he rode by. No one spoke until they arrived at the open gates of the Brannigan ranch.

"This is it," said Ontiveros. Not knowing that Kotkin had already been to the Brannigan ranch, he pointed and said, "Barn on the right, house over there."

Reilly said to Kotkin, "Just you and me. Although, I don't think they'd object to G. C. riding in with us."

"Go on ahead," Kotkin replied. As they started up the road, he turned to Finley and Hopkins. "Jed, you go first. Take the main road—I doubt they'll be any trouble, but Luke will be following you, just in case." He looked to Hopkins, "You take the same road but give him a half-hour. Any sign of trouble, you and Jed get back here. Otherwise, be at Brannigan's saloon at noon tomorrow." He wheeled his horse and caught up with the others halfway up the road.

As they rounded the corner of the barn, Kotkin looked around. Even in winter, the ranch looked well-maintained. He asked himself what he expected. Had he thought that the older son's death would cause an observable change in the Brannigan's standards? Kotkin realized that he was disappointed that life went on after the tragedy he'd inflicted.

Ontiveros led to the back of the house—allowing Kotkin and Reilly to dismount as he looked around. Kotkin noted the Indian's scrutinizing look and asked, "Notice anything?"

"Yeah," said Ontiveros. Pointing to the tracks leading from the house, he said, "Somebody's taken the back way and not too long ago. The tracks are from two horses, but only one of them was rode. Sometimes the back trail is used for hunting, which would explain why." He pointed in the direction of the ranch road. "And three horses there—with riders—the tracks back on the road say they're headed to Butte."

Reilly looked at Kotkin. "No surprise," he said.

"It makes me wonder if Finley and Hopkins will be running into trouble."

Inside the house, Brannigan and Kindred had been waiting. They drank their coffee at the kitchen table and had tried a few hands of poker to settle their nerves and help pass the time. Stevie had done his job and let them know that Kotkin and his men were on their way to the ranch. At the first sound of horses coming up the road, Kindred took his cup to the tub, washed and dried it before putting it back on the shelf. He returned to the table, pulled his coat from the chair, and started out the door. "Yawl be careful."

Brannigan nodded. "It isn't like I've got a choice," he said. "If something goes wrong, I know you'll take care of my family."

"Ah promised, an' ah'll live up ta it," said Kindred. He walked down the hall to the back bedroom and climbed out the window. When he heard Brannigan greet the visitors, he walked away from the house into the cover of a stand of aspen trees. His horse that had been tied to a tree an hour ago was waiting. Kindred led the horse deeper into the trees before swinging into the saddle and starting off in a direction away from Crested Butte. He followed a route he had scouted the previous day and turned east to cross a neighbor's ranch and then turned on a diagonal that would lead him back to the main road to Crested Butte, well beyond the Brannigan ranch.

Brannigan stood as the three men entered the kitchen. His normally ruddy face lost all color as he stared at his son's murderer. He could taste the satisfaction of reaching for his gun hanging on the back of his chair, aiming between Kotkin's eyes, and pulling the trigger. Brannigan's color returned when he took in the rest of the party. "What's that half-breed doing here?" He pointed at the Indian. "He's not staying in my house."

As if by magic, a knife appeared in Ontivero's hand. He waved it back and forth, the steel gleaming menacingly. "You want to die, old man?" he snarled. "I've had my fill of you and your stinking family."

Reilly stepped between the two. "You didn't tell me you were acquainted."

"Put the knife away," Kotkin ordered. He sounded almost bored. "This man is my guide."

"What do you need a guide for?" Brannigan asked. "You managed to find Crested Butte before."

Kotkin didn't answer. He moved around the kitchen and noted the single cup, checked out the washtub. He pulled out a chair. "Finding the town is not what concerns me," said Kotkin. He casually leaned back and crossed his arms over his chest, resting his hand inches from the gun hidden beneath his coat. "Perhaps we should get down to business," he said. "Ontiveros, step outside."

Brannigan sat in the chair that Kindred had left warm and reached for his cup. There was no way to hide his shaking hands. They did not go unnoticed by Kotkin. *Is it fear or rage?* he thought. "Why should I believe that you have Bates? If Charles is dead, there's no deal and no need to keep you around."

Pointing at the windowsill, Brannigan said, "See for yourself."

Kotkin opened the envelope and emptied the contents. A gold watch with chain and fob still attached slipped out, along with a heavy ring. Kotkin meticulously examined the items before placing them in a row on the table. "These trinkets don't prove he's alive."

"Guess you're gonna have to go on my word," said Brannigan. "There's a letter in that envelope. You'd better read what Charlie wrote."

Kotkin quickly scanned the letter. "It seems he's quite concerned over his predicament. I must applaud Cassidy for having Charles expound on some of the personal issues only he and I would know. And while it doesn't necessarily mean he's alive, it does make it more plausible. Therefore, for the time being, I choose to believe you."

"You ready to do business then?" asked Brannigan. Kotkin nodded. "You're gonna go to Crested Butte and meet with Butch. I'm staying here with this young fellow?"

Reilly spoke up. "What's between you and Ontiveros?"

"Damn renegade's been stealing my horses," said Brannigan. "I can't prove it, but I know it's him. In the old days, I would have shot him or had him hung. Oughta do it now."

"Andrew will have the honor of guarding you. Should there be any trouble from you, it will be no surprise that, on my orders, Andrew will kill you," Kotkin said. "Andrew, search the house. He could have someone lurking about."

Kotkin did not look at Brannigan when he spoke. "You and Charles have to be brought together for the exchange. The location is unknown, at least to me. I assume it will be highly visible and safe for both parties." Brannigan didn't reply.

Reilly had his gun drawn when he came into the kitchen. "House is clear. I'll tell the Indian to check the barn."

"Very good," Kotkin said. "You can put your gun away. So far, they've lived up to their end of the bargain." He motioned to Reilly to follow him to the back porch. Once outside, Kotkin tried to gauge the young man's resolve. "You know what to do."

The weather had turned colder and the wind was raw. Reilly tightened the collar of his coat around his neck then pulled his watch from his pocket, checked the time, and said, "I'll take care of Brannigan. After that, I'll be watching from the background in Crested Butte. Should be no problem to blend in, no one knows me except our people."

Ontiveros handed the reins to Kotkin and watched him swing up into the saddle. "We're going to take the back trail," Kotkin informed him.

Reilly watched until they disappeared into the trees at the end of the pasture. Prior to entering the kitchen, he checked his gun, making sure all cylinders were loaded.

Brannigan sat nursing cold coffee and anxious for the answer to one question. "Which way they going?"

"Up the trail," Reilly replied. "Kotkin's sure that Cassidy has something planned for the road." He filled two fresh cups with coffee and, after a hesitation, reached for the bottle sitting on the shelf. He poured whiskey in the cups and slid one across the table. "Drink it," he ordered. "You'll need it." The older man didn't need convincing. Reilly pulled Brannigan's scarf from the jacket slung over the chair beside him and wrapped the ends around each hand.

❧

The ride to Crested Butte had been uneventful for Finley and Hopkins. It was impossible to remain behind Finley, and Hopkins soon caught up with his partner. In addition to his remarkable lack of riding proficiency, Finley had to dismount to stretch his cramping legs. The two men rode into Crested Butte side by side, making Josh Brannigan's and Trenton Carver's job easier.

Trenton and Josh waited on a bluff two miles outside of town—Josh, tired of being stuck at his father-in-law's ranch, was happy that Cassidy had allowed him to help. Cassidy's plan was for Carver to follow his man to whichever hotel, or whorehouse, he put up in, and then catch up with Josh, who would be following the second man. Both were disappointed when their respective assignments appeared in tandem on the tree-lined road. This was too easy. They dutifully followed Finley and Hopkins to the San Franciscan, an establishment on the north edge of town that featured a Victorian façade and the fanciest array of prostitutes in the county. For the right price, a man could rent a bedroom, as long as he also rented one of the fifteen working girls for his stay—payable in advance.

The proprietor of the San Franciscan was a rotund middle-aged woman who went by the name of Gaylelynn Schneider. After her lumber-baron husband met an untimely death when he ingested arsenic delivered in his coffee, the madam had become proficient at her trade in the fleshspots of San Francisco. A few years later, after the suspicious death of her second husband—the house bookkeeper—she left California. In 1895, Madam Gaylelynn arrived in Crested Butte on the noon stage. Within a month she and

Tom Brannigan were business partners. He helped her resume her career locally by selling the enterprising widow an interest in the brothel. A few years later, she'd convinced him to sell the remainder.

Luckily for the male population of Crested Butte, the madam developed a taste for her own staff and never sought a third marriage. Over the years, she had gained some measure of acceptance by the businessmen of the mining town. Brannigan considered her a friend and important confidant.

Recalling their first visit to Crested Butte, Finley and Hopkins headed directly to the San Franciscan and reserved two back rooms for their stay. Without Kotkin's constant evil eye on them, they forgot or ignored their boss's admonition not to be seen together.

Josh and Trenton sat bundled up in the barbershop rocking chairs across the street to wait for their prey to leave the brothel. When Finley and Hopkins reappeared, they headed toward the Bucket of Blood. Carver and Brannigan watched them settle into heavy drinking and left, setting off in the opposite direction to the back door of Brannigan's establishment.

Kindred opened the door just enough to look through the small crack and say, "Ah thought ah wuz gonna have ta come lookin' fer ya." He stepped aside to let them enter.

Hands clasped behind his head, Cassidy leaned back in a cane chair, his boots resting on a barrel of pickles. It was hard to tell whether Carver was excited or just proud when he launched into explaining in detail the arrival and whereabouts of Kotkin's men. "You boys did good," said Cassidy when the young man had finished. His blue eyes twinkled in the light shining through the window as he said, "Acorn doesn't fall far from the tree. Your pa would have been proud of you, Trenton. You two might as well go back. You need to keep those bastards in sight from now on."

Kindred stood and stretched. "Ah'll hep the boys with thet." He led them through the saloon and out the back door. Kindred waited to speak until they were outside. After minutes of intense back and forth—much of it by Josh—the young men were soon nodding in agreement. Kindred slapped them on the shoulder and sent them on their way.

Cassidy hadn't moved when Kindred walked back into the storeroom. "You must have done some kind of riding to get past those guys."

"Nah," said Kindred. "They wuz so bad, ah past 'em 'fore ah caught up with the road. Truth be told, ah coulda walked ta Butte fasta than them boys rode here."

"Kotkin and G. C. should be getting here soon. Wouldn't you think?"

"Yessir. G. C. said he'd keep him outta Butte 'til nightfall. If Kotkin does what he done before, he'll be stayin' at Sanford's hotel," said Kindred. He peered at Cassidy. "He'll be lookin' fer ya soon as he gits here."

The grin reappeared and Carlisle's eyes again twinkled. "You think Kotkin's going to need G. C. to scout, or do you think he can find this place on his own?" he asked.

Kindred almost laughed, but the truth was, he was nervous. "Ya best be gettin' serious," he said. "This Kotkin ain't a man ta be trifled with. He's gonna try an kill ya quick, an' ifen he's got somethin' to say 'bout the matter, it ain't gonna be no fair fight."

Cassidy looked over at the cowboy as his smile disappeared. He was about to speak, but Kindred interrupted him. "Ah ain't tellin' ya nothin' ya don't already know," he said. "Tom's tole me all about ya. He says ya kin talk a bear back to the cave ifen it's what ya want. But Kotkin ain't no bear—he's a killa. An ah'll say it 'gain: he's comin' ta kill ya. Ta say nothin' of Tom. An' me an' Josh throwed in fer good measure."

"Silas, my friend, you say it well," said Cassidy. Feet hitting the floor with a resounding thud, he stood and said, "Sooner we get up to the mine, the better I'll feel."

A mile out of town Cassidy spoke. "You know, what it comes down to is I kill Kotkin, or he kills all of us." The brim of Kindred's hat dipped, acknowledging the truth. Cassidy continued, "I won't mind if he gets me as long as I take him.

I don't figure any middle ground in this deal. He's dead, I'm dead, or we're both dead. But there's no compromise and no turning back. That's all there is to it."

Flakes began appearing in front of their hats and it wasn't long before the snow turned into a flurry. Cassidy reined in his horse and stopped. He looked up at the gray clouds, amused expression had returned to his face. "Well now... look at this. Things are starting to go our way."

XXIV

The ride from Brannigan's ranch over Indian Pass had been long and arduous, and though many of the trees were snow covered, their lower branches brushed Kotkin's coat with dirt and grime as he followed Ontiveros. Closing the door to his second-story hotel room overlooking Elk Street, Kotkin made sure the curtains covered the solitary window before tossing his coat and shirt on the bed. He poured water into the washbasin and scrubbed his face and upper body. As he toweled off, he heard someone in the hall.

Reflexively, Kotkin turned down the lamp and reached for the gun lying on the bed under his coat. He slid it out of the holster and backed into the corner to wait. When the footsteps stopped outside his door, he silently thumbed back the hammer. A light knock was followed by the whispered words, "It's Reilly."

"Come in," said Kotkin. He remained in the shadows until the door opened and the light from the hallway showed the figure to be his assistant. The gun hit the bed with a thump and he turned up the lamp. "When did you get here?" he asked.

"About two hours ago. Ontiveros must have taken you the very long way."

"He was doing what I asked. One cannot be too careful," Kotkin said as he pulled a starched shirt out of his bag. He slid the shirt over his shoulders and buttoned the front, meticulously avoiding creasing the smooth material. "Did you take care of Brannigan?" he asked before stepping to the mirror to examine the collar for smudges.

"We'll not be bothered by him again," said Reilly. He slouched against the door staring at Kotkin's back. He could feel the greasiness of sweat across his forehead. When

Kotkin turned from the mirror and eyed him, Reilly said, "It wasn't easy."

Kotkin nodded as though he understood. "It never is the first time," he said. "How did you do it?"

"I used the scarf he wore in cold weather. It was hanging with his coat." Reilly pulled his handkerchief from his pocket and wiped his face as he said, "There wasn't a struggle. He seemed resigned to it. I carried him down the hall and laid him on the bed. Perhaps his children will think he died of natural causes."

"Good. Less likely that any suspicion will be raised. But do you care what his children think?" Kotkin asked, as he put on his coat.

"The end will justify the means, but cold-blooded killing is unnerving."

"It had to be done," he said. "Let's move on. Tomorrow I'm meeting Cassidy at the saloon, and if all goes well, I'll have the journal this time tomorrow. I assume you and Hopkins will be taking care of the other arrangements?"

Reilly straightened, then nodded. "He and Finley disobeyed your instructions and are staying at the whorehouse, just as you said they would. It's a wonder no one knew they were with you the last time, to say nothing of my wondering how they've managed to stay alive as long as they have," he said. "I caught up with them at the aptly named Bucket of Blood saloon. They weren't drunk yet, so I was able to confirm that Hopkins has the explosives. We'll leave in the morning as planned."

"You've done well," said Kotkin. He paused once again to examine himself in the mirror. "I'll be having dinner here in the hotel. As I said earlier, there's nothing to be gained by taking chances, so make sure you keep Jed and Luke out of trouble—the best thing is to encourage them to make use of the whorehouse. Luke, in particular, has to be able to destroy that mine." After a slight pause, he added, "And everyone in it."

Reilly started out the door but stopped to ask, "How are you so sure the mine is where Cassidy has hidden the journal?"

"Where else could it be? In the mine it would be impossible to find. Plus, it makes a perfect killing ground for him and his men," said Kotkin. "But look at it this way, if I'm wrong and the journal is elsewhere, we'll still end up with it. And as for Charles, now that Brannigan's out of the picture, things do not seem to be going in his favor."

⁂

The following morning, Reilly stepped into the bitter cold. He'd taken a room at a boardinghouse on the edge of town, as far away from the shenanigans of Hopkins and Finley that he could get and still watch them. When he rolled out at four-thirty, with no moon, and the sun an hour from rising, the darkness made the air even more frigid. Reilly saddled his horse and led her out to the street where he tied the reins to the rail. He returned to the stable to retrieve the three boxes Hopkins had left under a pile of straw in the pack mule's stall. Reilly wasn't nervous about loading the dynamite, the cold air made him think the material would be less volatile and safer to handle.

Leading the mule out to the street, he was relieved to find Hopkins waiting. Reilly ignored the whispered greeting by untying his horse and vaulting into the saddle. He tossed the pack rope to Hopkins and said, "I'll lead. You handle the mule."

"Aren't afraid of a little dynamite, are you?"

"Just do as you're told." Reilly turned his horse and started down Maroon Street before turning north on Butte Avenue. Five minutes later, they'd cleared the outskirts of Crested Butte and Reilly was already watching for the cross trail that would lead them to the Sadie Mae Mine.

It wasn't until the trail began to climb that Hopkins spoke. "How far up is this place?"

Reilly swiveled in his saddle. "Why?" he asked. "Does altitude affect dynamite?"

"Shouldn't," he replied. "The only thing that can really hurt is if it starts to sweat." Pointing at the snow-covered trees, he said, "But there's little chance of that happening. So how far do we have to go?"

"Not far," conceded Reilly. He reined in his horse and waited for the other man to pull even. "Listen, if you don't get this right, none of us will get paid. Of course, that won't be a problem because we'll all be dead."

"I'll plant this stuff in a way that nobody will see," said Hopkins. "And I'll guarantee something else. I'm not going to be around when it blows. There won't be nothing left after I get done."

They came over a rise and spotted the old cabin nestled in the valley. The sun peeked over the top of the mountain with enough light to make the entrance to the mineshaft, carved into the face of the mountain halfway up the trail, visible. Reilly stopped his horse and dismounted, tossing his reins to Hopkins. Walking in the shadows that covered one side of the road, Reilly approached the cabin. The corral and lean-to that served as a shelter for horses were empty. At the door of the cabin, he called out. There was no answer, not a sound of any kind, but he still pulled the pistol from beneath his jacket and cautiously entered.

Hopkins waited until Reilly reappeared before leading the horses and the pack mule down to the cabin. He tied the mule to the post and then led the horses to the corral, shutting the gate behind them. Reilly was waiting on the porch, a lantern in each hand. Gesturing at the trail in back of the cabin, he said, "The entrance is up there. I don't think the mule can make it all the way."

"We'll take him as far as he'll go, then we'll carry the dynamite together," said Hopkins. Calm had settled over him—when it came to explosives, he knew what he was doing. "Wouldn't be good if we dropped one of them. Even if it made it halfway down before it exploded, it'd kill us."

The altitude and poor footing on the last fifty yards of the trail made the work dangerous, and even Hopkins was breathing heavily by the time the boxes of dynamite had been set at the entrance. Taking one of the lanterns, Hopkins went to examine the mine. Reilly went back to retrieve the third box that contained the rolls of fuse cord. Reilly was waiting with the cord when Hopkins emerged from the mine. Hopkins opened the first box and began bundling the dynamite into groups of five sticks using the cord to secure the crude bombs.

As Hopkins worked he explained what he was doing. "The second level is held up by heavy timber—God knows how long it took them to build that—which, with charges in the right spot, will blow easy. The main shaft will go a few seconds behind and cover the lower level. There's no chance a man could live though this."

"How are you going to control the explosions?"

Hopkins held up a piece of fuse. "By making sure the length is right," he explained. "The safest way to blow this is from right here. I'll light the second level, give it a five count, and then the other gets lit. That'll give us a couple minutes to get our asses down that trail." He went back to work, using the length of his arm to measure the fuse.

Reilly explored the shaft to orientate himself in the event something went wrong. Upon return, he found Hopkins waiting, bundles of explosive set in each box. "I'm taking the cord. You're going to carry a box," he explained to Reilly. "Once I'm down to the ladder, you hand me the charges, bundle by bundle. Got that? You're not carrying that box down the ladder."

"Whatever you say," agreed Reilly. There was no fear in his voice and his hands remained steady, but proximity to the explosives was not easy. Part of his uneasiness was the realization that his life was currently in the hands of a man who Reilly did not considered to be the brightest of operators.

Hopkins, however, was all business and placed the dynamite without a hitch. Reilly admired the professional attitude Hopkins exhibited. He directed Reilly, and in less than two hours the charges were placed. Hopkins ran the cord, covering all traces with a light coating of sandy dirt.

In the days when the mine had been active, the search for gold had included digging behind the support timbers. This was helpful to Hopkins as it provided more space to secure the bundles and less handling of the dynamite. When Reilly followed Hopkins out the entrance he was relieved.

Hopkins coiled the end of the cords and hid them behind a pile of rocks. He brushed his hands on the seat of his pants and said, "Unless you want to go in there again, we're done."

Once back at the cabin, both men stopped to wash in the stream. The cold hadn't stopped them from sweating while they handled the dynamite. They mounted their horses and headed back to Crested Butte.

The trip back went much faster than the ride up. As they entered Crested Butte, Reilly pulled his watch from his vest. It was eleven o'clock—plenty of time left for his next job.

***

When Kotkin pushed through the swinging doors of Brannigan's, he had no expectation of recognizing Butch Cassidy. He expected Cassidy had altered his appearance as much as possible and was convinced the former outlaw would not resemble the photograph he'd seen. As he stepped inside the establishment, all talk came to a halt. Kotkin smiled to himself. He knew his dress, if not his demeanor, would call attention. In fact, had Kotkin been wearing a peaked military cap, most would have assumed the tall man was a lost Army engineer. Looking around the room, he spied Finley leaning with his back against the bar, and Hopkins sitting in a chair in front of a window, pointedly ignoring Kotkin by looking out to the street. Pleased his men were in place, but wondering where Reilly could be, Kotkin's eyes went from face to face around the room until he saw a man sitting by himself at a table in the corner.

He had found Butch Cassidy.

As Kotkin weaved his way through the tables to Cassidy, he realized that other than a well-trimmed beard that matched the silver of his hair, the outlaw had changed little from the photograph. Cassidy didn't appear to be watching as Kotkin approached. He let Kotkin get within a foot of the table before saying, "You must be Kotkin."

"That's correct, Mr. Cassidy. Or should I call you by another name?"

"Butch," said Cassidy. "There's no need for you to know

the name I'm running under." He stared at Kotkin, thin-lipped smile in place.

"Very well," said Kotkin. He leaned back in the chair and measured up his adversary. Kotkin expected the hatred that radiated from Cassidy, but he was momentarily taken back when Cassidy's smile turned into a grin. In exasperation, he said, "Are we to play games?"

"Don't think so," replied Cassidy. "Just wondering. Do you use guns? Or would a knife be your favorite?"

Kotkin hesitated for a moment. "Whatever's appropriate and will get me the kill I need." Now irritated, he said, "What difference does it make? Frankly, what I do or how I do it is of no importance. Gun, knife, hand-to-hand—it's all the same." Leaning forward, he went on, "Let's stop this nonsense. We each have a hostage, so let us get down to business and get this over with. You have an article, and I want it."

"You in a hurry?"

"Not particularly, but I fail to see why we should prolong this."

Standing, Cassidy said, "Come with me." He led to a door at the back of the saloon and entered. Kotkin glanced back at Finley before following. Three feet inside the storeroom, he stopped as Cassidy shut the door behind them.

A small man—who Kotkin knew to be Silas Kindred—stood in the far corner, a gun in his hand. In the center of the room, Bates sat trussed in a chair with a bandanna securely tied around his mouth. If he was surprised or relieved to see Kotkin, he didn't show it. Kotkin looked him over, raised an eyebrow, and said to Bates, "You seem to be in a predicament."

Cassidy walked behind the chair and removed the gag. Bates tried to swallow, then turned his head and spat on the floor. "About time," he said to Kotkin in a raspy voice. "Have you made the arrangements to get me out of this?"

"Perhaps," said Kotkin. He looked at Cassidy.

Cassidy replied to both men. "As long as we reach an agreement on future reprisals. You people created a situation that didn't need to exist. One way or another, me and the boys are going to make sure the situation is resolved. It's your choice. Otherwise, neither of you get to go home."

In the silence, Bates was first to speak. "Elias, I fail to see an alternative," he said to Kotkin. "Your usual methods won't apply in this situation, you'll have to negotiate."

A shadow crossed Kotkin's face before he said, "You know I'll do whatever it takes to get us back to New York. And when we do, rest assured we'll be in possession of the journal." He stopped as Cassidy pulled the bandanna back over Bates' mouth. "I assume this means we're finished here," said Kotkin. Without looking back at Bates, he followed Cassidy into the saloon. As they entered the room, he made sure that his men were in the same spots. Reilly was standing at the opposite end of the bar.

Cassidy looked straight ahead as he continued through the saloon to the street. Outside, he asked, "Which horse is yours?"

"Where are we going?" countered Kotkin, as he pointed at a roan tied to the rail.

"Mount up," ordered Cassidy. He pulled himself into the saddle of the dark gray horse that had been tethered near Kotkin's. "You'll know when we get there," he said. Cassidy turned his horse and started down Elk Street, leaving Kotkin behind.

Before Cassidy reached the end of the street, Kotkin caught up with him. He settled in the saddle for the ride, secure in the knowledge that whatever Cassidy's plan, it had no chance of working.

In the saloon, Reilly waited ten minutes before signaling the small bartender, who had returned to his bartending duties after Kotkin and Cassidy left, and quietly asked, "Care to talk about a journal?"

Kindred gave a nod and walked toward the storeroom. Reilly locked eyes with Finley and followed the cowboy. Finley tossed off his whiskey and headed for the door while Hopkins remained at his table, his full attention now shifted to Reilly.

Kindred was holding the door when the barrel of the gun hidden under the heavy coat jammed his ribs. "Just go on in,"

whispered Reilly. "And don't even think of reaching for it." He
slid the gun from Kindred's holster and quickly glanced back
at Hopkins. To the other patrons leaning against the bar,
nothing seemed out of the ordinary. In fact, no one in the
room paid any attention.

Once the door closed, Hopkins went out to the street,
hurrying down the block to where Finley held their horses.
After mounting, Hopkins waited for the stringy man to
struggle into the saddle, before asking, "Will Reilly take
care of him?"

"Which one?" asked Finley. "The cowboy or Bates?" They
started down the street in the same direction as Kotkin and
Cassidy.

XXV

It had been snowing lightly since early morning and a smattering of snowflakes continued to drop. But even in the cold air, the flakes melted against the warmth of exposed cheeks and Kotkin had to continually wipe the wetness with the back of his glove. The cold and wet caused him to become more irritated than he'd been at Cassidy's irksome grins. By now, Kotkin had guessed their destination, but the ride to the mine took much longer than his first trip — even the terrain seemed different. Ahead of him, Cassidy never once looked back, leaving himself exposed to an attack.

Kotkin was about to protest the length of the ride when they crested a hill and Cassidy spoke. "You know where we are," he said, pointing at the cabin. "That's where you killed Will."

With the knowledge that whatever he said to Cassidy no longer matter, Kotkin said, "I don't deny it." He saw a way to get under Cassidy's skin and made no attempt to hide his delight in the memory of his last visit. "Your young friend wasn't as forthcoming as I'd anticipated. He never revealed your identity or whereabouts, which means he knew neither. No one could stand up to that type of punishment."

Cassidy swallowed his hatred and asked, "What'd you use?" From inside his coat, Kotkin produced the cosh. After a glance, Cassidy said, "You're a brave man."

"Are you trying to 'rile' me, Butch?" asked Kotkin. With his quarry in hand, his dead eyes were now shining as his anticipation welled up. Hoping Cassidy had help, the cosh went back inside his coat—Kotkin wanted to prolong tormenting Cassidy. "You can't upset me. This is my game."

"If it's your game, why haven't you killed me?"

"Need I remind you that you have Charles," he said. "Besides, I assume the journal is well hidden within the mine, and that I'd never find it on my own."

Cassidy grinned, knowing that it would irritate Kotkin. "You're not as dumb as I thought." He prodded his horse and led the way to the cabin. "We walk from here," he said to Kotkin. The mine entrance loomed like an open tomb above the cabin.

The snow was falling harder and sections of the trail were crusted with ice making each step more treacherous than the last. The threat of slipping over the edge into the dark canyon was constant. Cassidy remained in the lead, causing Kotkin to marvel at the outlaw's steady tread and steadier nerves. He seemed not to care about the slippery trail, Kotkin's presence, or the fact that only one man would leave the mine. Halfway up the trail, Kotkin became obsessed with the idea that by reaching out he could push Cassidy over the cliff. Just like that. One little push. But he had come for the journal, not for amusement, and it would be impossible to find the journal without Cassidy. Kotkin reined in his urge. But the need to kill ate at him.

At the entrance of the mine, Cassidy found the lone lantern and lit the wick. The light cast a dull-yellow glow into the mouth of the cavern illuminating a small area in front of the men. Without a word, he led Kotkin through the second tunnel. They reached the hole in the floor that led to the tunnel below, then stopped.

Kotkin's anticipation again rose, a precursor to a killing rage. As his heart began to race, he bit the inside of his cheek to calm himself, savoring the coppery taste of blood. He looked at the ladder and picked up two small rocks. Flipping them back and forth in his hands, he asked, "How do you propose we do this?"

"I'm going down first. That leaves you in the dark, except for the light coming up the shaft," said Cassidy. For a brief moment, a grin appeared, before he said, "The ladder's been fixed. I'll even hold it for you when you come down." Secure in the knowledge that Finley and Hopkins were now outside the mine and would soon be following, Kotkin agreed.

Holding the lantern in one hand, Cassidy swung his leg over the ladder and climbed down. Before the light disappeared and blackness descended around him, Kotkin stepped in the direction of the entrance and knocked the rocks together. Seconds later, he was rewarded with a low whistle. His backup was in place. Cautiously finding his way back to the top of the ladder, Kotkin was confident that Reilly had also done his job and would have by now followed to the mine. Bates and Kindred were assuredly dead and of no future bother. That left only Cassidy. Kotkin had no illusions about the outcome; he even hoped the old outlaw had the sense to arm himself.

"Come on down," called Cassidy. He stepped back up on the first rung of the ladder and held the lantern over his head.

With the light shining the length of the ladder, Kotkin had no trouble reaching the floor of the tunnel. Cassidy backed far enough away from the ladder to make it harder for Kotkin to jump off and overpower him. Kotkin stepped off the ladder and moved in Cassidy's direction. "Where is it?"

Cassidy lifted the lantern until the light shown on a metal box in the center of the floor, not hidden at all. "You'll need a key."

Kotkin stopped. Even in the poor light he could see the movement of Cassidy's hand and reached out to catch the small key attached to a black ribbon. Watching Cassidy out of the corner of his eye, he knelt next to the box. He opened the padlock, held his breath, and lifted the lid. "Bring the light over here," he demanded. He lifted the book out, opened the cover, and tried to read the print. In the poor light, he couldn't make out if he was holding the journal of E. H. Harriman, or, for all he knew, Cassidy's bible. "I said, bring the lantern, damn you."

Cassidy had moved back toward the ladder. Lifting the lantern, he said, "It's your journal, you bring it over here."

Kotkin moved to the center of the light and furiously began turning the pages. In only a short time, he was convinced it was his father's journal. Looking up at Cassidy, who was staring at the book, he was about to speak when Cassidy said, *"That's* what caused all this killing?"

Kotkin slipped the journal into the outer pocket of his coat. "It's time to finish the game."

Cassidy stepped backwards until he came into contact with the ladder. "If I didn't know better, I'd think you're throwing Charlie to the wolves."

Kotkin showed his teeth and snaked closer to Cassidy. "I could care less about Charles," said Kotkin. He pulled the cosh from his coat. "I have all I need right here." Even as his thirst for blood came to the surface, he could see that Cassidy had no fear. Perturbed, Kotkin stopped. "Perhaps you fail to understand me or what's about to happen here. I prefer my victims show fear. It stimulates me."

"Why should I be afraid of you?"

"I killed Brannigan's son and the bartender. I killed your partner and his beautiful wife," he said. "And let me give you additional news: Brannigan is dead, Charles is dead, and your man Kindred is dead. All by my order." Still no reaction. Kotkin continued in his venomous voice, "And after I finish here, I'll be visiting Brannigan's other son. And Molly, of course. I believe that's her name. That should be quite entertaining."

Ready to give the first blow to Cassidy, Kotkin lifted the cosh over his head. From the corner of the cavern a match flared and light from a second lantern flooded the room. Kotkin whirled and came face to face with Kindred. Next to Kindred stood another man cradling a double-barreled shotgun pointed at Kotkin's chest. "You won't be visiting nobody," said Brannigan.

Kotkin was frozen in place. The silence was broken only by the unsteady breathing of four men, and for a long time no one moved. Brannigan cocked the second hammer of the shotgun, and Kotkin let the cosh slide out of his hand. It landed with a thud against the rock floor. Kotkin looked wildly from face to face. Knowing Brannigan would pull the shotgun trigger before he'd be able to reach the gun strapped to his leg, Kotkin gauged the distance between him and Brannigan. He had nothing to lose.

At the last second, Kotkin jerked himself back from the certain death of the shotgun blast. His men, who had been at the mine entrance, should now be at the top of the ladder. When Kotkin turned to face Cassidy, he found the outlaw now held a rifle. The rifle had lain hidden in the shadows behind the ladder. Working the lever of the Winchester, Cassidy chambered a round, and asked, "How you feeling?"

Ignoring the rifle, Kotkin stepped toward Cassidy. "If you're going to shoot me, do it and get it over with." His voice came close to anger as he shouted toward the tunnel ceiling, "Do it!"

Cassidy laughed. He looked up at the hole and called, "Send him down." The sound of a voice and a shuffling noise drifted down the shaft before legs appeared on the ladder and started down. Cassidy called up to the man, "You've got a rifle staring up your ass."

Finley reached the bottom and helped guide the body of his partner, who was being lowered by rope. Once Hopkins' body was on the floor, a cowering Finley stood with his head down. His weapons had been removed, including the hidden stiletto, at the mine entrance. Hopkins hadn't been quite as lucky. His resistance had necessitated knocking him unconscious. Blood oozed out of one ear and trickled down his cheek.

A minute later Trenton Carver jumped off the last rung and joined the growing group in the cavern. He was followed by a second man. Kotkin couldn't believe what he saw. He clenched his fists and demanded, "What have you done?" His fury was evident as he again looked for a weapon. "You bastard, I'll kill you for this!" he screamed. Sweat poured from Kotkin's face and ran down the collar of his shirt.

Reilly ignored the man and the threat. He waited until Brannigan jammed the barrel of the shotgun against the back of Kotkin's neck before he pulled a piece of rope from his pocket and roughly tied Kotkin's hands behind his back before retrieving the pistol strapped to Kotkin's leg. He removed the journal, found the folded straight razor at the bottom of the same pocket, and tossed to it Cassidy.

Carver reached for the coiled rope from his shoulder. He trussed Kotkin from neck to feet, shoved him to the floor, and jerked him to a sitting position. Kotkin now experienced the total helplessness that many of his victims had suffered.

Cassidy inspected the ropes. He ceremoniously set the infamous cosh in Kotkin's lap. Satisfied, he nodded at Brannigan, who lowered his shotgun and stepped in front of Kotkin. "Reilly is my sister's married name," he said. "She and Andrew lived in New Jersey until his daddy died, and then Sophie moved back to Missouri."

Words froze on Kotkin's tongue. "He's...he's...your nephew?" he stuttered. Kotkin's mouth opened and closed, but no more words came out.

Brannigan's face hardened as he stared into the eyes of his son's killer. "That means my son was Andrew's cousin, and in Missouri, we kinfolk lived by the feud," he said, grinding the words out. He slowly cocked both barrels again, before brandishing it in Kotkin's sweating face. "You killed one of ours, so now you're gonna die, you miserable son of a bitch." There was silence in the cavern as the others waited. This was Brannigan's moment.

Brannigan didn't see enough fear. Releasing the hammers, he shouldered the weapon and said, "Shooting you in the face would be too easy. You got to pay the hard way." Brannigan walked to the ladder and climbed to the tunnel above, followed by Kindred and Reilly. Only Carver and Cassidy remained.

Cassidy said, "Go ahead and tie the other two." Carver tied Finley in the same neat package Reilly had tied Kotkin. When Carver turned his attention to Hopkins, he found the strongman was no longer breathing, so Carver didn't bother. Cassidy told him, "I'm almost through here. Wait for me with the boys outside."

Kotkin's sweat-streaked face was sheet-white as he stared pitifully at Cassidy. Aristocratic supremacy long gone, he pleaded, "What are you going to do?" Behind his back, Kotkin's bound hands were wet and shaking uncontrollably.

"I'm going to do what you intended to do to me. Leave you here."

"But at least I was going to kill you first!" cried Kotkin, voice rising to a shriek.

"You're more thoughtful than me," said Cassidy. "Look at the bright side. Maybe you can chew your way through those ropes." He thought for a moment, and then said, "Nah, you'll die of thirst before you get loose—that, or hunger, not that anyone cares." He bent over and checked the knots again. "Well, just like you said, it's time to end this."

Cassidy stepped over to the ladder, but he stopped. "You know, thinking about it, maybe we did rob Harriman too many times. Hell, he was probably right putting LeFors on us." He placed his booted foot on the rung and paused again. "The sad part is, we eventually changed our ways and became upstanding citizens, so all of this was for nothing. All Charlie had to do was buy that damned journal from Will. Then he and old Harriman wouldn't have had to unleash you." He started climbing the ladder.

"Wait!" yelled Kotkin. "Wait!" When Cassidy didn't stop, he screamed, "Don't leave me down here! Don't let me die like this! You can't—!"

Brannigan was waiting when Cassidy stepped off the ladder. The screams echoed throughout the cave as Finley's cries competed with Kotkin's. Ignoring the pleas, they made their way to the entrance where Josh was waiting. Josh lifted the two fuses and showed them to Cassidy. "Everything's ready," he said.

"Just give me time to get out of here," Cassidy said. "Me and dynamite don't do well together."

Josh pulled matches from his pocket and handed one to his father. They stood together and watched until Cassidy reached Reilly and Carver waiting at the bottom of the mountain, the three then hurried past the cabin to the corral. Looking back once again, Josh watched as Kindred, Ontiveros, and Bates joined the others. He scratched his match on the rock face of the mountain, saying, "This is for Will and Jimmy," as he lit the fuse.

Brannigan counted five seconds and then lit the second. "And this is for Sundance and Etta," he said. "How long?"

"Andrew said a couple of minutes—give or take," said Josh. He grabbed his father by the arm. "Let's get the hell out of here!"

They made it down the slippery hill with time to spare, joining the others away from the danger of falling rock and debris. The little group waited and watched for what seemed like an eternity before a muffled explosion sounded, followed almost immediately by a second. As always in a blast, at first nothing happened. But then smoke poured out the entrance—seconds later, the upper part of the mountain caved in, and with a roar, the mine was sealed forever.

The men stared, deep in their own thoughts, until the echo died. Cassidy broke the silence. "Unless somebody's got a better idea, we might as well go back to town."

An hour later, Cassidy, Kindred, Reilly, and Bates sat at the corner table of Brannigan's saloon. Shortly, except for Ontiveros, the rest of the men joined them. G. C., having seen Horace Aker's killer die, was already on the way back to Gunnison. At first there was little talk; no one wanted to admit to it, but regardless of how bad they wanted Kotkin dead, killing him had not been an easy thing. Josh, being the furthest removed from the plan, asked, "How'd Andrew get hired by Kotkin? Doesn't seem like that'd be possible."

"It was easy," said Cassidy. "Once Charlie got involved."

Bates voice was subdued as he explained. When George Nelson, the Pinkerton chief of detectives, suggested a candidate for Kotkin's bodyguard request, Kotkin didn't know that Nelson's brother-in-law was Herman Caudill, head of security for the railroad. The two men were close. They met for dinner one night, and the next day Caudill passed the information on to Bates.

Kotkin had told Bates that Brannigan was following him. But Kotkin didn't believe Brannigan posed any danger, although he did offer Bates a description, along with the advice to avoid traveling alone.

Making contact with Brannigan had not been difficult. Bates approached him on the street and afterward met with Brannigan several times. Bates convinced Brannigan that Kotkin was becoming a dangerous liability for the company and Bates personally.

Bates bribed Nelson into recommending Reilly as Kotkin's bodyguard. Accepting the position with the Union Pacific Railroad, Reilly would later admit, had been more than he bargained for. His real job was to stay in close contact with Bates, and working with his uncle, direct Kotkin into falling for the scheme to get him back to Colorado.

But there was one flaw. Kotkin had not been as forthcoming with Reilly in the beginning of their relationship as he would later become. Kotkin's plan for the Longleys, including the abduction of Hattie, was unknown to Reilly. Subsequently, Reilly had to be talked out of taking action into his own hands. Brannigan did so by pointing out that killing Kotkin in New York might backfire, and Reilly could even hang for it.

Through a series of telegrams, Bates hatched the scheme for his own kidnapping with Cassidy. Bates reasoned that even *he* might be one of Kotkin's targets and came up with a plausible story to force the assassin's hand. Trenton Carver had been dispatched as a backup for Brannigan for the trip west. To further cover his plans, Bates had arranged for a private car from the Baltimore and Ohio Railroad. The president of the competing railroad company was a college chum who happily made the accommodation. "—and the rest is today's results," finished Bates. He looked around the table.

Josh wasn't satisfied. "Why didn't you just buy the journal from my brother?"

"If it had been my decision, I would have," Bates said. "For better or worse, I felt obligated to inform Mr.

Harriman. He'd confided parts of his past to me. Over time, I was able to piece the rest of the story together."

Cassidy disagreed. "You could have always made more money."

"It wasn't that," said Bates. "Well, not entirely. The fact is—and surprisingly, Elias understood—Mr. Harriman believed the disintegration in the confidence of our banks would destroy the country."

Bates continued. "But Mr. Harriman didn't know of his son's proclivities. I doubt he could have even conceived the extent of the havoc Elias wrought. I, however, am convinced that the random murders perpetrated in the city were Elias' work. I'm betting the murders will cease now that he's dead, never to be solved."

When Bates slowly looked around the table again, it was like a weary old man. "Does that explain everything?" When no one answered, Bates stood. "If that's the case, I'm going back to New York." As he started to walk away, he paused for a moment. "Cassidy, I'll be in Denver for a few days." He left without looking back.

The group watched Bates walk away before Cassidy said, "Time we all get back to our lives." Carver stood first. "Keep in touch, Trenton," said Cassidy. He shook Carver's hand.

"I'd like that," he said. He grinned at Reilly. "Glad to have gotten to know you." He then turned back to Cassidy. "The Carvers will always be there if you need us."

An hour later everyone had slipped away except Cassidy and Brannigan. Reilly and Josh left with Kindred to go back to the ranch. Kindred would soon return to Crested Butte to take up his bartending duties.

Cassidy tried to think of anything he'd missed. "Did G. C. get his money?"

Brannigan nodded. "He got his guide money up front. Plus, Andrew was carrying the travel funds for Kotkin's boys. He split them between G. C. and Carver. And Charlie's gonna see that the reward money goes to Horace Akers' family." He stared out the window at the falling snow. It made the town seem clean, almost pristine, but still depressed him. With a sigh, he said, "It's been a bad time. It always is when people get killed for nothing."

"That's the way life is," Cassidy said. "You lost your boy and Jimmy. We both lost Sundance and Etta. Funny thing…the way we lived, I always figure we could go early, but I never thought any of us would die living a straight life."

Brannigan's smile held some sadness. "Legends always come true," he finally said. "Doesn't seem to be any way around it." He looked across the table at his friend, who was staring back. "What?" he demanded.

"I don't know about legends always coming true," said Cassidy. He suddenly grinned. "Maybe for Sundance. He was one hell of a man." There was a pause. "He made my life a lot more interesting, that's for sure." Cassidy looked around the room before deciding to say more. "Sundance and Etta were closer to being family than friends. And they would have said the same about me. I'll always regret they're gone, but I'll be damned if I'm going to grieve them. I can't change a thing, so the best thing I can do for Sundance, for Etta, and myself—now that Kotkin's dead—is go back to my family."

Brannigan sighed again. "That might be your best idea yet," he said.

"I tell you, I'm loaded with them. And you haven't seen the half of it," said Cassidy. "Let's go down to the hotel and get some dinner."

They'd almost finished their rabbit stew when Brannigan thought to ask, "You planning on seeing Bates in Denver? Sure sounded like he wanted to."

A grin rolled across Cassidy's face. "Well now, that would be polite of me, wouldn't it?"

The beauty of the Colorado Grand Hotel was unmatched at any time of year. This was true for the outside as well as the luxurious interior. However, it was unusual for guests to conduct an outdoor meeting once winter had set in, and Cassidy was surprised when he was directed to the back

lawn of the hotel. Bates was standing on the far side of the
dormant brown lawn next to the stream that ran through
the hotel property.

Cassidy skirted the damp grass by walking on the rock
steps that encircled the lawn. "Afternoon," he called, and
stepped onto the gravel path leading to the water's edge.
Without looking up, Bates waved. He was staring at the
water running over and through the rocks. When Cassidy
reached his side, Bates said, "Even though the water is cold
and will eventually freeze, fish are still running down-
stream. How will they survive?"

"Probably find a hot springs downriver to hole up for the
winter," said Cassidy. Two chairs were placed under a bare
cottonwood. He walked the few steps to the chairs and said
as he sat, "Although I've never given it much thought."

Bates picked up a stone and tossed it in the water. He
joined Cassidy and pulled his chair away from the tree. "I
hope you don't mind the weather," he said. "In New York,
I've always hated the cold. Here, I want to be outdoors all the
time. The difference in the air, I suppose." He took his time,
before adding, "Or, perhaps it's because it helps me think."

The wind picked up just enough to cause snow to slip
from the branches and softly plop to the ground behind them.
After Bates looked to see if more would fall, he said, "Or it
could be the beauty of the West makes me realize how small I
am." Cassidy gave a short laugh even while he acknowledged
to himself that Bates was trying to figure something out.
Something important to Bates. Embarrassed, Bates smiled
and said, "Or perhaps I've become a maudlin child."

"What's on your mind?"

Bates rubbed his hands together. "It would be helpful if
you returned the journal." He reached in his coat and
brought out the book that Kotkin had scrutinized so intently in the mine. "This is a wonderful copy. But it is a copy."

"There goes the plan," Cassidy muttered under his breath.
He took the book from Bates, flipped through the pages as if
seeing it for the first time, then he handed it back. "What
tipped you?"

"Other than the fact that this fifty-year-old document is in perfect condition?"

The wind increased, causing the branches to release more snow, this time leaving a dusting on their shoulders. Glancing down, Cassidy sighed and said, "It's strange Etta didn't think of that. On the other hand, once it became apparent that you weren't the problem, we didn't think Kotkin would notice."

Bates smiled at that. "But in any case, what are we to do about the journal?"

"Don't you think that damn thing has caused enough trouble?" Cassidy was growing impatient. "Can't you understand that you—or some other moron in your organization—could cause more trouble with it, than without?" He paused for a response. When none came, he continued, "It's going to stay with me. You're going to have to go on faith that this arrangement is in your best interest."

Bates wondered how much leverage he had. He calculated there was none. "I suppose there's no sense in arguing. Perhaps you have a point that the journal is just as safe in your hands as the company's. I thought for so long that I had to have its return, it's strange to give up that notion, much less leave it in the possession of someone whose name I don't know."

Cassidy stood and brushed the snow from his coat. The wind was picking up again and he was growing uncomfortably cold. He looked up at the gray sky. "Gonna storm real hard tonight," he commented. Turning back to Bates, he said, "Unless you do something stupid, my name will never be important to you. You'll never know where I live, or what I do for a living, but you'd better believe that I'll know all about you." The blue eyes blazed as the steely voice continued, "We're not friends, Charlie. You killed my partner. Maybe you didn't pull the trigger, I'll give you that, but you let that killer loose. If you ever cross me, my family, or any of my friends, I'll kill you. And that's a fact."

With that, Butch Cassidy walked out of Bates' life.

Portland, Oregon—Summer 1936

E ven though the sun was beginning its descent into the rugged forest, it was still bright on this early summer day. So far the season had been warm and dry for Portland. As the temperature dropped, Carlisle sat alone at the cloth-covered table dappled with food stains and cake crumbs. Bits of festive paper and ribbon blew around the yard. He was alone for the first time all day. A few minutes earlier, Thea had returned to the house to help the last of the guests find their unused coats and umbrellas.

The celebration of Carlisle's seventieth birthday had been an all-day affair, attended by friends, well-wishers, and rela-tives. David and Lawrence and their wives had come early with their daughters and sons-in-law. Carlisle's grandchildren were all girls—three for David, two for Lawrence. Carlisle enjoyed teasing his sons over the lack of a male heir, but they knew he loved his grandchildren as much as he loved them.

He turned to look across the lawn to the river. The entire clan was preparing to take the motorboat upriver. When they returned, he'd see them for a light supper before they left for their respective homes in town. He waved to the grandchildren who shouted, "Happy Birthday, Granddaddy!"

"Doesn't get any better than that," he said to himself.

The shadows of the trees were covering the picnic area. Carlisle had been comfortable until the shade crept around him. He was dressed in a white linen suit with a starched blue shirt, open at the collar. He had discovered that as he got older the cold bothered him more, and he rarely ventured outside without a coat. It was time to go inside.

Carlisle rose with a grunt and looked down at the belly that protruded around his belt. No longer active at the mill, he'd gained weight—or so he said—although Thea thought it *was because he'd developed a fondness for wine, or a glass or two of beer, if the mood took him.*

He walked up the steps to the back door. The kitchen staff was bustling as they washed and dried the dishes before returning them to the pantry. Not wanting to talk with anyone, Carlisle hurried down the hall to his study and closed the door. Once inside, he saw that a fire was already lit, so he settled into his leather chair. He sought solitude; today's celebration had brought back memories, and he wanted peace and quiet to examine them.

Josh and Molly Brannigan had been the first to arrive, bringing their son, William Harrison, whom they called Harry. It was the first time Carlisle had seen the couple since Tom passed away. At the funeral in Gunnison, Molly had confided to him that she didn't think Tom ever got over the loss of Will. And today, when Carlisle asked about Kindred, Josh had laughed and said the cowboy had vowed never to leave Colorado again, other than an occasional trip to Texas to see his sister and her family. Kindred was in good health, wished Carlisle the best, and had taken up with a retired professional lady who was keeping him in style in Crested Butte, though he still tended bar in the saloon that he now owned with Josh.

Andrew Reilly arrived shortly after the Brannigans. He had continued his career with the Union Pacific Railroad and developed a close relationship with Charles Bates. He married a New Jersey girl who had died shortly after the birth of their only child. He never remarried, raising his son on his own. Reilly brought the news that Bates had succumbed to pneumonia last winter, but that his replacement was equally competent. Bates had never married and left his considerable fortune to Father Flanagan's Boys Home in Nebraska.

The clock chimed and startled Carlisle. He realized he'd been reviewing the day and dozing for an hour. He marveled how time could pass so quickly when he was daydreaming. He got up and gave the fire a poke to restore the flames before dropping a log on it. As he returned to his chair he glanced at the armoire in the corner. Telling himself he didn't want to read it, he nevertheless used the key hidden on top of the armoire's crown molding to open the middle drawer.

The pages of Harriman's journal were stiff with age, the leather cover cracked and split on the bias. But the words were the same. Carlisle had returned to the book so often that he could almost recite the pages from memory. He hated the journal and the havoc it had caused, but reading it again and again convinced him that Bates had been right about its power to disrupt the American banking system. Although in the last few years he conceded that the power of the journal diminished as the country grew. The Great Depression had been difficult, and Carlisle was grateful that his mill had survived. He believed America would emerge as a world leader, and not only from a financial point of view. For that he was grateful.

Still, he was often drawn to the journal. Perhaps because it represented his last adventure, the tail end of his days as an outlaw leader. Many a night Thea had gently pried the book from his hands after he had fallen asleep, taking care to lock it back in the drawer and return the key to its hiding place.

Carlisle settled once more in his chair but refrained from turning the cover. Instead, he fell to reflecting on his life—something he did fairly often now. He would be the first to admit that some things could have turned out better. On the other hand, considering where he sat now, he couldn't complain about much. The loss of the Longleys was certainly something he wished he could have changed. There were few days when he didn't think of Sundance and Etta. In one of his last conversations with Tom Brannigan, Brannigan told him the Longleys' will had left their estate to their employees.

His life as an outlaw was another part of his life that Carlisle often dwelled upon. The friendships and loyalties that developed between him and his men were a thing of the past. Even as time passed and as the memories became tarnished and faded, he still reveled in the excitement of the old days. In his more generous moments, he found he was even able to forgive Harriman for setting LeFors and his posse after them. Although he couldn't forgive the railroad magnate for spawning Elias Kotkin.

Kotkin. *Never for a moment did Carlisle regret the mad-man's death. In all his reading Carlisle had been unable to find anyone more evil than Harriman's bastard son. He never thought twice about playing a part in putting an end to Kotkin's miserable life.*

He wondered what was keeping Thea. He liked to know she was close. Another change with age, *he thought. A chill swept down his back. He stood and moved to the fire, warming his hands as he rubbed them together. Although it was early, barely twilight, he was tired—strange for him, he often stayed up late at night to read, or think.*

He sunk back into his chair as his thoughts turned again to Brannigan. A good soul—*and a fearless, tenacious, and loyal friend. He reached for the comforter Thea used to cover her legs while she read. The fatigue was setting in now, and it took him a moment to recall what he was thinking.* Oh yes, Brannigan, *he reminded himself.*

When Brannigan returned to Colorado with Bates, there had been plenty of time for talk while they waited for Kotkin. At first Tom had been withdrawn and reticent about the Longleys. He had eventually opened up and described the scene to Carlisle, the only other person who could feel their deaths as Brannigan had.

Carlisle struggled to recall something Brannigan had said. Then it came to him. Legends always come true. *"But that's not right," Carlisle said aloud in a voice that had grown hoarse with the years. Surprised at the sound, he struggled to sit before giving up and pulling the comforter up to his neck. "Legends don't become true," he whispered. "Legends become lost. It's only the passage of time that makes legends true." He would have laughed, but the truth of his words stopped him.*

The cold permeated his body and a deep weariness made it difficult to think. Casting a final look at the book, he set the journal aside as sleep overcame him. At peace, the last outlaw closed his eyes.

THE END

CHARLIE MAC began writing as a second, or perhaps, third career. His first careers were as a marketing executive and entrepreneur. Charlie is a native Californian who now lives in Colorado Springs, Colorado. He was inspired to write a novel to answer the question, 'What happened to Butch and Sundance after Bolivia?' Charlie heard actor Paul Newman say in an interview that no one actually saw Butch and Sundance die in the film. That was inspiration enough for Charlie, long fascinated by the tale of the amiable outlaws.

While Charlie worked on *Legends Lost*, three more adventure novels took shape. Look for *A Minor Inconvenience*, *Traveling the Flatland*, and *A Major Concern* to follow *Legends Lost*.

Follow Charlie on Facebook and visit his website, CharlieMacBooks.com, for appearances, special events, and new titles.